A JOURNEY IN TIME

A STORY WRITTEN BY

PETER BAINES

ISBN-13: 978-1976460364
ISBN-10: 1976460360

You are born with a Beautiful Mind

Keep it safe

Always think to use it wisely

It will last you a Lifetime.

This story is dedicated to you.

CONTENTS

ACKNOWLEDGMENTS

First of all I would like to thank my wife, Susan, for all her hard work and help with my Novel. How she puts up with me I don't know.

Secondly, I would like to send my appreciation and thanks to Jessica Grace Coleman of Coleman Editing Ltd., who was an invaluable contributor to this Novel. Her editing and ghostwriting skills are second to none.

Without these two people this book would not exist.

Thank you also, to my friends who read certain parts of my novel, and sent me in the right direction. You know who you are!

Prologue

James McKenzie slid into the comfortable leather chair, nodding at the middle-aged man who was sitting on the other side of the large, walnut paneled desk.

"It's going to be one of those days," said the huge husk of a man in front of him. "I can feel it in my bones. Roll on retirement, eh Jimmy?"

McKenzie nodded again, this time allowing a small smile to creep onto his lips. "You've got a while to go yet, Sir. You don't look a day over sixty!"

"Smart ass," came the reply. "Now, the reason I got you in here is that I need your report early this month. By the end of the day, in fact. Can you do that?"

"The end of the day?" asked McKenzie, feeling his stomach drop. This was all he needed. "I'm not sure that will be possible. Why do you want it early?"

The man smiled at him, though it wasn't a comforting smile by any stretch of the imagination. "We're just trying to get on top of a few… what shall we call them… *anomalies* that have cropped up."

"Anomalies?" asked McKenzie, a small line of perspiration popping up on his top lip. "What kind of anomalies? I can assure you, my staff are just as efficient as always, and they never leave a stone unturned. If something's wrong-"

The man held his hand up, stopping McKenzie mid-sentence. "There's nothing wrong with your staff," he said, smiling again. "Believe me when I tell you they're by far the most competent employees I've ever had the pleasure to work with. You've done a good job with them, James."

McKenzie relaxed a little at that, though it hadn't escaped his notice that his boss and old friend was now referring to him by his actual, full first name. He hadn't done that in years. "Thank you, Sir. I'll make sure I get that report to you by the time I leave."

The man cocked his head, whistling through his teeth. "Well, I'm afraid that might be a bit of a problem. I'll inform your staff about the report – I'm always happy to help out an old friend – but it won't get done before you go." His eyes wandered to the door behind McKenzie's head. "There are two gentlemen waiting for you outside, and I'm guessing they'll want you to leave…" the man glanced at his watch, "right about now."

McKenzie swung round, his heart beating fast as he saw the silhouettes of two rather large men standing beyond the frosted glass. He turned back to face the desk. "Waiting for *me*? Who are they?"

"I think you can guess." His boss reached down into his drawer and brought out several leather-bound folders, which he proceeded to throw onto the desk with a loud thud. "You've been careful – very careful – but I'm afraid your luck's run out. All these fake business names and offshore accounts? All these false expenses? How long did you think you'd be able to get away with this? Really, James?"

McKenzie shot out of his chair and bolted for the door at the side of the office before his boss could say another word. Thinking there was no way that the door wouldn't be locked, he was delighted to find that it actually opened quite easily.

His delight, however, was short lived.

There were two police officers waiting for him in the adjoining room, and when he looked back at the office he'd just been sitting in, he saw the other two as well. One of them was holding a pair of handcuffs in his hand.

"We'd like you to come down to the Precinct," he said slowly and carefully, as if McKenzie were stupid. "We've got some questions for you regarding the sum of \$3.2 million."

McKenzie stared at the police officer, knowing he had no options left and feeling remarkably numb about that fact. It was almost a relief.

Almost.

So this was it. The game was over. The rush of adrenaline he'd felt just moments before as he'd tried to escape was long gone, and he sighed in defeat as he walked over to the police officer.

Being careful to avoid eye contact with his boss, he nodded at the man with the cuffs. "Let's do this."

Chapter 1

Paris 'Den of Thieves'

It doesn't really matter what your view of France is, it all depends on who you are. It is a vast multi-cultural country of many nationalities, people all living together fairly peacefully and whether you live in one of the major cities, or in the countryside or if you are a tourist, a business man, straight or gay it doesn't really matter, there is something in France for everyone.

If you live in Monaco you may think you are someone special, and you are, but at the end of the day you could still be classed as French.

You may live in the Vatican City and think you're someone special, and you may be, but really you're just an Italian with a different zip code.

Now if you are a Parisian, well, in your own mind you're someone special, and you are. But you don't really see yourself as living in France. 'You live in PARIS'. It is one of the most cosmopolitan capital cities in the world. A huge portrayal of how a European city should be, vast expanses of art and culture, an unrivalled business center. Vibrant and alive.

The inner sanctions of the city with its fast extortionate living pace, and the thoughts that we are only upon this earth for a very short time, so let's make the most of it, wasn't to everyone's values of how you should live your life.

But one person cruising the city center was loving it, as he had done the last time he was home. He loved just slowly touring the streets, watching the young and vibrant dreamers enjoying their turn to be the generation of the future, and then watching the middle aged men and women, drinking at the bars still thinking that they were the future generation, but had somehow missed the cut off point. Then there's the people who had seen it all and done it all. However, no one really knows what they had done or seen as they were now classed as the obsolete generation that knew nothing and had done nothing in their lifetime. Funny old world, how one generation portrays another, and so it shall continue.

As our man leaves the City Center, chest pushed high, well as much as he could, considering, he was full of pride as he has received more than a dozen admiring glances. His thoughts however register that the admiring glances are not for him but are for the car he drives. He had scrimped and scraped a few years ago, to get enough money together for the deposit on one of the most prestigious automobiles you could ever wish to own in his line of business.

It was the six door *'Mercedes Benz S-Klasse Pullman V140'* a beautiful piece of German engineering, which had the looks and grace of Venus de Milo, and for the rich and famous to be seen driven around in the comfort of the Pullman was the show stopping image they wished to portray to the newspapers, the tabloids, and the News film crews.

He had been chased all over Europe by the paparazzi on many occasions. Life was sweet. Over the past few years he had worked hard in his legit operations, and even harder in, let's say, the darker side of his work. Over the years he had managed to pay off the loan for the car, and to give him his dues it was the only possession he ever had in his life.

You couldn't just park one of these heavenly creations at the side of the road. No sir, so he was heading towards the secure compound where he would keep the *Mercedes* parked over the weekend.

As he flashes his headlights at the small compound security hut, encouraging the guard on duty to open the electronic gates. The car phone rings.

"Shit I know who this is going to be," he says quietly under his breath, picking up the phone.

"Bonjour," he says.

"Bonjour," is the reply. "Is this the great flamboyant Louie Arnett, chauffeur to the stars?" Everyone knew Louie by this title and he loved it. "This is Dominic your personal security gate operator, with a message from our manager – *Go Get Stuffed.*"

Louie, shaking his head knowing what's coming says, "I've got the money Dom. Just open the fucking gate."

The reply from Dominic came short and fast, "You better have comrade, or that car may turn out to be your coffin."

"Ha, Ha, very funny." After a few seconds the automatic gates begin rolling back, Louie sets off into the compound.

He parks up, switches the engine off, and begins to check that all the cars' unique systems are closing down, making sure he wouldn't have a flat battery on Monday. Opening the rear passenger doors, he begins to empty the contents and rubbish from his last customer. The people who used him to chauffeur them around had a great respect for the car and would always make an effort to keep it as tidy as they could. Louie opens the fridge and takes out three bottles of champagne that had been opened. He didn't want the car smelling of stale alcohol on Monday.

He retrieves two envelopes from the glove compartment above the fridge. They are addressed to him. Opening them reveals a stash of cash. He quickly counts the money. Stuffing it into his jacket pockets, he picks up the champagne bottles and throws them into the trash cans of the compound.

Returning to his car he activates the alarm systems with the keys, and blows a kiss towards the Mercedes saying, "Goodnight my beauty."

Approaching the security cabin he takes out €1,650, the funds to pay Dominic his debt for parking.

"So Louie, you have robbed a bank?" says Dom as he counts the money.

Louie, leaning on the fencing trying to impersonate Humphrey Bogart, as he lights a cigarette with his Zippo says, "I wouldn't tell you if I had would I?"

Dominic finished counting, "Ok Louie all here… that just leaves tonight's parking charges."

Louie looks at him frowning, "No problem Dominic," he says putting his hand into his jacket pocket, he then pulls out his fist all tightly scrunched up, just with his middle finger proudly standing up from it, "can you just give this message to your manager?" as he thrust the finger in Dominic's face.

Dom laughs as he presses a release button allowing the single pedestrian gate to open, Louie steps out into the street. A man with a mission thinking 'right which generation shall I be tonight?'

Just round the corner is one of Louie's half-way bars, he enters, and the barman sees him, "Hey Louie, you're back, what is it tonight just your usual?" says the man. Louie stops in his tracks thinking, no, tonight I feel good. This is going to be my night to remember, we shall make it special.

"No, no my friend, let's celebrate." Looking round the small bar he notices that there are only three other people in. That's not bad he thinks, "No, no Monsieur, drinks all round, make them doubles!" When Louie has money in his pocket he is everyone's friend. A second round of drinks are ordered and Louie enjoys the company and attention that they bring with them.

But now he has money to burn, he must be moving on. His main objective tonight is to hit the casino. Feeling his luck this particular night will be *'the making of the man'* leaving the bar to the cheering of the patrons, he's loving it being in the spotlight.

It's about a kilometer's walk to the casino, and

these days Louie could only shuffle along at a snail's pace. Taking a short cut off the main drag he is now travelling down the sleazy back roads of Paris. To many these streets would put the fear of God in you, with the dark shadowy corners and the dark shadowy individuals lurking in them, but to Louie this was part of him and he loved it. He had been born and brought up in these streets and always thought he was one of those dark shadowy individuals just waiting to pounce on the unsuspecting.

Leaving the back streets, he greets the bright lights of the row of clothing and wine boutiques. Here on the main route there's more people milling around, enjoying the evening. The casino is only a few more meters now next to the old war memorial. His vision now picks up a few familiar faces gathering round the back of the memorial. It's an encounter that Louie was hoping he could avoid tonight. Trying not to make eye contact and shielding his face, edging round the people on the walkway, he finally makes it to the casino entrance unnoticed, or so he thinks.

"Hey Louie, come here you devil!" shouts one of the girls.

'No, no,' he thinks, *'not tonight,'* his eyes drop onto his cheeks. *'Not tonight,'* his vision focuses on where the voice was coming from, it was Carmel behind the Memorial, his favourite prostitute.

"I've had a poor night tonight Louie, you can change all that," she shouts, "do you fancy a bit of this?" as she lifts up her skirt exposing her underwear.

Louie waves his hand in a *'not tonight Josephine'* gesture as he stops outside the plush casino entrance, which is totally out of character for the district it is located in.

He steadies himself, tucking in his shirt and pulling up his trousers. The man looks quite respectable as he straightens his tie, he glances back at Carmel. She is blowing smoke rings from the cigarette in her fingers, teasing him with those dark amber eyes, no Louie no, not tonight, be strong, are his thoughts, his shoulders drop, or should I?

He stands there contemplating what to do when the casino doors swing open, this invites him forward to enter the gaming rooms.

The bright lights instantly attract him, the view of the tables are so inviting to him that he cannot resist it, standing at the threshold taking it all in – the sights, the smells, everything.

It was just the same as the last time he was here, and will probably be the same the next time. He had no will-power to resist the pleasure of the glam and glitz of the tables.

After all, are his thoughts as he marches forward, it's not going to continue for much longer, as he makes a grab for his chest.

The pain racks through his torso as he'd forgotten to take his morphine in the early evening. Never mind, he thinks, a few whiskeys will soon take the pain away.

His mind made up, he walks confidently towards the reception area. Staff member's acknowledging him as he breezes past.

Everyone knew Louie as he spends most of his

waking hours at the casino; well this is when he has any money, it was kind of hard to miss him.

He has forgotten how much his debt is to the casino but last time he was threatened by the casino enforcers, it stood at almost €1.5 million. This was quite a sum to be in the shit by, but Louie, as always, just shrugged it off.

He knew that if the casino management stopped him from playing the tables they would never see any of that money. As it went at the moment, however, if they allowed him to continue, they may get some of it back.

Louie had just finished a long drive out of Paris, through Germany and Poland and on into Russia all the way to Moscow, as he was chauffeuring a rich Russian Diplomat who had to get out of the Capital pretty darn quick. This was one of Louie's specialities, he knew which Autobahns to use and which to avoid, he was very skilled at fast driving and the rich and famous were very aware of this and hired him quite often when things were a bit – let's say, difficult. He kept his mouth shut and never asked questions.

His gentleman passenger from this last excursion had been involved with a group of Carmel's friends. They had been having one of those 'anything goes' parties and that word 'anything' included some of the most depraved sexual antics you could imagine even for Paris.

Carmel had told Louie that one of her girls had been choked in an erotic sadomasochistic game and had consequently suffocated. He knew the girl from the streets where she had worked but hey, it was nothing to do with him.

Louie had received a call – shortly after the girl's death – to get the murderer out of Paris as quickly as possible in order to avoid any Diplomatic incident. He realised straight away that this was going to be one of those big money earners, and he'd arrived to pick up the Russian Minister before the poor girl's body had even gone cold.

He had been paid quite handsomely for his troubles – €50,000 were his fee for the drive – but he had also been handed a €100,000 tip as a 'thank you very much and keep your mouth shut' gesture. This was the bundle of cash he had in his pocket for his night of entertainment.

Louie marches on into the *'Den of Thieves'* so to speak, he is heading towards the banking area to change some of his ill-gotten gains for chips to play on the pontoon tables. He loved the cards and always believed that he understood the predicable way the cards sometimes fell and of course, sometimes didn't.

As he walked on he felt a rattling sensation deep in his chest, it seemed to be getting worse as the days went by. He thought, I must try and get back to the doctors to restart my treatment for this, but then he thinks what is the point?

He had been told fifteen or so months ago it was the smoking that had caused the lung cancer and was also told that if he gave up the cigarettes and started with the chemotherapy, it would extend his life expectancy by three whole years.

This thought then makes him fidget in his pockets just to make sure he had his cigarettes and lighter standing by to pair up with his first whiskey.

"Damn willpower," he says to himself, something he had nothing of, he then makes a small coughing sound to clear his throat which surprisingly brings the taste of blood into his mouth, "damn cancer," he says under his breath.

On the edge of his peripheral vision he sees his reflection on the mirrored wall as he approaches the casino banks and this makes him turn his head to look at the man in the mirror, he could hardly recognise the figure reflected back at him, "Damn cancer," he says again to nobody in particular.

How it had changed him from the handsome, young and fit man who could pick up a new conquest just by using his steely blue eyed stare, and his movie star rugged features – to the wreck of a man who was now only able to attract the charms of his dear beloved Carmel.

Still that was something else he also had to pay for so perhaps it wasn't his charming personality she was after! It was just his money.

HA! Money he thought as he reached the bank. Didn't it always come down to money?

Thrusting his hand into the inside pocket of his jacket he pulls out a wad of crisp new €100 bills. Hope they aren't counterfeit, he thinks looking at the new, freshly printed notes – that would be just his luck.

Louie focuses his vision on the attendant at the banking tills who is serving a group of ladies acquiring some chips for the tables.

As he waits his turn, his eyes refocus on the mirrored wall behind the bank, he knows that this particular area consists of the manager's offices and the mirror is a two-way system that is used to keep an eye on who is coming and going from the casino.

He knows this as he has been interrogated in there by the management as to when he was going to start paying his debt with the casino. He also knows they will have been watching him through the casino CCTV system as he entered the premises and now he knows that they would be clocking him through the two-way mirror.

Just to be clever Louie pulls a second wad of notes from his inside jacket pocket and begins waving both fists full of money at the reflected image of himself – knowing full well that he would be winding up the manager who he could just imagine being in the office watching him, cursing and swearing to the Enforcers.

'Look at that bastard Arnett! He is taking the piss out of me!' he imagined the manager saying. Louie laughs to himself, however the excitement starts him off coughing again, and the returning taste of blood makes him feel sick at the back of his throat.

He sees a waitress close by carrying a rather large tray of complimentary drinks. He stops her then attacks the free drink samples, one small whiskey swallowed fast, and then another that he slowly sips at.

"Thank you, mademoiselle." The taste in his mouth now reverts back to something familiar.

Regaining his posture, Louie hands a wad of cash to the attendant who straightens out the pile of notes and feeds them through a currency counting device.

The attendant then turns his head and gives an 'all OK' nod at the two-way mirror.

Looking through the mirror from the office side are four men: two of them well-dressed and respectable, the other two more rugged in their appearance – action type men, you might say.

The casino manager – sat in his oversized chair at his oversized desk speaks to the well-dressed gentlemen. "You are in luck tonight Messieurs; that is the greasy, flamboyant Louie Arnett, chauffeur to the stars."

This was the third night that the four men had occupied the manager's office and here was the prize they had been waiting for.

Nodding, one of the gentlemen replied, "You can hardly recognize from the dossiers, that this is the same man; the disease is ravaging him."

Their gaze follows Arnett as far as the two-way mirror would allow. Returning to the manager's desk they pick Arnett up on the CCTV system that covers almost the entire casino.

Back in the gaming room, Louie was fumbling around in his pocket for his cigarettes, he put one to his lips and lit it. Breathing the smoke in deeply, he leans back against a supporting rail surveying where his favourite Croupiers were hiding.

He always enjoyed playing the tables where he knew that sometimes he would get a wink or a nod to make a good bet – especially if he was well down that particular night – but there was no-one dealing at the tables that he recognised. A little disappointed, he just made his way to the nearest card game.

"That croupier, Monsieur, is not a normal in-house man, is he?" said one of the gentlemen to the manager in the office.

"No Sir, he is not. There are no normal staff here this week, as you requested. They are all from our club on the West Side," the manager replied.

"Excellent. What do you think his chances of winning are?"

The Manager shrugs: "The house always wins and these dealers know what is expected of them and are on a special bonus tonight."

"But we have got to encourage him to play," replies one of the well-dressed men.

"Don't you worry, you English always think that we French have not much idea in, how do you say it, 'Pulling the wool over the eyes'… well, we have been stitching you British up for years!" the manager laughed.

The two well-dressed men exchanged meaningful glances. The heavy blue smoke hanging in the casino gave a rather toxic feeling about the atmosphere. It was a very unhealthy place to be. They just wanted to get their job done and get out of there.

Louie Arnett sits on a stool at the pontoon table, extinguishes his cigarette, places his bet and receives his first card, the other players are also dealt in.

The dealer lays his own card down then deals the second round to the punters. Louie studies his cards keeping to his well-practised emotionless expression so as not to give any signals to the Croupier.

Louie decides to stick on twenty – an Ace and a 9,

the dealer continues firing cards at the remaining punters, then turns his cards over scoring twelve.

He deals himself another card – the 4 of diamonds scoring 16 then another, the Ace of Clubs, this gives him 17.

He looks up at the four players at the table, two at the far end are staring at the dealers' four cards, he can tell that they are expecting him to announce that he will play 18's which he more or less knows they have, he gives the third punter a disguised glance.

The croupier believes him to just be there for a laugh as he is flashing his two cards in his mate's face, laughing as he expects to get paid out in this opening game, so he must have a score of 19, maybe 20.

He then turns his head towards Louie, and is not surprised to find him staring right back at him.

This man, he thinks, is playing a game of wits with me, so it's going to be a challenging night. However, the dealer then picks up a paper napkin from a small stack to his right.

"Bonjour Monsieur," he says to Louie. "I think you have a split lip; the corner of your mouth is bleeding," as he passes the napkin across to Louie. "I do not wish to damage the deck my friend," he says, as Louie takes the napkin.

The dealer then turns his fifth card and without even looking at his hand he announces, "Five card trick to the table. The house wins. Please place your bets and we shall go again."

Damn, thought Louie, come on let's get going with this, as he dabs the corner of his mouth. He's a top Croupier, thinks Louie, but he has not come up against the great *Louie Arnett* before, Louie smiled; so let me make him squirm. Five card trick! That's not proper gambling.

Louie holds on to the napkin in his left hand then puts his bet on with his right, the croupier then deals a further hand of cards to the now five punters as another player joins them.

The fifth man is ruggedly dressed with a distinctive English accent. He is sat at the table just to the left of Louie, who looks across at the man and says in his best English, "You're from England my friend, you over here for a good time? I can show you a good time. That is my speciality."

Louie is then cut short by the Croupier. "Monsieur, I must ask you to discard the soiled napkin. I cannot risk the cards being marked by your blood."

Louie has now got the two cards from his next game in his right hand and is looking left and right for a trash can.

"Here you are," says the fifth man in his best West End of London accent as he picks up a trash can from the floor to his left and shows the open container to Louie, who throws the soiled napkin into it.

Just at this moment as Louie's gaze is distracted by the open trash can, the fifth man makes eye contact with the Croupier which is the signal that this is the target man for the evening. The fifth man returns the bin to the floor.

"Thank you my friend. I love that London accent," says Louie.

"Bonjour Madame," says the fifth man as a joke, trying to break the ice with the Frenchman.

Louie laughed, glancing back at his cards, *brilliant* were his thoughts, *21 scored*. Back came his blank expression.

The croupier announced: "Pay 21."

This was better, thought Louie, and as the game progressed he began to win in every hand; perhaps the Englishman is my lucky charm. Louie won again and again, *fantastic!*

The fifth man and Louie were getting on very well, the drinks were flowing, the friendly atmosphere was a pleasure to Louie, but to the fifth man it was all business. He had the knack to gain people's confidence or rather it was his special training in the job he did that gave him the edge.

The fifth man wasn't doing as well as Louie but then again he wasn't supposed to be, they have another game and Louie wins, the fifth man loses.

"Hey Madame! This table is unlucky for me," says the fifth man for a bit of fun.

Louie laughed again; he liked this man and his strange sense of humour. "It's Monsieur Arnett my friend, or Louie to those with a passion for life."

"Well Louie I'm going for a slash mate," says the fifth man looking round for the restrooms.

"You are going for a what 'a rash'? What is a rash?" says Louie.

"No, no, you mad Frenchman I'm going to the toilet for a pee!"

The ice was broken, and Louie and the fifth man were getting on like old friends.

"Ah yes," says Louie, "you are going for a piss, you crazy fool. Well don't be long, you are my lucky charm. Hurry back!"

The Englishman tosses a €25 chip towards the croupier, who knows that this is the signal to change Louie's luck. The fifth man leaves the table and makes his way to the restroom.

Louie continued to play on the table, and no matter how hard he tried to hide his expression the croupier could tell that he was enticing him, encouraging him, as he begins to deal cards to him that he knows would be too tempting, even for Louie to resist increasing his bets.

A picture card, an Ace, a 9 or a 10. Louie keeps thinking, *I've got him here*, but the dealer is always one count ahead and the house keeps winning, then the croupier feeds him a welcome win and he recovers some of his losses, but the law of averages always favours the casino.

The plot was all being watched on the CCTV system in the office. One of the well-dressed men glances at the other who then turns and leaves, and heads towards the restrooms. In one of the cubicles he meets the fifth man.

"I've almost got him, I'VE ALMOST GOT HIM! Just another poor spell for him with the cards and he'll be mine," says the fifth man.

"Yes Rowan, we can see him being drawn in on the monitors, but you must get him across to the Roulette tables, that's where we will trap him. Get some more whiskey into him as well. That will give him more courage."

The well-dressed man paused for a second, reaching up as he receives a message over his ear piece. "Arnett's left the table and he's heading your way. Repeat he's heading your way, you have 12 seconds."

Arnett enters the restroom and there standing in front of the urinals zipping himself up, is the fifth man.

"Hey are you coming back my friend? I need my lucky mascot. I might as well have a piss while I'm here," says Louie.

As he approaches the urinals he spits into the basin and sees his saliva mixed with droplets of blood, "Damn it," he mutters under his breath. At that moment the cubicle door opens and out steps the well-dressed man.

"Hey my friend I cannot keep calling you 'my friend' do you have a name?" shouts Louie.

"My name, my name Louie, yes it's…" replies the fifth man, as the well-dressed man walks behind Louie on his way out, "…it's *Armitage*. You can call me Armor."

The well-dressed man is puzzled as to *what sort of name is that. Armitage?* Then he sees the name on the toilet urinal pottery *'Armitage Shanks'*. Well at least it's original he thinks, the well-dressed man leaves the toilet area, then is followed by Louie and Rowan (or 'Armor'), the fifth man.

As they are walking back to the pontoon table a girl with a tray of complimentary drinks passes near to them. Rowan takes two whiskeys from the tray, one for himself and one for Louie, his new best friend.

He passes one across to Louie who raises the glass up and in a toasting action shouts out, "*Vive La France.*" Rowan half copies Louie by raising his glass, bowing his head and clicking the heels of his shoes together.

Louie can't stop laughing at Rowan's antics. They both down the drinks in one. Rowan shudders inside, trying to disguise his grimace, he hates whiskey, but puts on a brave face.

"Come on, Louie, let's break the bank!" said Rowan. He steers Louie back to the card table.

Louie climbs onto his stool. In front of him are his remaining chips, he had lost a lot of money since Rowan went to the 'John'.

"Good grief Louie, the Gods aren't in your corner tonight. Where has all your money gone?"

With that Louie pats his jacket pocket. "Don't you worry my friend, tonight the Gods are in my pocket!"

The two friends have four more games of cards, Rowan loses all four, Louie loses the first two, then wins the third, he plays the forth and loses on a five card trick by the croupier.

"Damn you! You have beaten me tonight," says Louie to the dealer as he stares down at his few remaining chips. He tosses a €25 chip to the croupier, "That is for you, you slug!"

Louie then pushes the remaining chips on to the table for the final game, and loses the lot as the croupier turns the fifth card over, and shows another five carder!

"The house wins. Place your bets," says the croupier with no feeling at all in his voice for the poor dejected Louie, but why would he, he's just doing his job. Louie finishes another whiskey, gets up from the table, and gives a big sigh as he faces Rowan.

"Come on Louie, let's get something to eat, I will treat you to some supper."

They walk towards the food preparation area passing one of the Roulette tables.

"Oui, Oui, Magnifique!" shouts a man at the table. Clearly excited at the way *his* evening was going.

"That's where I'm going to make my fortune," says Louie, "after something to eat." They sit down and have some pate on toast and a pot of strong coffee.

Watching a few punters on the Roulette table having some good wins, encourages Louie to rush his last mug of coffee.

"Come on Armor let's gets some more chips and get on that table." With that Louie is striding out towards the casino bank.

"Slow down Louie, just a minute!" Rowan has to rush the last mouthfuls of his coffee and catch up to Louie who has already reached the bank.

There are a few people already waiting for chips so Rowan and Louie wait in the queue.

Rowan pulls out a comb from his pocket, and faces the two way mirror to tidy his hair up. He knows he will be directly facing the two well-dressed men, and raises his eyebrows in a *'hi guys'* manner. Louie then turns to the mirror and sticks out his tongue in the most vulgar way you could imagine thinking he would be looking at the manager.

The second rugged man in the office jumps back in surprise. "Jesus, look at the state of him," he exclaimed, shaking his head. "I almost feel sorry for the guy."

One of the well-dressed men turns to the rugged man and says, "Don't you ever feel sorry for this man, he is the lowest form of life and is just an excuse for a human being. His poor wife has to go out begging to try and keep a roof over their two children. His father died a pauper and his mother lives in poverty off the state.

All their lives they have had to try and pay his gambling debts off, it broke them, it broke their hearts, and here he is gambling more money away in one night than most people would earn in a lifetime. So don't feel sorry for him because of the way he looks! He's scum!"

The rugged man looked even more surprised at the outburst by the well-dressed man. "I'm sorry to go on so, Steve, it's just that people like that just wind me up!"

Back in the gaming room Rowan and Louie have changed their cash for chips, Rowan, €25,000 but Louie, all his €100,000.

"Good grief," said Rowan, eyeballing the fat stack of chips Louie had acquired. "That's a fair wedge of money Louie. You could buy a house in Wales with that!"

Louie is settling himself down at the roulette table. With a puzzled expression on his face, he replies,

"But who would want to live in Wales? Easy come, easy go, Armor, easy come easy go my friend."

Rowan stands next to him, and clicks his fingers in the air; one of the waitresses walks over.

"Two whiskeys please Mademoiselle."

Louie studies the table, his favourite number at the tables is 32 on the red so what is he going to do? Rowan places €100 on 14, and 50 on its four corners.

"What sort of bet is that Armor? That's never going to rock the foundations. Look and learn: what you should be doing is this!" says Louie grinning as he places 5,000 on 32.

There are another 3 people playing on the table who all place their bets, then the Croupier spins the ball. All eyes are watching the wheel spinning and everyone is giving the ball encouragement to drop on their number or colour.

The ball slows down dropping into the path of the spinning wheel, '*Ching, Ching, Ching,*' as it bounces over the dividers between each number, everyone is holding their breath in silence as the ball stops and then drops into 32.

"Yeah!" shouts Louie punching the air. "This is it Armor! This is going to be my night, just follow my lead my friend."

Louie stacks his winning chips, picks up his whiskey and takes the last mouthful from the glass. He spins round on his stool to order a further drink.

Just at this moment as Louie is distracted, the Croupier makes eye contact with Rowan. Just a wink but enough for Rowan to realise that this was it, it was on: the entrapment of Louie Arnett had now begun.

"Place your bets." This statement brings Louie back to the game.

Back in the office the roulette table is being watched closely by the two well-dressed men and the casino manager on the CCTV monitors. "Is that table fixed?" asks one of the well-dressed men.

"Mon Ami! Do you take us for fools?" says the Manager. "I know this is Paris but we still have gaming rules. The inspectors make frequent unannounced visits. If we got caught doing those stupid things we would get closed down immediately!"

The well-dressed man holds his hands up apologetically, "Sorry, sorry I didn't mean to be disrespectful. It's just that how are we going to trap Arnett if the table is not fixed?"

The manager gives a long stare to the well-dressed man, "You English, you English! I bet you don't even play on the fruit machines. The skill on the tables is in the hands of the Croupier. The man we have on tonight is one of the most sought after in Paris. He can really make money for the casinos," he says puffing his chest out proudly.

The well-dressed man looks puzzled. "Well how can he influence the game?" he says.

"Argh! You English! How you managed to conquer half the world I do not know," replied the casino manager. "A skilled Croupier has the ability to pick the number he wishes the ball to land on. He spins the wheel at a certain pace – the same every time, he looks on the table to see where the punters have placed most of their bets and works out roughly the cost to the casino. Then, as our man will do here tonight, he will release the ball at a certain point as the wheel spins round and at a certain pace which will then land onto a given group of numbers. Some Croupiers can even hit eight given numbers out of ten! Watch this."

At the Roulette table Louie is still in good humour but isn't doing as well as he'd hoped, however, Rowan is holding his own.

"Come on Armor be a bit braver than that," says Louie as Rowan places €1,000 on number 5. "This is where the money should be tonight," as he places €8,000 on 14 red.

"You mad Frenchman; you're going to lose all your money!" Rowan replied, laughing. Using his training to keep the atmosphere ticking along in good humour.

The wheel spins, the ball is released; it spins for a few seconds then *Ching, Ching, Ching!* It drops into number 5.

"You aren't part Irish are you Armor. Was that the luck of the fairies?" says Louie as he is assessing the damage to his 100,000 chips. His happy go lucky attitude had dropped a level. Realising he had taken a few hits on his stack of chips, *I've got to be less gung–ho*, he thinks

Rowan counts his chips, "37,000, hey that's not bad at all," smiling at Louie. "How are you doing my friend?" as he sees Louie's dishevelled expression.

"Don't you worry about Louie Arnett, my friend," as he puts 10,000 on number 23.

Rowan shook his head. "You're mad Louie. What are you doing, put five on 23 and the other five on… I don't know, 32! Split your bet up a bit, increase your chances of winning."

Louie stares distantly at Rowan. He is beginning to feel the whiskey now and the taste of blood has returned to his mouth.

Picking up a napkin from the side table, he wipes his lips which leaves the faint colour of red on the white material. He throws it into the trash.

Looking back at Rowan, rocking slightly on his stool, he says in a tipsy French way, "Don't ever tell me what to put my bets on you English pig," before laughing loudly.

Shrugging his shoulders, Rowan puts 5,000 on number 32 as he told Louie to do. The wheel rotates, and the ball is released, again, to more encouragement from the punters.

"Come on, come on you beauty."

If you didn't know better, they could have been watching a horse race.

"Come on, drop into 23!" shouts Louie. A hint of desperation in his voice now.

Ching, Ching, Ching the ball rattles on the wheel then drops into 32! Louie stares at the wheel disbelieving, as the croupier slows it down.

"I told you Louie, spread your bet, you should have stuck to your plan and played 32," Rowan tells Louie. "Spread your bet man!"

Louie slowly turns his head away from the table, then focuses his gaze on Rowan, he edges one step closer to him then stares square into Rowans face, eyeball to eyeball.

"Don't you ever tell me how to play the tables, do you understand? I would never ask an Englishman for *shit*, so don't tell me how to play roulette."

Rowan now knows that Louie's temper is taking over his reasoning, this response from Louie was all in his files, and it was all going to plan, Rowan also knows he's got to keep Louie on the edge. *'Just on the edge'.*

"Louie, look at my stack of chips." Rowan puts his hand on the back of Louie's neck and pivots his head round.

"Look at them Louie! Look at them. There is over 55,000 there now. Look at your stack," Rowan grabs hold of Louie's jacket lapel and turns him, Louie is now looking at his own bedraggled pile of chips.

"Look Louie, look, what is there?" Rowan knocks one or two of Louie's chips around with his fingers, as if to count them.

"You will be lucky if there's 23,000 there!"

Rowan places his hands either side of Louie's face and holds him still, then he looks very meaningfully into Louie's eyes.

"Look mate, just cash your chips in and go home with something. Please just go home." Rowan knows that Louie can't just walk away from the tables. If he has money burning a hole in his pocket he will have to play it, he was a complete gambling addict.

Rowan, still holding Louie's face, looking deep into his eyes, begins to realise that Louie has begun to cry. This caught Rowan off guard. He didn't expect this, he releases Louie; however, Rowan must have been supporting Louie when he was cupping his face, because he then had to make a grab for him as he almost fell.

Rowan sits him down at a table, then sits opposite him. Louie's tears had turned into quite a spell of emotion. As he takes some napkins off the table to dry his eyes, he coughs very quietly then spits the blood that he had just gargled up into the napkin as he looks at Rowan.

"I'm in the shit my friend. I can't go home, I lied to my wife, I told her I had this really lucrative job on this week, and that I would bring home almost €500,000. You see I'm so far behind with our mortgage that we are going to be evicted at the end of the week, unless I can come up with the €380,000 that we need. I came here to try and double my money but I should know better – it never works!" Louie wipes his mouth again looking like a lost soul.

Now if Rowan was a weaker minded man he may have felt sorry for Louie, but he knew from the dossier on this man that he was in shit street and that was the reason why Rowan was there. But it was just that this new information about Louie's debts, may make Rowans job easier.

"Look Louie," Rowan replies trying to give himself some time to think.

"You've got to find almost €400,000 by the end of the week to pay your debts off." *'Think Rowan, think. Just stick to the plan. Don't feel sorry for the man. Just stick to the plan'.*

Louie regains his composure. "That's not all Armor, my friend. I've got almost €1.5 million in debt to the Casino."

Rowan looks at Louie and tries to put on a very shocked and sympathetic expression.

"Then I've got debts to the sharks of Paris. Oh Armor, I'm really in the shit!" Louie makes a motion to grab Rowan's arm, Rowan turns quickly and grasps Louie's hand.

"That's not all that's wrong. I've seen you struggling for breath, and you've been coughing up blood. It's not looking good for you Louie is it?"

Louie is looking incredibly lost and dejected. "I'm dying Armor, I'm dying. It's lung cancer and it's getting worse as the weeks go by, but I must try to make things right for my wife before I die. I've been a bastard to her, and just thought of myself. Where I come from the debt belongs to the family."

Rowan already knew this, but he must keep up the deception, he must appear to be genuinely concerned. "What?! So they will still be pursuing your wife even after you have died?"

Louie is now staring intensely into Rowan's eyes; his fingers entwined in front of his mouth, tears streaming down his face as he can no longer contain his emotions. In a garbled splutter of whispered words, he opens his doomed soul to the betrayal of his family.

"You don't know the half of it Armor. I have two children and they also will be hounded for the debt as soon as they reach 18 years of age."

Rowan also knows this, but again he must convince Louie it's more dreadful news.

"They're going to make your children pay for this as well?! That's a total bastard's trick! Go to the police Louie. Go to the police you've got to put a stop to this!"

Louie gazes at Rowan, but doesn't speak. "What Louie, what? There's something you're not telling me?"

Louie's eyes glaze over again, his face awash with tears. "I can't go to the police Armor, I can't. You see it was me who signed the family up to the debt. I didn't know that I was going to contract lung cancer. I've got to get back to the table!" Louie's words are garbled from his emotions, as he gets up from his seat, wipes his face down with another paper napkin, staring at Rowan.

"You fucking idiot! Who in their right mind would sign their family over to a lifetime of debt?" Rowan spat. He couldn't help it; he was just so angry.

Louie rests his hand on Rowans shoulder, "You are right Armor *'who in their right mind'*? Come with me to the table and bring me some luck my friend."

Louie and Rowan re-join the game. Louie looks down at his miserable 22,300 worth of chips, he studies the table, *maybe Armor's right, spread your bets,* he thinks, this focuses his mind.

"Place your bets gentlemen, place your bets," says the croupier, so Louie in desperation puts 5,000 on 14. Spread your bets he thinks, 5,000 on 23, but on his favourite number he places €10,000, number 32.

Rowan looks at Louie, and taps him on the shoulder. "What the hell are you doing? You're going to lose the lot, that's 20,000 just on one game!"

"No, no, Armor I'm taking your advice and spreading my bets." The ball is released, Rowan doesn't get chance to lay a bet down.

The two men stare at the Roulette wheel spinning, "Come on Louie, come on," Rowan is encouraging the ball for his dying comrade. The high pitched zinging tone of the ball drops down an octave, as it slows and drops into the plate of the wheel, '*Ching, Ching, Ching*'.

It bounces on the dividers, Louie thrusting his hands forward, fists clenched tightly, "Come on, for me, just for me, please?" he shouts in desperation.

The croupier stops the rotation of the wheel, Louie now staring at the ball as it sits smugly in its pocket, unable to react, unable to even breathe. He cushions his forehead in the palm of his hands as his head drops.

"House pays 5 on the red, the house pays number 5," says the croupier.

"No, no, no," he cries, his voice full of anguish. He took a deep breath, trying to get himself under control. It didn't work. "Oh God, what am I going to do?"

Rowan sees Louie's desperation. *We've got him, we've got him*, Rowan thinks, but just to cement Louie's downfall he slides €10,000 over to him.

"Here Louie, take this money. I will lend you 10,000. Try once more," Rowan says, knowing full well that the croupier would ensure that Louie would lose that too.

Louie looks up at Rowan, then pushes the chips back to him.

"No, no, my friend I cannot take your money, I have just one last chance." Louie fidgets in his pocket and takes his car keys out, he throws them on the table, and looks up at the croupier.

"Monsieur, this is my final desperate chance to win. Will you take my car as collateral for an €80,000 bet, my final bet?"

The croupier picks up the phone linked to the manager's office. The two well-dressed men look at the manager as he answers the call. They had been watching the croupier on the monitor and were concerned over what was occurring at the table. Here was the answer.

"He's what? Put his car up for a final 80,000 euro bet?" says the manager looking at the two well-dressed men, who in turn look at each other, a half frown and half smile appears on their faces.

"He's put his car up for a final bet," repeats one of the well-dressed men, "this couldn't be any easier!"

"You would think he would have realised by now that… Oh never mind," says the other.

They nod in approval at the manager to go ahead with the deal.

"He has that *Luxury Mercedes Pullman?*" The manager asks the croupier.

"Yes, I think he does," is the reply.

"Well that will easily cover the bet. Go ahead," says the manager. "Go ahead." He then turns to one of the casino enforcers, "Get down there and bring Arnett up here as soon as he loses his car."

One of the well-dressed men speaks up, "Can you bring his car keys with you?"

"Yes boss," was the reply.

Louie is given the go ahead to make the bet. Rowan can't believe this, the man is already drowning but he's now attaching a lead weight to his feet.

Louie stares at the table, he makes a slight coughing noise deep in his throat. The taste of blood returns to his mouth. *Nothing I can do about that now*, he thinks, *'shit or bust' I can't keep losing, I can't. Number 32, do it Louie do it*. Slowly, he leans forwards and places his keys on number 32.

By now quite a few patrons of the casino had gathered around the roulette table, interested in what was going to happen. Louie laughed to himself; it was just like the old days. Him being the center of attention, everyone else coming to see the car crash as it happened.

"Final bets," says the croupier, making eye contact with Louie. The wheel spins, a few seconds later the ball is released; everyone at the table is in silence. All you can hear is the zinging of the ball as it spins round and round the wheel, it seems to be going and going and going. Almost in slow motion the ball drops down onto the thin dividing blades between each number, *'Ching, Ching, Ching,'* it bounces once, twice, three times before finally coming to rest.

Louie has to refocus his eyes as the coughing in his

throat had brought tears to them. It's 32! It is, it's 32! He can't believe it! The croupier then announces, "The house pays 23 on the red, pays 23."

Louie seems to freeze, a couple of seconds pass; he looks up from the table towards the croupier. "No Monsieur, you are mistaken! The ball is on 32, it is on 32."

"The house pays 23 sir. That's 23 on the red."

Louie looks at Armor. "You saw it Armor you saw it, that was on 32, it was!"

Louie was becoming more and more hysterical, he had lost everything! All the money and his beloved *Mercedes* car. He began to feel physically sick, blood was beginning to trickle from Louie's nose.

Rowan passes Louie a napkin, looking as sympathetic as he could. "Here Louie give your face a wipe. I'm sorry my friend, but the ball was never in 32."

Just at that moment Louie felt a strong hand on his shoulder, he turned his head to see who it was.

"Hello Louie. Remember me?" says the casino enforcer. Louie doesn't answer. "The boss wants to see you." With that the enforcer stretches his hand out towards the croupier.

"The *Mercedes* keys please Simon," he is handed the keys. Louie then turns back to Rowan, but there is no-one there, he looks left, he looks right, no-one there. That's strange, thought Louie, where's Armor? Then in no rush he is half nudged and half directed away to the office.

As Louie enters the manager's office he is expecting to perhaps lose a finger or an ear, as a warning to others, but all he could think about were his two children, his wife and perhaps a slight thought for Carmel.

The two men reach the manager's oversized desk, Louie is aware of three other people in the office. He thinks the worst as he holds the now blood sodden napkin to his face.

The enforcer places the *Mercedes* keys on the desk in front of the manager, who then waves his hand at the enforcer in a direct order to leave the room, which he does.

The manager is now tossing the keys from one hand to the other, not saying anything for a minute or so, just staring at Arnett the whole time. Louie on the other hand is becoming more and more concerned for his own safety. Shuffling from one foot to the other, feeling very vulnerable.

He had heard in the past of people that had just disappeared, vanished never to be seen again, or was that a rumor started by the casino? Who knows?

"You've had a shit night my friend," spouts the manager, holding his hands up with the palms open in a sympathetic manner, "but that's how it goes sometimes." With that he stands up from his desk and with a slight gesture of his right arm he invites Louie over to the comfortable area of the office.

"These gentlemen have come all the way from England to see you Louie. Why you, I don't know, and I don't care, but do not think you are some sort of celebrity. To me, you're just dog dirt on someone's shoe."

The manager then turns and walks towards the

office door. He is caught up by one of the well-dressed men who thanks him for the use of his office and gives him an envelope full of cash. Returning, the first well-dressed man passes the oversized desk, picking up the *Mercedes* keys, he slips them into his jacket pocket.

The manager leaves, and the other well-dressed man invites Louie to make himself comfortable on the sofas, then he asks Steve, the second ruggedly dressed man, to bring a bowl of warm water so Louie can clean the dried blood from his face.

Immaculately dressed in his three piece suit is the first well-dressed man.

Standing dominantly in total control of the frightened, captured creature before him, he studies Louie for a moment, then breaks the silence. "So Monsieur Arnett, we meet at last. I bet you're thinking *what is all this about?* Well my friend we've been keeping an eye on you, and the truth is you think yourself quite a bit of a rebel, don't you?"

Steve returns with the hot water and a flannel. Louie begins to clean himself up. "Can I get you a drink Monsieur Arnett?" says Steve.

Louie is now looking completely vacant in his expression. "Look, I don't know you guys, but you seem to know a lot about me."

"No Louie, you don't know who we are and you never will. Do you mind if I call you Louie?" Arnett shrugs his shoulders in a *'no I don't mind'* response.

"Well Louie we do know a lot about you, we have files and dossiers on half the population in Europe but we have picked you out of all those people because we believe we can help you, and in return you can help us."

Louie recognizes the thread of this conversation. He had been involved in so many bent deals over the years, that he knew exactly where this was going. Straight away he is seeing dollar signs.

He begins to regain his self-esteem, feeling more like his old self, 'Louie Arnett, chauffeur to the stars.' If only he still had his beloved *Mercedes*.

The second well-dressed man turns to face Louie. "Yes Louie," he says reaching into his jacket pocket, "we cannot give you too much information just yet, but we have a proposition to put to you that will put everything right for you, for your family, even as far away as your grandchildren, and to start with, here are your car keys back…"

Chapter 2

California Dreamer

The car slipped silkily through the bright Pacific morning, the brand new engine running like a dream.

The day was light and clear, the early summer heat not yet having settled over the Californian countryside. There was a stiff breeze coming off the ocean – bringing a sense of freshness and that salty tang that told of long, hot beaches and coves where the water was clear and blue.

There was something exquisite about the way the sunlight struck the vibrant scarlet bodywork and polished silver hubcaps of the *Jaguar* as it hugged the coast road, high above the sea. It shone brightly down upon the leather seats and dark, honey-colored walnut interior. It glinted off the sparkling handles of the golf clubs in the backseat and scorched the arm of its driver, which was already sporting a rich tan – the product of countless previous journeys and many days spent out on the course.

Josh Banner – the proud owner of this fine car –

whistled along to the song on the radio, the corners of his mouth turning up as the wind ruffled through his hair.

Life was sweet.

He chuckled as the song changed to an oldie but a 'goodie' – *If I Could Turn Back Time* by Cher. It seemed particularly apt.

He followed the coast road until it headed inland into a valley sheltered by a slight ridge, then pulled off the main drag. It wasn't long before the chain link fence came into view – the first herald of one of the most high-tech research facilities in the world. In many ways, it was Josh's own private kingdom, and the sight of the building never failed to give him a bit of a confidence boost.

Though, of course, some days it gave him the shivers too.

After all, how many people could say they worked in a facility like this? How many people were working on something so huge, something so potentially life-changing? World-changing, in fact? He was one of the privileged few, and he knew it. Not that he'd ever tell the others how he felt, of course – he had a certain image to uphold at work, and feelings and emotions didn't usually come into it.

Pulling up to the main gate, Josh nodded cheerfully to the Security Guard on duty, the start of his daily ritual.

"Good morning Professor Banner," the man said, leaning down to Josh's window with a big friendly smile.

"Morning Stan," Josh grinned. "How's it going?"

"Pretty quiet, Professor." Stan shrugged his shoulders affably. "You're in early today."

"Well, it's the kind of morning where you just can't wait to get out of bed," said Josh, jerking a thumb out of the window at the clear, sapphire skies above them.

Stan chuckled, though he didn't seem quite as enthusiastic as Josh; he did have to spend most of the day in his little security hut, after all. "You got that right."

He checked Josh's ID – though since they'd both worked at the facility for several years there really wasn't much need anymore. The protocol, however, was important: it reminded every member of the staff – scientific, security, janitorial or technical – that security was paramount. It was also part of the structure of the facility, the daily routine, the repetitive predictability that was vital in order for somewhere like this to work. If one person stepped out of line, if one person dropped the ball or disregarded their specially thought-out routine, who knows what could happen in a place like this.

Not that Josh was all that bothered about security himself, however. In fact, he hadn't been for some time. While he wouldn't share the secrets of his work with anyone outside the complex, he just didn't think there was any point in worrying about it anymore.

Even if he did happen to spill one or two secrets regarding his work, there was no way in hell anyone would ever believe him. The disbelieving, close-minded natures of his friends and family were the most powerful security tool he knew of, and he assumed it would be the same for most other members of staff here.

Even in 1997 – with just three years to go to the millennium – a lot of people were still stuck in their old-fashioned mindsets.

Josh drove into the parking lot – which was already filling up with the cars of his colleagues – and parked a short distance from his building.

It was just far enough away to enjoy the sunshine on the way over, and just close enough that his mind wouldn't wander too much before he got there – a habit of Josh's that he was trying hard to lose. Plus, sometimes it was just good to be able to stretch your legs, something he didn't get to do too much of once he was sitting at his desk.

Opening the car door, he grabbed his briefcase from the passenger seat and set off, still whistling that Cher song – a song that had been whistled, sung, and hummed more times around here than you could count, thought Josh as he entered the building.

Striding past the reception desk, he headed straight to the coffee machine, the first port of call for every member of staff throughout the complex. Someone once said that scientific discovery was driven by money, and while that was at least partly true, Josh knew better. Off the beaten track in San Diego, it was driven primarily by caffeine. And lots of it.

He breathed in the rich aroma as he made his usual – cream and two sugars, to get those brain cells firing – before peering into the lion's den.

The room beyond was where a lot of the action

happened, and today it was uncharacteristically noisy, which meant that no one had bothered to actually turn on their computers and get down to work yet.

They were all too busy gossiping, and Josh supposed that was the mark of a successful team: people who would come up with ideas that could change the world and still be able to laugh at the antics of a co-worker's kids.

You didn't want too much work and too little play, no matter what field you were in, and especially when you were in one as mind-bending and overwhelming as this. Sometimes you just needed to talk about silly things, like what you watched on TV and how long it took you to get to work today. Sometimes you just needed to talk normally, like you were in a normal office doing normal, mundane office work.

You could even believe the whole 'normal' thing for a while, too, until you got back to work.

In many ways the research facility was like a village, and for the most part, everyone rubbed along pretty well, with the odd, inevitable exception. Just like every village had an idiot, every office had that person you'd rather not sit next to. This office had several.

Yes, changing the world was hard work, and being able to blow off steam occasionally was a release valve from the stress and pressure of it all. Not that there had been many world-changing ideas of late, he thought, frowning.

Putting that unhelpful thought at the back of his mind, Josh finished making his coffee as he eyed Becky, the beautiful secretary, in his peripheral vision.

Becky was everything the research facility needed in a secretary: she was brilliant, intelligent, thoughtful, and had the managerial skills of a fleet commander. She kept them all in check, which wasn't the easiest job in the world – and she didn't take any crap. When she needed to be, she was tough. Really tough. She was good at her job, and she knew it.

And, although she was much desired and adored by pretty much everyone who worked there, she still managed to keep them all at arm's length, never getting too close to anyone. Josh was sure she had her reasons for this, though he hadn't yet found out what they were.

She was also drop dead gorgeous – which none of the all-male engineering team had failed to notice – and although she dressed impeccably and clearly put a lot of effort into her appearance, her looks seemed to be almost secondary: for Becky, the job always came first. As a woman in a male-oriented field, she radiated professionalism – while some of her colleagues did not.

Feeling his covert gaze, she looked up and betrayed only the faintest hint of annoyance that someone was, yet again, staring at her. If Josh hadn't been watching carefully he'd have missed it, but as it was, he saw an almost imperceptible twitch at the corner of her mouth. It was her irritated twitch, and it was kind of cute.

"Hi Josh," she smiled. "You're looking like the cat who's got the cream – you must have a promise on today."

He picked up his coffee and turned towards her,

unconsciously puffing out his chest a little at the same time.

While he knew that nothing would ever happen between them, it wouldn't hurt to try and impress her a little. Of course, he'd been trying for years and he didn't think he'd impressed her even one bit in all that time. She was a hard nut to crack, despite her polite exterior.

"I dropped the kids off at camp for a couple of weeks," he explained, trying to sound smooth as he smiled at her. "I've got the clubs in the car for an afternoon on the green at Santo's and I'm taking Mary Lou down to Mexico tomorrow, so you bet! I'm on a different planet entirely today!"

He grinned, inching up to her and winking in what he hoped would be a charming and adorable kind of way. Unfortunately, at the same time he managed to tilt his coffee cup, spilling the hot liquid all over himself and making him shout out loud in a rather effeminate manner.

Becky stared at him, looking distinctly unimpressed, but he managed to laugh it off, giving her a big smile.

After a few seconds of steely silence, she shook her head at him, chuckling. "Nice one, Josh; you're a source of endless entertainment."

He coughed at the unexpected – and sarcastic, it had to be said – compliment, before stumbling back over to the coffee machine and refilling his cup, resolutely trying to ignore the brown stains that were currently flowering on his shirt and tie.

Drink refilled, he made a hasty retreat into the

laboratory beyond, where Bradley, Jerry, and Zachary were milling around, getting their brains into gear for the working day.

As Josh said a general hi to the room, he looked at his fellow workmates.

Brad was a slightly plump, genial sort of fellow. He was still a kid at heart, though he was in his early forties now. He was always up for a laugh, but that had never stopped him from furthering his scientific knowledge – he had a real thirst for it, and his desire to learn was what kept him motivated. He'd learned his trade working on the Apollo program, which made him something of a celebrity among the younger engineers on the base. He spent most of his lunch breaks telling stories that they'd all heard a thousand times, but no one minded.

Jerry – who was currently rearranging the papers on his desk – was a quiet, sometimes distant man, far more comfortable with data than with other people. In terms of social dynamics, he was a little clueless, but if you wanted to know where Mars was on any given day or how the asteroid belt was behaving, he could give you an answer in under a minute.

He spoke mathematics like other people could speak French, and any scientific problem any staff member ever had was always taken to Jerry. Josh had a great deal of respect for him, though he felt that occasionally he took life a little too seriously. It was one of the reasons there was sometimes tension in their little office, when Brad's jokes got out of hand and Jerry didn't know how to react. When that happened, awkward silences were common.

Zackary – the fourth member of their little scientific quartet – was Josh's best friend. He was a laid-back, easy-going sort of guy who could trace his family back to the Nazi occupation of Europe, where they had lived at the time.

Like many of their contemporaries in the Jewish diaspora, the majority of them had been murdered in the war, and Zackary might never have lived if the Americans hadn't liberated the camp his mother was imprisoned in – just at the very moment she had given birth to him, as it so happened. It was one hell of an origin story, that's for sure.

His mother had died very soon after and it was the unlikeliest quirk of fate that had led to an American soldier picking him up and taking him back to their medical team, unable to ignore the cries of an hours-old babe in arms. He'd been taken back to America where he was adopted by a Jewish family – as many lost babies were after the war – and he'd been given a good education. A great education, really. He was smart, but Zackary's main gift was his imagination, something which had pulled them out of intellectual ruts time and time again.

Although they'd come from different places and had various backgrounds and upbringings, all four men had keen scientific minds and were close enough in age that they got on very well. Josh was glad – and felt very lucky – to work with them.

They all looked up as Josh greeted them, and both Zackary and Brad high-fived him as he made his way to his desk.

"Hi Josh, just seen you performing for Becky,"

Brad sniggered. "You never give up, do you? You've no chance anyway; she's out with a *real* man tonight." He waggled his eyebrows suggestively as he grinned, running a hand through his thick, brown hair and showing off his ridiculously expensive sparkly gold watch. That thing was his pride and joy, but Josh thought it looked tacky and ugly on his wrist.

"In your dreams, Brad," Josh scoffed. "She's only got the hots for that 'special one'."

"Yeah, 'special' being the operative word," replied Brad, laughing. "She's waiting for 'Mr Right' and you, my friend, are not it. You're Mr Wrong, or Mr Not-In-A-Million-Years or…"

"Yeah, yeah, I get it," said Josh, chuckling. How many times had they had this same conversation? This exact throwing about of insults in relation to Becky, almost word for word? Somehow, it never got old. That was when you knew that you actually liked the people you worked with, instead of fantasizing about ripping their heads off and kicking them around the office like footballs.

Next in line was Jerry, whose attention was completely focused on his desk, as usual. And – again, as usual – Josh crept up behind and poked him in the side, scaring the living daylights out of him. He clutched at his chest, giving a shout of fright. It was the same every time.

Josh waited for his friend to recover before asking, "Got all your gear with you, Jerry? We're going to Santo's today to flex the old irons." It had been a while since they'd all gone, and Josh was looking forward to it. Had been all week.

"Not me, man," Jerry shook his head sadly. "I'm going through all these calculations again – I want to make sure we achieve the finest degree of perfection."

Ah, perfection. That one thing everyone strives for, thought Josh, *especially around here.* But could perfection ever really be achieved? Most things in life weren't perfect, and in their field of work it was seemingly impossible to get to that level. A pipe dream. A fantasy.

Perfect! If only.

"Hey, give it up, Jerry," Josh told him. "You know they'll never use the missile."

The room went silent for a moment, Brad and Zackary looking over at the sound of the 'M' word.

"Josh," said Jerry, shaking his head slowly, "we *don't* know that, and if anyone ever asks me, I'm going to pretend you never said those words."

Josh sighed before glancing around the room to check no one else was there. Even though the coast was clear, he still lowered his voice to a whisper. "What I mean is, what's the point of trying to achieve perfection on something that *probably* isn't ever going to get used? It's never going to become a reality, because it's not possible! The best we can do is get close to achieving it, so the 'perfection' you speak of isn't worth chasing. I know that, you know that, everyone knows that… so why not relax a little instead of beating your head against your desk? Come on, let's all go down to Santo's, it'll be fun!" He raised his voice again on the last sentence, smiling at his co-workers and raising his eyebrows suggestively.

Jerry's shoulders slumped a little as he dropped down into his chair. "I'm sick of this, Josh," he snapped. "We *can* launch the missile, we just need to iron out the navigational problems. The new engines are ready, the rocket boosters are ready, the fuel tanks are ready – all we need to do now is get our heads around how we tell the darned thing precisely where to go."

Josh shook his head. Jerry had never been able to leave something alone if it wasn't exactly perfect. And while it may be true that in a scientific context that was a very good thing, right now it was mostly just annoying.

"Oh, give it a rest," Josh urged. "The missile is never going to travel through time because *time travel is not possible*!" he hissed. "Now can we please just let it go and enjoy the fruits of our labor? We've come pretty damn close, and that should be enough."

Jerry sighed, staring at Josh as if he were mad. "I didn't sign up for 'pretty damn close'. We don't get paid to come 'pretty damn close'. Don't you want to change the world?"

Josh shrugged. "If I could, I would, but let's not get sucked into some kind of sci-fi fantasy, OK?" He was trying hard not to lose his temper; they had the same argument every so often, and this particular one was something that *did* get to him. This one got old fast. "Look, they won't keep us on these paychecks forever – not once they realize we're flogging a very large, very dead horse – and I for one intend to make the most of it." He pretended to swing an invisible golf club, then put his hand to his forehead as if he were watching his golf ball land meters away.

Jerry put his head in his hands, and once he'd

finished watching his imaginary ball, Josh patted his shoulder consolingly. "You always were a bit of a dreamer, Jerry, but hey – you're one of the best guys to have around if we have a problem. You should be proud of the work you do, even if it's not *exactly* what we're supposed to be doing."

He shook his head at Jerry one more time before turning his attention to Zack. He, too, looked tired and frustrated, and Josh frowned – something he seemed to be doing a lot lately. Jerry was always a little sensitive about his work, sure, but it was usually different with Zack, and Josh's sixth sense told him there were problems here. Big problems.

"Zack, you're looking a bit down, man," he observed. "You look as if you've fallen into a barrel full of nipples and come out sucking your thumb." He laughed, the smile dropping from his face when he realized he was the only one finding his words funny.

"Don't mess about," Zack told him, uncharacteristically stern. "Billy's had some bad news; he's been waiting for you to get here." With that, Zack lifted himself up from his desk and met his friend's eyes. He didn't just look tired; he looked absolutely exhausted, like he hadn't slept in days.

Josh felt the color drain from his face. This was bad. This was serious. This was…

Yeesh, and it had looked like it was going to be such a good day. That song on the radio had lulled him into a false sense of security, the thought of the golf making him almost goofy with happiness, and now it was all coming back to bite him on the ass.

"He's in the missile bays," Zack said, looking grim.

"Let's go."

Josh followed him out of the office, sparing a backward glance at Brad and Jerry, who were watching his expression carefully. He saw them share a dark look before the door closed behind him, and an unpleasant nauseous feeling started to take up residence in his stomach. Just what the hell was going on here?

He didn't have time for this.

He and Zack strode silently out into the hall, picked up Becky as they passed reception, and then left the office building, walking briskly across the open area towards the missile bays.

Josh looked up at the sky as they went, the sun taunting him now with its blaring hot rays, rather than fueling his good mood as it had when he'd been in his car. He should have just driven past the facility that morning, headed down to Santo's early and called in sick.

If only he knew this was going to happen, he could have avoided it.

Though Josh took his responsibilities (reasonably) seriously, he wasn't averse to running away from a problem if it was particularly big or particularly bad; he was a strong believer in facing his issues head on, unless it was easier to leg it in the opposite direction, which most of the time, it was.

As a result, Josh found that if he ignored his problems for long enough, they usually went away. It was what he was doing with the time travel missile too – that venture had far too many problems and issues to deal with, and no one had time for that. Pun intended.

As always, Becky walked very properly, her arms primly folded across her chest, her expression and demeanor not giving anything away; Zack strode forward like a man on a mission, his chin up and his sleeves rolled back. Josh, on the other hand, kicked out at imaginary stones, his good mood now entirely punctured.

As they walked, Becky glanced between the two men, curious. "Any idea what's wrong, you two?"

Josh frowned. He'd been assuming that Becky would know all about this, but if even their resident battle-axe wasn't in the loop, then…

"Don't really know," said Zack evasively. "But Billy's been really pissed off all morning."

"I've got an idea," Josh grumbled. "I bet it's the Government Funding Agency."

He felt the rhythm of his co-workers' gait slow for a moment as they digested this possibility, and they both turned to stare at him, looking faintly horrified, before picking up the pace a little more briskly than before. If he was right, they all had quite a lot to lose here.

A problem with the GFA had always been a possibility, of course, but Josh – like the others – tried not to think about it too much. He liked living in the moment rather than worrying about the future or dwelling on mistakes made in the past, but it was quite possible that the moment was about to get very sticky indeed. The sick feeling in his stomach intensified.

The missile silos were a little way from the office building for safety reasons – along with security, safety was paramount around here. While they may not be able to get the perfection that was required to make the time travel missile work, there was plenty that could go wrong in the pursuit of it.

On the other side of the parking lot, the business end of the industrial park was arranged around a series of connecting paths and walkways. From the outside, it could have been a University campus or a technology park, but inside it looked like something out of a sci-fi movie, with acres of clean concrete and painted metal gantries leading to mysterious steel doors. Everything that was in here surrounded the revamped *Saturn 5* spacecraft.

Upon passing through the normal security checks – of which there were several in this restricted area, and more than a guy in a little hut – Josh, Zack and Becky turned inside, entering the great missile bay.

For a moment, all three of them paused inside the hangar doors and simply stared at the machine they were building: the culmination of years of their work. The very stuff of dreams, they'd thought at the start, and as it turned out, they were right – dreams were all it was ever made of.

Josh stared at the impressive-looking machine. Was it arrogance to believe that time travel was possible? That almost every preceding generation of physicists had been wrong? Josh had his fair share of arrogance, but he wasn't so sure about the science needed to get this thing off the ground. Making it work in theory was a whole different kettle of fish to actually getting something to the point where it could travel in time.

Or was Jerry right? Did everything hang on getting that last line of equations squared away? In here, with the enormous weight of history upon them, it was easy to fall in love with that dream, however far from reality it might seem the rest of the time.

Shaking his head, he tried to concentrate on the present.

At the moment, the spacecraft was on its side, having been divided up into five equal parts. It seemed as if a magician had had the thing volunteer for the saw-the-lady-in-half trick and been called away halfway through. It looked a little forlorn, a little vulnerable, lying there like that.

The central section, however, was coming along nicely: the engines had been inverted to direct their mighty propulsion force back towards the time travel missile with the intention of pushing it *through* space instead of out into it.

The time travel capsule itself sat atop of the central stem, looking relatively small compared to the massive equipment surrounding it and gleaming in the bright, clinical light.

The view had floored Josh the first time he'd seen it, but it almost bored him now that he'd been there so many times. It was amazing what human beings could get used to, amazing how quickly the magic went out of things.

The four remaining parts of the rocket were being moved into position around the central stem, acting as extra fuel tanks. They would need it, if the missile ever worked; where that was going, it would need all the propulsion it could get, and breaking the laws of physics took quite some oomph. It had all been painstakingly designed to fit inside the loading bay of the Space Shuttle, ready for deployment – and, if it worked, ready to be collected again at the other end.

Of course, that was a lot of ifs.

Together, they walked along the narrow metal gantry that passed beside the time travel capsule. Josh and Zack stroked reverent hands across the outer hull of the capsule, and Becky rolled her eyes. Whether it ever worked or not, she knew it was their 'baby'. Men and their toys.

"Come on, you two, stop day dreaming," she admonished them lightly. "Let's find Billy and get this over with."

As soon as she'd said that, her eyes caught and rested on a group of men below; Zack and Josh followed the direction of her gaze and saw Billy, shaking hands with several technicians who had been with the company for many years.

"What's he doing?" Josh asked, frowning for what felt like the millionth time that day, and it wasn't even lunchtime yet. "He's shaking those guys' hands as if he's just met them."

"He looks like he's going to burst into tears," Zack remarked, his voice low and quiet. Josh wasn't surprised at the tone of his colleague's voice – the whole scene looked off, and as he watched the men below, his stomach churning went up a notch.

They followed the secretary into the open-caged lift at the end of the gantry, and it took them down two levels, where Billy was waiting for them.

Billy was a senior scientist in his mid-fifties, though these days he looked much older. He was the Project Director for the Time Travel Project and the strain of keeping the enterprise going was clearly affecting his nerves, aging the man prematurely. Josh felt for him.

Today in particular, he looked like he was on the brink of a mental breakdown, his hair in disarray, his face pale, his eyes bloodshot. This was not a healthy man, not at all.

"Hey Billy," shouted Josh. "What's up?"

Billy turned and gave them an awkward little wave, something that seemed to take up far more of the man's energy than it should.

The four of them met near the engines of the craft, where Becky grasped Billy's arm, concerned. "Seriously Billy, what's wrong?" she asked, surprised. "You look dreadful."

Billy – who might normally have taken mock offense to her words and shot back some witty remark – instead said nothing, but he took Becky's hands in his, staring woefully at her worried face.

Josh eyed them a little jealously. Becky was such a stunner, and every man working at the complex envied how close she and Billy were. They had been close confidantes for years, although Josh wasn't sure when their friendship had started, or how.

It was clear that Billy was close to tears; pale and trembling, he looked like he was facing his own personal apocalypse.

"God Billy, what's wrong?" Josh asked. "You look

like shit, man!" He said this in a jovial tone, hoping to lighten the mood, but it didn't exactly have the desired effect.

Instead, Billy shot all three of them a miserable look before leading them to a nearby workstation where they could all sit down together. It was almost a relief – Billy looked like he might have simply toppled over if he'd remained standing up for much longer.

The workstation – like all the other things in the missile silos – was overshadowed by the *Saturn 5* and its unusual capsule. It was impossible for the eye not to be drawn to it – it was as if it had its own gravity.

"I *feel* like shit, Josh," Billy said heavily. "My buddy from the Government Funding Agency was over last night. Apparently the Head of the Agency has been *encouraged* to retire. Millions of dollars have disappeared from the accounts; it looks like he's been embezzling funds for years." He shook his head in disgust. "From what I gathered, he was interviewed by the police but they're not going to lock him up – they need to save face for the government. Bastard."

Josh gaped at the Director, trying to absorb this new information. The silence that greeted his statement was profound.

Fuck! Where does that leave us? Josh wondered. Up shit creek without a paddle, no doubt…

So, it was happening. It was really happening.

Reaching up, he loosened his tie; he was suddenly feeling very hot, and more than a little claustrophobic.

"So what?" Zack asked, breaking the uncomfortable

silence. "That doesn't mean anything. How does that affect us? No one's going to be bothered about what we're doing. Come on, Billy, pick yourself up, man!" They were encouraging words, but the tremble in his voice betrayed what he was really feeling – what they were all feeling.

Billy made a disconsolate sort of noise: a kind of desolate bleat, like a wounded animal who knew it's time was nearly up.

"I can't go on, Zack," he moaned, looking wretched. "I've lost it. I've been down to the medical center – they think I'm having a breakdown."

Called it, thought Josh, before immediately giving himself a mental slap. Now was not the time for those kind of stupid, childish thoughts.

Billy looked around, his eyes hollow and exhausted. "My buddy told me last night that the man taking over is a very clever, well-respected businessman, and that the government are having a crackdown on spending money. It's practically a guarantee that they'll be coming here, poking their noses around – and what've we got to show them?" He waved at the hulking missile above them, his tone a little hysterical.

Becky put her hand on Billy's arm again, wearing an expression that clearly indicated what Josh was currently thinking: that they were all responsible for destroying this man's health. They'd all worked hard, but not hard enough, and they'd lost sight of the goal.

And now this was happening.

Billy sighed again. "His instructions are that everything has to be gone through, and that he has to abandon any project that looks a bit suspect. So, that's us gone for a start. I've let you down – all of you."

"Billy, please stick with us," Becky pleaded soothingly. "We're a team! After all these years you can't just walk away from us. We'll be fine."

Billy stared at her, eyebrows raised. "Fine? Becky, how can you even think that? As soon as they start investigating us, we're toast!"

His voice was starting to have that hysterical edge to it again, and Josh leaned forwards, lowering his voice in an attempt to sooth the Director. "Come on, Billy, it's not that bad."

Billy shot another disbelieving look at Josh. "You know, for someone who works with scientists and mathematicians, I sure am surrounded by a load of idiots!" He stood up, his nervous energy stopping him from sitting any longer. "We've been cooking the damn books – how is that 'not that bad'? Did you not hear how this whole mess started? The Head of the Agency was embezzling! He got found out, so we're definitely going to get found out! How do you not see how bad this is? We could all go to jail!"

Becky shot nervous glances at Zack and Josh before turning back to Billy, placing her hand on his shoulder and giving it a comforting squeeze. "Billy, try and chill, OK? This isn't your fault, and no one's going to jail."

"Yeah, come on, Billy," said Josh, trying to encourage him. "All that shit I've been putting in those three-monthly reports – no businessman is ever going to understand that. They'll take one look at it and wish they'd left us well alone. Come on, man;

we're golden!"

"I'm serious, guys, I can't take any more of this," Billy cried, wringing his hands. "They're going to lock us up when they find out we've been living the dream with their money! Especially if there's no actual time travel to come out of all this. I don't want to go to jail… I think I'd rather…" he trailed off, looking up at Becky with tears in his eyes while he ran a shaking hand across his sweaty forehead.

Seeing her friend look so distraught broke something in Becky, and her eyes also filled with tears as she patted him on the hand once more. "Don't say that, Billy, and don't you dare do anything stupid. For now, we just need to wait and see what happens; there's no use doing anything drastic until we have all the facts."

It was as if Billy wasn't even listening to her. "I've spoken to the Government Department this morning and I'm taking my pension *now!* This very moment! I don't want to stick around and see this place go to the dogs, it's too hard, we've put too much into it…" He suddenly slapped his hand on the table, making Becky jump. "No! I'm leaving."

"No!" Josh exclaimed, taken aback. "Let's keep this going! I'm telling you, we've got it good here – this new guy at the top's not going to change anything. He'll probably have a look around, be impressed with the machine, and leave us to it."

He waited for a response from one of his colleagues, and when he got none, he shook his head. No matter what he said, Josh was perfectly aware that this new businessman was bad news – particularly for his bank balance. A man gets used to a certain standard of living, and if they gave this up, his lifestyle just wouldn't be possible anymore. He highly doubted that anyone would just 'leave them to it', either; anyone with half a brain could see this wasn't going anywhere. Most people didn't believe in things like time travel as a rule, and no amount of flashy equipment was going to fool them without concrete proof that it was possible.

Billy let out a loud sigh. "And you, Josh, you'd better start thinking of what you're going to tell them, because they'll be coming here later this week to have a look around." He gave a hollow chuckle. "They want to see where all their money has gone, and what your solution is to get this fucking thing off the ground. So if you don't have one – which I know you don't – you'd better think of something, fast."

Billy gestured wildly towards the time travel capsule, and it was clear that his frustration – built up over years and years of trying to hold a ridiculous project together – had finally boiled over.

His face was crimson with fury, and he was glaring right at Josh. As if Josh were the only person here, the only person responsible. He may have been there right from the beginning, but there was a hell of a lot of other people involved in this too.

Well, thought Josh, *everyone needs a scapegoat.*

"And another thing," Billy shouted, really getting into his rant now, "all you ever think about these days is going down to Santo's for your *freaking* golf, day after day – and when you're not doing that you're off down to Mexico! What about this place?" he demanded. "I mean, it was you who put all this together a decade ago. This is all you! All of it!"

Josh stared at the angry Director, unsure of what to say, which was a first.

"Anyway, all of that – Mexico, Santo's, your precious high life – will be coming to an end because you'll be sharing a *freaking prison cell WITH ME!*" he roared, pointing a trembling finger in Josh's face.

"Hey, come on," said Becky, in her best calming voice, but Billy ignored her. He had lowered his finger now, but he was still staring at Josh like he wanted to kill him.

Zack hovered worriedly beside them, more than ready to jump in and stop them brawling should the need arise. No one wanted a punch up at work, but he was also thinking of the equipment in the room, most of which cost more than some countries' GDP. No fight was worth destroying that kind of kit.

Josh – who had been getting pretty riled up during all of Billy's accusations – was sorely tempted to sock Billy in the eye, but just before he could, Billy tutted to himself, relaxing his posture out of fight mode. "Ah, fuck it!" he exclaimed, before turning and stalking away. "Fuck all of it. I'm done with this. I'm done with you, I'm done with this whole fucking place!"

Once Billy had gone, Becky sighed, glancing at Josh and Zack before walking off in the opposite direction.

Josh turned to Zack, shrugging. "That went well."

Chapter 3

Bo was actually 'Dutch'

The office block of the Government Funding Agency was fairly quiet at 12.30 a.m., which made paperwork significantly easier to go through. There were far fewer opportunities for interruption, for one thing, and no meetings to disrupt proceedings. Security personnel had also been posted outside the doors of the main office to ensure that the two men closeted within weren't disturbed. It was quiet enough for a man to think – to *really* think.

The two men had been going through as much paperwork and as many records and files as they could find in relation to the projects the Agency had been funding under the tenure of the outgoing Director. It was a lot like sifting through an endless snowdrift of paper, and in many cases, an endless pile of shit.

Most of the staff had been given extended leave in order to better facilitate the research without interruption – and more importantly, without records being 'lost' before they could get to them. This was a job that had to be done properly, after all, and neither man intended to leave any stone unturned. It was a matter of pride, really. Pride of a really slow, boring job, but pride nonetheless.

The newly appointed Head of the Funding Agency, Bo Nick Olsen, and his right-hand man, John Dillon, were on their knees, surrounded by mountains of folders and documents, a sea of white sheets and manila envelopes.

They had settled in for what they knew would be a long and arduous – but ultimately vital – records search several hours earlier and now, in the dead of night, they were still at it, their eyes tight and red from the dust and from squinting at the tiny print, their muscles cramped from sitting on the floor for way too long.

Every hour or so they would shift position, or get up and do a lap of the room (or as much of a lap as they could manage with all the paperwork taking up most of the floor space). Their backs hurt, their necks ached, and they'd both had pretty much permanent headaches for the last few hours. Still, they had to push on.

Bo was an extremely competent, confident man, much respected by most of his allies and utterly loathed by those who counted themselves his enemies. Fortunately, there weren't too many of the latter: if you were sensible and had any ambition at all, you made sure that Bo Nick Olsen stayed your friend.

He had been appointed Head of the Funding Agency due to his thoroughness and determination to see a challenge through right to its conclusion. After the scandal of the previous Head's little money-making schemes, the government had needed a man they could trust, and Bo was that man. Over the past few years, Bo had served (and still served) on various government committees and panels, and he had the Vice President's ear on many subjects. He had, in short, made himself indispensable. Bo was a very smart man.

One of Bo's other postings was as part of a panel for a department that examined the ways in which the government could improve the global opinion of America and the American people, and he often found his work in other areas overlapping with that particular cause.

After all, when you worked in Bo's field, you were a representative of your country wherever you went and whatever you did *(despite the fact that Bo was actually Dutch)*. You were always on the clock, always being scrutinized. It was an exhausting way to live, but Bo was used to it.

The global opinion of his much-loved adopted country wasn't always as he'd like, of course. The United States of America was a big place – almost a continent in its own right – which left a lot of room for the dangerously stupid, and as with most governments, trying to improve or maintain public image was something of a full-time job.

John Dillon – the other man currently up to his eyeballs in the driest of reports – was Bo's closest confidante, almost his Man-Friday. They had been working together since their younger days on the New York Stock Exchange, where both together and individually they had been very successful, and consequently had made tidy fortunes. Recognizing similar qualities in one another, they had become fast friends, and Bo had persuaded John to keep on wanting more of a challenge.

Bo seemed to have something of the 'Midas Touch' – everything he worked on just seemed to fall into place – and John hadn't been able to pass the opportunity up. They had been operating together for years now, John happy to work for a man for whom success and common sense were a kind of instinct.

The nature of their present project and the lateness of the hour meant that they were both dressed very casually, which was good because every inch of their clothes was covered in paper dust.

Dust, a faint trace of mold, and the bubbling coffee pot in the corner were the predominant essences of this tiny but industrious office. It left a curious taste in the mouth, reminiscent of used bookstores, parish records, and the archives of accounting bodies.

John stretched his back, popping his spine for what felt like the hundredth time that night. It made a loud crack, muffled only slightly by the vast quantity of files around them. He looked around, exhausted. A whole forest must have had to come down to produce this crap.

"Come on, Bo, let's call it a day," he said, yawning. "It's gone midnight. We've been sorting this lot out for over ten hours now. I'm forgetting which pile is which."

"Yeah, I suppose you're right," said Bo, looking up

from the report he was working through. "You old folks can't do full days anymore," he teased, trying to look innocent.

"Full days?" John gasped, and they both laughed. "You cheeky bastard! We've been up since five this morning – and anyway, I'm younger than you are."

"You wouldn't think so to look at you," Bo cracked, earning a nudge in the ribs. He paused then, looking over at his friend. "Hey, I think you're putting these in the wrong piles. You're going senile, Johnny-boy."

John glanced up as Bo shuffled forwards on his knees, heading toward the piles of files they had already stacked up.

"Look at this on the 'must investigate further' pile," he said, picking up the top sheaf of papers. "*A Study into the Changes in the Calcium Content of the Sea Water from Alaska to the Gulf of Mexico* – now, who gives a fuck about that?" he asked with a grimace.

He flicked through the pages of the report, leaning against the table. "Just have a guess how much this has cost us, over what?" He glanced at the file in his hand. "The last eight and a half years? Go on, Johnny-boy – how much? How much do you think for calcium content?"

"I don't know, let me think," said John, sitting back on his haunches, glad to be having a break from reading. "You take a sample of sea water in maybe about fifty locations, test it in a lab, put the results on a graph, analyze them, write to the Waters, Marine and Oceans Society with the results… so it can't be more than say, three million over eight years," he guessed. "Yes?" He looked at the unimpressed expression on Bo's face. "No? *No?* What is it then? Four million? Five?"

"Wrong and wrong again!" Bo exclaimed. "You're miles away. It's nearer nine point five million dollars."

"Fuck me," John swore, astonished. "How can that be?" he asked, gawping at the stacks of reports around them. "God, that's only one – there could be over two thousand projects to sort out here – and all of them with a price tag like that!" The amount of money flying around was incredible; no wonder they had to whittle them down to the bare essentials.

"You're not wrong," Bo mumbled, as he continued to thumb through the files, rapidly reading the title pages as he went.

"Here's another one on the wrong pile, John – *A Further Understanding of the Language of the Orca Whale*. Now come on, what's been going on here? Has no one been checking these projects before they've been approved for funding? They can't have been. This one's to the tune of four point three million! I mean, what's that going to contribute to humans as a society?"

By this time John had climbed stiffly to his feet, his muscles protesting from hours of bending over the towering stacks. Watching his friend's face as he read, he decided that Bo Olsen was genuinely enjoying himself. God help the scientists.

"Huh, that's strange," Bo frowned. "Both of those last two projects are based in Mexico, and their accounts – get this – their accounts are in a bank in Switzerland. Jesus. That's got tax-fraud written all over it. The FBI's going to have their hands full investigating this lot."

He'd just moved to drop the files onto the 'no hope' pile when he spotted the top file on that stack. He picked it up, his face a picture of exasperation.

Yep, John thought, *he's definitely enjoying himself* – the things Bo found interesting were a little different to that of normal people, that's just one thing he'd learned about the great man himself these past few years.

"What's this one? *To Believe a Dream/A Journey in Time?*" Bo asked, waving it around. "Hang on a minute. I've heard of this before!"

Grabbing his nose, Bo closed his eyes tightly, going deep into the old grey matter inside his head. "I have heard of this before," he repeats to himself. "Where was it? Where was it? Aha! That's it!" He opened his eyes again and stared at his friend. "About five years ago, we were at one of those government-funded lectures on how the future will look in the next ten years, compared to how it had looked in the *past* ten years." He thought for a few more seconds. "That's it! Eddie Daniels was the chair, and he was introducing the boffins who were predicting the forthcoming, ground-breaking, world-changing discoveries!" He laughed, "That was a mouthful John! Who was that guy?"

John watched, amused, as his friend tried to cast his mind back. He'd clearly given himself the challenge of remembering every last detail from that lecture.

"That's it John, a Dr Banner. He was the nutty professor boring me to death, rattling on about

71

quantum physics. I remember Eddie telling me afterwards, that it was one of those projects to keep an eye on, because it only takes one nutcase to change the world!"

"Oh, I've flicked through that," said John, nodding. "Can't understand a word of it, but I know it's about time travel – what a load of bull crap. I mean, can you see that ever happening?" he paused, recalling his friend's taste in fiction. "Hah, actually, I bet you can."

Bo rolled his eyes, saying nothing.

John grinned and started to sing, "There's Klingons on the Starboard Bow, Starboard Bow, Starboard Bow, there's Klingons on the Starboard bow, Jim!" He broke off, laughing. "I'd forgotten about your penchant for science fiction, Bo – or should I call you Captain James T Kirk of the Starship Enterprise?"

"Shut up, John," said Bo affably. The truth was that he did like science fiction, but that was exactly what it was – fiction. Why there was a project on time travel in the pile, he had no idea, but he was more than a little intrigued about it. "When you say time travel, are we talking past or future?"

John thought for a moment. "The past, of course. The future – now that's crazy talk."

Bo laughed. "Come on, let's call it a day. I'm going to take this file back to the hotel, and see how Banner's getting on spending your money, John! Another financial sinkhole I bet." He arched an eyebrow, radiating an air of mischief as he added, "It will make for some fascinating reading, Mr Spock!

We'll meet at Terminal Five at Dallas Airport, oh-nine thirty hours tomorrow for a mission debrief."

"Message received loud and clear, Kirk," said John, rubbing his eyes as he straightened up. He desperately needed some sleep and some food. And a shower.

The two men took the files they'd decided to treat as bedtime reading, tucking them into their briefcases before locking up for the evening.

"Don't let anyone enter that room without my say so," said Bo to the Security Personnel as they walked out into the crisp, silent pre-dawn night.

The man nodded back, looking like he could use some sleep too.

Bo also needed to rest up, but the name of that file kept coming back to him – *A Journey in Time*.

Exhausted as he was, he couldn't wait to read it.

Chapter 4

I'm not Stupid, Navigator!

At about the time Bo Olsen and John Dillon were heading back to their hotels to sleep, dusk was falling over the great, dusty city of Astana, the capital city of Kazakhstan. International relations here had never been particularly friendly, but for the past eight years, the American, British and French security forces had been shoulder-deep in a United Nations conflict with the rebel group *pışaq – jïegi*, or '*The Knife's Edge*'.

A top-level meeting geared towards establishing a long-lasting peace agreement was underway in the city, aimed at bringing a swift and decisive ending to the current crisis.

The usual suspects were all there: Presidents, Ministers, high-ranking military personnel, and other high ranking negotiators were being brought in from all over Europe. A group of British advisers were also to be flown in from an RAF base in Germany.

Over these past few weeks the conflict with the rebel group '*The Knife's Edge*' had created a feeling of excitement on the RAF base in Germany, almost like the olden days when it was the USSR plotting and conspiring to expand the iron curtain to envelope as much of Europe as it could.

There are many jeeps, fuel tankers and personnel milling about. Fighter planes and bomber aircraft are stacked up in the parking areas – all having their weaponry reloaded with the latest air to ground missiles and laser guided bombs.

The whole site is like a hive of hornets, people and vehicles rushing in this direction or that direction, no one having any time to stop and talk.

One particular mission to be carried out that day is to fly in a group of four high-ranking Officers who are participating in the peace talks in Astana, hoping to bring a diplomatic solution to end the conflict. Travelling with them are 22 British Marines who will be joining the security team to protect the meeting.

There are a lot of anxious people involved in these talks, all with a view that this latest genocidal blood bath must – at all costs – be brought to an end.

The Marines had already boarded the Transport plane, and the vehicle that was chauffeuring the Officers had just pulled up at the plane, and they were ascending the steps onto the flight.

There had been a short delay in finding all the flight deck crew who had been assigned to the mission: Captain Ben *'don't fuck with me'* Newson, a bully to his Junior Officers, was the man in charge today, along with his Navigator, Luke *'head in a book'* Alexander, a very confident man. They both had, for the last fifty minutes or so, been scouring the

Terminal complex, the accommodation blocks, the officers' dining lounges… in fact, almost the whole base, looking for the Co-pilot, Ali Singh.

They had almost given up and were about to find another officer to replace him when a message had been received in the control tower, transmitted from the flight deck of the Transport Plane. It was Ali Singh reporting in for duty.

Just like Mount Vesuvius, Captain Ben Newson erupts when he is told. Instead of the people near to him being covered in volcanic ash, they are splattered in spit and saliva as he gives the foulest description of what he is going to do to 'Singhy' when he gets hold of him.

The two men board a jeep and are driven to the Transport Plane. Luke Alexander sat in the back, is keeping quiet; he knows what Newson is like and he doesn't want his day ruined by the bully. To be perfectly honest there isn't a chance to say anything as Newson never stops ranting and raving about what he is going to do to 'Singhy'.

The best Luke could do was dodge the saliva pouring out of Newson's mouth as the wind catches it and blows it into the back of the jeep. Trying to tune the Captain out, Luke starts thinking about Ali. What on earth was he doing on the plane? It's one thing sitting there flying the fucking thing, but it's not the place to be trying to get your head down or escaping from the wife.

Luke has known Ali for many years – they had gone through RAF College together – and one thing he'd learnt during those years, was to stick close to Ali when you were out having a drink and a good time; he was such a handsome lad that the girls would always drape themselves in front of him hoping to catch his eye. You could always manage to pick up a girl that he had discarded. Ali was always looking to bed the cream of the crop which left many a conquest going, for second best.

Over the years, however, Ali had become a very different person, for one thing, he no longer dressed the same. Back in the day you could always count on Ali to be wearing the latest fashions, but now – when he wasn't in his RAF uniform – it seemed as if he didn't give a damn about his appearance. You sometimes caught him in what appeared to be a hessian sack, looking as if he'd been on the 'wacky baccy' most of the night.

The jeep stopped, and the two men got out, Luke looked at Ben Newson hoping to somehow have a reasonable conversation with him.

Newson clocks his expression. "What Luke, what are you trying to tell me?" His brow furrowed. "Spit it out man, what are you thinking?"

Luke composes himself for a few seconds. "I'm not completely happy flying with Ali Singh these days, I haven't been for a few months now. In the past you could always depend on him, but these days he never speaks to me, or anyone for that matter. He seems so removed from the unit."

Ben thinks for a minute, "Look Luke, you may think I'm a bit of a jerk, but I've always got the wellbeing of my crew and my aircraft at the forefront of my thoughts. I know what you are thinking because I'm thinking the same, what has Ali Singh been doing on the plane for the last fucking hour?" Luke shrugs his shoulders.

Ben continues, "This is the plan, you tell him that I want to see him here on the tarmac – that will get him off the plane – and while I'm giving him the special *'Newson fucking'* you run a full system diagnostics check through the whole plane. We can't just accuse him without proof. OK Luke?"

"No can do Captain," Luke replied, shaking his head. "A full diagnostics check would take over half a day to complete. Best I could do is a stepped system check over a few of the crafts systems."

Ben Newson thinks for a few seconds, trying to work out the most vulnerable components on the plane. "Right Luke, do your checks on Navigation, Fuel capacity – make sure we can get there with our 12% over valuation – also the engines Luke, get them fired up. I will give you as long as I can."

The two men part, Luke climbing the steps to the plane's fuselage, and Newson checking the flaps and undercarriage of the plane.

As Luke enters the cockpit he is stunned as the sight of Ali Singh hits him. Ali is knelt down on a Prayer Mat praising his religious leader. Luke, unsure of what to do or say just stands there through the cockpit door.

Ali hasn't clocked him as his eyes are tightly shut. Luke is just an easy going person and it doesn't make any difference to him what peoples beliefs are as long as it doesn't harm his family. But this, this is different, this is deeply concerning.

"Ali… Ali what on earth are you doing?" This startles Ali as he hadn't heard Luke enter the cabin. He quickly grabs his belongings and prayer mat. Rolling the mat up, he glares sternly at Luke, no words are spoken just the expressions on both men's faces writes a whole chapter.

Yet again Luke was hit with the realization of just how much Ali had changed from their RAF training school days; he was now completely unrecognizable as the friend who'd marched down the runway with Luke and the rest of their classmates during their passing out parade. His body language now visibly shows hatred and tremendous anger – but at what, or at whom?

That day, at the training school, *Harrier* Jump Jets were practicing landing and take-offs on the airfield and had given the new recruits the traditional Jump Jet bow twenty five yards or so in front of them. What a tremendous buzz that was. They had all piled into coaches after the parade and hit the town, and the man to be with, yes you guessed it, was Ali Singh.

Luke, looking at Ali now on the flight deck – could still see the handsome young man of those glorious days – when no one had a care in the world, but he had totally lost his charisma and self-esteem. Staring at each other made Luke more uncomfortable, it lasted longer than it should have done. Someone had to break the deadlock.

Luke cleared his throat. "Newson wants to see you down on the runway. He's spitting more saliva than a bloodhound."

Ali continues to stare at Luke. "Do you think I give

a damn about that man? It's people like him that have caused all this friction in our World, he can wait."

Luke thinks for a moment, I've got to get him off this bridge. "You better get down there. He thinks you tried to stitch him up, not reporting to the pre-flight briefing."

Ali putting his prayer mat into a locker says, "I hate that man, I fucking hate him, if I could do this any other way…"

With that Ali leaves the cabin to go see Newson. As soon as he is out of sight, Luke opens his flight case and takes out the pre-flight check flash drives, plugging them into the plane's computers and leaving them to do their work. Next he takes a small pre-programmed laptop from his flight bag and plugs that into the mainframe computer of the plane, setting this operating on a systems diagnostic check on given components of the craft.

While he worked, he thought of Ali's parting words: I wonder what he meant – *if I could do this any other way.* As he is looking out of the cockpit windows he can now see Ali, on the tarmac getting a right dressing down from Newson. Arms are waving around, fists are being shown in a threatening behaviour and no doubt a flood of bodily fluids will be heading in Ali's direction.

I'm glad I'm not on the end of that one, thinks Luke as he sits in the Pilot's seat, going through a pre-start check on each of the four engines. He begins to fire the engines up leaving them in an idle warm-up safety position, ready for the Captain and Co-pilot to take over.

That's if they had a Co-pilot to fly with, however, now time was running out. They would be unable to carry out the mission if Ali walked, because he couldn't be replaced in such a short time.

Luke was watching Ben and Ali on the ground, and as the engines had begun to run the two men looked up at the cockpit. Luke never responded to their wave of acknowledgement but he was surprised as both Ben and Ali shook hands, and tapped each other on the back almost like long-lost friends, then headed towards the boarding steps.

Luke went back to his Navigation station and very quickly checked through the diagnostic report displayed on his laptop computer. No anomalies on the systems he had checked, great that's fantastic were his thoughts. *But it didn't mean everything was as it should be.*

Newson and Singh arrived in the cabin. They were being friendly with each other – or as friendly as you can be with Newson – it was as if the last hour's grief hadn't happened. Taking his seat, Ali began concentrating on the flight controls as Ben swung round to make eye contact with Luke.

"All OK Navigator? Have you Pre-Programed our course?"

"Yes Captain, all looking good," replies Luke as he gives a thumbs up to the man. Newson nods in a clearly satisfied manner.

"Right, let's get this bird in the air," says the Captain as he begins to taxi his plane. In the next ten minutes as the plane was en-route to its take-off strip, the atmosphere in the cockpit was fraught with tension but at least they were on their way, at last.

The skies over this area of Europe were very busy, many families were taking advantage of the currency exchange rates on the British pound. Cheaper holidays over the continent had stimulated the tourism business and double the number of planes were being used to cope with the extra demand.

Luke was watching them on the Transport Plane's radar. "Look at all those lucky bastards! Going to Spain I bet – Benidorm will be buzzing this weekend. Captain, can I divert us to Alicante?"

"The only place you will be diverting to is the galley, to make a brew!" replied Newson. "Do you think you could navigate yourself that far?"

As the Captain finishes his statement an alarm begins to sound on Luke's instrument panel. *That's odd*, thinks Luke as he is trying to focus on which warning beacon is flashing.

"What's that? Talk to me Luke, what is it?" demanded Newson.

"Just a second sir… that's odd I've never seen that before, it's our transponder Captain, it's showing a malfunction," answers Luke in a puzzled voice.

"It can't be Navigator, check for system failure. That's never a problem," responds Newson, glancing across at Ali who has an expression of complete complacency.

"Ali, you're into programing, what do you think? Give Luke a hand with it."

Ali turns to face Newson with the same blank expression on his face. He doesn't respond verbally, just gives a cold stare.

"Come on Singhy, give Luke a hand!" Newson repeated.

That gets a reaction. "Don't call me Singhy! You wouldn't like it if I called you Benny, would you?"

"OK Flight Lieutenant Singh," said Newson through gritted teeth, "keep your dreadlocks on and get that fucking transponder working!"

Ali remains seated. He has no intention of assisting Luke, and is barely listening to the captain anymore – he had far more important things to think about.

The stress in the cockpit had returned, the tension levels high as Luke tried to figure out what was going on. He'd wished he'd been able to tell Newson about the prayer mat incident, but there hadn't been time, and it was far too late now – they were already at thirty-eight thousand feet.

"Yes, got it," he cries. "I've reset the program Captain, Transponder back on again." Newson looks across at Ali, who seems to be in his own little world. After a few seconds Newson answers the Navigator.

"Good work Luke give me the distance to Astana International."

Luke was feeling a bit smug with himself. "292 miles Sir, and closing."

Newson looks round at Luke, "Well it *would* be closing wouldn't it? That's the direction we're heading in."

"It was just a joke Sir, a bit of light entertainment."

"Light entertainment Singhy. What do you think

of that, by our 'Compere' Mr Luke Alexander?" Ben Newson is now trying to wind Ali up, trying to get some reaction from him.

Suddenly a loud, high pitched warning sound is emitted from Luke's instrument panel.

"Damn it Captain, the transponders off again. Shit!" an exasperated Luke shouts out.

"Singhy, get off your arse and give Luke a hand with those fucking transponder settings!" shouts the Captain as he throws a punch at Ali's shoulder.

"Leave him Captain," says Luke without looking up. "I'm resetting the program again – that should do it." A minute or so passes, the alarm stops blurting out its high pitched beeping. The transponder is reactivated once again.

The friction and anger along with the sound of the alarm increases the tension in the cock-pit.

"Back on again Captain, but we can't keep going on this course with that fault," a word of warning coming from Luke as he takes his laptop from his flight bag.

"I'm not stupid Navigator. I know that!" snaps Newson.

Luke continues, "I'm going to do a systems check on that transponder. It runs through the communications program, so if I can find the cause of the glitch, I can just reset it on the mainframe."

Luke plugs the laptop into the craft's main computers, causing Ali to spin around, staring at him. Ben Newson has spotted the interest that Ali has now shown in what Luke is doing – something definitely wasn't right here.

"What's your problem Singhy?" states the captain. "Worried that Luke will find your porno stash in there?"

Ali swings his gaze towards Newson. "Don't speak to me that way! You have no respect for other people. You're just a damn pig. A bully!" Ali finally responds.

Ali, hates his captain more and more.

Newson smiles to himself – happy he is winding Ali up – but inside, he's troubled.

Deeply troubled.

The atmosphere in the cockpit could be cut with a knife, 'the Knife's Edge'?

Chapter 5

A Bulldog Chewing a Wasp

The summit meetings for the peace talks were being held at the French Embassy in Astana, a large, fancy building in the Gothic style. It looked rather like the architect had read *Dracula* and tried to personify it in stone; it squatted in the street, like something out of a *Hammer House of Horror* film. Hideous gargoyles were mounted on the ridges of the tall, steep tiled rooftops, while inside, delegates reclined on plush velvet settees.

Security was a constant nightmare for the CIA, and consequently, the City was crawling with agents and personnel from every conceivable country.

The large, terraced area in front of the main entrance was accessed by steep, awkward steps that any number of the delegates could tumble down and twist their ankles. Luckily, no one had – yet. The large parking area was jam-packed with Limousines, *Bentleys* and *Rolls Royces*, all belonging to the array of dignitaries within, and all being watched over by conflicting security forces who were all a hair-trigger away from an international incident.

The light went quickly in Kazakhstan, and lamps were already burning in the numerous alleyways leading away from the main courtyard area. Everyone was so tense that none of them had even spared a thought for the beauty of a Central Asian sunset. Uniformed Kazakhstani Police patrolled the courtyard and gates, machine guns resting on their shoulders. Their plain-clothed counterparts were gathered in small groups, eyeing their charges unobtrusively.

The overall effect of the security personnel was one of a Mafia convention, with Mexican moustaches, jet black hair, cheap suits, oversized sunglasses and long overcoats; they weren't, on the whole, particularly subtle. One of the main challenges of the evening was trying to tell each other apart – without the usual insignia, they all just looked the same. It would have come in handy, one of the agents thought as he patrolled the perimeter, if there had been a multi-national briefing on the subject, but given the current political climate, that was fairly unlikely.

Several CIA operatives moved purposefully through the crowd, looking aloof and watching their particular assignments assiduously, with an air of superiority over their European cousins.

Two of them stood atop the terraces, surveying the danger areas below, stern expressions on their faces.

"Look at those cars down there, Jonesy," one of the men remarked, nodding at the parking lot. "How can a hellhole like this support automobiles of that quality?"

"That's where your United Nations funding ends up, Brady," his fellow agent groused, rather inaccurately. "At least it keeps the luxury car industry going. I bet your wife gives to the 'Help the Poor, Peasant Farmers Charity'," he scoffed. "Well, there they are – the poor peasants in their brand new *Mercedes*."

"This is a nightmare," the first man said with a light sigh. "There aren't enough of us to cover all the entrances and exits. I mean, look at this place!"

"Keep it together, Brady," his friend told him. "Don't forget the A-WACS above us. We've got to do the impossible here. They're counting on us!"

As one, both men looked up at the sky, hoping to see the Airborne Warning and Control System aircraft (commonly known as the A-WACS) where it was cruising, thirty-five thousand feet above their heads, but all they could see were the stars.

∗

Some of the nervous energy on the ground had, not unnaturally, passed on to the operators on the A-WACS plane; the personnel on the aircraft were, after all, responsible for all of the ground activity in Kazakhstan, along with any corresponding air traffic. There were a lot of lives on the line here – and not just the ones in the French Embassy. If this thing kicked off then the whole region could destabilize, and then they really would be in the shit.

For the last ten minutes, several rather tense officers had been watching the blip of an unidentified incoming aircraft on their radar. It was giving off an unclear transponder signal, which was a bit of a worry, given the event that was taking place on the ground. Generally, transponder codes were the first priority for any pilot after staying airborne, particularly when heading into airspace above such an internationally important event.

The operational controller – a big, burly man named Clark – frowned. The A-WACS was operating under radio silence and there had been nothing in their briefing about a flight matching with the description of this one. It was still over two hundred and eighty miles away, but it was heading straight for the capital.

They did, however, have some time – there were still a number of options open to them – and it wasn't a threat. Yet.

"Johnson, you're the man," the operational controller barked, coming to a decision. "Keep your eyes peeled on that incoming bogie and let me know if it changes course or speeds up – and tell me if it gets to within one hundred and sixty-five miles from the capital. You hear me, boy?" he repeated, adding for clarity: "One hundred and sixty-five miles!"

Johnson – a keen young man who was fresh from his AAF training – gave a sharp salute. "Yes, Sir!" he shouted, snapping to attention. He beamed into his monitors, his eyes glued to the radar.

Clark smiled slightly. He knew Johnson's ambition had always been to be part of A-WACS – including the status that gave him within the air surveillance community – and he could tell by the way the boy's ears tinged pink that the responsibility for tracking their unknown aircraft had given him a bit of a buzz.

Operational pride was a good thing in the small,

hectic world of the A-WACS, but that buzz was worrying. Clark ran a tight ship, as it were, and after so many years, his crew were rather like a family to him; the younger ones looked up to him as a father figure and the older ones saw him as a commander. He was reasonably sure that none of them even knew his first name anymore. To them, he was the very concept of 'Sir!' and that was just how he liked it.

It made them work harder. It made them want to succeed more. People with a clear line of command worked far more effectively.

As Clark looked back at the screen, he mopped his sweaty brow.

The operational controller strode over and picked up the radio transmitter that ran on a coded frequency.

"Yes, that's right," he confirmed, into the radio. "Two F-111s standing by, fully armed and ready to go on my word – got that, sonny? On my word."

He put the radio back in its holster and went to loom over Johnson's shoulder, thinking of the F-111s.

He hoped to God he wouldn't have to use them, but it was always better to be safe than sorry. If they were already on stand-by he could scramble them at a moment's notice.

"Johnson, how close now?"

"Two hundred and ten miles, Sir – no change in flight path," Johnson reported faithfully.

"Signaler!" the operational commander barked. "Transmit the position of that bogie to those F-111s. Do it – do it *now*."

"One ninety, Sir, and closing," said Johnson, his eyes still glued to the screen.

Clark paced up and down the flight deck, the tension in him building and infecting every part of the business-end of the A-WACS. Something didn't feel right about this whole thing. Something was off, and when something was off it made him anxious. He rubbed his stomach as it gave a painful twinge where his stress ulcer was.

"I hate this, I fucking hate this," he muttered, his face bright red. Looking like a bulldog chewing a wasp, he span towards the signaler. "Get those two F-111s off the ground," he snapped. "*Get them in the fucking air!*"

The signaler nodded her acknowledgement, already transmitting the request to the airbase, her calm expression the very picture of professionalism.

"One hundred and seventy-two miles and closing, Sir!"

The swagger in the young officer's voice jarred the operational controller's anxious thoughts. Delight was an emotion that had no place in control – not here and not now.

"Shit, Johnson!" he roared. "Don't you *fucking* realize what's happening? God, I *fucking* hate this." He whirled around again, this time pointing a trembling, red finger at the Sergeant at Arms. "Remove Johnson from his post! I can't have a man in my company getting a buzz out of what's about to happen!"

The Sergeant at Arms pulled Johnson up by the shoulders, and the young officer was escorted away with an undignified squawk, quickly being replaced by another man. Distantly, Clark could hear the kid sobbing, his dreams dashed.

He let out a growl of frustration. This was no place – and no bloody time – to be worrying about bruised feelings. Not when the shit was about to hit the fan in such a big way.

The trouble with Johnson was that he had no experience. Everyone else in the business-end of the A-WACS had been through enough missions to feel that something bad was coming and monitor their tone accordingly. The kid hadn't a clue. He'd learn. By God, he'd learn. One way or the other.

"One hundred and sixty-six miles and closing, Sir," said Johnson's replacement, as professionally as possible. He clearly didn't want to have the same treatment as Johnson. "No change in flight path, Sir."

"F-111s airborne and en-route, Sir," said the signaler. "Coming in from Turkey."

Clark nodded his acknowledgment as a trickle of sweat ran down his back.

Well, he thought, *this was it*.

Whatever was going to happen, it was going to happen soon.

Chapter 6

What's going on?

Back on the transport plane, Ben Newson had yet again been having problems with the transponder – it had failed a further three times.

Luke had reset the system again and again. At the moment the transponder appears to be working, he had been successful in gaining access to the communications program in the mainframe computers of the craft.

"How far from Astana now, Navigator?"

Luke, concentrating on his laptop, doesn't respond to the question.

"Navigator, I've still got to fly this fucking thing so give me a distance reading, not in a minute, not in five minutes, NOW!"

Ali answers the Captains request, "Two hundred and twenty," as he is looking at Luke's instrument panel. Luke frowns as he realizes that is a lie as he has already recorded that distance some time ago.

"No we aren't Captain," as he looks up at his panel. "It's one hundred and eighty five miles to go."

Ben Newson looks across at Ali. "Why did you say that, you arse?" Newson snaps at Ali.

"Well," replies Ali, "why do you say some of the shit you come out with?"

"Mr Singh! I'm Ben *'Don't Fuck with Me'* Newson, and you're fucking with me."

The captain and co-pilot glare at each other, Ben Newson smirking, knowing full well that he has got right into Ali's head.

Ali, on the other hand is wearing an expression of calm and peace, and a slight smile appears on his lips. This makes the Captain think twice, *what's going on?*

Suddenly, Luke excitingly shouts out, "Found it, got it!" As he locks onto the Transponder's program with his laptop. "Hang on, the program's been reset. It's at a five on and thirty-five minutes off intermittent setting! No wonder we couldn't get it to stay on."

"How's that happened Luke? Singhy have you any idea?" By now Ben Newson is very suspicious, and when you are in a plane, being 'very suspicious' never ends well.

Newson again looks at Ali who is concentrating on his instruments. Something is not right, this doesn't just happen on its own.

Luke speaks up, "Hang on Captain. I've got someone's electronic signature recorded here as the last operator."

Ali spins round, hand in his flight suit pocket.

"The recorded pass code is *'HGNIS 1'*." Luke suddenly looks up at Ali, he has just realized the threat and where it is coming from.

Just then there was a loud bleeping tone emitting from Luke's instrument panel. "SHIT, the transponders off again!

Ah Captain! More shit. I've got two planes on radar just taken off in Turkey I don't know what they are but they're moving very fast."

There's tension in Luke's voice as he makes eye contact with Ali, he notices his hand in his flight suit. Is he holding a weapon?

Luke's radar is now giving a high frequency bleeping sound, indicating that it has identified the two planes, he reluctantly focuses back onto his instruments.

"They're F-111's Sir and they're heading our way, fucking hell… FUCKING HELL DO SOMETHING, they're coming! Shit!" Luke, desperately shouting now.

Ben Newson, with stress and panic in his voice says, "Give me the distance to Astana Navigator, QUICK!" Once again Luke checks his instruments.

"One hundred and sixty five, what the hell are we going to do?"

"That distance is the first reaction response on an A-WACS. They've clocked us with no transponder. Shit!" The Captain glares at Ali who steadily returns the look, that same slight smile still lingering on his face.

"Break radio silence, Singhy, and transmit today's

Security codes. Tell them who the fuck we are," Newson roared.

Ali replies in an almost mocking manner, "Yes sir, at once Sir."

As Ali is fumbling in his flight case to retrieve the Codes, Luke is trying to attract the Captain's attention to tell him of his suspicions. He knew Ali wouldn't have the codes as he'd missed the pre-flight briefing. But would it make any difference, is the Transport Plane doomed anyway?

The Captain is now urgently shouting **"COME ON!** Singhy **COME ON!"**

Ali breaks radio silence, opens the microphone and begins transmitting the plane's details and the security codes for the day; however, he changes his well-spoken English accent to an Accent of his Motherland.

Disturbed by the change in Ali's voice, the captain thinks for a few seconds, then realises what has just happened. He shouts at the co-pilot, "Hang on a minute, I recognise those codes: they're yesterdays! You bastard, you've stitched us all up! It's you that's been fucking about with the transponder. You bastard and now that stupid accent!"

The tension in the cabin is like a standoff at the 'OK Corral'. Who is going to make the next move?

Suddenly, another high-pitched bleeping omits from Luke's instrument panel. He clocks the readings and in a strained desperate voice says, "They've launched missiles. **TWO MISSILES! OH SHIT!"**

The captain makes a lunge for the radio; it's not

too late he can still save the plane. If only he can get to the mic.

Ali thrusts his hand into his flight suit, pulls out a small handgun and shoots the Captain dead, Luke stares at him in horror, unable to move, Ali wasted no time in turning the gun on him. "Sorry Luke, but you're just another heathen."

Luke launches himself at Ali, but before he can get there, the whole plane is rocked with the power of two huge explosions. The missiles have hit their target.

The last thing Luke sees before he drifts off into oblivion is the triumphant look on Ali's face.

*

In the morning, the wreckage is spotted by local tribesmen who inform the nearby News reporters – covering the war – and cameras are set up to record and transmit the disaster round the World.

The Headlines read *'AMERICAN AIR FORCE SHOOT DOWN BRITISH TRANSPORT PLANE ALL PERSONNEL KILLED.'* This creates tremendous hysteria with the British people and a protest is quickly set up outside the American Embassy in London, which is also being transmitted by News Crews around the World.

Chapter 7

Dallas – 'Breaking News'

Bo and John stared at the monitor hanging from the ceiling in one of the many anonymous waiting areas in the airport, both of them completely mesmerized.

Kazakhstani tribesmen were showing the cameramen a vast field of blackened wreckage, in which vague impressions of twisted, charred limbs rested here and there amongst the warped metal.

"Flight K-43, an RAF transport plane, was carrying British personnel to the peace summit at Astana, along with several high-ranking officers who were due to speak at the event. The military haven't yet released the names of those killed, but what we do know is that thirty-one people were on that airplane when it was shot down by American Forces."

The screen changed to a video showing a pair of F-111s taking off from an airbase somewhere in Turkey. They shot through the air like hornets, their engines roaring.

"The American Air Force has apologized for this incident,

saying that an equipment fault was to blame. The White House has released a statement sending the deepest condolences to the British service personnel and their families."

This time, the camera was trained on hundreds of people – it must have been in a helicopter from the way it panned around the street in front of the American Embassy in London. The people in the crowd were clearly unhappy, waving banners and placards from where they stood. They were tightly packed together on the roads, holding up all of the surrounding traffic.

"Shortly after the statement was released to the British public this morning, a crowd began to gather outside the American Embassy in London. This is being called one of the worst military disasters in aviation history, and now people want answers."

The picture changed again, this time showing a lot of very angry people shouting at the staff who were trying to get into the Embassy building. In front of them, a news crew had somehow managed to shove their way through to where the British Prime Minister was making a valiant effort to placate the crowd.

"The British Prime Minister has called for a full review of procedure for all UN member states."

The presenter paused while the Prime Minister faced down a forest of bristling microphones and camera flashes, the sound of several thousand pissed off Brits clearly audible in the background.

"This kind of thing is utterly unacceptable," he said, trying to look stern. *"A number of British personnel have lost their lives in a senseless and violent fashion that was entirely avoidable, and I for one feel that we owe it to them and*

their families to press the issue. The Ministry of Defense has assured me that a flight plan was filed with all UN forces prior to take off. How many times are our allies going to be allowed to commit such mistakes?

"There should be measures in place to prevent a catastrophe like this from happening, and I think that some serious questions need to be asked: Why did this happen? Can we allow incidents like this to go unchecked? And how do we prevent such tragedies from occurring in the future?" He looked dead into the news camera, ever the consummate politician. *"If this is how we're treated, can we really trust our allies?"*

John winced. That was a direct stab aimed right at the American government, and if he was honest, he didn't entirely blame the man. His citizens were clamoring for answers – and they deserved them. He was just doing his job, but this wasn't going to help the world's image of America, not one little bit.

"This is the latest in a series of blunders by the American Armed Forces," the presenter resumed, soberly. *"People here in London are beginning to ask if these so-called 'friendly fire' incidents can be prevented in future. They're also beginning to ask what right America has to shoot first and ask questions later. The feeling across the country – and particularly here in London – is at its lowest point since the American War of Independence.*

"An investigation into the incident is ongoing…"

Bo shook his head, and John could tell what his boss was thinking because he was thinking it too: what an absolute fuck-up. You couldn't really blame the Brits – if it had been a member of his family out there he would have done absolutely anything to register his displeasure with the government – but America was in for a rough few months, that was certain.

"Did you see all that on CNN last night?" he asked, not taking his eyes from the screen; the picture had looped around once again to the blackened, smoking wreckage, about one hundred and fifty miles away from Astana. "Those poor people and their families."

"I did John, I did," said Bo, sounding wearier than John had ever remembered hearing him. "What a horrendous mess. It's fucked everything up. *Pıṣaq – jïegi* are going to love this!"

They watched the news for a few more minutes in tense, contemplative silence.

"Have you had a call from Ron Champion?" John asked, eventually, shooting Bo a sidelong glance.

This was exactly the kind of thing their Vice President would be sweating buckets over – and when people in high places started sweating buckets, they called Bo.

"Yeah, my old buddy," he said thoughtfully. "I'm off to Washington right now – they've called a meeting of the Cobra committee."

John nodded; he had suspected as much. His buddy tended to appear wherever the political shit was hitting the fan, and right now it would be raining effluent in Washington.

Bo rested a hand on John's shoulder. "You, my friend," he said with a wan smile, "I want you to fly out to San Diego and find out where this Time Travel Complex is. Don't go in – just find it and I'll meet you in the city the day after tomorrow."

"I never normally question your decisions Bo, and maybe I shouldn't this time, but why?" asks John, the change in subject momentarily throwing him.

Bo smiles and raises his eyebrows rather mysteriously, and replies, "That is something we'll discuss later."

John put his hand on Bo's other shoulder and the two friends indulged in their own, idiosyncratic form of farewell: they patted each other on the backs in a not-quite-hug before walking off to their respective gates.

John hurried towards the San Diego flight, wondering what Bo had up his sleeve this time. It was why people like Ron Champion called him in: he could be relied upon to find solutions, even when it seemed like the world was ending.

There would be something – there always was.

*

Bo made boarding in good time, despite stopping off to put a phone call in to a colleague on the way. He liked to keep as many options open as possible, and today's mess was no exception. He was *always thinking, always thinking.*

He needed to know that there was a body on the ground he could put his trust in, and today he had a particular skill-set in mind.

Having dispatched the air stewardess for coffee, he settled down to work. It wasn't very busy in first class – internal flights at this time of day never were – and it allowed him to spread out a little, which always helped him think.

Sticking his headphones on, he turned the in-flight TV to the news channel, just in case there were any new developments in the Flight K-43 debacle.

Pulling out the file entitled *A Journey in Time*, Bo flicked through it once again. It was a difficult read, as he'd discovered last night – despite his science background he found it tough going, and most of the math went straight over his head, but he ploughed through it nonetheless.

Of course, his lack of understanding didn't matter too much; his eidetic memory would allow him to pick up on anything coming up in conversation when the occasion called – a skill that had come in handy several dozen times over the years.

He'd got most of the way through the file when the TV newsreader's voice changed dramatically. The man sounded floored – there was no other way to describe it.

Bo's ears pricked up, sensing some new emergency as the big red banner at the bottom of the screen suddenly got bigger and started flashing the words: *Breaking News.*

"This just in, there has been a fatal car crash in the Paris underground road network. Sources have just confirmed that two of the people involved were Diana, Princess of Wales, and her boyfriend, Dodi Fayed, the wealthy son of Arabian businessman, Mohamed Al-Fayed – the owner of the world famous London department store, Harrods."

"Holy crap," he murmured. He put his file down and stared at the screen.

"CNN understands that the injured passengers have been taken to hospital for treatment and are thought to be in a

critical condition. Ambulance crews were on the scene within minutes, but…"

The reporter faltered, momentarily overcome with emotion. Around the first class section of the plane, people who had been watching the in-flight TV began to cry. Their neighbors fumbled for headphones, frantically pressing buttons, trying to find out what on Earth was the matter with their fellow passengers.

"The much loved Princess Diana – known throughout the world for her grace, beauty and kindness – has been killed outright, along with her boyfriend, Dodi Fayed, the wealthy Arabian Playboy. The bodyguard to the Princess is alive, though he remains in a critical condition. Doctors at the Paris hospital have released a statement saying that he has suffered severe brain damage and may not wake up…"

Bo turned the sound up on the TV, his eyes transfixed to the screen.

"It appears that no other vehicle was involved in the crash. The chauffeur seems to have lost control of the car while travelling at great speed, crashing straight into a concrete stanchion on the Paris underground motorway…"

Bo leaned back, his head whirling. This was big news, perhaps the biggest world news in decades.

For at least a few minutes, all thoughts of time travel left his mind.

He continued to watch the news, and by the time the flight arrived in Washington, the tragedy in Paris had quickly become the main news story on all channels in America, France, and Great Britain.

Even on the plane there was a tremendous outpouring of grief for the mother of the future King of England, a woman he was prepared to bet that none of them had ever met. He had: he remembered a charming woman, smiling and chatting easily with other guests at a White House garden party. Bo shook his head sadly. She had been so full of life. Why was it always the good ones who were taken early?

He sat back with a sigh while the plane taxied on the runway. At least one thing was guaranteed: her death had firmly relegated the story about Flight K-43 to the proverbial back pages, taking a bit of pressure off the American Government.

Unfortunately, it was for all the wrong reasons.

Chapter 8

Eddie who?

Bo sat quietly in his Washington hotel suite, mentally preparing himself for his upcoming meeting with the Vice President. He had showered and dressed smartly.

Things ticked over and over in his mind, the '*if onlys*' and the '*how can we avoids*'. One thing was clear – he needed options – as many as possible, no matter how far-fetched they might seem right now.

After a few moments the phone rang, startling him from his mental exertion and causing a smile to spread across his face – he had a pretty good idea of who would be calling him.

"Hello?"

"Hi buddy," says the man on the other end with little preamble. "What are we having for breakfast – eggs over easy?"

"Eddie, you beauty!" Bo exclaimed. "You made it then! Where are you?"

"Look, my old friend, when I get a call from Bo Nick Olsen, I know it's going to be atomic so I'm on the first flight in," he told him, a hint of humor in his voice. "I'm down in the restaurant of your hotel waiting for you to buy me breakfast."

"Give me a minute," said Bo, hanging up the phone.

Eddie was a good friend of Bo's and had been for many years. They had met nearly a decade earlier when Eddie was called in to sort out the security inside the computer network systems that the American Government had installed.

It was believed at the time that the Chinese and Russians could intercept the flow of information being fired down the lines, but it soon became clear to everyone that this was simply paranoia. Eddie had pulled off several computer-based miracles and had convinced the government that their secrets were safe – for the moment, at least.

Eddie was a genius when it came to computer science and physics and as soon as that particular security cock-up had been fixed, Eddie had been promptly snapped up by the CIA as a top scientist and analyst. He was quickly given the nickname 'Eddie Einstein' by his new colleagues, and Bo suspected he was actually quite proud of the new moniker.

Bo, now having left his room, was descending in the elevator, looking at his reflection in the mirrored panel opposite thinking to himself, *yes a smart suit is the right way to go today, I need to be aloof to my competitors;* he straightens his tie one more millimeter to the center, *perfect*.

The bell rings as the elevator reaches ground floor, stepping out as the doors open, his briefcase tucked under one arm, knowing that his appearance will gain admiration from anyone that should chance to cross his path.

A couple, stood in the reception area waiting to use the elevator, step to one side to let Bo pass. The man is dressed in shorts and a scruffy tee-shirt with *open-toed* sandals on his feet, the lady is dressed to match with huge blackout sunglasses wrapped around her face. They eyeball Bo over the few steps it takes him to reach the double doors to the restaurant. *Ping,* the elevator bell rings and the doors close as someone on another level has pressed the call button. The lady looks back to see the elevator ascending to the upper floors, "Stupid," she remarks in an English accent. As she smacks her gentleman friend on the shoulder with her handbag.

Bo senses the reaction of the two people behind him in the reception area – he smiles and immediately knows it's going to be a good day.

The restaurant wasn't very busy that morning; there were only a few families having breakfast. It was still a bit too early for most people. Not early for Bo, though – he was always ready to catch the worm.

He glances across to the reception area of the restaurant, and sees Eddie waiting for him. True to form he seems to have captivated one of the waitresses. No doubt thrilling her with his well-practiced (and made up) tales of bravado. Bo shook his head, smiling.

Eddie spots Bo who nods and indicates that they

should head towards the dining area. Leaving the girl with some reluctance, they both head towards one of the tables against the wall, divided from one another by booths.

"Eddie, my old friend," Bo declares happily, setting his briefcase down on the table, freeing his hand to shake Eddies as they greet each other. "Thanks for getting down here so quick. How's the family – Aiyana and the kids okay?"

"They're fine, Bo," Eddie grinned as he sat down. "But that's not why you're here, is it, you crafty old devil? I know what you're up to today, and I bet dressed like that, even Ron Champion fancies you."

For a moment they are both caught up in reverie, and then Eddie cracks a smile and Bo chuckles, tiredly.

"Sorry I'm not my normal self," Bo apologized. "I suspect you've guessed that we're deep in the brown stuff right now. I haven't slept; I'm spinning that many plates in my head at the moment that I don't know which day it is."

"Come on, Bo," Eddie cajoled him. "You always take on too much. There are other people on that committee, you know. Let them sort it all out for a change." He grinned, knowing full well that Bo Nick Olsen wouldn't ever let that happen. He just wasn't that kind of guy.

"I know what you're saying, Eddie, it's just that a ton of things are running through my head," Bo explained. "I feel like Superman running to save Lois Lane as the helicopter falls over the edge of a skyscraper and into the crowd below. I don't have enough time – or enough limbs. You know what I mean?"

"All too well, my friend, all too well," replied Eddie, who was always almost as busy as Bo himself.

Bo took the file on the Time Travel Project out of his briefcase, laid it on the table, and rested his hand on it. He then gave Eddie a long, considering look that put the scientist on full alert. Something is definitely cooking here – Eddie looks immediately interested – that's just how Bo wants it.

Bo takes a deep breath. "Do you remember about five years ago when you were doing the circuits with those seminars, predicting the future and direction that science fiction was going in, and how it was becoming science fact? Well we were in New York and one of the guest speakers was a Dr Josh Banner and these files Eddie, are the up to date reports on how that project is going."

Eddie holds up his hands, "Just slow down here Bo, just slow down. Give me a clue, who the hell is Josh Banner? I know I should remember but five years is a long time, and I've met a *lot* of people since then."

Bo throws Eddie a knowing smile. "You'll remember, Eddie. In those days it was coded 'To Believe a Dream'. Come on, Eddie get those old gray cells going!"

Bo fell silent as the waitress came across to take their breakfast order, surreptitiously dropping the napkin over the file, just in case.

Eddie smoothly changed the subject. "So, Bo, how's John doing?" he looked up at the waitress. "A full breakfast and a coffee please, darlin'."

"Just a coffee for me, thank you," said Bo. "I need to charge myself up for the meeting," he chuckled as she walked away. "John? He's good."

He waited until he was sure the woman was out of earshot before launching into his pitch. "Right, Eddie, so Josh Banner, he was that Geeky looking guy, boring the pants off me, rattling on about the relationship between 'space, time and velocity' how it was all relative or something like that."

Bo could just see a change in Eddie's expression

"I vaguely remember the man," says Eddie, "he had some groundbreaking revolutionary theories on how time travels, but it was all just theory. I don't remember the project name though *To Believe a Dream'*, I seem to have another name at the back of my mind."

Eddie's statement springs Bo into action, he begins to rattle his fingers over the folder, feeling a buzz as he was now getting through to Eddie.

Bo nodded, "I've been reading this file and at the beginning it seems to make some sort of sense. Well, maybe not technically – at least, not to me – but in the way it's written," he said, grinning excitedly. "The trouble is, after – what, six years? It seems to have lost all practicality. I don't understand where it's going anymore and I suspect the scientists on the ground don't either. They've lost the thread."

Eddie nodded back, intrigued now; he was beginning to build a picture in his mind of where Bo was going with this – Bo was clearly very excited about this project, and that infectious excitement was spreading. Eddie could feel himself being embraced by his friend's persona and it was infecting him, soon he would be swallowed up in 'Bo Nick Olsen – Se*a of Dreams'.*

Reading his friend's expression, Bo sat back still rattling his fingers across the file. "I want you to read this file from front to back," he said quietly, "and let me know exactly what's going on with this project. Is it feasible? Is it close to working? I want your take on this, Eddie Einstein."

Eddie reached across and picked up the file from the table, a curious expression on his face, like he was itching to get started. He spun the file round to study the front cover.

"*A Journey in Time*?" His face immediately lit up. "You're kidding me! That's the project title I remember. Now it's coming back, Bo! This is it! Dr Banner's very own theory on how time travels. How did you get hold of this? It's one of those projects so top secret, that the President won't even know about it."

"It's a long story Eddie, a long story," Bo said mysteriously.

Eddie immediately jumps in, "The theory is, it's all to do with generating tremendous velocity in space… this'll be right up my street! How far have they gone with it, Bo? Do you know?" Eddie turns the document's front cover over as he looks up at Bo who had the broadest of smiles on his face.

"I knew it, Eddie, I knew it!" replied Bo. "All I have to do is put the fuel in, turn the engine on and light the touch paper!" he laughed. "Do you remember that day in New York? We were at that seminar and you said to me it only takes one man to change the world. Well Eddie, you might be looking at the man who might be able to do just that. How far have they got with it? Well from reading that file, they've got the craft built. It's a working prototype."

Bo paused, scratching his nose. "They're now running tests on computer simulators, carrying out further calculations and perfecting the fuel components, but I get the feeling they've hit a snag somewhere. The research just hasn't really progressed in the last few years."

Eddie smiled, thumbing through the file, already lapping up the equations on the pages. "Leave this with me, buddy," he said, satisfied. "I'll get to the bottom of it."

"Good man. Now, here are the keys to my hotel suite," said Bo, dropping them into Eddie's hand.

Eddie laughed. "You always were pretty forward, Bo. Inviting someone up to your hotel room after one breakfast?"

Bo rolled his eyes, ignoring his friend's attempt at a joke. "You can have free run of my apartments, but you're not allowed to raid the bar, use room service, sleep in my bed, or use my shower! I know you, Eddie. Take it easy."

"Hey – come on, Bo," Eddie whined, not quite able to hide a smirk. "I won't be able to go all day without lunch and a glass of wine, my old buddy."

He knew full well that Bo didn't mean it. Nobody could be expected to produce their best work without sufficient fuel, and Eddie was no exception. He just needed a little more fuel than most, and the more alcoholic that fuel, the better things usually went. He found that it opened up his mind, loosened up his brain cells. And that's when the magic happened. Well, sometimes.

Bo grinned, eyeballing the waitress who was returning with the meal trolley. "Just kidding, Eddie," he said, as the woman started to unload the scientist's breakfast from the trolley.

"Thanks ma'am," Eddie said when she was done, eyeing up the huge plate in front of him.

"Your car is waiting at the main entrance, Mr Olsen," the waitress added primly, before departing at speed to the kitchens.

Bo grabbed his briefcase, shook Eddie's hand, and got to his feet, picking up his steaming coffee to take with him. "I gotta scoot," he said, clapping Eddie on the back.

"Give 'em shit, Bo," said Eddie, his mouth full of bacon. "I've already worked out what you're planning, buddy, but don't forget that this is so top secret it's practically imaginary. Be careful who you speak to – and don't make any promises you can't keep."

Bo smiled at his old friend. "I really believe this is possible, Eddie, I really do," he said, with a wink. "And you're going to tell me how. See you tonight."

He left Eddie laughing over his breakfast and headed out of the hotel towards the car that was waiting for him, feeling slightly more positive than he had before. Though Eddie was interested in pretty much anything science-related, part of Bo had thought his old friend would laugh in his face the very moment he mentioned time travel. He wouldn't have blamed him, either.

It was a crazy thought.

But sometimes, a little bit of crazy was exactly what was needed.

Chapter 9

Security clearance below level two

Bo's car pulled up at the White House without any ceremony. He nodded at the aide waiting for him and allowed the boy to escort him to the offices presently being used by the Department of American World Opinion Committee, or 'Cobra'. He was early, having beaten every other member of Cobra, so he let his mind wander, gazing out onto the immaculately maintained White House gardens from the windows of the comfortable offices.

He remembered that garden party again, a few summers before, where guests had mingled and played on the lawns, and a British Princess had laughed at the President's bad jokes.

The door opened, pulling him out of his reverie, and Bo turned to greet Ron Champion, the Vice President of the United States of America. They shook hands, and though it was going to be a somber meeting, Ron tried to break the ice with a half-smile on his face.

"Great to see you, Bo," he drawled in his Southern accent. "You look like you've come for a job interview." He paused, then laughed, his voice echoing around the room. "There may well be a lot of vacancies here soon if we can't sort this mess out!"

"It's nice to meet up again, Ron, despite the circumstances," said Bo tolerantly. "Your family all okay?"

"Yeah, Bo, thanks for asking. Well, as good as they're going to get," he said, shrugging. "Mags is still very ill – she's in a wheelchair now, poor thing. Still, you've got to keep going, you know."

Bo nodded, bowing his head a little in respect. Champion had an extremely time-consuming and stressful job, and Bo didn't know how he managed to deal with his difficult home life as well. He guessed some people just had more tolerance and patience, even in the direst of circumstances.

Ron and Bo had known each other for several years now, and had worked together for most of them. Bo Nick Olsen had made it his business to make ripples in a pond, and Ron Champion had made it *his* business to seek out the people making those waves before making them personal allies of his. He had been lucky with Bo, whose robust sense of humor and unwavering commitment to a challenge had steered them through many seemingly insurmountable crises. Once, jokingly, Champion had even referred to him as his personal Batman.

Well, the Bat Signal was well and truly up on this one.

Both men pivoted around when they heard the

other committee members approaching, their friendly catch up over.

There was the normal hand shaking, 'long-time-no-see' mutterings, and friendly back-slapping that you got in any group of people who only worked together twice a year at best, and while it grated a little, Bo kept a tight smile on his face.

He just wished they could get straight down to business. After all, time was running out.

Or was it?

The committee members all loaded themselves up with coffee and pastries before taking their accustomed places around the rectangular table.

Everyone here had been chosen because they saw solutions rather than problems. Their view of life was a little bit different than everyone else's: they were the kind of people who could turn an issue around and make it into an opportunity.

Bo, as he knew himself, was the best of the lot. He couldn't even remember all of the problems he'd solved over the years, sometimes with help from John or Eddie, sometimes by himself. He was proud of what he'd achieved, but he was only just getting started.

The Vice President positioned himself at the top of the table, not yet sitting. It was his usual routine – making himself higher than everyone else around the table to show his power, though he didn't really need to; most people in the room already respected him, and already knew their place.

After a few seconds he leaned on the table, his knuckles white as he pressed down on the highly polished wood.

There were a few moments of silence – a mutual pause where the members of Cobra sat back and mentally prepared themselves for what promised to be an interminable and difficult meeting.

These meetings always were, of course, but this one would be on a completely different level.

"You all know why you're here," Champion said soberly. "The fact is that Air Command followed the correct procedure in that field of operations. They were defending a high level meeting, but that means nothing outside this room. Trying to explain that to the British public is not going to be a picnic," he sighed. "And to be perfectly honest, I agree with them. Casualties from friendly fire – no matter how accidental – are utterly unacceptable."

He ran a frustrated hand through his thinning hair while the others around the table nodded in agreement.

"We've already started the procedure to offer compensation to the families of those killed, so now we have to put our heads together to come up with a scheme to raise world opinion of the American Government. Whatever it takes, people."

He took his seat, signaling the opening of the discussion. "Let's begin."

"We need to start with reducin' the media circus around the crash," said Ted Hayes, a large, affable Texan who had a history of taking on failing businesses and making them boom. "Get 'em muzzled, pull it back a bit and then we can start makin' waves of our own."

"Yes, but we don't want to be too overt," Marion Kinver advised. She had been the press liaison for the FBI for fifteen years before being asked to join Cobra, so she knew what she was talking about. "I think moderating the media response is a damn good start, but we don't want them to know we're doing it. We need to start with some small scale good news, flood the front pages with that and then hit them with something big."

"What do we have in terms of smaller stuff?" Vic Letterman – a man who had made a fortune in confectionary – asked.

"Uh, well the zoo in Louisville has a pregnant panda," Theresa Wolfe, a fortune five-hundred entrepreneur said, flipping through a stack of printouts Marion Kinver was passing around. "That always gets people's attention. Oh, and there's a whizz-kid in Michigan who's invented a new form of solar power – that could be something, we could lead into how good our education system is and give it a double whammy of saving the planet…"

"There's a guy in Portland, Oregon, celebrating his one hundred and eighth birthday," Stephen Oxford – the former and much loved Governor of Massachusetts – pointed out. "He was some kind of artist when he was younger, could be a 'good news' kind of story."

"How about this," Roger Carson – a property magnate from the south – suggested, holding up a report. "A veterans' organization that's raised enough money to house a bunch of its members."

"We could throw a bunch of money at them,"

Hayes, nodded, thoughtfully. "Make the houses really something. We could do the same for the families of the people on that plane too – they're military families, after all. I bet you anythin' the vets will be happy to go talk to them, and getting a housing project off the ground in the UK would be really good publicity."

"Let's make a splash with those," Ron Champion agreed. "I'll talk to the President, see if he'll meet the whizz-kid and the ancient artist. The panda's a good call, too, Theresa. People go nuts for those things – they'll lap it up."

"So we need our big story – or even two," Marion announced, moving the meeting on. "Any ideas?"

For a moment, the room was worryingly silent.

"Seriously?" Champion groaned. "Come on people, America's not called 'the Great' for nothing. We must have done something right in the last two weeks!"

Bo chewed the inside of his mouth, keeping his thoughts to himself. Thirty-two friendly fire casualties was a lot to bury.

"Uh, we're about due to help out *Doctors without Borders*," said Nick Richards, an ex-military man currently heading up committees for several charities. "They want to build a new hospital in the Republic of Congo," Richards continued, clearly seeing an opportunity to help out a worthy cause at the same time as shoveling shit for his government. It was part of what Bo liked about the man.

"As you all know, they're in the middle of a civil war and things on the ground are pretty bad right now. A couple of new pop-up medical centers for civilian casualties, and a central hospital complex would go a long way to mediating the total death toll. Not to mention the post-war refugee problems you get through disease and damaged infrastructure."

"That's not a bad start," Theresa agreed, cautiously. "As long as no one takes it as us trying to make a move down there."

"They won't," Nick Richards argued. "If we do everything through *Doctors without Borders,* it can't be seen as anything other than philanthropic. We're just trying to preserve human life, not send security forces in on the ground."

"Would this be a good time to pour our resources into worthy causes here, too?" Stephen suggested, making quick notes on the pad in front of him. "I mean, we definitely need to make an impact abroad, but we can use this disaster as an opportunity to do some good here, too."

Around the room, everyone smiled wryly: where charities were Nick Richards' pet projects, education was Stephen Oxford's. No one was surprised when he continued, "We could look at helping out a bunch of schools across the nation – the hundred poorest, that kind of thing," he suggested. "Set up projects aimed at keeping kids in school and off the streets, getting their parents to really engage with their future, that kind of thing."

"Another reading scheme, Stephen?" Marion asked fondly.

"You can't have enough reading schemes, Marion," he told her. "Literacy and education is a key investment in the future of America – sometimes they're what makes the difference between a kid growing up straight or dying in a gutter."

"I fear we may have come off track, slightly," Ron cautioned. "But I don't see why we can't look into improving facilities – it would send the right kind of message. Nick, Stephen, *Doctors without Borders* and the school things, they're your babies, I want you to run with them."

"They won't take this disaster out of people's minds," Marion assured them. "But they certainly can't hurt."

"What else have we got?" Ron asked.

"Well, if we're going down the humanitarian route," said Letterman, leaning his elbows on the table, "then we could do worse than sending aid and personnel out to Indonesia. That tsunami damn near wiped them out."

Around the table, several people nodded.

"That's on the news every day right now – we could make quite an impression that way," Marion agreed.

"So we need, what? Food supplies, medicine?" Hayes asked.

"Building materials, clothes, sleeping kits, cooking kits, water purification kits, tents, vehicles, doctors, nurses, personnel," Theresa listed, ticking each one off on her fingers. "We'll need to make it clear that we're not going in to give handouts; we're going in to help these people rebuild their lives – supporting them to build their own future."

"I think if we're going to do this, we're going to need to get the military on board," Letterman grimaced, foreseeing a potential problem. "Maybe going through the UN would be a plan, right now. Marion, if you can manage the press on this one…"

"That's what I'm here for, Vic."

Bo sighed as the conversation rolled on around him. They were all reasonable suggestions, but he was pretty sure that after accidentally shooting down an aircraft full of United Nations personnel, they just wouldn't cut it. Hardly anything would. These kinds of things were damage control, and pretty weak damage control at that.

Of course, Bo had something else in mind. He cleared his throat.

Marion sent a shrewd smile in his direction. "I thought you'd been awfully quiet, Bo," she said, sitting back and effectively giving him the floor. "What've you got up your sleeve?"

"I'm sorry, folks," said Bo, glancing around the table, "but I'm going to have to ask anyone with a security clearance below level two to leave the room."

There was a brief silence as all the members of Cobra stared at him, then, slowly and a bit reluctantly, Stephen Oxford, Theresa Wolfe and Roger Carson gathered their papers and left the room. Bo waited until the door had closed behind them before getting to his feet.

Ron Champion looked puzzled but intrigued, while Vic Letterman, Ted Hayes, Nick Richards and Marion Kinver waited with bated breath. None of them knew what was about to be discussed, but if Bo was insisting on secrecy, then there would be a damn good reason for it. Tantalized, they watched him as he stalked around the room, his hands deep in his pockets.

"Let me get straight to the point," Bo began. "Our committee has been funding a secret establishment that is studying the idea and developing the practical application of time travel."

He watched as the five remaining committee members exchanged incredulous glances. Plainly, the four secure members of Cobra felt that Bo might actually have lost his mind this time, which was pretty much what he'd expected. Ron, however, was watching him closely.

Encouraged, he went on: "I recently came across a file on this project, and I've been reading reports from the group going back the last ten years. The most recent entry is three months old, so they should now be closer than ever to a working model."

"I'm going to have to stop you there, Bo," said Ron, making Bo's heart stop for a split-second. He didn't, however, look like he thought Bo was insane, so that was something.

"What we've got so far is great," Ron continued, "and I want Cobra to keep working on those projects – Marion, Ted, you get them kicked off. Every little helps." He sighed. "Look guys, I know this is unusual, but Bo's project is of the highest sensitivity so I'm afraid I'm going to have to discuss it with him in private – I'm sure you understand."

Marion, Vic, Ted and Nick looked more like they didn't understand at all and that they thought both men were crazy, but they left with more grace than their colleagues, most of them smiling at Bo as they went.

That left the two men alone in the office. There was silence for several seconds after the others had gone, and Bo waited for the Vice President to speak.

"Let me lay it out for you, Bo," Ron said eventually. "All the other ideas Cobra has put forward have been pretty run-of-the-mill, but I have to say this one intrigues me. Sit down Bo – it will save me getting a stiff neck following you wandering round the room."

Bo refreshes his drink then sits back at the table.

"Right Bo, I'm going to tell you a story. When the President moved into the White House, and I became the Vice President, one of the most boring, time-wasting jobs I had to get through was to listen to all the department heads, medical personnel, Military personnel, and the rest of the heap of Government people. I had to take double rations of *Pro-plus* just to try and keep awake. But one thing that stayed with me, Bo – and I will always remember this – is when your predecessor came to see me about the government-funded projects. He told me about many of them, but it was the one on time travel that really stuck in my head. At that time the project was called…"

Ron, running his hand across the desk, chopping up an imaginary carrot says, "God what was it named?"

Bo, who now thinks it's time to intervene, speaks up…

"To Believe…"

"A Dream," Ron finishes the sentence. "That's it, Bo. Funny really, – I remember finding it so fascinating that I couldn't get it out of my head." He raises his eyebrows. "It sounds like you've had a similar reaction?"

Bo nodded. "I guess we must be quite a lot alike, you and I, Ron," he said, smiling.

Ron smiles back at Bo. "I take that as a complement."

Ron moved from the top of the table to a chair two seats from Bo, looking cautiously optimistic, going by the hesitant smile on his face. He rested his chin on the knuckles of his right hand, motioning his old friend to continue with his left.

"Time travel," said Bo, his eyes glittering. "Just think about it, Ron – we could prevent this whole goddamn mess happening before it even started."

Ron smiled. "You have my attention."

"I know this may sound far-fetched, but I believe we could kill two birds with one stone here: of course, the main thing is that we can stop that UN Transport plane from getting shot out of the sky."

Ron nodded, clearly thinking this through. "And the other thing? You mentioned two birds. What else have we majorly screwed up lately?"

"Well," said Bo, unsure of how the Vice President was going to take what he was about to say. "Not that anyone will know if it succeeds, but there has been another world wide story recently that we could change. Why save the lives of military personnel alone when you can save Royalty too?"

Ron stared at Bo, his expression unreadable. "You're talking about British Royalty? Diana?"

"That I am," said Bo, leaning forwards slightly. "She doesn't have to die."

Ron said nothing for a moment as he stared into the distance. "Princess Diana's different – that wasn't down to American citizens making mistakes. That was an accident, something that could have happened at any time."

"Yes," agreed Bo, "but the point is it doesn't have to happen at all. We can send a message back in time to stop the English Princess from ever getting into that car with Fayed," he insisted.

Ron rubbed his clean-shaven chin thoughtfully. "Surely that isn't our place, though? Diana's death had nothing to do with us."

Bo sighed; he wasn't sure if time travel could work yet, but if it could, it did raise some moral questions that he didn't particularly want to deal with. Such as: even if time *could* be changed, *should* it? What right did human beings have to play God? What would the consequences be?

How could they know that changing the history of the world wouldn't plunge them into some kind of terrifying dystopia in an alternate timeline?

But then, on the other hand, if they *did* have this technology and they *could* go back in time, shouldn't they use it to do something good for the world? And after all, saving lives was a humane act, no matter which way you looked at it.

It was enough to make your brain hurt, even a

brain as well put together as Bo's.

Still, he had to focus on the main thing here, and as far as he was concerned, the main thing wasn't what the rest of the world thought of America – people would always find some reason to pick on the superpowers of this world – but instead the lost lives of the people.

"Look," he said to Ron, "all I know is that if this works, we have it in our power to help people, to save people's lives. Why save those on the plane and not some people who were killed in a car crash? Are they somehow beyond our reach because of their status?"

Ron waved Bo's question away with his hand. "No, of course not, but when does this stop, Bo? Are you going to go back and save soldiers in the Great War? Kill Hitler? While you're at it, why don't you find out the date of every school and university shooting in this country and stop all the gun-wielding maniacs? This is way, way bigger than us."

Bo sighed – he knew the Vice President would have objections, but if they were going to do this, they had to agree on it as soon as possible. Before they lost their nerve.

"No, obviously I'm not going to try and save everyone who's ever died," explained Bo, "but the Transport Plane incident is our priority, and the death of the Princess occurred so soon after the shooting down of the plane that it is feasible to think we could stop both in one fell swoop. They're not years apart, they're hours. I really think we could do this." Bo took a deep breath. "And I think we should."

Ron stared at Bo, a small smile eventually

appearing on his face. It was certainly a tempting proposition.

"We could stop all this happening and get the American government back to the top of the tree with the British people," said Bo. "And not just with them – with the whole world. Of course, this is all totally top secret. The general public would never even realize that we had *rewritten history*."

Ron nodded. "And even if they did know, they wouldn't believe it."

"Bingo," said Bo, who suddenly felt incredibly tired; just thinking about the possibility of time travel was exhausting. "Still, I think it's our only shot. Our only *real* shot – old people and pandas will only do so much for America."

Ron laughed, the first real laugh he'd had in days. "You're right about that."

*

The discussion had been going on for hours, each talking point and proceeding argument becoming more enthusiastic than the last. Ron Champion was excited and positive, which Bo took as a good sign. After all, they had to be careful with this.

"So Bo, leave things with me," Ron said, firmly shaking his friend's hand as they got ready to leave. "I'm meeting with the President shortly, and you can expect a phone call one way or the other by the end of the day."

"You got it, Ron. Hey, send my love to your wife," Bo added politely, before walking purposefully down the corridor. He paused just long enough to stick his head around the door of the meeting room where the rest of Cobra had reconvened. Smiling, he wished them all luck with their various projects.

He tried not to let the smugness show on his face, but he was very satisfied with his day's work. Not only were they making an effort to mediate their problems in the here and now, they also had a shot at something even greater – something impossible!

It made him laugh just to think about it.

Not unexpectedly, Bo was getting quite a buzz from this. He loved his job, but he'd be the first to admit that it could be a little boring at times. This new project was anything but boring.

Not only that, but things were going his way, and – if he had any say in the matter – the American people would soon be back on the top of the pile.

He remembered Champion's expression – a combination of amusement and shock – and was smiling again.

It wasn't every day you could astound a Vice President.

As Bo left the building, he started whistling.

Chapter 10

You can't beat these French Wines, Bo

Bo was still on a bit of a high when he got back to his hotel suite.

Eddie, true to form, was sparked out on the couch in the lounge, wearing only his jockey shorts. There were two bottles of wine on the table beside him, one empty and one still about half full. It wasn't the best sight to be greeted with after a long and tiring meeting, and Bo was suddenly very glad that he wasn't married to Eddie – he couldn't imagine putting up with this every day.

Still, he hadn't really expected anything less from his old friend; Eddie had always been happy to take advantage of a working relationship if it meant a decent meal and a bottle of wine at someone else's expense. Besides, Bo knew him well: wining and dining Eddie meant getting faster and more accurate scientific assessments than anywhere else in the country – probably the world. The man was a genius, and spending a few bucks on room service could mean the difference between success and failure. Bo thought it was a very wise investment indeed.

Moving quietly, Bo set his briefcase down and crept over to his friend. He then picked up the wine bottle, emptying its contents into the sink in the kitchen-area of the apartment. Carefully refilling it with water, he replaced it beside Eddie and stealthily made his way back to the door, which he proceeded to slam as loud as he could.

He laughed out loud when Eddie shot up from the couch, his hair sticking up everywhere and his eyes wide. He'd clearly been quite deeply asleep, lulled there by one and a half bottles of wine. He clutched his head, which looked like it might be swimming right about now.

Hopefully he'd got all his scientific thinking done before his hangover, thought Bo.

"God! What the hell was that?" he shouted, turning and catching sight of Bo. He clutched his chest dramatically. "Oh, you're back. Shit, you scared the life out of me. What time is it?"

Eddie reached for his empty wine glass and collapsed back onto the couch with the air of a man who had been very much put upon. Meanwhile, Bo stretched out in one of the plush armchairs and watched his friend, a wry expression on his face.

"You still like your white wine then, Eddie," he observed. "Oh, and by the way – there are children in this hotel, so don't be going outside dressed like that or you'll frighten the life out of them. You'll have the FBI after you, and we all know how much of a mess that'll be."

Eddie grunted his agreement, pouring himself a glass of what he thought was wine. Bo watched, amused, as he lifted the glass up to the light like a true connoisseur and examined the liquid.

"You can't beat these French wines, Bo," he said indulgently. "Look at that – a living, breathing angel about to dance on my tongue." He took a mouthful of the 'wine' and immediately sprayed it back out, shocked.

Bo burst out laughing. "Some wine connoisseur you are, Eddie," he exclaimed, still chuckling.

"What the hell was that?" Eddie demanded. "You trying to poison me?"

Bo couldn't help it; he threw his head back and roared with laughter. Eddie was a hoot sometimes – particularly when he was still feeling the effects of a midday drinking session – and Bo sure felt like he needed to let off some steam after his intense meeting with Ron.

"That's water," he declared, wiping tears of mirth from his eyes. "That's drinking water, you ass!"

"What? Water?" Eddie cried. "Who on earth drinks water? That'll never catch on!" He shook his head as he brushed the spray of liquid off his legs, where most of it had landed. "Oh, and I hope you haven't told–"

They were interrupted by the ringing of the telephone, and Bo held up his hand to prevent Eddie from talking while he picked up. Eddie clucked at him impatiently.

It was Ron Champion.

"Ron! Hi – thanks for getting back to me so quickly," said Bo. "How did your meeting go with the President?" He listened for a moment, his spirits rising. "Oh yeah? That's fantastic, Ron – so he's impressed, eh?" He laughed. "Well, you won't believe this, but I've got Eddie here at this end so we'll pair up and fly down to San Diego to get this moving. Fantastic news!" He nodded as Champion went through the usual conversational motions. "Yep, yep, yep – get back to you ASAP!"

He hung up, grinning at Eddie like he'd just won the lottery.

"Yes! Yes! Yes!" he exclaimed, before calming down a little. "Sorry for interrupting, Eddie – what were you going to say?"

"What I was going to say, Bo," Eddie told him wryly, "was that I hoped you hadn't told anyone that the Time Travel Project is a goer."

Bo's face dropped at roughly the same time as his stomach did. "What the fuck?" he asked, astonished. "You just heard that conversation with Ron Champion – the President himself has given us permission to put the wheels in motion!"

Eddie nodded. "I heard, but you were right," he explained. "There definitely is something missing. I warned you not to make any promises on the back of this project, but you never listen." He paused for a moment, shaking his head before continuing, "Something held the project up after about six years of testing and evaluation – I'm not sure what, but it's clear from the reports, that it halted. Everything seemed to be going great for them, but a major problem must have raised its head, because after that the quarterly reports go scientifically stale."

He shrugged. "For the last four years the contents of these reports is just bullshit," Eddie went on. "It may sound good to the layman, but it is bullshit, pure and simple. It means nothing, it's just there to fill up space on the paper."

Bo gaped at him, uncharacteristically anxious. "So what are you saying, Eddie?" he prompted. "That there's something dodgy going on?"

Eddie nodded. "Something like that."

"But what are we going to do? The President is expecting results."

Eddie shrugged. "You shouldn't have told him, Bo."

"Well I did," said Bo, getting a little frustrated, his previous good mood gone. "So will you help me out, please? Think of your duty to the country, man!"

"Well," said Eddie, considering, "if you can get me into the Time Travel Facility so I can take a look at the proper records of the project, then I'll have more of an insight into what went wrong. Then maybe – *maybe* – I can help them figure out where they go from there. I can't promise you anything, mind."

Bo clapped his hands, breathing out a sigh of relief. "Right answer, Eddie!" he declared. "Get your bags packed and we'll be on our way. John's already there – I told him to reccy the facility, so it's all go at that end."

Eddie groaned, looking at the wine bottles next to him. "Do you have to be so loud?"

"Come on, buddy; pull your finger out and put some pants on. We're booked on the eight o'clock flight to San Diego."

"How did that happen?" Eddie gasped, flagging a little. "We're booked on a plane? But we've only just decided to go to San Diego! Bo…"

"You're not dealing with an effing amateur, Eddie," Bo scoffed. "Do you really think I hadn't thought this through? I've got a plan, old buddy. I've got a plan! And you, my friend, are part of it. Always have been."

"Alright, Bo," Eddie laughed, shaking his head. "You know, it's almost like you can see the future!"

Bo sighed. "If I could, we wouldn't be in this mess."

"Right. Just give me a minute to make a call to my friends at the CIA – they're understanding about national emergencies, but I do need to check in before I leave the state, you know."

Bo sighed again as Eddie picked up the phone. He wanted to be in San Diego now, but he had to be patient.

They had time. And if this thing worked – if it actually *worked* – they'd have all the time in the world.

Chapter 11

Here come the Cavalry

It was six a.m., the sun was still low in the morning sky, and at that angle the rays were bouncing off the sands of the desert making the grains sparkle like jewels.

Bo, John and Eddie had just left the confines of San Diego, and had now filtered down onto the coast road. It was only a few miles to the Time Travel complex, the three men were in complete silence as they absorbed the radiant splendor of the serene image portrayed in front of them. It was wonderfully hypnotic.

After several minutes, Bo broke the spell. "You know some people always knock America but one thing's for sure, it is a beautiful country."

The rental car slid past the unobtrusive wire fence of the Time Travel Complex.

They'd arrived.

It was so early in the morning that it wasn't even

hot yet, though the three men in the car knew the heat would quickly pick up in the Californian desert. At six a.m. there were also very few cars on the streets, meaning they'd had a smooth, easy journey to their destination. It made a nice change from the chaos of the last twenty-four hours, anyway.

The buildings they could see in the distance were vast, which was promising; it looked like there might actually be the infrastructure in place to make the project feasible.

Bo looked at the nearest building, smiling. Despite the distinct possibility that this was all a spectacular government pipe dream, he was rather enjoying himself. He grinned at Eddie, who rolled his eyes.

"Come on, man," the scientist complained. "You might be able to survive on a three hour siesta, but some of us need our beauty sleep! Or at least some caffeine. Quit being so goddamn perky, will you?"

John Dillon – who was driving – laughed. "He doesn't have another setting, Eddie," he quipped, glancing at the man in the rear-view mirror. "Or don't you remember?"

John was about to turn the car into the drive approaching the security gate when another vehicle – travelling far too fast – screamed out of nowhere and wedged itself between them and the gate.

"Here come the cavalry – right on time!" Eddie observed, amused. "You're not the only one who can call in favors," he added, as Bo and John both gaped at him. "I made a call before we took off last night, spoke to my old buddy in the San Diego Field Office – I helped him on a fraud case a while back."

Eddie chuckled, looking tremendously satisfied at having surprised his two old friends, both of whom were usually so unflappable.

"Moonlighting for the FBI, now, are you?" Bo asked, entertained. "What will your handler say?"

The three friends watched as six burly FBI agents scrambled out of the SUV and secured the security office, much to the astonishment of its occupant – a tall, friendly-looking, black security guard.

He sat in his chair and stared up at them all. "What the fuck is going on here?" he asked, not unreasonably, eyeing the badges that were being thrust in his face.

Bo let Eddie – who had experience with the FBI, after all – explain, and after a few minutes the security guard nodded offering to escort them into the facility.

It was as easy as that – it was amazing what one little badge and three little letters could do.

Three of the federal agents followed their little party down the drive and into the main office, while the others took over from the security guard on the front gate.

"What's going on?" a sharp, female voice enquired, as they walked through the main foyer of the Time Travel Facility.

Bo looked up to discover a primly-dressed, professional-looking secretary, eyeing them with an air of deep suspicion.

Becky shook hands with the three men, which was a mark in her favor in Bo's opinion. He smiled, admiring the lady with her professionalism. Every facility should have a person like that. Especially one that showed up so early in the morning.

Bo was a great believer in first impressions, and this woman had certainly impressed him. Bo, the true professional, was thinking she's very pretty, but a pretty face won't make me stray from my relentless pursuit of right and wrong…

Ah that's bullshit, a pretty face wins every time, am I mad? he thinks.

Bo wondered how far up the engineering ladder she'd got – and whether anyone here treated her as anything other than a pretty face. He hoped they did: this woman looked like she wouldn't stand for any less.

"It's okay, Becky; they're with the government," said the security guard, waving at her. "I checked their identification – these gentlemen are FBI agents. This is Eddie Daniels, a top scientist at the Bureau, John Dillon, and Bo Nick Olsen."

Bo saw her eyes narrow when she heard his name; she, it seemed, knew exactly who he was.

"You may have heard that I took over the Government Funding Agency a few days ago," Bo said with an easy smile, before continuing with the normal government spiel.

Becky nodded, giving away nothing with her poker face.

"Well, I don't want anyone here worried about being shut down," he said, trying to reassure her. "That's the last thing I want – I find this project fascinating. John here's my second in command, and

Eddie's – well, he's Eddie." Bo shrugged.

"We have top security clearance, ma'am," John said politely.

He may as well have bowed down and doffed an imaginary hat, thought Bo, who – as always – was trying to evaluate the situation.

"So I see…" She assessed them all with a piercing look, and after a few seconds or so, she appeared to make up her mind. "Are you an occupying force or just here for a visit?"

Bo chuckled at her bluntness. "A little of both," he admitted.

She nodded, impressed, perhaps, by his honesty. "Fair enough. What do you need, gentlemen?"

Then, just for a moment – just for a fraction of a second – Bo saw her as a different person, as someone beyond the professional and helpful company secretary. It almost seemed she was struggling with her thoughts as much as he was with his. Their gaze held in each other's eyes just for an extra beat, just for a moment longer than a breath.

Bo now was stammering – "Well… erm… yes… Well what we need…" Bo recovers, clearing his throat, "Eddie here needs a look at your files – all of them – and somewhere private to do it," Bo told her, clapping Eddie on the shoulder with a resounding smack. The physicist winced. "And John and I would like a tour of this very impressive facility."

"Very well," the woman said. "If you'll follow me, gentlemen, I will show you to the laboratories, where Mr Daniels can find the records."

She walked off before anyone could answer. John and Eddie set off quickly to keep up with her, but Bo's legs froze, they wouldn't work, he couldn't help it he had to watch her as she set off walking, not in a rude way but with tremendous admiration, her movements were so graceful. She suddenly stopped, looking round.

"Keep up," she says, "we need to get through these security doors together."

Bo quickly shifted his gaze, hoping that she hadn't seen him watching her, but he knew she had. This made him feel terribly embarrassed. *Damn it I think she saw me. Here am I trying to look super cool and I mess it up. Hang on a minute why am I trying to look good when I know I already do… I don't think that one will work though, not this time. She probably thinks I'm acting like a horny schoolboy.*

Which, to be fair, wasn't that far off the mark.

Did she smile? Maybe not, observed Bo. He was a few paces behind, watching as she raised her hand to use her security access card to open the doors.

No ring on her finger. Bo noticed. Why was that, a girl like Becky?

They left Eddie in the laboratory, already engrossed in the paperwork and under guard from a rather bored-looking FBI agent, while the remaining two agents, Bo, and John followed Becky for their thorough tour of the research facility. This was what Bo had been waiting for, and it didn't disappoint.

"This really is incredible," he said – for about the seventh time – as he and John gazed out over the time travel capsule in the missile bays.

John nodded, letting out a long, low whistle. "Jeez, you can see where all that money was going, huh?" He nudged Bo in the ribs. "I gotta say, this beats salt water concentration hands down…"

The agents, too, seemed impressed – despite their training, wonder and amazement had broken through their usually impassive demeanors, and now they were staring around them like teenagers on an unexpectedly interesting school outing.

During the tour, Bo had more opportunity to watch and admire Becky without feeling guilty – he had spotted other engineers on the site glance across, but no one would approach her.

He supposed that was a little odd – she seemed so out of everyone's reach – but then again, it wasn't that odd at all. Her cold and unforgiving persona seemed to be just that; it was probably a mask she wore to stop anyone else from seeing the real person behind it, but Bo thought he'd seen a small tear in it earlier.

At that moment, he knew he'd like to see more tears in that mask of hers, if he was ever given the chance.

As well as his thoughts about Becky, Bo had been battling with his inner child all morning, but the Time Travel Facility was just a bit too exciting to keep it under wraps; he couldn't resist being caught up in the dream of it all, and he didn't care who knew it.

He trailed his hand along the hull of the nearest, vast engine, a delighted smile upon his face. "This… this is the thing, Johnny-boy," he murmured. "This is where it's at."

He could just imagine the crew of the USS

Enterprise (NCC-1701) being transported down from the Starship to battle alien invaders, in this very hangar, led by Captain Kirk.

As the tour was coming to an end, John decided to have a bit of a laugh with Bo; grinning, he started singing, "There's Klingons on the starboard bow, starboard bow, starboard bow…"

Bo rolled his eyes, laughing. Looking across at Becky who was joining in the fun, their eyes met, laughter turning to pleasant smiles, then her smiling expression vanished.

I caught her out there, another tear in her mask. If only I was brave enough to ask her out… Hell what am I thinking? I'm the bravest person I know, if I can't do it no one can, he was just about to make his move…

Did Becky see this coming, maybe she did, quickly she turned then marched out of the building, not a word was spoken.

John had seen it too, he realized, as he glanced back at his friend. He must have been able to sense the friction between them.

Bo sighed. He was puzzled. *Have I read this all wrong? A girl like that must have a boyfriend, it must be me that's just being stupid. I've no right to think that she may even be sweet on me? That's it… It's just me being an idiot; the curse of the Olsen's strikes again.* He looks across at John, and shrugs his shoulders.

"Come on John let's get back to Eddie." They walk out of the missile bays.

Heading back to reception, John keeps glancing at Bo, "You look a bit lost Bo. Anything to do with

Becky?"

Bo couldn't help but smile. "So I *was* being obvious." He took a deep breath, shaking his head. "I'm a bit disillusioned, I honestly thought… Oh never mind, you're right John, let's just stick to the plan. History is being made here, buddy – I'm not going to spoil that by thinking about romance!"

Chapter 12

That is one hell of a game plan

After the tour they joined Eddie in the laboratory, where his head was full of physics. It was getting on for nine a.m. now and the other staff members were beginning to trickle in through the unexpectedly reinforced security gates, for work.

Bo was still beaming from ear to ear, like a kid in a candy shop. "You want to come and see this, Eddie," he declared, even more excited – if that was possible – than before. "It's unbelievable – there's a fucking spaceship in there as big as the Hoover Dam!"

"I know there is," said Eddie, distracted. "But never mind that; I think I've found the missing link!" he laughed. "It's almost as plain as how we moved from *Homo-erectus* to *Homo-sapiens*, if you catch my drift?"

Bo shared a puzzled expression with John, who just shrugged. Eddie had a way of confusing people.

"Plain as mud, Eddie," he remarked. "Enlighten us, would you?"

"I–" Eddie had just opened his mouth to speak when a loud crashing noise prevented him from going any further.

The three men and their FBI attendants turned, startled, as the doors to the office burst open. Doctors Josh Banner and Zack Bookerman strode in, the security guard close behind them.

Bo immediately recognized Banner from the seminar they'd attended five years ago, and Bookerman from the personnel files he'd been studying on the flight over with Eddie, though his photos from the files had obviously been taken many years before.

They both had an air of slightly unhinged defiance around them, the kind scientists got whenever they thought their work was under threat, and Bo could understand why.

They must think we're here to shut them down, he thought, before steeling himself for what he suspected might be a rather interesting ten minutes. Not quite as interesting as the spaceship in the other building, of course, but still…

Sensing trouble, the FBI agents immediately placed themselves between Bo, John, and Eddie and these new faces, and upon seeing this, the scientists checked their stride, bristling at having their progress blocked and a little wary of three suited men with guns. This was clearly no ordinary day at the office, if such a thing was possible around here.

"Who the *hell* are you?" Doctor Banner demanded. "And what the hell do you think you're doing? This is a secure complex requiring a high security clearance;

you can't just walk in here and take over the place! The FBI are on their way so you can just put up, shut up and *fuck off!*"

Bo – who was taller and more physically imposing than anyone else – firmly moved one of the FBI agents out of his way. Then, in a voice that commanded respect, he pulled Doctor Banner up short. "Whoa, whoa, whoa!" he began, holding his hands up. "For Christ's sake, these men *are* the FBI. Calm down – no one here wants any trouble!"

He stepped lightly around the remaining wall of agents and jabbed a finger in Banner's direction, pretending to be mighty angry. "You, you're Doctor Josh Banner – I've met you before – and you," he continued, pointing at Zack, "you're Doctor Zack Bookerman. I'm not stupid," he added, upon seeing their identical and comedic expressions of surprise.

"I've been studying the files you've been presenting to the funding committee and I know that they've been fabricated for the last four years, so I know that you have problems here. That, gentlemen, is simply unacceptable."

He made a show of pacing about the room, sternly, before shooting Eddie a covert wink. He was having far too much fun.

"But," he continued, "I'm a reasonable man, and I'm interested in this project. I'm sticking my neck out for you, so don't you give me any grief as to why we're here. I know – I *know* what you guys are expecting," he went on. "You think we're here to close you down; I can see it in your body language. You're expecting us to shut you down for the mistakes you made in your little reports – or should I say, lack of reports."

John smiled to himself. He had seen Bo do this before, sensing a bad situation before it could develop and utterly dominating all of the personalities in the room. He enjoyed doing it and he was good at it: Bo had always been the kind of man who could immediately engender respect. It was a skill John hadn't yet acquired, but if he kept learning from the best, he would soon.

Becky, the company secretary, was stood at the rear of the office as Banner and Bookerman burst in through the swing doors. She was observing the events as they played out in front of her, and observing one man in particular.

Who was this man with the unusual name? Becky knew that he had taken over at the Funding Agency but she had expected a much older person – someone with many years under their belt.

There was something about him. He was so commanding in his manner and so strong in his demeanour. When Josh and Zack had started to try and belittle him, he made them both seem like children who had been very, very naughty. They were going to have to say sorry or be sent to bed without any dinner!

This thought made Becky smile to herself, but was it fate that played its part, or was it something deeper? For just at that moment as Bo spun round to view his captive audience, his gaze seemed to lock onto Becky's eyes as her smile had just lifted the corners of her lips, a ray of sunlight shone through the office windows and brushed her face.

Bo was captured, his well-practiced and rehearsed speech forgotten, his thoughts elsewhere entirely, only for a brief moment, but long enough for him to realize that something had just changed in his well-managed lifestyle.

Becky on the other hand, almost fell over, the feelings in the pit of her stomach made her grasp the corner of a table for support. *What happened then, this isn't me?* She had to sit down at the desk, the nervous feelings had made her legs go weak. It happened so quickly, looking round the room she hoped no-one had noticed, but someone did.

Tearing his eyes away from Becky – which was much harder to do than he thought it would be – Bo recovered his composure, trying to get his thoughts straight as he continued. "I'm Bo Nick Olsen – Mr Fix-It from the government, you might say, and the new Head of the Funding Agency that keeps you in business," he declared in his best 'important voice'.

"This is John Dillon, my number two, and this is someone you already know, Mr Banner: Eddie Daniels, or 'Einstein' to his friends."

Josh had a vacant expression on his face trying to place Eddie. "Yes I remember now," he replied after a while, "I was invited to speak at one of those 'Kiss my Ass' seminars which was just an excuse for a free-for-all in the bar afterwards. I remember because you got through half a carafe of wine and then you got up on one of the tables, pretending you could dance, and if I recall you had stripped down to your underpants, then thankfully you crashed to the floor.

You had to be carried out."

Bo tried to suppress a smile while Eddie gave an awkward wave. "Well, I'd like to say I remember, but…"

Josh laughed. At least now the ice had been broken.

"Now," Bo said, clapping his hands together. "Can you please get me a cup of coffee? Black, no sugar."

True to form, Bo had bewildered his audience into submission. No one was demanding questions now or threatening to throw them out. They'd been well and truly put in their place.

Bo saw Zack Bookerman visibly relax, trying to fit these new concepts into his head. It looked like it was taking quite a while. "What? A coffee? Er… yeah," he stammered, frowning. "Er… let's go through to reception."

Bo smiled benevolently. Behind him, he heard John poke Eddie in the ribs and say, "How does he always do that? One minute it's DEFCON Three and the next we're taking a walk through the garden of Eden!"

Bo grinned to himself. God, he loved an audience.

Today was a good day, and it was only just starting.

While everyone was leaving to get their drinks, Becky slipped away to the lady's restroom. Maybe it was Becky's luck – good or bad – but Bo, the one person who she didn't want to see her leave, did. He was very concerned, but couldn't get across to speak to her as everyone wanted his attention just at that moment.

Feeling flushed as she enters the restrooms, Becky places both hands on the sink below the mirror. Looking at the image staring back at her, she sums it up. I know what's wrong she thinks – this isn't me it's someone else; men don't have this effect, not on me. I've got to stay in control of my feelings. I've got to try and keep up the appearance of the professional in charge, in control of the situation, I've got to…

Damn that man!

Her eyes begin to fill with tears. Come on Becky stop this, she dabs her eyes with a napkin, then tries to regain her composure. Right she says to herself, I'm ready to step back out into the fray.

One of the problems she has is working in the engineering complex – she understands the attraction between positive and negative charges – and boy could she feel them working that particular morning.

Damn that man!

She leaves the restroom with a mission, *'I've got to control my feelings, I can't risk getting too close to him'.*

*

They reconvened in the reception area, where coffee was dutifully doled out to all parties, including the FBI agents, who were perfectly friendly once they'd established nothing exciting was about to happen. It wasn't half bad, either, for institutional coffee.

Bo let them all mill around for a minute or two, relaxing with their drinks – their arrival had come as a bit of a shock to the resident scientists and Bo wanted co operation. He could afford to allow them to collect themselves a little if it meant he got the most out of them in the long-run.

He, John and Eddie had a habit of creating shockwaves, after all.

Becky rejoins the affray, trying to keep out of Olsen's way, and avoid any eye contact with him. Perhaps keeping busy is the way to neutralize her thoughts, but she can't stop herself glancing over to where he is, catching his air of superiority, his body language.

She always thought throughout her adult life that she would never meet anyone that could erupt the feelings she had only read about in magazines, during her teenage years.

Was this it? How do you know? Perhaps it's only me, that's it, it's just me being silly, forget all this, that's it, put all this out of your mind, silly girl.

Eventually, Bo called them all to order, and – still trying to avoid eye contact – Becky helped herd everyone towards a meeting room.

As she was walking backwards at the time, showing people where to sit, she hadn't noticed the group of people behind her suddenly stop moving as someone a little overweight got stuck at one of the tables. She nudges into the person directly behind her because of the hold up.

Turning round to apologize, she comes face to face with the person who had received her shoulder charge, he has also turned round to make his apologies. Becky froze, for stood only a foot away from her, yes you guessed it, was Bo. She couldn't speak, her lips moved but no sound came out. She tried to release herself from his gaze, but couldn't, his steely blue eyes had a hypnotic effect over her thoughts.

The crowd of people in that little area are pulling and pushing their way through, which dislodges Becky from her trance. She has to escape. No way could she remain in that room.

The crowd of people also pushed Bo forward to the rostrum at the front. He looked for Becky, but she had gone.

I've got to find her. The strange thing is, I have never felt this way before over anyone, and I can't just ignore it. I must speak with her – I've just got to find her.

He turns away from the audience to regain his thoughts, he sees the speech in his mind written on the blank wall in front of him. *I've got to give this everything, come on Olsen lock and load – here we go.* He spins round and begins to address the hoard of engineers and scientists.

"Now," he started, "you all know the mess this country is in; you all watch the news. The President has instructed us to find a way to put things right, and I believe that this project is *the* answer. It's our best shot, and I believe in it 100%."

"Gentlemen, I'm here to tell you that we are going to put America back in its rightful position: right back at the top of the pile. And how are we going to do this, I hear you ask?" Bo allowed himself a little smile. "We're going to use the time travel missile to send a message backwards in time to prevent the shooting down of the RAF transport plane, and stop all this from occurring."

His pronouncement was met with a kind of awed

silence. He guessed that it had been a long time since any of these scientists had believed they would see this day; by the looks of the recent reports, everyone here had given up hope of ever getting their amazing spacecraft working the way it was meant to work.

"So, my good men – and woman," Bo said expansively, raising his arms to include everyone present in the discussion, "let's hear your views of my plan."

All was silent.

Doctor Josh Banner in particular had gone as white as a sheet, and he raised his hand slowly, as if he were at school.

Bo invites him forward to address the audience.

Josh stands up, tentatively taking his position at the rostrum while Bo takes his seat, watching the young doctor expectantly.

It was a bit of a role reversal from his meeting with Ron Champion, and it felt good to be on this side of things for a change. "Right, Doctor Banner, let's hear it," he said. "I want nothing but the truth, please."

Josh took a deep breath. "You're right," he said simply. "We do have major problems. No matter what we try in the simulator, we can't get it to work. We have everything ready to go, but we can't proceed." He sighed. "In the most basic terms, Mr Olsen, we've hit a snag, in that we cannot tell the capsule where it's supposed to go. No matter how we approach it, the navigation is shot. We can launch the thing okay, but we can't guarantee it will actually go anywhere."

He heaved another heartfelt sigh as he looked around the room at his colleagues. "So, I'm sorry, but I'm going to have to piss on your bonfire," he added heavily. "Your master plan just isn't going to work."

Bo gazed at him for a moment, thinking hard. Of course, this was about what he'd expected. "Well, well, Doctor Banner, it looks to me like everyone here's had their finger in the pie," he said silkily. "Mr Dillon and I know to the nearest ten cents how much money has gone into this project and I would say that you, Professor Banner, are very much in mine and the government's debt."

He leaned forward to emphasize his point. "I think that if you want to save your ass and stop your colleagues from further disappearing under the weight of all the brown stuff currently accumulating around them, then you ought to be as helpful as possible." He gave Banner a very stern look. "Don't hold anything back, Doctor Banner. Now, first of all, you can explain to us the finer points of the theory driving the Time Travel Project. How is any of this even possible?"

He stood up, rather enjoying Banner's wide-eyed expression – like a schoolboy who'd just been caught napping in class – and crossed to the white board at the front of the room. He grabbed a pen from the board's ledge and handed it over to the doctor.

"Right, Josh," he smiled, Bo's voice more gentle now. "Just explain to all of us on the board how this is supposed to work. Oh," he added, glancing at the FBI agents – he'd forgotten about them entirely, "I think you gentlemen can leave now."

Doctor Banner stood there, clutching the pen unhappily as Bo retook his seat.

Once the FBI agents had left the room – already shifting their focus to their next assignment – the doctor shook his head as if to clear it.

Bo waited with bated breath; this was a life-changing moment. He could feel it.

Banner took a moment to pull himself together, then he stepped forward to the whiteboard and began his explanation: "Right," he said, clearing his throat, "I'm going to try and keep this as simple as I can for you heathens; most of it is hard math, even for people with multiple physics degrees." He cleared his throat again, obviously nervous. "Now, you have to understand that this is how it would work in theory – all of this is theoretical at the moment. The capsule is supposed to prove that it works in practice, but… well, you know how well that's going."

He drew a small, simple dot in the center of the board. "Okay, so we have the sun here in the center of the universe, and around it there are the planets and other large bodies of our solar system," he told them. "They all orbit the sun clockwise, apart from Venus, which is the second planet from the sun and which has an anti-clockwise rotation. We're the third. Now, let's say Earth is here at position 'a'."

The pen squeaked as Banner marked the Earth at the top of the whiteboard. Bo stared at it, fascinated as to what was going to come next.

"Over the course of several months, the Earth moves in an arc around the sun to position 'b', here…"

Another squeak. He tapped his pen against the Earth's new position at the bottom of the board.

"The distance travelled by the Earth is approximately three hundred million miles," he continued.

"It takes six months to make this journey, so if you take the distance travelled and divide it by the time to give you the speed, then you'll know that the speed that the Earth moves around the sun is approximately sixty-seven thousand miles per hour."

He looked around at them all, over the top of his glasses, smiling; despite everything, he appeared to be starting to enjoy himself. Bo supposed that it had been a long time since Banner had had the opportunity to play the mad professor, and as soon as he'd had that thought, he suppressed a smile. Everybody had a button – you just had to know what to press.

"Are you all following me?" he asked, without giving them chance to respond. "Good. Right, so what we do is launch our time travel missile from – say – point 'b', and the trajectory of the capsule has to take it in more or less a straight line to point 'a'. This is a significantly shorter distance – though, of course, the sun is in the way. Kepler's second law of motion tells us that the distance is approximately one hundred and twenty million miles less than the distance travelled by the planet in the standard arc of its orbit."

"You keeping up with me?" Again he didn't leave enough time for them to answer before he carried on. Bo's head was already starting to spin.

"In order to comply with Einstein's theory of relativity – 'E=mc^2', the mass-energy equivalence – we need to have a maximum velocity of the speed that the Earth is travelling through space. Sixty-seven thousand miles per hour." He wrote the number on the whiteboard and drew a circle around it. "Or eighteen point five miles per second. Then we add the velocity of the calculation 'c', the constant, and divide it by 'm', the mass of the missile, and with that we can calculate what energy, 'e', is required to push the capsule back through time – and it's feasible. Totally feasible.

"We have produced a Hydrogen based fuel mixture that is so powerful, it is equivalent to a small atomic bomb exploding in the Saturn Five's inverted rocket chambers every 93 seconds.

"At that velocity the time travel missile will reach point 'a' before planet Earth has had time to leave that particular time zone." He paused and eyeballed his audience. "Do you follow me?"

He did leave a gap this time, and taking the rapt silence as encouragement, he went on. "The Saturn Five rocket is so vast that it will be influenced tremendously by the gravitational pull of all the large objects in space – the planets, large space debris, the sun, and so on, which will affect its velocity. The five engines on the rockets have been inverted pushing the craft through space rather than into space. This allows the capsule to increase its speed to the rate required following each gravitational encounter."

Taking a breath, Banner continues, "When the missile gets past Mercury…" marking this planet on his rudimentary map of the solar system, "the gravitational pull of the sun will increase the speed of the capsule even further."

He paused for a moment, looking around the room. "Now, I know what you're all thinking – the Saturn Five system will just disintegrate because of the radiation and extreme heat generated by the sun, but what we have done is borrowed the magnetized force-field, heat resistant shields from the Mercury Probes, which we have then passed through the huge magnetic flux generated by the Hydrogen power-house of the engines to increase the force fields, equalizing the high field density, thus demagnetization will occur around the craft." He paused again to take a breath. "At a given point the booster rockets on board will activate, deflecting the missile onto a new course."

Bo nodded, hoping it looked like he was following everything. He sneaked a glance at his friends – while Eddie was smiling knowingly, John was sporting much the same expression as Bo imagined he himself was. At least he wasn't the only 'heathen' at this table.

"This new course will allow it to skim the surface of our star," he continued. "At this point, all the excess baggage is jettisoned – the engines, the huge fuel tanks, and so on – just leaving the smaller time travel capsule to continue onto the second stage of its journey. Because this is such a comparably insignificant object, the influence on it by the gravitational pull of the sun and the planets is negligible.

"This means that the enormous velocity of the capsule can be maintained," he went on, gesturing wildly. "If our calculations are correct, it will arrive at point 'a' before Earth has left that zone – effectively travelling back in time – and Hey Presto! That's that."

He turned and looked at Bo.

"So what do you think?" he asked, fiddling with the pen. "As I said, we've got some problems with guidance, because according to Jerry's calculations, the capsule will leave our time zone within an hour and a quarter of it launching. After that, there will be no way to make a course correction – even if we can direct it properly – and if it makes it to position 'a' then the Earth's missile defense system will probably shoot it out of the sky."

He shook his head. "Of course, we won't know it's worked even if we do succeed – the nature of paradox and all that. If the disaster is avoided, we will never have sent the missile to correct it. *It will only exist because it's in a time zone six months earlier.*"

Bo nodded, now very excited by the concept, and while he'd followed most of what Banner had told them, he was sure that Eddie had missed none of it at all. It wouldn't do to let it show, though. Got to keep them on their toes.

"That is one hell of a game plan, Josh," he said, before making eye contact with Eddie, who was applauding the presentation. "Eddie, don't let me down on this – I know you've got a handle on it. So go on, man, what can you bring to all this?"

Eddie strode to the front of the room as Josh Banner sat back down. There was a slightly awkward handover of the pen – like a slow-motion relay race, and then Eddie held the floor. He nodded at the four key scientists on the program.

"You lot have been living in a scientific cocoon

these last ten years," he admonished them mildly. "I have not. The world has moved on a pace. Ten years ago we couldn't have done it, but today we *can* do this. Let's start with the navigation issues."

He smiled, locking his fingers together and pushing them out in front of his chest, stretching his hands like a concert pianist. "Right guys, this is completely top secret – and I mean *top secret*. My good friend Bill Gates and the team at *Microsoft* have been working on a series of revolutionary new microchips that – if you connect them together in a particular configuration – they can rewrite themselves, over and over again." He paused for dramatic effect. "Think about it – a new program written fifty times a second! Flexible programing – a program that can adapt, that can shift and fix itself when it encounters a problem, or moves out of a time zone."

He wiggled his eyebrows at Bo, making him laugh. Eddie was enjoying himself too.

"With self-correcting software, travelling back in time can't affect the core program; if we give it all the information it needs before it leaves, it will rewrite itself so it can complete its mission. That's the beauty of flexible computing! We have a chance at getting this capsule to exactly where it needs to be."

Eddie was so enthusiastic about what he was saying that he was rising up on the balls of his feet, bouncing up and down like an excited child at a carnival. Here, he was in his element, showing off his genius to people who could really appreciate it. Bo smiled. This was exactly where Eddie was supposed to be.

163

"All we need to do is speak to Bill and see if we can borrow the blueprints – or, better yet, get him to send us over a couple from *Microsoft,*" he went on. "This is government business and he owes me a favor – I can't see that being a problem. Now, when it comes to a missile defense system shooting the time travel capsule out of the sky, I think I have a solution for that too, though it will take a bit more planning before I'm certain."

Bo clapped his hands, reveling in the positive atmosphere Eddie's announcement had produced. This was going to work – he could *feel* it!

There was a moment of silence around the table as everyone tried to digest what they'd just been told, a moment that was broken by Josh Banner, who was staring at Eddie in awe. "Can I ask you a question?"

"You can ask me three, if you're lucky," said Eddie, his good mood still very much evident.

Josh glanced around the table, his gaze lingering on Bo slightly before turning back to face Eddie. "Do you really know Bill Gates?"

Eddie rolled his eyes. "I tell you I can help make time travel possible, and all you want to know about is Bill? Come on!"

Bo laughed as he joined Eddie at the front of the room. "Alright people, we have a way forward now," he grinned. "Let's get this show on the road."

The members of staff stood up, glancing at each other with a newfound hope illuminating their faces. It was almost as if the air conditioning system had started pumping through some fumes from a South American marihuana crop, everyone was on a high.

Eddie catches Josh's eye. "I'm just trying to work all this out Josh," says Eddie, "you might end up with two Time Travel capsules every time one is used. The one that has just been returned to you, and the one that is about to be launched?" Eddie shrugs his shoulders.

Josh nodded. "That's about it, yeah."

Eddie grinned. "Tell me, Josh, did I really strip down to my underpants and dance on a table top that night in New York?"

"Well," replied Josh, "it was either you or John Travolta strutting around, but someone was certainly suffering from Night Fever!" He laughed loudly, and Eddie couldn't help but join in.

For the first time in years, they were excited about what they could achieve, and it showed. Everything was coming together. Finally.

Bo watched them leave the meeting room, a satisfied smile on his face, but inside, he was thinking of something else. Or, to be more accurate, some*one* else.

He couldn't match the feelings he was having to anything, even the drama of the Time Travel explanation hadn't helped.

Bo looked all over the Office complex, in the canteen, the reception area, but nowhere could he find her.

As he was heading towards the missile bays to check for Becky there, John Dillon shouted across the parking lot. "Come on Bo, we're on our way back to Sans! Gotta catch a plane early in the morning."

"Go without me, John," he shouted back. "I can't leave, not yet. I need to do something…" He trailed off vaguely. "Tell Eddie we'll all meet at the airport seven sharp."

Smiling, John ran over to Bo, stopping him before he could enter the missile bays. "This is about Becky, isn't it?"

Bo shrugged. "I'm not sure what you mean."

John laughed. "You're a bad liar, Bo." He paused, thinking for a moment. "Look, even I could tell there's something between you, and you've only just met! That kind of thing doesn't happen very often – I should know. In fact, some things only happen once in a lifetime, and if you miss it, or don't see it happening, it may never come your way again. Go and find her, Bo. I'll cover for you." He smiled again. "Keep in touch."

Bo couldn't help but smile back, and they shook hands before John disappeared off to the car.

Bo entered the Silos. Security wasn't a problem and Bo passed through into the Missile Bays. The place was very well lit and he could see a lone figure stood at the base of the Saturn Five Engines.

As he entered the open-caged elevator, the noise of the lift operating made the figure on the floor turn in the opposite direction.

Bo, unsure where this was going, felt he could not just walk away.

The lift reached the ground floor, Bo raced across to the figure, it must happen here, I can't let this moment be lost. He arrived alongside Becky, standing in front of her, so she had to stop her relentless march to the lower exit doors.

"Hello Becky," he started, before adding quickly. "I'm afraid I don't know your second name – may I call you Becky?" He was babbling, and he knew it.

She raises her face to look at Bo, and he immediately realizes she has been crying. She said nothing.

"I don't really know why I'm stood here," he said eventually, "I don't know what I'm supposed to do or say."

Pulling a tissue from her pocket to wipe her eyes, Becky replied, "I think you have misread the situation, Mr Wholeson; I do not wish you to do or say anything."

Bo smiles. "My name is *Olsen*, Bo Nick Olsen. I'm normally so confident in what I do or what I say, but now I just don't seem to be able to find the words that will help me… Look, this may sound a little crazy… I don't know you, and you don't know me, but does that mean we can't take a chance? I felt something special in that office, perhaps something that dreams are made of. I'm not really sure what it was, a connection of souls perhaps?"

Becky was staring at the floor now, unable to meet Bo's eyes. She didn't respond.

"Look, I'm not suggesting marriage or anything," Bo joked, even more nervous now, "I was just thinking, if we just take one step at a time and see how far it will take us?"

There was still no response.

"Or," said Bo, the fight rather leaving him now, "If I step to one side and you go through those doors and leave, then I will never cross your path again. Is that a deal Becky?"

Becky still didn't say anything. Of course she'd felt the connection Bo was talking about – or rather, rambling about – and that was exactly what was scaring her. Those feelings she had in the office were still with her, and she didn't like it. She'd been hurt before, and some of those wounds still felt fresh. She vowed she'd never get involved with another man… and leave herself vulnerable, but here was 'another man'!

All her strength and charisma had gone, she no longer felt in charge of her life. Someone else's heartbeat had just matched her own, and she had no idea what to do about it.

With a very nervous movement Bo steps to one side, Becky's eyes follow him, a few seconds pass as her heart is battling her mind. Becky stands still, her vision moves back across, looking at the exit doors, she thinks 'shall I leave through those doors?' Her heart was losing the battle. Bo is trying his best to hold on to her thoughts, he reaches his right hand across, a few seconds pass, she looks across and their eyes meet.

"Who are you?" she says, Bo's hand drops to his side.

"Right now Becky, I just don't know… I've always tried to help other people, and never asked for anything in return… But just this once… just this once, I feel I need to ask the question… If you can honestly say you never felt anything in that room then please, I can only wish you all the luck for your future, but if, in your heart, you did miss a beat and wonder where it went, then I would love to help you find it."

Becky smiled back, her eyes sparkling with tears that hadn't decided to fall yet. The emotion begins to overwhelm her. Her gaze is now locked together with Bo's.

"I've always tried to suppress these types of thoughts," she says, "always believed that this is not for me, but this time I can't hold them back… yes, I felt the connection. Of course I did!" Her smile widened. "I'm glad you came to find me… that missing heartbeat, Bo… are you keeping it safe for me?"

Becky smiles, she reaches her hand across to Bo, "One step at a time Mr Olsen and let's see how far it will take us."

Bo smiles, as relief floods through him. Taking her hand he says, "One step at a time is fine with me."

The romance begins, but how long can it go on? Or can it last?

Chapter 13

And your point is, William?

The party at the White House was in full swing: balloons and streamers were hung in tasteful wreaths about the walls, and the tables were decked out with pastel-colored flowers and the best silverware in the building. It was extremely elegant, but with just a hint of carnival flavor.

The dinner and dance in honor of the First Lady's birthday had gone well so far, and most of the guests were either dancing to the musical stylings of the big band on the modest stage in the ballroom, or relaxing after an excellent meal with glasses of wine, brandy or whiskey. There was an air of pleasant exhaustion in the atmosphere and people's guards had most definitely been dropped. A lot of the guests were more than a little bit tipsy.

Bo Olsen was not a frequent guest at these events but he did attend some of the more personal shindigs such as birthdays, anniversaries, and the odd governmental entertaining of foreign ministers and diplomats. Ron Champion was the main man who kept Bo in the inner circles of Government and ensured that his face was recognizable.

Whenever Bo attended these functions, he presented himself well, often giving off an air of superiority he wasn't even aware of. Heads turned when he entered a room. Some women couldn't take their eyes off him, some men also having the same problem; he is a very handsome man.

Over the years, many people at these functions had tried to catch Bo's eye – including the daughters of ministers and diplomats – and while some succeeded, it never went anywhere. Bo always found them to be too flirtatious, or more interested in collecting 'trophies' than in getting to know him as a person.

This particular night of the First Lady's birthday party was different. Bo had arrived at the White House in his normal chauffeur-driven limo as usual, however, he was not on his own – with him was a very, very special lady.

Bo was dressed in his tailor-made tuxedo, looking as cool as ever, and the lady with him was dressed very elegantly indeed, though not over the top like some of the people there. She had applied a small amount of makeup, but not much; just enough to enhance her already striking looks.

They walked arm in arm as they entered the ballroom, Bo with a natural flair in his step and the lady gliding along effortlessly, as if she did this kind of thing every day.

As they went by, people stopped and stared – it

seemed they both commanded the same air of admiration. Just in their near vicinity there was an unannounced noticeable silence.

Bo smiled at his partner. "Did you feel that? I think everyone's wondering who you are."

Becky smiled back; it was hard not to feel good when you were the center of attention.

Consequently, tongues that probably should not have been wagging had been loosened by good alcohol and good company. The happy couple knew exactly what the topic of the moment was, *Who's that lady with Bo'?*

Bo spotted Ron Champion – he was leaning against the buffet bar; Ron noticed Bo and his lady-friend, waving them over. He reaches across to greet Bo and shakes his hand.

"Great to see you Bo, how come you look so good in that monkey suit?"

Bo laughed. "It's in the genes Ron," with that he releases his left hand from the lady who is with him. "I'd like you to meet Becky, someone who just happened to catch my eye very early one busy morning."

Ron smiled at Becky, clearly captivated by her sparkling eyes and stunning appearance. "Hello Becky," he said, as he took her hand in his, "I'm Ron Champion, Vice President of the United States of America."

Becky held Ron's hand just a little bit longer than you would expect in a handshake.

"Pleased to meet you Mr Champion, I can do one

better than that. I'm 'President'... of our local Tennis Club!"

Bo shook his head, trying not to laugh, as Ron froze, he was just momentarily lost for words; then a small, naughty smile appeared on Becky's lips. Ron realized that he had been duked – the ice was broken. He returned Becky's smile and they ended the handshake.

"I'm sorry Becky," said Ron after a few seconds, "but when I pitch that 'Vice President' speech the girls normally go weak at the knees."

Bo *did* laugh at that. "Well, Ron, you'll have to do better than that – this is one special lady."

"I can tell," responded Ron, clearly already impressed by the way Becky handled herself. "So how did you two meet?"

Bo and Becky began telling the story of how they had got together, and soon all three of them were talking like old friends.

Bo and Becky were very much an item, even though they had only known each other a short time. The morning they first met at the Time Travel Complex, Becky was so entranced by Bo's appearance and demeanor, she was almost overcome as the butterflies were dancing around in her stomach. She still felt the same every time he looked at her, but was now managing to control her feelings.

They were obviously in love – this was easy to see – both in the way they looked at each other, and the way their hands constantly sought out the other, gently touching an arm or brushing a strand of hair away from the other's face.

Ron Champion had to stop himself from laughing on a number of occasions – they were just like a pair of teenagers, so in love and clearly unable to hide that fact. Ron was glad – he'd wanted Bo to find someone for a while now, and Becky certainly seemed to be the right someone.

Bo excused himself and went to the restroom, Ron kept Becky entertained and although Becky always replied to Ron's enquiries; he began to realize that she in fact had never told him a single thing. Where she worked, what she did for a living, who she worked with. She answered all the questions, but Ron realized that the answers, although very convincing, didn't relate properly to the questions. Just like a true politician, Ron thought, he held his hand up and stopped the conversation.

"I surrender Becky, I surrender, I've only just realized that you've been giving me the run around for the last ten minutes, you're good Becky, you're damn good."

Bo returned, a big smile on his face, he put his arm around Becky's waist. "How are you two getting on. Has Becky been trying to get you sorted out Ron, because she has me, that's *'trying'* I mean?" Again all three had a good laugh, the conversation jumped about with one thing or another and one of the topics was the British Transport Plane being blown out of the sky.

Just at that unfortunate moment the British Foreign Secretary was passing behind the trio of friends. He was currently touring the States, and had been surprised to get an invitation to such an important event.

"Ah, Vice President Champion." A booming English voice made the three people spin round abruptly. "Mr Champion I feel you are avoiding me." His words were slightly slurred; he'd clearly been enjoying the free alcohol available at the party.

Ron didn't give his thoughts away. "Oh. Hi there Mr Secretary, so pleased you could make it."

"Don't bullshit me Ron. I know the invite didn't come from your office."

"And your point is, William?" asked Ron.

"Look, I just overheard you discussing the disastrous mess you lot made shooting down that transport plane," says William, as he turns waving his hand at Bo and Becky. "Do you really think discussing that topic with the likes of these people is going to help you come up with a solution? I mean, they're only government groupies!" With that, William reaches out, poking Bo in the chest. "Excuse me young man I need to speak to the man in charge. Alone."

Bo doesn't move, standing his ground, so William steps squarely in front of Bo to face the Vice President.

Becky is evaluating the situation. She pats the Foreign Secretary on the shoulder hard enough for him to notice the infringement. Startled, he looks round – mildly confused – and Becky, with her professional *'I'm in charge demeanor'*, which is very clear and precise, tells him, "Look! I don't know who you are, and personally I don't give a damn, but you will never, ever be so disrespectful in my company again, do you understand?"

Bo is stood firmly at Becky's side. The British

Foreign Secretary, just for a moment is put in his place *'by a girl'*. However, with the authority thrust upon him, he feels the need to apologize.

"Oh," replied William, his cheeks slowly coloring, "I'm sorry, my dear. I just need to speak to the Vice President. Please do accept my apologies."

William turns back to Ron. "I'm telling you, my government simply can't believe that you've managed to mess up everything we've been working towards. After all the effort that we have put in trying to get the public on our side over the conflict going on in Kazakhstan! That plane had most of our top people involved in the conflict and peace process on board and you lot muck it up good and proper!" he scoffed, his face getting redder by the second.

"Even the Queen has summoned the Prime Minister for talks about the tragedy in Astana," he continued. "You have no idea how high feelings are running back home right now. You're not exactly Britain's favorite people! In fact, I'd say you're on the bottom rung of the bloody ladder at the moment. You do know that, don't you?"

Bo decides to stay out of it, he rests his hand on Becky's arm to avert her from the two men. The conversation wasn't exactly aggressive – at least, not yet – and he rather felt that the British Foreign Secretary had a point.

"Yeah, yeah," the Vice President said in what he clearly felt was a consoling manner – which obviously wasn't. "We do understand your position. It's a terrible thing to have happened. Just awful. There's a top level inquiry going on as we speak, but we all know it's never quite as it seems, is it?"

He paused, taking a sip of his champagne before carrying on, "And then there's that awful crash in Paris. Your Princess…"

At the mention of Diana, Bo stepped forwards again, thinking he should intervene to take some pressure off his friend. "Yes, the death of the Princess," said Bo, lowering his head in respect. "That was a dreadful thing to have happened. A real loss. Your country must be devastated. My condolences, Mr Secretary." He swirled his own drink around in his glass a few times, lost in a reverie of sunshine, where a British Princess had smiled and laughed. She had been a kind, elegant woman. Bo remembered that very clearly.

"You know, I once met the lady at a charity function in the White House gardens. She was a lovely lass. Really lovely."

The British Foreign Secretary pivoted round and fixed Bo with a petulant stare. He had clearly been spoiling for a fight, and he didn't particularly care who it was with. After all, he'd been rubbing the Vice President of the United States up the wrong way, and he didn't seem to have a problem with that.

"Look, young man," he said, in high dudgeon. "I don't know who the hell you think you are, but you just can't describe the future King's mother as a 'lovely lass', like you're talking about a showgirl. And yes, speaking of the death of the Princess, that's another bloody problem for you Americans. The British tabloid press are going all out to try to blame that on you lot as well. Although that's clutching at straws if you ask me."

Bo smiled as the man squared up to him; the old fool seemed to believe that the British Empire still ruled the world.

"Anyway, don't you start being clever with me, young man," he added, prodding a bony finger in Bo's chest. "You Americans are always so bloody cocksure. It's arrogant and inelegant."

Bo raised his hand up in apology, carefully schooling his features into puzzlement. "My apologies, Mr Secretary, I didn't mean any disrespect – it's probably just my Dutch accent."

Becky looked on making mental notes. *Is this how foreign policies are made'?* She wondered.

But there was more deliberation to come.

Ron has now listened to the British Foreign Secretary's ever so righteous rhetoric for long enough. Removing his spectacles, he begins to clean them with the handkerchief he has just taken from his pocket, a gesture that Bo notices straight away. He knows exactly what it means: Ron Champion was about to let William Harcourt have it with both barrels!

The British Foreign Secretary realizes that Bo has made eye contact with Ron. Pivoting round he sees Ron replacing his glasses.

William is caught by surprise as the Vice President takes one step closer to him.

Suddenly, full in his face, and without hesitation, Ron reverts back to the hardened politician. "Right. Now you listen to me Harcourt! I do not feel any love for you, so I'm telling you this, do not come into our country and expect me to bow and scrape to the likes of you. How many times have you lot come to us to save your precious, pompous, idiotic holier-than-thou asses?"

The British Foreign Secretary steps back from Ron, and bumps into Bo, he looks round possibly hoping for some support.

Bo just stands his ground, giving a meaningful glance at the British Foreign Secretary. Becky catches Bo's eye – she has tremendous admiration for him – as he can stand his ground with these high ranking politicians. Becky then holds the Secretary's gaze for a few seconds.

"And look at me when I'm talking to you," bellowed Ron, causing William to turn back to him. "So, here you are again, holding out your challis hoping to pick up a few pieces of silver."

The British Foreign Secretary is almost lost for words.

"Look I've been invited here by the First Lady as a sign of respect…"

Ron is now reloading both barrels.

"Respect, respect?!" repeats Ron, the vein in his temple now pulsing. "You wouldn't know what respect was even if you fell over a sack of it. For the past five hundred years you've treated this planet like it's some sort of playground, and now when things aren't going quite your way you come here looking for retribution. Well, there won't be any pickings here for you, when we're again going to have to put right the mess you've made of things. You see Mr Harcourt, we've got time on our side in ways you could never dream of!"

Bo closed his eyes for a moment, letting the stunned silence wash over him. He couldn't actually believe what had just happened. I hope the British Foreign Secretary isn't any good at working out *cryptic clues*, he thought.

The very controlled exchange of differences by Ron and the British Foreign Secretary had attracted some attention from FBI Agents mingling with the guests, the Secretary's personal Aide had been brought over to address the problem. The agents stationed themselves at Ron's side, ready to intervene if needed.

Bo put his arm around Becky and brought her closer to him to keep her safe – not that she really needed protecting, of course; she'd made it quite clear that she could look after herself.

The British Foreign Secretary has without doubt been humbled by Ron's forceful, not humiliating, but forceful political address. He was now being led away by his Aide to regain his thoughts. Perhaps he had picked on the wrong person.

With great restraint, the British Foreign Secretary made his way to the First Lady to pay his respects and wish her many happy returns, but quickly left thereafter, his aide trailing after him like a faintly bemused comet.

Ron, Bo and Becky watched them leave, all three of them relieved to see him go.

"Well," said Bo, "that could have gone better. I think you caught him with his pants down there." He gave his old friend a grim smile.

"I know, I know," said Ron heavily. "Perhaps I should have been more sympathetic. I just couldn't help myself – he was pissing me off with his holier-than-thou attitude."

"You and me both, Ron. You and me both," Bo added, shaking his head.

"What you must understand Bo," continued Ron, "is that when you sit in a seat of power, it's no good letting someone like that come along and cut a couple of inches off one of your chair legs making your seat unevenly balanced because you will fall Bo, you will fall one day, it would then be unhelpful turning around with crocodile tears in your eyes and pleading, *'I never saw that coming'*, you've got to take the lead roll Bo and stop them when you have the advantage."

Bo smiled. "I always enjoy the time we spend together, Ron; there's never a dull moment when you're with Ron Champion. I've got a lot to learn from you, my old friend."

Ron gives a light hearted smile at Bo and Becky. "I'm sorry, Becky, maybe that was your first introduction to politics, but I hope you don't mind me saying that I don't think it's going to be your last!"

Becky gives Ron a cheeky smile.

He continues, "The dressing down you gave William back there Becky, along with that facial expression was a classic piece of work, you left him searching for his next sentence, which gave me chance to fire some more bullets at him."

Now standing in between Bo and Becky, Ron put his arms casually around the two of them before stating, "You two, come with me!"

He walked them outside, into the White House gardens, which looked beautiful under the starry, moonlit sky. When they'd got to one of the small water fountains, Ron stopped, and invited his party to sit down.

"I know we've only just met Becky, but as Bo said earlier you're one very special lady, and I trust Bo with my life – if he says you're one of the good ones, I believe him. If my gut feelings are right, what I'm about to say will affect both of you, I want you to listen to my proposal." Ron pauses to gather his thoughts.

Becky exchanges a confused smile with Bo, raising her eyebrows as if to ask, 'Where is this going?'

Bo replies with his own smile and a brief shrug – he has no idea.

"Right Bo this is what I've been thinking and you must fully consider what I'm about to say. In two years' time Bo, the Presidency of the United States of America is coming up for re-election."

"Yes, in the fall," answered Bo.

Ron scratches his forehead. "Yes Bo that's right. Well I'm going to be put forward by our party as the candidate for that position and I've been asked to nominate a Vice President. I've been racking my brain trying to find an American who has that drive, that persona, that charisma to take the job on, and there is no one who I could consider more suitable than you my friend. You have always been a loyal, dedicated, and committed friend to me, and you are the one man who I can trust to be at my right-hand when the knives are unsheathed and my back is exposed."

Ron paused briefly to catch his breath. "The problem I'm having, of course, is that the Vice President must be born of American Citizenship." Ron looked at Bo with an air of sadness. "I've had my trusted legal team look at this from every angle, and under no circumstances can it be overruled.

"However, my friend, I still want you at my side. We will be scrutinized by all the politicians in America, no doubt, so we cannot be seen to make any mistakes, and you will also be studied closely by all foreign governments to see why you are standing so close to me on the world stage. They will eventually realize what your role is, but government diplomacy should protect you. However, knowing how you handle yourself, I don't think you'll need much protection from those sharks."

He smiled. "I've spoken to the party hierarchy on the committee, and as they know you, and as they are aware of your reputation, they understand and have agreed to my request. A candidate for the role of Vice President will be chosen later by the committee, but this will be in name only. He will be a man who can speak and address himself very well, and he will be able to present your views in a very clear and professional manner.

"So, Bo, I wish you to be my true right-hand man if I'm elected. I know you love this country as much as I do, so, my friend, what do you say? Do you want me to leave you to think about your decision?"

On the outside, Bo didn't appear to be giving much away, but inside his own head, it was a whole different story. There were cheerleaders dancing around, the Washington Redskins were running out at the Super Bowl, and fireworks were exploding in every single one of his brain cells.

"Think about it, Ron? You mean, think about how much of an honor it would be? Let me give that a millisecond to digest. There, now that's done. To be perfectly honest Ron, it's always been one of my dreams to serve this beautiful country in government."

Ron holds his hands up, "Whoa there Bo. There's a long way to go yet, we've got to ensure that our party gets elected; it's not going to be a walk in the park. Do you think you will be able to persuade John Dillon to come with us?"

"Take that as read Ron," said Bo.

The men stand and shake hands, but instead of heading back into the White House as Bo expected him to, Ron turned to face Becky. "Right, Becky, now it's your turn. I know we have a long way to go, and it's only early days at the moment, but I think that together, the three of us could really achieve something."

Becky nodded slowly, not quite sure how to react.

Ron carried on, "You are a brave and clever lady; standing up to old Harcourt really showed your courage in a tight situation. Now," he said, getting down to business, "I don't know if you can, but tomorrow, would you be able to accompany me to a meeting with the party leaders? They're putting together a team that's going to orchestrate my climb up the White House steps, and I feel I need someone strong, shrewd, clever, and persuasive to head it. Not to mention – and I'm sorry to say this – appealing physically. This person's image will be in every house, mobile home, factory, office, and place of work in the country, and Becky, I want you to be that person. I can arrange an interview for you with the party leaders, but only if you wish. There's no pressure on you at all, I want to emphasize that."

Bo holds his hand out for Becky to grasp as she lifts herself up off the garden seat. Her eyes wide, sparkling in the moonlight, she holds her left hand across her lips.

"Well?" asked Ron, clearly too impatient to wait any longer, "what do you say? Will you please work with me, Becky?"

Becky smiled as she gently shook her head. "But you don't really know me!"

"Oh yes I do, Becky," Ron replied. "After all, I am the Vice President of the United States."

Ron smiles as Becky leans over, giving him a small kiss on his cheek.

"I would love to work with you Mr President."

The three companions stroll back to the Ballroom, Bo and Becky locked arm in arm, with Ron, strolling beside them.

'It's been a good day's work.' Ron thinks.

But how is it all going to work out in the end?

Chapter 14

Project Update

In San Diego, plans were moving on a pace.

Years of inertia had given way to weeks of extraordinary activity following Olsen's, Dillon's and Daniels' visit to the Time Travel Complex. The first couple of days, however, had been purely administrative, with everybody gearing up for what would be a last big push to get the time travel missile operational. Half of this concerned arranging transport and accommodation for resources and personnel as they transferred operations to several new locations across the US.

The biggest move, out of necessity, was getting the Saturn Five rocket to Cape Canaveral. What was essentially a cross continental journey had further been complicated by the sheer size of the module and its immense engines. Even partially dismantled, it was impossible to transport them covertly.

Each shipment was classed as an extra-wide load and needed police escorts through each state, plus the occasional road closure to get them safely through. Both Bo Olsen and Ron Champion had pulled some strings with NASA and the Secret Service, and several feel-good new satellite stories had been carefully filtered through the press. They seemed to be doing their job pretty well: so far no one had had any uncomfortable conversations about time travel, and NASA was busy trading on the subsequent upsurge in press coverage.

Where the rocket went, the technicians went – for many of them, this was the longest they had ever been away from their families, and with the added stress of their project finally coming to fruition, weekly meetings had been set up for the scientists to vent. Becky – that paragon of system operations – was organizing it all.

There was talk among the higher ups that if they pulled this off, Becky would be snapped up into a top government position. She sure as hell deserved it.

Of course, in the madness of trying to get everything ready, they all seemed to have forgotten that if this all worked out, no one would even remember any of it.

The launch pad – which was integral to the mission – was the one bit of kit that hadn't been under construction when the launch date of the project was brought forward. Bradley was now overseeing that project in a NASA facility on the cape.

Luckily, it had been one of the first things they had designed, and the plans for it had been established and approved for some time. So, when the time had rather unexpectedly come for the project to move on, all that they'd needed to do was start the build. One of NASA's top teams of construction engineers had been taken off the building of a module they were intending to send past Neptune and the Kuiper belt, and were brought in to get the pad finished in time for the installation.

It was so big that it had to be constructed in five parts, each one to be carried separately into orbit and put together in situ by several teams of astronauts who were getting a bit of an operational workout on this project.

This thing was big in every sense of the word.

As time moved forward, there was less and less activity at the Time Travel Facility in San Diego and more and more teams working in facilities on the East Coast of America, leaving the buildings in California mostly empty, like some eerie, abandoned ghost town.

Things were beginning to come together, and the closer they got to the proposed launch window, the more people were starting to get a real buzz from the project again.

It was beginning to feel real.

It was going to work.

Chapter 15

If I had my time again

It was good to be back in England.

As much as the Right Honorable William Harcourt enjoyed state visits (as a rule), he always missed the country of his birth. It was silly and drizzly and set in its ways, but it was home.

He had never married – given the rigors of the job – but his sister's family was always happy to see him and made a point of welcoming him home. It steadied him – that little ritual of catching up on family news and gossip – and reminded him that there was more going on in the world than the vast, sweeping decisions that governments made day to day. It helped keep him down to earth. Well, more or less.

The British Foreign Secretary had spent the last half hour dozing in the backseat of the car while they were stuck in the interminable London traffic jam. He'd just come from a slap-up breakfast at Claridges with his sister and her husband, and after a start like that and a strong cup of tea in hand, he felt like he was ready to face anything, or almost anything. The slippery and somewhat aloof Director of MI6 is expected later in the morning for the normal debriefing session, he was someone William detested, he could really make your skin crawl, but it was all part of the job, dealing with oily creatures like Graves. He always got the impression that Graves thought he was a complete idiot, and Harcourt didn't like the idea of that at all. He happened to think he'd got it the wrong way round.

Finally, he got to his destination, and the short ride in the lift to his office on the third floor – where their meeting was being held – was a good opportunity to get his head in order, but the only thing he could think of was the sooner this meeting was over, the better.

After exiting the lift, he walked the few steps towards the suite of rooms used by the Foreign Office. A number of colleagues – who were dodging up and down the corridors – acknowledged his return.

Home at last, were his thoughts as he eased open the huge oak door to his private office.

As the fresh smell of polished leather hit him, he couldn't help but grin – it was like a fix. Yes, he was back, and he was ready to tackle the huge backlog of paperwork that had no doubt accumulated since his excursion to North America.

As he hung up his trilby hat and umbrella, his gaze landed on a somber-looking man in a dark pinstripe suit, who was sitting comfortably in one of the dark leather upholstered armchairs. He was almost camouflaged against the oak bookcases and dark curtains.

Having to look twice and refocus his eyes, he was alarmed to see Samuel Graves – the Director of MI6 – *how the hell did he get in?* William thought.

"Samuel," exclaimed William, "what are you trying to do, give me a heart attack? You know it's my first day back after a month across the pond."

Samuel just gave a kind of 'Humph' in response, stood up and shuffled to a nearer seat adjacent to the highly polished antique desk. "I was just practicing my covert maneuvers; I was a dapper hand at it in my day, though I suppose I was about eight stone lighter then. So, how did it go in the colonies?"

"Give me a chance, Samuel; I've not even sat down yet," William replied as he put his briefcase down, then eased himself into his comfortable leather chair. "Ah yes, it's good to be back."

Just then, there was a knock on the door. It was Margaret with the early morning coffee and tea trolley.

"Great to have you back, William; it hasn't been the same without our early morning ritual. Shall I pour?" she asked, to which William smiled in response.

"Ah Margaret, I sure have missed you these past few weeks, though I'm afraid we'll have to give our normal chit chat a miss – Mr Graves is here for the de-briefing session."

Margaret nodded. "Yes I know, William; he's already ordered his Earl Grey." She pours the drinks out, then passes the cups across to the two men. "Earl Grey," says Margaret, "I don't know how you can," then heads towards the door to leave adding, "It's not my cup of tea, I'm afraid!"

Samuel was shaking his head. "That woman William, why don't you pension her off? She must be in her seventies," he says.

William smiles. "This Department was built on loyalty and so it shall remain."

Samuel readies himself, clasping his hands together in front of his chest as he says, "Right William, let's get going with this."

They spent an hour or so discussing his tour of North America, most of which had been quite enjoyable despite the recent tensions between the two countries. They went over security arrangements, regional appointments, and up and coming politicians who were worth watching. Eventually, talk turned to Washington, as it inevitably always did.

Harcourt's face clouded when he recalled the early conclusion of the First Lady's birthday party.

"I was chatting with Ron Champion," he said sourly. "He's a fool, that man, trying to blame us for the transport plane disaster. He said to me – *but we all know it's never quite as it seems, is it?* And he had some new faces with him, so he tried his best to embarrass me in front of them. But don't worry – I gave him as good as I got." He laughed, shaking his head. "The gall of the man! He shouldn't have tried to bully me. He was going on about how our Princess had suffered and died in that car crash on the Paris underground road system, and how *they* were going to put things right for us. Arrogant bastards. He kept spouting some rot about having time on their side. *All the time in the world.* Something or other that we would never dream about!"

The MI6 director laughed. "Time on their side! What on earth is that supposed to mean?"

Harcourt nodded. "Exactly!"

The MI6 Director is not a stupid man. His gut feeling was telling him that Champion's words meant something, though he couldn't for the life of him think what. But he did know that if the American's do say something off the cuff describing an action or an event, then behind that remark is a line of thought that he just can't ignore.

Harcourt continued, "What I couldn't understand was why the Vice President seemed so excited by it all! What an absolute oaf!"

He scoffed and the MI6 man chuckled. *Americans. Honestly.*

"Typical yank bullshit!" Harcourt added. "Anyway, I gave him a piece of my mind – and his colleague, too. Some fellow called Olsen – I don't know what he was doing there; he wasn't even American. Some Dutch fellow. They made a perfect pair of buffoons."

"Olsen?" The MI6 Director sat up straighter, a light frown creasing his forehead. "I've heard that name before. You don't mean, Bo Nick Olsen do you?" he asked, after a moment's thought.

"That's him," said the British Foreign Secretary, unimpressed. "He was hanging around the Vice President most of the night, although he did have a rather attractive lady with him."

"I wonder what he was doing at the First Lady's gala," Graves reflected. "He must have moved up the ladder a rung or two since the last time I heard about him. Anyway," he shook his head, "you're right. What a sick joke to make about the Princess. Typical of them. Bloody Yanks! They've no respect for protocol. Arrogant and slipshod, the lot of them."

Harcourt nodded. "You can say that again."

*

Samuel left the meeting, deep in thought. That man could bore for England, and he was a bit of an idiot most of the time, but his general ignorance could often come in handy; people let their guard down around him, and he never failed to bring back information he didn't understand.

It was a very good thing that Harcourt was sufficiently stupid enough to never take anything at face value. It was a stupidity he had cultivated, and one which Graves could use.

Marching down the corridor towards the lifts, he passes Margaret's small office. "Thanks for the tea, Margaret," he said, grinning. "One thing I always love about coming here is that I get to see you; you know you still stir my loins."

"Samuel, you beggar!" replies Margaret looking up from the keyboard, "If I had my time again I'd be chasing you down that corridor!"

"Ah Margaret, if we could all have our time again, I'd let you catch me."

He continued along the corridor to the lift, pressing the button and waiting for the doors to open. Once inside, and as he descended to the ground floor, he leant back against the side panel and reminisced of days gone by when he and Margaret once had a romance together, smiling to himself – those were the days – she'd been a bit of a doll back then. If only we *could* have our time again, he thought.

As the lift descends, Samuel ponders over Margaret's words. Our time again… That would be a dream – if we could only have our time again… There was something niggling at the back of his mind, but he couldn't quite wrap his head around the meaning… our time again… time… that's it! That's what they meant – time, yes they've got time on their side.

His heart started thumping fast. That's what Champion was on about, having time on their side! He took a deep breath as he realized what this meant: they'd commissioned the Time Travel Project to change history, to rescue the transport plane and the Princess!

The lift reaches ground floor, the doors open, and Samuel rushes out. A group of people waiting in the entrance lobby are directly in his path. As his mind is focused elsewhere, he doesn't see them. It's quite amusing to watch as Samuel crashes into the group, knocking them over like skittles in a bowling alley. He doesn't stop to make any apologies, just continues his relentless march to the exit doors.

He is now outside the main entrance to the office block, waiting for his limo. "Come on, come on," he is saying under his breath. His car arrives. Like a beached whale he falls in the back seats, speaking to the chauffeur. "I'm in a rush George get me back to H.Q. as quickly as possible."

"Yes sir!" replies the driver.

The sleek black *Jaguar* pulls out of the office

complex, and continues its journey on the main road. Samuel is surprised to see a peddle bike overtaking them. He watches the bike carry on into the distance, pondering on this for a moment, he speaks to his chauffeur, "George does this effing car go any faster?"

"It has two speeds, Mr Graves," George replied, "and that's this speed, and stop."

Samuel shakes his head, thinking the word *cretin* as he closes the soundproof window between him and the driver.

Lifting the receiver from his in-car telephone he starts on his phone calls. The car was sound proof, had tinted windows, and he had it swept for bugs every morning, so he knew he could be confident of never being overheard.

Taking out a pad of paper and a pen, he twirled the expensive writing implement between his fingers as he waited for his call to be answered.

"I've just had some startling news," he said into the mouthpiece. "We need to meet within the hour."

He waited for the person on the other end to make the appropriate noises before hanging up, aware that arrangements would already be being made. That was the thing about having the right people in the right places: when the chips were down, they could be relied upon to do exactly what was needed at a respectable speed.

In this business, time was almost always of the essence, and Samuel Graves didn't like to be kept waiting. By the end of the day, his team would have everything in hand, he could be 100% certain of that.

"Can you meet me at my offices in an hour?" he asked of his second phone contact. "Yes, yes – a major problem. The biggest. Quick as you can, yes. Thank you."

The third call was more trying; sometimes it was astonishing how little people seemed to appreciate the urgency of a situation.

"No, no – look, forget about that," he said, exasperated. "If we don't sort this new problem out right now, the repercussions will be never-ending. Yes – yes, be there within the hour!"

He rolled his eyes as he hung up, exhausted by his colleague's incompetence, before picking up the receiver for a fourth time.

"Yes, Major General Peterson, please," he said, and then waited for the voice at the other end to stop babbling. "Look, could you put me through straight away, please? I appreciate that he is busy, but this is a matter of some importance. Thank you… Daniel, my old friend – I need your help. I need you to get across to my offices as soon as – yes, classified. Top level."

He paused for a moment, then chuckled. "Yes, that's right – follow standard protocol. Look, I'm sorry about this, but it is a threat to national security. Within the hour, Dan, within the hour!"

He ended the call and leaned back in his car seat, sighing deeply.

One way or another, this would be sorted out.

Chapter 16

Graves was not an idiot

An aide was waiting for Samuel before he even got out of the car at the MI6 headquarters, and gratified by the efficiency to which Graves was accustomed, he passed the time of day with him until they were safely inside their building.

The mood was already somber, as befitted the desperate circumstances; even without proper clearance and full information, the urgency of a given situation had trickled down throughout the organization, and there were more than a few tense agents milling about that morning.

Graves and his aide reached the edge of the foyer together and stepped into one of the vacant lifts.

Smoothly, as was normal practice in the foremost spy organization on the planet, the conversation altered as soon as the lift doors closed.

"That chauffeur, Louie Arnett, have we paid out compensation to his family yet?" the Director asked. "Because if we have, they better not be able to trace it back to us."

"Yes Sir, of course we've paid them," said the aide promptly. "That was all part of the deal. We had to pay them before he would carry out our orders. We were very careful, as usual. Why, what's the problem?"

"I've just been in an endless de-briefing with the Foreign Secretary, and he gave me a line or two of a conversation he had had with Ron Champion." He raised his eyebrows. "It was a bit like the cryptic clues in *The Times*. He kept spouting some rot about having time on their side. Something or other that we would never dream about. Basically, Champion was saying that they were again having to put right the mess the British had made of things."

Graves took a deep breath. "But what intrigued me the most was the words he was using, like *'having time on their side'* and *'in a way we would never dream about'*. That's not Champion talking; that's someone else. And I know who it is."

The aide – who had read the Intel about the top secret site in San Diego and had therefore had time to get used to time travel being something that was actually possible – let out a low whistle.

"Shit. For God's sake, why can't the Yanks just leave things be? It happened, it's done. Just let it go. They're always trying to save the damn world!"

"We can't let this happen," Graves said quietly. "Not after all the planning that has gone into this. Not after everything we've risked! It's simply unacceptable." He scratched his head wearily.

"I laughed it off, of course, because that old tit has no idea what's going on in this world." Samuel shook his head.

The aide looked up at him and frowned. "But he's the Foreign Secretary."

The lift doors open. "Exactly," replies Samuel.

The two men just had a short walk to Samuel's secretary's office, where two more men were waiting for the Director, their suits crisp and their faces subdued. They didn't bother with pleasantries, but simply walked together into the Director's office, ahead of him and his aide.

Graves nodded a greeting to his unflappable secretary.

"Major General Peterson is about five minutes away, Lucy," he instructed her. "Show him in with the utmost urgency, please. This is important. Oh, and Lucy we must have an agent in the time travel complex in San Diego can you bring up his latest evaluation report for me, and make contact with him through the normal channels? As quick as you can please."

"Yes, Mr Graves. Of course, Mr Graves." She smiled her polite, professional smile, and Graves wondered for about the millionth time if she even liked working in his office. He guessed she was only there for the money, and that was fine. Money made the world go round, after all.

The four men sat at the table in the large office. The somber atmosphere had permeated into here, too, and where there would usually be at least some catch up chat and polite formalities, no one was saying anything. Graves was glad – he didn't have time for all that bullshit anyway.

He rested his forearms on the table in front of him, his fingers intertwined as if he was praying. "Gentlemen, Project Avalon might be about to rear up and smack us right back in the face," he began, choosing his words carefully. "Now, before we go any further, I need to tell you of a top secret American project, and I need you to believe what I'm going to say. We don't have the time to discuss the intricacies of it, and I sure as hell don't have time to listen to you if you're going to tell me it's impossible. OK?"

The two men who hadn't ridden in the lift with them exchanged confused glances. This wasn't usually how these kinds of meetings started.

Graves went on, "Simply put, the Americans have been working on a Time Travel project for several years, and I believe they are close to figuring it out, if they haven't already. If it *is* possible, then this is bad news for us – to put it lightly." He took a deep breath.

"We've worked out that the Americans are going to try and save that RAF transport plane they shot down as it was approaching Astana, which would be all well and good – except that *at the same time* they want to use the opportunity to save Diana from the car accident in Paris. It seems they can't stop themselves from interfering in the affairs of other countries – poking their noses in as always. As soon as I get that report from Lucy, I'll know; certain names are in the frame, and if they appear on the report…" He shrugged. "That, I'm afraid, will be that."

There's a slight knock on the door and the ever efficient Lucy pops her head into the room. "Latest report from San Diego coming onto your screen now,

Samuel," she said, adding, "it's three days old." The Director looks up as Lucy is disappearing out of view.

"Thank you, Lucy. Right, gentlemen – just give me a minute to read this," Samuel says, before concentrating on his monitor for a few moments.

"Just listen to this! A party of American government personnel were present at the complex last week, accompanied by a number of FBI agents. It is unclear at the moment as to why, only the people above level two security were aware of that information – efforts are ongoing to establish reasons for visit. For the record personnel from the government were… let's see… Mr John Dillon." Samuel looks up at his team. "Anyone recognize that name, I don't?" The reaction from everyone is quite negative. "A Mr Eddie Daniels? What about him?"

"Yes I know that name," one of the agents replied. "He's the FBI boffin involved in that communication scandal; he was brought in to eradicate a virus in the computers at the American Government sites."

Nodding, Samuel continues, "And here he is – Mr Bo Nick Olsen! This is the man who keeps coming into the frame on every occasion, so my assumptions were correct. It is the Time Travel system that's been commissioned. Definitely."

Samuel turns his monitor off before re-addressing the group round the table. "This is a technology that I knew they were developing, but I had no idea they were this close to perfecting it. I was briefed about that project five years ago," he continued darkly. "We all hoped that it had been abandoned, that it was the usual American arrogance of thinking they could control more than they actually can. It seemed like a bit of a money sink at the time – their research had reached a dead end, and it looked like it would stay that way. Apparently, that isn't the case. So, gentlemen, I'm looking for suggestions here. There is no way we can allow this to happen – absolutely no way!"

At that point they were interrupted by a prim knock at the door, which opened to reveal Lucy.

"Major General Peterson, Mr Graves," she announced, showing the military gentleman in before quickly evaporating from view.

The Director rose from the table and shook the Major's hand, gesturing for his old friend to take a seat.

"Daniel, glad you could make it!" said Graves, sitting back down. "Now, I won't mess about with small talk; we haven't the time. This is a top secret meeting. Naturally, whatever you hear inside these four walls will never leave this room, and there must be no written record of this meeting. No matter what pressure is put on you, you may never reveal a thing – if you do, you will be in breach of the Official Secrets Act, and effectively guilty of treason. Are you okay with that?"

"You know me, Samuel," said the Major General, who was used to this particular spiel. "You don't get to be in charge of the SAS by having a big mouth, but I do know one thing – you don't get me into a hush-hush meeting if you only need someone with a little pea shooter, so this must be pretty bloody important. What's got your knickers in a twist?" He was blunt and to the point, as usual – something the MI6 Director respected. He was a man after his own heart.

Graves nodded soberly. "Right you are, Daniel," he said. "I'm not asking you to judge us – I'm not. In fact, I'd rather you didn't, if I'm honest. I just want you to listen, and at the end, give me a solution." He sighed. "The MI6, as you know, is tasked with keeping our country safe and acting in the United Kingdom's best interests, even if the means can sometimes be distasteful."

He rubbed a hand over his face, heaving a frustrated sigh. "We were asked – no, we were *ordered* – by someone so high up in the hierarchy of our country that we could not refuse, to ensure at all costs that the mother of the future King did not marry a member of the Muslim faith."

Major General Peterson frowned, deeply. This wasn't the direction he expected this meeting to be going in at all.

Graves went on, "Whatever it took, we were to prevent the Princess from marrying Dodi Fayed, the man who was courting her," he continued grimly. "We were told that an engagement was imminent, and that no matter what it took, we had to ensure it did not happen."

Daniel Peterson's expression was one of utter astonishment, but he motioned for Graves to continue.

"We found and hired the services of a chap called Louie Arnett," the Director continued. "A chauffeur who had been driving for the rich and famous in France for several years. This poor man was dying of terminal cancer and he had accumulated some heavy gambling debts. He was coerced into agreeing to crash the car in return for particular debts being cleared and a fund being set up to take care of his family. It was a solution that seemed to suit everyone, at the time. Win-win, as they say."

"He was contracted to ensure that the man in the car – the Princess's boyfriend – died, but that the Princess survived. The most effective way to crash the car to ensure the death of one passenger and protect the other was discussed at length, and Arnett followed the plan to the letter. He knew, of course, that he would be killed too. As you know, gentlemen, he did just that, though the one thing that was not supposed to happen *did* happen." He bowed his head respectfully as if thinking of the Princess's last moments.

"I'm sorry," said the Major General, abruptly. "I'm sorry – I just can't sit here and listen to this. It's preposterous. What you're saying is you've managed to *kill* Princess Diana, *by accident*. What sort of idiots are you?"

He shook his head, almost violently, before continuing, "Samuel, I have known you for years, and you know I have a great deal of respect for you, but I never imagined you could be capable of something so idiotic – or something so cold! Who the hell told you to do this? Who? You lot must be fucking brainwashed!"

He was getting angry – his face slowly becoming the color of beetroot – and honestly, Graves didn't really blame him. It was an incredibly messed up situation, he knew that.

"It wasn't supposed to happen like this," said the Director, holding his hands up. He hadn't expected the Major General to be particularly understanding, but even though he'd been prepared for this reaction, he could still feel a small, intense headache forming immediately behind his right eyeball.

"The car's seatbelts had been adjusted. The Princess's belt was strengthened so she should have been safe in the car, and Fayed's was weakened to ensure his swift and preferably painless demise. The accident was rehearsed time and time again without a hitch – the Princess should have been perfectly safe!"

"Well, what the bloody hell happened then?" Peterson demanded. "I mean, the Princess is dead for God's sake! *Dea*d! The British press had to suppress the news recordings of her taking her dying breaths, for fuck's sake! My God, man, don't you feel for the poor woman? For her family? Her children? And why shouldn't she be with someone she was in love with, for crying out loud? This is the twentieth century, not the bloody eighteen hundreds!" He took a deep breath, trying to calm himself down.

"And how the hell did you expect to control a car crash when the vehicle was travelling at those kinds of speeds? If you *had* to kill him – and I'm sure there are a million other things you could have done to break them up before resorting to murder – why not do it in a way that didn't involve the Princess at all? Seriously, I think this is the most insane plan I've ever heard of in my entire life. So tell me, what happened? What went wrong?"

"What happened, Dan? I'll tell you what bloody well happened," Graves groused, now just as angry as the man in front of him – he'd only been following orders, after all; he didn't say it was a great plan. He knew it wasn't. "No one other than the MI5 man put their fucking seatbelts on, *that's* what happened! It was totally out of character for the Princess. I can only assume they were canoodling in the back seat."

He ran a frustrated hand through his hair. "Don't get me wrong, it's not an excuse, but the incident was planned down to the last detail – which stretch of motorway it would be, which stanchion the driver was to aim for. We even made sure they would be near to a hospital for Christ's sake. And all that planning was for nothing."

A ringing silence followed Graves's exasperated statement. The three MI6 men were wisely keeping their mouths shut – this was as much their fuck up as it was his, after all.

Major General Peterson shook his head, staring at the four men, appalled and dumbfounded. He wasn't a man who approved of killing people, unless it was honorably and in battle, and this was about as far from that as it was possible to get. It was senseless murder, and no one had gained from it. No one at all.

There was no honor in that.

After a few minutes of digesting the scale of this epic calamity, Peterson finally broke the silence. "I have two questions, Samuel," he said, sounding like he was very much losing patience with the whole situation. "One, why am I here? How can I possibly help undo what you buffoons have managed to do? And two, who sanctioned this ludicrous course of action? I mean, who put forward the request to have the boyfriend of the Princess assassinated? And in such an idiotic, haphazard way?"

The Director stared intently at the Major General for a moment. He couldn't answer the man and both of them knew it.

Instead, one of their colleagues decided to try and help the Director out, "You are here to give us an option," he said quietly. "Not to ask questions you know we can't answer. We *can* tell you this – the Americans have perfected the operation of a time travel missile. They have put together a project and are going to try and save our ill-fated transport plane, saving themselves the humiliation of carelessly murdering a plane full of British citizens. At the same time, they are going to use the opportunity to save the Princess from the car accident."

There was a moment when Peterson looked at the man speaking as if he'd gone insane; Graves watched the expression of incredulity chase across his face.

Peterson glanced at his colleagues and decided that they really did believe that a time travel missile existed – and if they believed it, it was probably true. They were MI6, after all, and stranger things had happened. Like the ridiculous plot to kill Diana's boyfriend.

"Well, why not let them?" the Major General suggested, clearly feeling that if people were simply going to repeat the situation at him, he might as well speak his mind.

"That way you could still kill Fayed if you absolutely bloody have to – which I still don't think is the only option here – but in a way that doesn't put anyone else's life at risk. Say, when the Princess isn't even in the fucking vicinity! Or – and here's an idea – why don't you just tell whoever it is that asked you to murder him in the name of your country to get stuffed? I mean, come on! Grow some balls!"

He sighed, exasperated. "No, never mind, I know you can't do that or you would have done it in the first place. Look, I realize that you lot will have done your homework on this, so you must believe the Americans can pull it off. Yes? No?" He shook his head. "Well, if they can that's fantastic – they could save all those personnel on the transport plane. I'd say that's a positive outcome. So tell me again, why am I here?"

"No, no, no, you don't understand," said one of the other MI6 operatives urgently. "We have got to ensure that the Princess's boyfriend remains deceased. He has to be kept out of the frame. However you want to put it, *that* is the outcome it is imperative to maintain."

"So – and I don't mean to be callous, gentlemen, since I don't agree with the operation in the first place – just rearrange things and kill him again," said Peterson, getting annoyed. "Think about the transport plane – thirty-odd people died who didn't have to. You can't just dismiss the fact that they could be saved. I knew some of those people. So did you."

Samuel interrupts, banging his fist on the table top in annoyance. "Look, Daniel, the situation is this: we are where we need to be, we have our goal, the man is dead, that was our orders, we are men who achieve results, we are not men who cry and blubber over who stands, or who falls as troops are ordered out of the trenches, and above all, we are British! We will have to sacrifice that transport plane," Graves insisted.

"You have to work with us on this – you must," he continued. "I hate to be indelicate, but I outrank you, Major Peterson, and I'm giving you a direct order. You must help us to ensure that this time travel nonsense is an outrageous failure – this project has taken up so much time and effort already, and the five of us have to ensure that it fails, whatever the cost." Graves threw his arms up in frustration. Why couldn't Daniel understand the importance of this mission?

The other MI6 man – who had up to this point been silent – now addressed the Major General, who was beginning to look really quite angry indeed. "As to your second question, Major General Peterson – the person who instructed us to put this into operation? You know that we cannot reveal that, Sir, but what I can say is that it's not the government and it's not the royal family. I mean, it isn't Henry the eighth that wears the crown, is it?"

"Forgive me, young man," the Major General began, turning his steely, dark eyes on the MI6 operative who had spoken, "but what the actual fuck does Henry the fucking eighth have to do with anything? He's been dead for the past four hundred and fifty years – and when he was alive, I have to tell you, he *did* wear the crown. He had quite a lot of people executed, in fact, for less reason than you are giving me now." He shook his head. "For God's sake, don't tell me that the Yanks have gone back to resurrect him, too?"

"No, it's not Henry the fucking eighth," the Director agreed. "It's not the royals and it's not the government, so who does that leave? Who do you think it is? The real power in the UK?"

Graves waved his arm in the direction of the office window; everyone followed his gaze to the towers of Westminster Abbey.

Daniel Peterson stared at him. "The church. The church?" he demanded. "You can't be fucking serious. A bunch of clerics, who have chosen to spend their lives serving God, their community and their country? You're telling me they're the real power in Britain? That they ordered you to murder someone based on their faith?" By now his face had gone a little pale. "You've lost your minds. This is not why I joined the army; this is not what I signed up to fight for!"

"Of course it's the bloody church, Daniel!" Graves snapped. "Those hypocrites sit up in their ivory towers, thinking that the whole world owes them," he complained, sounding very much like an aggrieved London cabbie. "They've done this before – I mean, for Christ's sake, just think of the number of people who've died because of the church! I suppose they tell themselves that it's just one more person, and that it's okay if it's in the name of God and if it keeps things right. I'm telling you, we had a direct order from the Archbishop that we couldn't disobey." *So much for keeping that classified,* thought Graves, but he simply had to convince Daniel, or they were all screwed.

Peterson shook his head in utter disbelief. "I'm amazed that you lot have gone along with this," he declared, before crossing his arms, effectively closing himself off. "I'll give the necessary orders, but I want it noted that I think this whole fucking enterprise is completely insane. For God's sake, since when does the Archbishop have the authority to issue a kill order?"

"Let's stay on point here," said Graves, wondering if this meeting was ever going to end. "And that point is, we need Fayed to stay dead, at all costs, and while we could kill him again if we needed to, there's a whole other side to this that we haven't yet discussed." He paused for a moment, looking around the room. "Do you really want the Americans to have this kind of power?"

Peterson coughed. He knew Graves was not an idiot, if you tried to think in the same vein as he did, you'd miss it, because he was British, but British from when Britain was still an Empire, from the days of the Great War. If he needed to gain three hundred yards on the battlefield, he would sacrifice three hundred men to achieve that, one for each yard, but then he and his brigadiers would drink a toast 'to their success', but if they lost 300 yards on the battlefield they would still drink a toast to celebrate not losing 600 yards.

'Crazy Days', however he might have a point there. If the Americans were the only Super Power to have this technology, then the world balance would definitely be disturbed.

These thoughts troubled Daniel as he relived days gone by, when the secrets of the atomic weapons were passed to the Russians in the crazy idiotic days of post-World War II.

Back in the room, Samuel continued with his speech, "Do you want America to be *the only* country in the world who can change history at the touch of a button? Just think what they could do! They could rewrite the past to benefit themselves, they could use the knowledge from the history books to go back and do… well, pretty much whatever the hell they want to do. They could kill other world leaders before they got a chance to do anything nefarious, they could change the outcome of wars, they could change who's President, change laws… the possibilities are endless. Don't you see that?"

"This is bigger than all of us," continued the Director. "This missile – assuming it works – will give America more power than even they've ever dreamed of. It could be more dangerous than a thousand nuclear bombs, worse than a million dictators the world over. They could change *everything*."

He stopped talking then, giving the Major General a chance to think, and the man was just about to open his mouth and say something when there was another knock at the door.

All five men turned to stare at Lucy, who had stuck her head around the door.

She immediately gauged the atmosphere of the room, and when she spoke, it wasn't much louder than a whisper. "I'm sorry to disturb you, Sir, but a report is coming in from America. It's from our man in San Diego – code name Prince John Do you want me to put it through to your office?"

The Director waved a confirmation in her direction, nodding, and the communication panels on the back wall lit up a couple of seconds after Lucy closed the door.

Graves flicked a switch on the end of the desk and

a few moments of crackling static sprang up on the monitors, quickly clearing as the signal improved.

"Good morning, Sir," said a crisp voice across the loud speaker.

"Good morning, Prince John. Receiving your transmission, please proceed," said the Director.

"I've been briefed by Lucy as to your concerns Mr Graves and the latest reports coming out of the Time Travel complex are quite alarming, they have transported a huge amount of materials and components from the complex – the fuel tanks, engine blocks, and the Capsule have all disappeared. Reports say that they have all been transported to Cape Canaveral not by time travel personnel, Mr Graves, but by NASA and government departments."

There were a few seconds of silence as Samuel absorbed the information. "Thank you Prince John. Do you have anything else constructive to add?"

"No Sir, investigations are ongoing."

"One point you mentioned in your last report was that Bo Nick Olsen was at the complex last week. Has that any significance?" Trying to sound casual.

There was a slight pause in time delay, then the contact replied, *"Yes Sir, everything seemed to go crazy after he arrived; he definitely seems to be what's driving these events."*

"Thank you, Prince John," said Samuel, before adding, "ending transmission."

Samuel thinks for a minute, *it's not looking good.* But then he thinks on another point, *how can Lucy brief an agent over my concerns, she won't know my concerns, unless she is psychic.* He looks up at the group of men in front of him.

"Lucy," he shouts.

"Yes Mr Graves, I'm just bringing the team on line from Cape Canaveral."

Samuel scratches his head, whispering, "How does she do that, I'm in charge here, not Lucy. Thank you Lucy," shouting the last syllables. Daniel smiles.

"Are you sure about that Samuel?"

Just at that moment the main door to the office burst open *clang, clang, rattle, rattle* – coming in with the tea trolley is Edna, dressed in her old green overalls, fifties style head scarf, just one pop sock on and odd slippers to match.

"Tea up Mr Graves," she shouted breezily. "Oh, you *have* got an office full this morning, haven't you? What can I be getting you gentlemen? I've got some nice sponge cake today."

Before anyone got a chance to reply, Lucy popped her head around the door. "Morning Edna! Black tea for me please, and I'll try a piece of your sponge cake as well."

Samuel shook his head, exasperated. "Look Edna, I'm sorry to be rude, but this is a very top secret meeting and you simply must leave. *Now.*"

Edna – who was already cutting Lucy a piece of sponge cake – looked up at Samuel. "Oh, don't go on so or I'll put you over my knee like I did when you were a little boy. Lucy, here's your tea and cake, love, and here's a nice cup of Earl Grey for you, Sammy. Your favorite."

Samuel's face had gone extremely pale, and he took the cup from Edna without a word. After all, what was the point in arguing or trying to get out of this one? He was sure they'd all have a big laugh about it later – although, going by the looks on their faces, it might be sooner than that.

"And here you are, Sammy, a nice piece of cake for you too," Edna added.

Samuel took it, again without saying a word.

Edna smiles. "As if your *Time Travel Missile* is going to make any difference to me," she says, attending to the other men.

Samuel, having just taken a mouthful of tea, splutters and almost chokes. "EDNA! How do you know about that?"

Daniel can't hold it back any longer, he starts tittering.

Samuel stands, fists on the table top. "Look this is a Top Secret meeting, so that last encounter with the tea trolley comes under the Official Secrets Act as well!"

Edna shakes her head as she continues to serve the other men. "Don't worry, Sammy, your secret's safe with me." Muttering under her breath, "Along with all the rest," as she exits the room, leaving behind an extremely flummoxed-looking Samuel Graves.

Lucy has just received confirmation that the contact with Cape Canaveral is now established on a secure line.

"Mr Graves," came Lucy's voice, cutting through the awkward silence. "The line is now open with Cape Canaveral code name Prince Albert."

"Thank you, Lucy," replies Samuel, glad to have something to distract him from Edna's little performance. "Put them through."

The wall mounted monitor springs into life once again. *"Good morning, Sir."*

"Good morning, Prince Albert. Receiving your transmission, please proceed," said the Director.

"Latest reports on Time Travel project, Sir," said the agent. *"We've discovered through our contacts that the launch platforms have been built in NASA's Engineering Plant, at an unbelievable pace, and are being placed in orbit and established there. Two more shuttles are taking up the fuel tanks and engine blocks in the next couple of weeks. That would only leave the Time Travel missile itself, and the fuel it needs for the journey. A suitable window for launch is coming up in the next two to three weeks."*

The Director nodded as he took all this in. "Just out of curiosity," he asked thoughtfully, again remembering the briefing with William Harcourt earlier in the day, "have you had any dealings with a Dutch chap called Bo Nick Olsen?"

"Yes, Director," said the agent in America, *"we always keep an eye on him – he's a bit of a mover and shaker when it comes to government projects. They recently made him head of the Government Funding Agency. He seems to be the driving force behind this project – before he came on the scene a few weeks ago, the whole thing was floundering. We don't know how he's gained as much influence as quickly as he has, but he's certainly one very intelligent man. People trust him."*

"I knew it," the Director declared, slapping the table in triumph. "I knew it! So that's what he's been up to."

"Yes, Director," said the agent. *"He's working very closely with Vice President Ron Champion – I've heard that*

the President himself has a lot of faith in him. He's a man who gets things done."

The Director tried not to laugh as he looked around the room. If Olsen was known for getting things done, he probably didn't have a group of people he had to convince of his intentions every step of the way. "What is he involved in at the moment, do we know?"

"Our informant in the White House says Olsen is working with Ron Champion and the President, to put together the information to be inserted into a Presidential Communicational black box that is to be sent back in the time travel missile. He seems to be overseeing the whole project, and they're doing it at the White House itself for security reasons, before sending it off."

"Hmm," said the Director. "That's one thing we should be looking into, Daniel. If we could interfere with the information being programmed into the black box, that would certainly mess their plans up." It seemed simple enough in the grand scheme of things, and it could be their only shot at stopping this.

"That could be it, Samuel," said the Major General reluctantly. "If we can keep an eye on that and interfere at just the right moment to change the information it contains… or, of course, destroy the thing outright."

"No, no, Major General," said one of the MI6 agents. "We've got to ensure that the Americans have no idea we're trying to interfere."

Graves nodded. "Yes, any action we take cannot be connected back to us; secrecy is imperative in this matter. We need a plan to put this course of action into operation immediately," he instructed the agent sternly. "Let's do this. Daniel, you have copies of the blueprints for the White House, yes? Let's get a team in there as soon as possible and get this show on the road."

"I will be going offline in a few minutes, Sir," said the agent in America. *"The satellites are moving out of position."*

"Find out where that communication black box is being worked on," the Director instructed. "The exact room it's going to be in, you hear me? We'll exchange it with an empty one. Simple."

"Copy that, Sir," said the agent's voice. *"I'll check in with you tomorrow at the usual time."*

Graves leaned back in his chair, feeling positive for the first time that day. For the first time in a long time. He even allowed himself a little smile.

Across the table, Peterson just stared at him, expressionless.

Chapter 17

Microchips, cutting edge technology

Eddie 'Einstein' Daniels reclined in one of the comfortable office chairs in the *Microsoft Corporation* headquarters in Redmond, Washington, smiling to himself. Bill was late, but that wasn't unusual – he had the kind of mind that worked in overdrive and would often be distracted by something complex that needed immediate attention or resolution.

It didn't bother Eddie at all; he had that sort of mind, too. He knew how it could take you on wild and wonderful journeys, even if you were scheduled for a very important meeting.

Currently, he was engrossed in the latest briefings from the disparate teams around the country. In terms of the scientific content of the project, Eddie was overseeing most of it, with the four Doctors from the original project – Josh Banner, Zack Bookerman, Bradley Cranmore and Jerry Mills – as his foremen.

He had dispatched Jerry to Redmond almost as soon as he had met him, recognizing the kind of mathematical mind that would make mincemeat out of the core mathematics behind the software they needed to design. That was another skill Eddie had – he could see the potential in people almost immediately, could read them and see where they'd best fit, where they'd be most successful. It was a skill that had worked extremely well for him over his career.

Eddie brought his thoughts back to the matter at hand. He and Bill had been working on this idea for the last few years and it was exciting to think that their flexible in-series sequential software would soon be put to good use. To brilliant use, in fact.

Bo Nick Olsen had convinced Eddie that this project was vital for the continued dominance of their country in the modern world, and when Bo believed something with that kind of conviction, Eddie tended to trust him. In truth, he would trust Bo with his life, and there weren't many people he could say that about, no siree.

Eddie put down the last report with a slight smile and closed the folder, satisfied.

"Things going well?"

He looked up and grinned, finding his old friend, the multi-million dollar entrepreneur Bill Gates, lounging in the doorway.

"So far so good," Eddie told him as he got to his feet. The two old friends shook hands. "How's it coming at this end?"

"Not bad," Bill assured him, taking a seat at the table; Eddie followed suit. "Jerry's a natural – where did you find him again?"

"Oh, just some top secret project in San Diego," said Eddie, off-hand, and both men laughed.

Bill knew exactly which project he meant; security clearance had been one of the caveats of Gates and his team's involvement. The sequential microchip system was cutting edge technology that no one wanted to part with without a damn good reason, and once one or two of their top brass – Bill Gates included – had been given a guided tour of the San Diego facility, they had been falling over themselves to be a part of the project.

This was science's chance to be daring, and everybody with clearance wanted to have a hand in it. This wasn't your normal, run-of-the-mill project they worked on every day; they would be making history – albeit a history that none of them would ever remember. As proof of concepts went, this was a fairly unusual one.

"We're moving forward into production now," said Bill, passing Eddie the schematics. "Because the mission parameters are so specific, we've had to scale everything back – I think you'll find this interesting."

"Yeah," said Eddie, quickly absorbing the information in front of him. "This is perfect, Bill."

"Hey, anything we can do," his old friend laughed. "That rocket is incredible. How's the launch pad coming along? We all set?"

"Should be," said Eddie, sitting back. "There's a tropical storm working its way north that might put us a couple of days out, but so far the window looks clear. The last section of the launch pad was sent up last night – they've got a team of engineers up there right now, tying it all together. I gotta tell you, Bill, it looks incredible."

Eddie beamed, and Bill joined him.

"I mean, I know we work in what people may think is science fiction, you and me, but this is *actually happening*," Eddie laughed. "It's like finding yourself in an episode of *Fireball XL5*!"

"Steady there, Eddie," said Bill, amused. "You get too excited about these things and something goes wrong. Keep your cool – you'll need it if there's a crisis."

Eddie shook his head. "No – I've got Bo for that, Bill. He can be calm and in charge – I'm just a lowly scientist; I'm allowed to be excited!"

"Now, this sequential programming," Bill said, bringing them back to the topic. "I think we've got the last few kinks worked out for the navigation system…"

He continued on, and Eddie sat back and listened to one of the wealthiest men on the planet talk about a device that would make time travel possible.

Sometimes, the world could be a very strange place.

A very strange place indeed.

Chapter 18

Evans, Evans calm yourself down

Evans had been a staff member at the White House for a number of years, and all things considered, it wasn't a bad place to work. He had been a very familiar face around the food preparation and kitchen areas, and was thought to be a very conscientious employee.

Whenever there was an opportunity to become more involved in the House itself, he was one of the first to volunteer, and this led to him having been asked to take on more responsibility in other staff roles – and it also helped him find his way around the building.

Of course, this was all a charade, as his real employer was MI6. Evans was in fact a *'covert'* or *'sleeper'* agent, just waiting there for whenever he was needed and now his years of training would come into play.

He had been briefed by his handler as to the mission parameters, and it had sounded more suited to a *James Bond* blockbuster movie, than the small covert operation of which he was normally used for. However, if he could pull this off his standing in the MI6 community would leap allowing him to pick and choose the more lucrative postings.

But was that what he wanted? Over the years he had become quite content working at the White House, and other things had now become a distraction to him.

The White House was a surprisingly huge complex of offices, corridor's, staff living quarters, areas for social events, swimming pools, sports training and exercise facilities.

Evans sometimes got lost, but this time it was different – on this occasion he had been studying the White House layout, and knew exactly where the authentic black box would be located on the day of the mission.

Over the past few days, he had spent some time in the storage areas of the building. You could easily disappear in some of these forgotten sections of the White House. They may send a search party out to look for you, if not you might be found some years later, just a bag of bones.

Of course, he couldn't just ask where the stock of White House black boxes were kept, so he had to search quite extensively to find the hoard.

During his excursions, he had been stopped and questioned a number of times by the FBI and White House Security. Having the right passes and paperwork helped to kid on the *'henchmen'*, also an old trick he used was to put a shirt and tie on, and with a clip board under his arm, it made him look like someone important.

He told people he'd been employed to carry out an audit of the piles of junk stored away. This enabled him to have even more free movement around the building.

It didn't take him too long to find the room where the additional black boxes were stored. They were not thought to be an 'at risk item', and luckily for him, there was no security guarding them.

The black boxes were not too heavy, just a bit bulky, perhaps the size of a boom box. He got one off the racking, put it onto a sturdy table, and opened it.

Inside it was divided into padded compartments, designed to keep any item inside, safe and secure. In one of the compartments he found a sealed tin foil envelope. Feeling the shape of the items it contained, he realized they were the copper date stamp seals he was looking for. He slipped these into his pocket.

He carried the box to an area that he knew was not covered by cameras, slipping it into a small storage cupboard piled high with kitchen cleaning products, which he then locked.

Evans was quite pleased with himself, his plan to retrieve a second black box had worked. So far, so good.

From there he went back to his sleeping quarters, no-one stopped him as he had become a very familiar figure wandering around, carrying out the audit.

Once inside, he changed his clothing, removed his false moustache, and put his kitchen uniform on. On his head he placed his cook's hat. Looking at himself in the mirror, this got him thinking, *what I should have been was an actor, I love dressing up – but that's another story for another day.*

He goes back to working in the kitchen area as Evans the conscientious dreamer. After the evening meal had been served, and all pots and pans loaded into dishwashers to be cleaned for the following day, he then volunteered to stay behind to clean one of the large ovens. It had been badly contaminated by a spill of apple sauce earlier in the day.

Evans had a long coffee break, giving the remaining kitchen staff chance to leave, then he set to, and worked hard cleaning the oven. It was almost finished when he disrobed the protective clothing he had been wearing.

Loading a trolley with white linen tablecloths, he set off to recover the hidden black box. The journey was uneventful, but at the storeroom, just as he was about to unlock the door, he felt the pressure of someone's hand on his shoulder.

"Shit," he'd been rumbled, his knees buckled, his legs collapsed, down he went. A security man had crept up behind him, scaring the crap out of him. The man had to catch Evan's before he hit the floor.

"Evans, Evans calm yourself down, you're like a shitting dog! What's wrong with you man, I've only come for a share out."

Evans – breathing and wheezing like a sixty-a-day smoker, tries to pull himself together. "Holden, you nob head what the fucking hell do you think you're doing just leave me alone and fuck off!"

Holden stands back. "Evans don't spit your

dummy out, you better have something for me tomorrow boy. I'm watching you."

Holden then struts off like the cocksure nob he is. Evans watches him, making sure he leaves. *Idiot*, he thinks if only he knew what tomorrow will bring.

He opens the cupboard and starts loading cleaning fluid onto his trolley, then in a casual action, just slips the black box across and covers it with the linen. Locking up the storeroom, he wanders back to the food preparation area.

Making sure he's alone, Evans begins to unload the trolley. He hides his 'prize' round the back of a huge stack of pots and pans that never get used. His last part of tonight's plot before retiring to his rooms, is to finish off the oven. That done he takes a deep breath. *I hope tomorrow goes better*, he thinks.

As he made his way back to his rooms in the White House complex, his thoughts were with his little collection of reptiles that he'd amassed over the past eighteen months. He had become fascinated – almost obsessed – with these creatures after his visit to a travelling zoo that had displayed weird exotic animals from distant areas of the world. He'd felt they were only being used and abused by the zookeepers for profit, which was pretty much like his own life story, he thought.

Upon entering his apartment, Evans started his usual evening ritual. His rooms were in almost total darkness, and he knew that his *'friends'* in the rear bedroom would have heard him coming in. He stumbled, his eyes not having yet adjusted to the almost zero light level. He preferred it this way; it gave him a feeling of being a fearless adventurer traveling deep into the African jungle.

He entered the second bedroom, making pursing noises with his lips to encourage his *'friends'* to join him. The fear that he could at any moment be attacked and killed by these beautiful poisonous creatures gave him a second buzz; at least that would be a glorious way to leave the restrains of the truly shit life he had.

Reaching for the light switch, he slowly increased the light level by using the dimmer device. It was just light enough now to see his way around, but not too bright to alarm his 'siblings'. His eyes focused on the area where he could hear the rustling of foliage in one of the tanks, then the four pairs of eyes of his favorite spider emerged from behind the mass of rolled-up leaves. This was the nest of 'Sultan', his prized South American spider.

In some of the other tanks, the snakes and spiders had also begun to wake up. Evans knew what they were expecting – it was *'feeding time at the zoo'*.

So, he went over to the two large cages in the corner of the room. It was in here that he kept the white mice he bred.

The left cage held the breeding pairs – that kept the food chain moving – and in the right cage were the offspring, who were fed and watered by him, to serve up to his menagerie of creatures for lunch. The young mice never recognized the dangers of their surroundings until it was too late, so they gladly gave themselves up.

He opened the shutter to the right cage and put his

hand in. As usual, one or two of the baby mice scurried onto his palm, expecting to receive some attention. Lifting his hand out of the cage, he raised them up to eye level.

Making squeaking noises to keep the mice focused on his actions, Evans picked them up by pinching the loose skin behind their necks.

Then, one by one, he dropped the mice into the one-way feeding shoots attached to the tanks. Still they never realized what the outcome would be as they settled into their new homes.

Evans loved to watch as the hunt began; he was always almost as mesmerized as the mice when the snakes made use of the hypnotic effect they had over the rodents. The mice would more or less crawl into the mouth of the snake, looking for a snug place to keep warm and safe.

On the other hand, the spiders would stay motionless, waiting for the mouse to run almost over their bodies. Then they'd pounce, injecting their poison into the poor creature and rendering it paralyzed but still alive. It would be encased in a fine, silk web, the creature still breathing as it was carried back into the spider's lair. Then, over the next twenty-four hours, the spider would eat parts of the mouse, piece by piece, leaving it alive and fresh for as long as it could until the inevitable bite that would finally put it out of its misery.

Whenever Evans had the chance to watch this event happen, it always made him think of the movie 'Aliens', where the crew of the spacecraft had been wrapped in silk cocoons and were kept alive as a food source for the alien creatures. He loved that movie.

When everyone was fed and watered, he made his way to the door. There was a bit of a mess on the floor, but he knew the cleaning lady would be in tomorrow. She too, had a curious affection for the creatures, especially 'Sultan'.

Turning the light off, he left the room and went into his bedroom. Relaxing, he strips off and has a well-deserved shower. On leaving his wet-room he towels off, and studies himself in the full-length mirror. He doesn't really recognize the man looking back at him.

What's happening to me? he thinks. The person in the image is a bit too portly – his hair is thinning on top and going grey on his temples – he could even be starting with a double chin. *Who is that man for god's sake? I'm only thirty-five, and I'm well past my best.*

The thought of Holden pissing him off made him feel really depressed. *Ever since we first met, he's had it in for me, and no matter what I do,* thought Evans, *he always comes out smelling of roses.*

These thoughts always had the effect of lowering Evans's self-esteem, at the moment it was just above zero.

A lot of his problems stemmed from the fact that he spent most of his spare time on his own. Either in his rooms or in the local bar, but here in his room, at least he had a friend who could help him.

He looks to an area of his bedroom, where he can see the reflection in the mirror, refocusing his eyes on to a biscuit tin sat on the shelving above his bed. He doesn't want to do this, but when he is so low, his will-power hides as well.

He pivots round, reaches up to the shelving and grasps the tin. Sitting on his bed, he removes the lid.

Evans had convinced himself that these little packets of white powder were the one thing that got him through his shit life. That and his other mate, Jack. He stares into the tin, not wanting to touch the few remaining packets. *But in this case it's different,* he thinks.

Keith Holden has so pissed him off that he had to have some help, so he takes an eighty-five milligram packet from the stash, opens it, then pours it on to his bedside table in a neat line. He looks at the drug, just sitting there, teasing him.

"No, No!" he says out loud. Standing up he walks into the kitchen, takes a glass off the shelf and half fills it with whiskey from a bottle of Jack Daniels. He studies the contents, then raises it to his lips. As the glass tips and pivots on his bottom lip, he feels, *yes this is where it's at,* as the liquid slides down his throat.

He slips back into his bedroom, still naked from his shower, catches his reflection in the mirror and convinces himself that he's looking good at thirty-five.

He has a 9.00p.m. meeting with a guy at the local bar so he hurries to get dressed ready to go out.

Throwing on his jacket, Evans grabs the envelope with the copper black box seals in, slips it into his pocket, and leaves his rooms for another night of loneliness.

He is now sat in his local bar continuing his main objective which is to destroy his liver. He is on his third tot of whiskey, recalling the night he had with

Holden. A feeling of 'why me?' is running through his mind. *He's always so cocksure of himself, and it's always me that comes off second best.*

"Evans," his 9.00pm meet had just arrived – twenty minutes late. *Never mind,* were his thoughts, *at least it's someone to talk to.*

"You look a bit pissed off buddy. You had a shit day?" Evans just looks across at his handler.

"Look at me, just look at me." He tips his head forward to show his thinning crown. "Look at my hair," straightening his neck and using his hands to express himself. "See the gray in my temples, the crow's eyes, the double chin, I can't keep going, I'm getting old before my time. It's been one of the most stressful days ever!"

The handler looks up at the barman, "Just a Bud for me, and whatever he's drinking." Putting his arm over Evans, the handler says, "Come on let's sit in one of these Booths."

They pick up their freshly poured drinks, shuffle across and get reseated next to the windows.

Evans, clasping both hands on his whiskey, is staring out of the window into the darkness, not really looking at anything, just the darkness. This refocuses his vision onto the reflection staring back at him in the glass. Shaking his head, he turns, then looks across the table at his handler.

"I had a run-in with a White House security guard today. This man creeps around the building and finds it ever so amusing, scaring the shit out of people. I almost had a heart attack with him today, look at me, I must have aged five years. I can't take the stress of all this." His handler takes a sip of Bud, thinking, *I've got to treat Evans sympathetically here, can't afford to lose him at this stage.*

"Who's that Evans, do I know him?"

"No boss you won't know him he's just one of those nobs, idling his time away until his pension comes in. Holden is his name. Agent Holden."

The handler smiles, "Oh yes, you mean Keith. He works for me."

Evans's eyes narrow, his face locks. "You know Holden, he's the most annoying man you will ever meet. He's what we call back in England, 'a Twat'."

The Handler put his glass down. "The thing is Evans, he's only playing a role. He's good at it though. He was what you would say, *'Top of the Twat class'* at college."

The Handler smiles and raises his eyebrows. "Anyway must get on Evans, have you got the black box seals, my friend?"

Taking the foil envelope out of his pocket, Evans passes it across the table to the handler, who runs it between his fingers to feel if it contains what he requires.

"Right Evans, I will be about an hour, so see you back here, and slow down with the drinking."

Now alone, Evans stares out of the window. He watches the handler being picked up by a car, and driven off. His vision focuses once more, onto the reflection staring back at him in the glass. *Why me?* he screams inside his head.

Chapter 19

Evans was already way beyond spooked

It was a good job that Evans had put all that whiskey away the previous night, as it was the only thing that got him to sleep.

It was now 6.30 in the morning; his alarm was ringing its head off. He could hear it, and he knew what it was, but he couldn't put that altogether in one package to stretch his arm out and turn the damn thing off.

"Shit," was his first word of the day – although that may have been a description of what was inside his head.

He rolled his legs over the edge of the bed, half sat up, and held his head in both hands, "What is that fucking ringing in my head?" he straightened his neck, lifted his shoulders back then tried to look around his room.

"God I've gone blind! What the hell's going on?" Then he realized that he hadn't opened his eyes yet, "Jeez that's a relief." He prized open his left eye and the blurred image of a flashing light on the bedside table helped him gauge the position of the alarm.

Turning that off didn't make his head feel any better, but it stopped that infernal ringing.

He showered, and dressed in his kitchen uniform, hoping this might make him feel a bit better, but no he was dizzy and light-headed. Feeling faint he sat back down on the side of the bed. *Shall I ring in sick today? Oh shit, no I can't, the black box, what time is it?*

He was meeting a second agent in the food preparation area at 10.30a.m.

"What fucking time is it?" he says in a panic, scrambling around on his bedside table for his watch. As he found it he also saw the line of coke that he had placed on the table the night before.

Staring at the white powder neatly lined up, so inviting, so tempting, crying out to him, *'I'm here Evans, I'm here'*. He convinced himself that this was going to be the only thing that would help him through the morning. Taking a short straw out of his top drawer he then proceeded to snort the drug from the table top.

He remained in that crouched position for a few moments, then *bang* it hit him. He grinned happily – *here we go!*

Standing up straight, he caught sight of himself in the full-length mirror, which must have changed to a fairground version overnight, because what Evans was looking at, wasn't what most other people would see.

He looked at his watch, 9.10a.m. plenty of time.

Evans felt totally focused now on the day's events, perhaps he had gone the other way and was now too hyped up, and a bit jittery. He felt his movements to be a bit sudden and jerky, his chest was pounding as his heart was trying to get out from the confines of his ribcage.

Stepping out into the corridor linking those rooms to the main house, his door closes and locks behind him. *Shit I've left my keys on the worktop, never mind,* he thinks. *I'll just get a new set from the caretaker's office.* He sets off at a pace ready for the day's events.

He was quite cumbersome on his journey to work, banging into objects that had been there for years, but today for some reason they kept jumping out at him, still he beat them all, and got to the kitchen. However, he must have picked up quite a few bangs and bruises on the way.

The kitchen manager corners him. "Evans what time do you call this, it's almost ten!"

Evans spins round trying to focus on the point where the voice was coming from. However, thinking he could carry out such a maneuver having a headful of cocaine and a bellyful of Jack Daniels was his first mistake – down he went – like a sack of potatoes. As he fell he caught a number of pans from the breakfast trolleys waiting to be washed. *Bang! Clatter!* What a racket as it echoed round the room and down the corridor.

The kitchen managers' reaction was, "Abrahams! Get a brush and pan and sweep this bag of shit off my kitchen floor!" The manager lent over Evans, "Fool, I was going to make you my 'Head of Oven

Cleaning' but you might be better just putting your head in one now."

As the manager is walking away, Abrahams passes him carrying a brush and pan.

"What are you hoping to do with that?" asked the manager. "I meant it hypothetically, you cretin!" He shook his head, amazed at the idiots he had to work with. "Just help him put everything away."

Just then, a White House security agent rushed through the double doors to the kitchen area, his hand on his revolver, he saw Abrahams picking up a bag of rags from the floor.

"What's going on boy, heard the ruckus down the way?"

"Nothing going on here boss, just getting this man back up on his feet. He's a bit worse for wear." The Agent looks again at the bag of rags.

"God, it's Evans." He steps in, "Leave him, Abrahams, I will see to this." The Agent half picks him up and props him in a corner against a wall. "God! Evans, what the fuck are you doing?" he asked.

"I'm alright, I'm alright, just leave me for a few minutes," says Evans, unsure of whom he is talking to. "I'll be OK in a minute." Raising his head and opening his eyes, he suddenly recognizes Holden. "Oh Shit, no!" His body jerks back where there is nowhere for it to jerk to. He bangs his back and head on the wall behind him, which makes him drop to the floor, where he is promptly sick and brings up most of last night's whiskey. The stench is pretty ripe.

Holden rolled his eyes, before taking a twenty-dollar bill out of his wallet and walking over to Abrahams. "Clean that mess up young man. Here's twenty for your trouble. No-one needs to know about this." He then helps Evan's to his feet and drags him into the next room.

"I don't need your shitty remarks Holden, I'm feeling OK now," Evans hissed, his breath smelling like a Whiskey Distillery.

Holden has to take a step back to breathe some clean air. True, he does look a bit better now he's been sick.

Holden was staring at him intently. "Hang on a minute… your eyes… what's wrong with your eyes? They're huge! You idiot, you're on a fucking high! Evans what the fuck have you taken? If you compromise the mission today, you're a dead man!"

Evans steadies himself. *The mission… what's he talking about? Mission, he's thinking. Oh yeah, the black box… must get that sorted, but why is Holden talking about the mission – he wouldn't know about the black box.*

Then in some distant brain cell far, far, away Evans remembers the handler's comments from the previous night – *he works for me.*

"You know about the black box Keith!" as Evans is looking at Holden, he realizes that over the past six days wherever he had been, Holden had also been nearby. *He said the other day, that he was watching me, that's what this is all about. He was keeping an eye on me, protecting me but still keeping under the shroud of 'I'm also a Twat'.*

"Yes Evans, the box, the black box, where is it? You know the plan you've got to get it to those unused doors."

He nodded, and together they set off to recover the black box, Evans admitting to Holden on the way that he might have had a tiny line of coke that morning. He needed it to get him through the day, he explained. Holden just shook his head, exasperated.

The two men arrive at the kitchen utility storage area, quickly becoming aware of a third person over by the black box's hiding place. The man is just lifting the white linen covers off the trolley. As he hears the footsteps behind him the third person looks over his shoulder.

"Evans! Glad you're here mate, I'm looking for those big roasting pans we use for the pigs' heads." He paused for a moment. "Hello Agent Holden, what are you doing in here?" Holden didn't answer. "I've just found this trolley which I may as well use to take those roasting pans back, I'm just about to empty it." With that he lift's the white linen off the trolley, an action that would determine the poor boys fate as the communicational black box is revealed.

There was a moment of complete silence, "What's this?" he asked.

He begins to turn, looking round for Agent Holden to answer the question. He didn't, however, get an answer. Holden had swiftly positioned himself behind the young man. In a well-practiced procedure that only takes seconds to orchestrate, the Agent, wrapping his right arm across the young man's chest, an action which locks both people together, and in a continuous move he reaches up then jerks the boys head at ninety degrees to his left, breaking his neck.

Holden doesn't let the body fall, he supports its

dead weight.

This action causes the dead boys eyes – which are still wide open – to stare at Evans causing him to freak out and scream, "What the hell are you doing? That poor lad was a friend of mine. He was kitchen staff!"

Holden then drags the body to a store cupboard, placing it inside and closing the doors saying, "Look Evans I get no pleasure out of doing that, but the mission Evans, the mission, it's the only thing that matters."

Evans is now pulling at the white linen to re-cover the black box.

"No Evans, no. We might as well fit the dated copper seals while we're here."

Evans froze, the look on his face giving him away in an instant.

"You haven't got the seals, have you?" Holden asked angrily. "Don't say you've forgotten to bring them, just don't say it!"

Evans looked down at the floor. "I don't have them, Keith."

His face getting redder and redder, Holden almost growled as he said, "Evans, I could break your neck just as easily as your buddy's, and if I didn't need you for this mission, I would! Tell me, where are the fucking seals?"

"I don't have them, I never got them back off our handler last night!"

Holden shook his head. "I know now why they stuck you in the White House – 'cause you haven't got any balls." He took a deep breath. "I saw our handler slip them into the inside pocket of your jacket, as he told you last night."

Evans paused, thinking. "You were there last night?"

"I'm everywhere," said Holden, smiling. "Didn't you notice your whiskeys seemed a bit weak? I had them watered down as much as I could, though of course you still drank so much it didn't make any difference."

Evans raised his eyebrows, trying to get his head around this new information. "You've been following me?"

"Yes, and it's a good job too," replied Holden, getting more exasperated by the second. "So where's your jacket?"

"Just in my rooms, Keith."

"Key, Evans. Key!" shouted Holden.

Fumbling in his pocket Evans replies, "Keys, yes, er, no, I've locked them in my rooms by mistake. You'll have to go to the Caretakers Office for another set!"

Holden, staring at Evans answers, "You're a fucking ass! Take the trolley to the double doors and I will meet you there." He sets off at a pace not running – he didn't want to attract any unwanted attention.

"Wait!" said Evans, catching up with him. "My rooms are number 23 in the dorms."

"I know – I've been watching you, remember?" Holden replied, before rushing off.

*

Evans sets off to the double doors and Holden races back to room 23.

It doesn't take Holden too long to get to the dorms.

As he walks down the corridor where Evans's quarters are, he sees the cleaning lady just coming out of room 19. *That was lucky*, he thinks. *It's saved me having to kick the door in.*

He reaches into his pocket to retrieve his pass and flashes it at the lady. "Do you have a key for room 23, my dear?"

Picking up the bunch of keys, she passes him No 23.

"You going in there boy?. On your own?!" her expression is one of alarm, "Be careful, be very careful." Holden takes the key from her.

He pauses. "What's that supposed to mean?"

"The hobo living in there, he's a fruit cake," she replied, clutching the golden crucifix that was hanging around her neck. "I emptied his trash a couple of weeks ago and pushed down in to the bottom of one of the trash bags was the remains of two kittens – ripped to pieces, poor things."

As Holden opens the door, he remarks, "Well everyone has something to hide. What's your secret lady, sorting through other people's rubbish?"

It was dark inside – thanks to all the blinds being down – but a soft glow coming from the hallway just allowed him to see Evans's jackct, which was hanging up on the coat pegs.

He started walking towards it, suddenly feeling the uncomfortable heat in the apartment – it was unbearably hot, and Holden had to loosen his tie as he walked.

Lifting the jacket down, he could feel the weight of the copper disks, and relieved, he retrieves them from the inside pocket by ripping it open thinking, you don't stick your hands into other people's pockets, you never know what could be in them.

As he turns to leave, he is confronted by the cleaning lady, hovering in the doorway. "What do you think?" she asks. "It's always like this. He's a mad man! The place is always in darkness, and the heat!" She steps in, blocking Holden's escape route.

"Excuse me, lady," said Holden, "I'm in a rush."

"You're not going anywhere until I've shown you this," insists the cleaning lady. "Have a good look in that room at the back."

Quite alarmed at the cleaning lady's brashness, Holden opens the door to the second bedroom, just a few inches. It's also almost in total darkness – he reaches along the wall to find the light switch.

"Careful, young man! Make sure none of them are out of their tanks!"

Holden eyeballs the cleaner. "I'm Delta Force trained, lady. We do not flinch at danger." With that he found the light switch, and just as he turned it on, he felt the legs of a giant spider running up his forearm.

"Shit!" he cries, pulling his arm back out of the room faster than Concorde breaking the sound barrier. His elbow smashes into the wall behind him and his arm wedges into the broken plasterboard.

On his wrist, tapping its one-inch poisonous fangs onto the pulsating vein just above Holden's imitation Rolex, is the most gruesome, hairiest creature God had ever created.

"Get it off me!" he screams. "For God's sake, kill it!"

Beads of sweat were forming on Holden's face as the creature – with its four pairs of eyes – staring him out, almost daring him to make a swipe at it. He could feel the stabbing sensation from the spider's venomous fangs almost breaking through his skin. "Kill it, woman!" he screeched. "Before it attacks!"

In response, the cleaning lady starts laughing. "Delta Force my ass," she said, reaching out her hand and resting her palm alongside the spider. It promptly walked onto her hand, and she cupped it safely to her chest as she stepped into the rear bedroom.

"Look at all this," she said, as if nothing unusual had just happened, "it's crazy! Snakes, spiders! He's even breeding mice, which I think he uses as food for these poor creatures." She lifted the huge spider up towards her lips, kissed it, and then placed it back into one of the tanks. "There you are, my beauty – you're back home now."

Holden takes a step backwards, well away from the cleaning lady, edging slowly towards the door. *She's mad! As mad as Evans!* he thinks.

"I'll just be off now," he said as he went.

"Oh no, young man – I want to show you my

favorite first." With that she lifts a three-foot snake out of its tank. Turning round to face the door, Holden had gone. She hears the hall door bang shut as Holden makes his escape!

She laughed. "Delta Force my ass."

*

The British MI6 agent known as White Knight pulled up to the rear double doors of the food preparation suite at the White House, getting out of the fruit and vegetable van with a quick glance around to ensure he was unobserved. He was dressed as a delivery man.

Opening the rear doors of his truck, he expects to see the inside man at the exterior glass doors, but there was no one there. He approaches to look through the glass, hoping to see Evans, 'his inside contact' waiting to open the doors and let him in.

"Oh shit, no-one's there," he says under his breath, then just as he is about to try the handle, Evans turns the top corner – running down with the trolley – waving his free hand in a 'No don't touch it' action. This stops the agent.

Evans is now at the doors, speaking through the rebait where the two doors meet. He whispers, "Don't touch anything the alarm's on a movement sensor." White Knight studies Evans' demeanor, the man looks deranged almost spooked, looking far more nervous than he should be, his gaze flicking left and right, he continues whispering, "When I open these doors we will have forty-five seconds, then the guard will appear."

"I know Evans, I've read your valuation report.

Have you got the black box?"

"Yes, under these sheets," replies Evans, whispering. White Knight jumps onto his tail-lift, turns to Evans and holds up one finger asking for one minute before opening the double doors. Dragging eight fruit crates onto his tail-lift, he lowers the tail down, then positions himself ready to go when the doors open.

Thumbs up to Evans, and go. The doors open, Evans whips the cloth off the counterfeit black box concealed on top of the trolley, White Knight stops dead in his tracks, looking at the black box.

"Come on, let's move it," spouts Evans, knowing full-well that he has seen the copper seals are missing.

White Knight passes the first crate of oranges – that has the false bottom on it, to Evans who lifts it straight over the counterfeit black box. A second crate of oranges is immediately stacked on the trolley. They had planned for this moment; the whole operation hinged on it, and they couldn't afford for it to go wrong.

As another crate was passed across, Evans went to take hold of it, but misjudging the distance, he caught the doorframe with the corner. He watched in horror as the whole thing fell to the floor, oranges rolling along the carpet like they were trying to escape.

"Dammit Evans!" hissed White Knight. "Pick it up, quick; he'll be here in twelve seconds."

Evans bent over, but as he did so, the remaining Jack Daniels suddenly surged in his stomach, making him stumble and fall into the wall. His head hit it with a smack, leaving behind a small but obvious patch of blood.

Exasperated, White Knight steps over him to retrieve the crate, and just as he placed it over the top of the first two, the security man jogged around the corner, fully armed. He immediately started shouting at Evans about protocol, pointing at him aggressively in a highly unnecessary way – after all, it was clear whom he was talking to. He struck White Knight as quite an unpleasant individual.

Evans had now sat himself down on the tail-lift of the truck, cradling his head, blood running down his face.

White Knight throws a dirty old rag at Evans that he'd been using to wipe the windscreen. "Here Evans, clean yourself up."

The White House security man watched for a moment, then started laying into Evans with a vengeance.

White Knight stooped back into the delivery van, taking the opportunity to pick up another box – he needed something in his hands to prevent him from reaching for his gun too soon.

"What the hell are you doing, using these doors?" the guard demanded, looming over Evans, who was not a small man. "You know we haven't got cameras covering this area! You can't use it for deliveries!"

"Sorry, boss! I'm sorry – we're just bringing in the fruit for tomorrow's shindig – you know the normal delivery entrance is being decorated. There's no other way in." He shrugged.

"Damn decorating. What you got there, Evans?" the guard asked, calming down as he holstered his weapon. "Anything for me?"

The guard smiled, clearly of the opinion that he was about to enjoy one of the perks of his job. He tapped the orange box – which was sealed with various colors of tape – and the agent felt his heart leap into his mouth.

He shifted the fruit box in his hands, anxiously. If push came to shove, he could always drop the fruit box and shoot the guard, though he'd really rather not. A dead or missing guard would raise the kind of suspicions that they could do without, not to mention the sound of the gunshot attracting unwanted officials to the very spot they were standing in.

"Only some oranges, boss – no, no, don't break the seal, boss! I won't be able to go any further if the seals are broken," Evans exclaimed, hastily trying to prevent the guard from opening the box and revealing its covert contents.

"Evans, Evans," the guard soothed. "Don't be a fucking idiot – I'm the security guy you'll be bringing it past, so don't bullshit me about security protocols. I want some oranges, and you're going to let me have them."

The guard knocked Evans's hand away then ripped the tapes off the box. He opened it to reveal the top layer of perfect oranges – all wrapped in blue paper to prevent them from bruising – and grinned, oblivious to how profusely Evans was sweating. White Knight's gun hand started to itch. It was down to the guard now: if he was greedy, then they'd have a big problem, but if not…

He moved his hand marginally closer to his gun – hoping he didn't have to use it – then watched as the guard pulled out three oranges, shoving them in his jacket pocket.

He closed the flaps of the box with a flourish and tried to refit the security tapes. He didn't do a particularly good job of it.

"There you are, Evans. Oh, don't pout – you know the rules," he said, winking at both Evans and White Knight. "So much for them and so much for us! Just leave a couple of boxes at my desk; there's a good man."

White Knight grimaced internally; it looked like Evans was already way beyond spooked, which didn't bode well for a smooth operation, and this needed to be the smoothest of the smooth. He hadn't worked with this White House contact before, but he'd heard from other operatives that Evans could be dangerously jumpy at times – not what you wanted on a covert mission, and definitely not when the President was around.

It put White Knight immediately on edge. He checked his concealed weapon, just to be sure.

With that, the guard turned and walked cockily back around the corner, fondling his oranges as he went.

"Lock those doors when you've finished, and let me know when it's done so I can reset the alarms. Oh, and Evans, if I was you I would go to sick bay with that head injury."

The agent watched him go, hand still hovering over his gun holster. He was almost tempted to use it.

"What a jumped up, brainless moron," Evans

muttered, a bit too loudly. "How these sorts of people get jobs in places like this is beyond me."

"I heard that!" the guard snapped, not even bothering to turn around. "Make that three boxes or you'll be looking for a new employer, smartass!"

White Knight shook his head. "I don't feel this is going well." Then he paused, looking anxiously at Evans. "The copper seals for the black box – where are they? We can't use it without them!"

"They're on the way, Agent Holden is bringing them to us. We should have them in a few moments," replies Evans.

"I don't have any confidence in you, Evans, I really don't." White Knight stared at him meaningfully.

Evans shrugged. "Well, it is what it is, so make the best of it."

Evans and White Knight loaded up the trolley with more boxes, making sure that they had ready access to the two pistols tucked among the fruit, just in case something went wrong. They shared a look: so far, so good.

"Let's hope it's plain sailing from here on in, yeah?" Evans muttered, as they maneuvered the trolley onto the access ramp.

"Hear, hear," the agent responded, as they trundled inside.

Together, the agent and his contact wheeled the trolley down the corridor past the security guard.

"Hey Evans, over here!" the guard barked self-importantly. "Where's my contribution, you little shit?"

Evans gritted his teeth, unloading three boxes of fruit from the top of the stack and depositing them beside the man's desk with a certain amount of bad grace. "There you go, boss," he said grumpily. "I hope you choke to death on these and all your children develop rickets, you asshole!"

"Thanks Evans," said the guard, aiming a kick in the direction of his shins. "And fuck you, too."

They carried on through the service branches to the corridors of power – slowly, so the wheels of the trolley weren't overly squeaky. Approaching them from the other direction was Agent Holden.

As they get closer to each other Holden opens a door to his right and invites Evans and White Knight to join him. He shakes hands with the latter.

"I'm glad you're here. The potential success rate of this mission has just jumped from zero to fifty percent," he says taking the envelope holding the copper seals out of his jacket pocket. Opening it, he checks that the White House emblem is stamped onto the disks, along with the date.

At the same time, Evans and White Knight exposed the black box from the crates stacked around it.

Carefully, Holden then slips the four disks over the locking device that will hold them in place, he looks up at Evans. A cocky smirk on his face. "I think I've just met your twin sister, Evans! A crazy woman, down in your rooms, kissing the ugliest eight-eyed zombie I've ever seen."

"Oh, you mean 'Sultan'," replied Evans. "He's got tons of character, that one."

Holden then clamps and locks each disk in place on the black box. Once finished, they begin to reload the trolley.

"Right. You guys are on your own now. Whatever happens in there, I can't back you up; I need to protect my cover." He shook hands with the two men, adding, "Good luck," and then left the room.

Evans and White Knight finished reloading the trolley, then they left the room too, setting off to their destination.

*

Voices could be heard filtering out of the doorway ten feet or so in front of them, they slowed down with the trolley to stop the noisy wheels rattling – and eventually came to a halt outside an anonymous-looking door.

With practiced skill, the two agents concealed themselves on either side of it and then carefully peeked inside.

Their target, the genuine black box, was on a table surrounded by four people who were having what looked like a very serious conversation. White Knight recognized two immediately, and the other two from the files he'd been studying for the better part of the last week: the President of the United States of America, Ron Champion – the Vice President, Bo Nick Olsen, and Edward Daniels, who did something scientific for the CIA. There were also two eagle-eyed Secret Service agents lurking by the far wall, keeping an unobtrusive eye on proceedings.

From their hiding places, the two British agents watched the President carefully lift the black box up and examine the seals on its edges. At the same time, Daniels moved away from the little group surrounding the black box and collected a disk from the adjacent table. Cheerfully, he twirled it in his fingers, showing off for his friends. Olsen was on the phone, clearly conversing with a colleague or underling on the Time Travel Project.

"Yeah Josh, it's just about ready to transport over to you at Cape Canaveral," he said into his phone. "How's the *Microsoft* team doing?" He laughed. "That's good to hear, Doctor."

"God, these boxes are heavier than you think," the President remarked, chuckling. "Eddie, tell me you're happy that we have all the information they'll need stored away in Pandora's Box here?"

"Yes, Mr President," said Eddie. "I've gone through my check sheets, and all of the necessary information is in place. The programs with the six digit security codes you requested have also been installed," he continues. "That was a clever piece of work, Mr President."

The President nodded in acknowledgement.

"Navigation controls have also been ironed out and finalized, so that's all set. We've got the location of the RAF transport plane and its security codes, so stopping that disaster, should be pretty straightforward. It's the death of the British Princess that's a bit trickier," he added, scratching his nose. "I've been working with the head of the CIA and I do believe we've got everything they're going to need on the disks. Then it's up to the people at the receiving end – it's a pretty big ask for them to believe in this to begin with, as I'm sure you know."

"It'll be okay, Eddie; we're smart people, we'll figure it out," said Ron Champion, a small smile on his lips. "Right, we can do no more."

White Knight and Evans nodded at one another: this was their moment. They backed off from the door a little and pushed the trolley around enough to attract the attention of the Secret Service agents. Sometimes the best disguise was hiding in plain sight.

"Hey, you two!" the first Secret Service agent demanded. "What the hell are you doing out there?"

"Just waiting to dress the room for the Spanish Flamenco Dancing Exhibition, Sir," said Evans briskly. "It's been relocated here because the East Wing is being decorated right now."

"Get on your way!" the Secret Service agent snapped. "You two don't have the security level to be this near to the President!"

Olsen – who was watching them in the background – frowned, and White Knight tensed, hoping he wasn't onto them.

From his reputation alone, Bo Nick Olsen was the kind of man who noticed things – and then did something about them. He didn't say anything, however – much to White Knight's relief, he finished his phone call and hung up, watching them with an air of nonchalance that the agent hoped was entirely natural.

"Hey, it's okay, Agent Bering, we've finished here," said the President cheerfully. "Let them prepare the room – I've got to move on to rehearse this week's State of the Union anyhow. Agent Roberts, you stay here and keep a watch on the black box," he added, pointing at the device. "We can't let it out of our sight."

Bo nodded, though he was far from happy having seen the two men who were there for the dancing event. You just didn't get staff members without clearance this far into the White House; they knew better.

If the President was feeling magnanimous, that was just fine, but Bo wasn't about to just ignore the two staffers: they may have been dressed like a waiter and a delivery man, but they didn't move right. The first man, whom he thought he might have seen somewhere around the White House before – seemed a lot more anxious than someone preparing a room for Flamenco dancing ought to be, and the delivery man looked completely out of place.

Bo couldn't quite put his finger on what it was, but the man clearly couldn't hide his athleticism. Not that grocery delivery men couldn't be athletic, or strong – for all he knew, the man could be a body builder or karate teacher in his spare time – but still, there was something undeniably covert about his movements.

For one thing, he was hyper vigilant, trying to keep something solid at his back at all times. Bo knew the signs because he often had to be on a higher level of awareness himself in his line of work – just like he was doing now. The other man seemed almost spaced out for the want of a better description; he wasn't acting normally at all.

Bo was being covertly vigilant, thinking, *people don't*

act like this, not normally.

Yes, the two men were clearly up to something, and he had too much riding on this project to let anyone interfere with it.

Bo kept his face carefully blank when the delivery man glanced in his direction, managing his micro-expressions. If they noticed him noticing them, things could go downhill very rapidly – and the President was still close enough to be at risk.

Thinking quickly, he put a call through to Eddie's mobile, deftly dropping his cell phone behind the precious black box, as he passed it on the way out. He then jogged to catch up with Eddie, who was fumbling for his phone. He peered at the screen and looked up at Bo, confused.

"It's you, Bo – on the phone… What are you doing calling me when you're standing right there? What are you up to? Another practical joke?"

"Give me that, Eddie," Bo ordered, taking the phone out of his friend's unresisting fingers. "I'm not happy – something funny's going on here."

He put the phone on loud speaker and held it up so both he and Eddie could hear it.

"What are you doing?" Eddie asked, bewildered. "Who's on the phone?"

Bo shook his head urgently and covered the mouthpiece with his hand. "Shush, Eddie, shush," he insisted. "I've left my phone in the Vermeil room by the black box – I'm not happy about those two staffers. There's just something not quite right about them."

There was silence for a moment, and then a voice floated from out of the cell – it was the athletic delivery man: *"Hey Roberts, how're you doing, man? Your wife okay? We've left you a case of French wine at your buddy's security station,"* Bo and Eddie study the conversation. *"You'd better get down there fast or he'll sneak it all out at the end of his shift. You know what that stuck up bastard is like."*

"I can't," said the Secret Service agent, with a voice full of regret. *"I can't leave this room until the black box is collected. Direct orders."*

Bo and Eddie stood listening to the cell phone, glancing at each other with expressions of puzzlement. Ron Champion and the President are marching on down the corridor, completely unaware of events.

"Don't worry, we're going to be here for at least half an hour – there's a lot of setting up to be done. Go and get your share of the bounty. We'll keep an eye on things for you. No problem at all."

"That's mighty kind of you," said the Secret Service agent, sounding gratified. *"Cheers bud – it's not often I get a share out. I'll be right back!"*

Bo and Eddie listened to the man's retreating footsteps, sharing puzzled, worried looks across Eddie's phone.

"This isn't right, Bo," whispered Eddie. "That guy should be staying put. Did he not hear what the President said? You've got me worried now."

They pivoted around and watched Agent Roberts stalk briskly along the corridor in the opposite direction before turning round the far corner, out of sight.

There were some muffled sounds, then Eddie and Bo listened, wide-eyed, as the two men in the Vermeil room had a quick, nervous discussion. A discussion about the black box.

Then, there was a hiss and a click, followed by silence. A rather worrying silence.

"The cell phone transmission has stopped," said Eddie, staring at his handset, his heart in his mouth. The black box was intrinsic to the Time Travel Mission; if someone managed to tamper with it... But who in the hell would? And why? Who even knew about it, for that matter? His mind was a whirlwind.

"That means they've moved the black box and discovered my cell phone," said Bo urgently. "Come on, Eddie, let's get back."

They hurried back to the Vermeil room, and Ron Champion and the President – who were currently much further along the corridor – stopped, startled. Hearing Bo and Eddie turn back, they did the same.

Agent Bering, belatedly sensing trouble, followed his nation's leaders at some speed.

Something was wrong, alright.

*

Meanwhile in the Vermeil room, the agent disguised as a delivery man was having an epiphany. He was in the wrong line of work.

"Evans!" shouted White Knight. "I'm not a real delivery man. Come and give me a fucking hand." As he was humping and dumping the orange crates from the trolley to reveal the *dummy* black box, Evans was just staring at the *genuine* black box.

White Knight moved around to confront Evans, pausing when he saw his face. He'd clearly lost it; his expression was blank and distant. His nerves had gone. Upon realizing this – drawing his hand back – White Knight slaps Evans in the face, momentarily bringing him round. "Come on, Evans, don't lose it now," he said, trying to get through to him. "Help me get these orange crates off the trolley."

Evans, very slowly helps as White Knight picks up the replacement black box.

"Bring the real one over to the trolley, Evans – Evans!"

Evans froze, staring at him as though he didn't know who he was.

"Just do it, Evans!" the agent snapped, beyond annoyed. "For God's sake, just do it – we haven't got much fucking time!"

He watches as Evans wanders back to the trolley empty handed. "Just get out of the bloody way!" he snapped.

"Some fucking spy you turned out to be – move it! Move it, for fuck's sake!"

Elbowing the other man out of the way, White Knight forces the real black box across the table, this action exposes Bo's cell phone.

This time it was White Knight's turn to freeze.

"Shit! There's someone's phone here!" White Knight exclaims. His heart begins to race; someone was onto them, but who? And how?

"What the hell? Whose is this?" He places the fake Black box down, picks up the phone, snaps it shut ending the call, and puts it in his pocket, then in a smooth action he picks up the real black box and carries it swiftly back to the trolley.

Still fuming at how badly this whole thing was going, the agent gently places the original black box onto the trolley, waiting for Evans to cover it. Unfortunately, Evans had frozen again – he was now just staring into one of the boxes on the floor.

Shaking his head, White Knight grabbed the orange crate with the false bottom and placed it over the real black box. He gritted his teeth; they were running out of time.

Looking at Evans his face all twisted, still staring vacantly at the boxes on the floor, White Knight follows his gaze, then realizes he is mesmerized by the two guns, part hidden by oranges in that particular box.

This didn't look good.

Just at that moment…

Bo and Eddie skid into the room, only to find one of the highly suspicious men dressing tables, and the other just knelt on the floor in front of some boxes. Despite their mundane task, both of them looked extremely uneasy.

Bo took a deep breath. Ron Champion, the President, and the second Secret Service agent were still a little way behind them; he could hear their soft footfalls on the carpeted corridor outside the Vermeil room. At least they weren't here yet.

Eddie and Bo walk towards the counterfeit black box as nonchalantly as they can, both men eyeing it suspiciously.

261

"This looks like the real black box, Bo," Eddie whispered urgently. "The date stamps are correct. Although…" He paused, frowning. "Jesus, look at these scratches on the table – someone's moved this box." He glanced at the delivery man. "Who are these people?"

"I don't know," Bo hissed, keeping an eye on the *waiters*. He frowned, "My cell phone is gone, too."

Eddie reached over and took his own phone from Bo. "Keep your ears open and your eyes peeled," he said quietly, tapping the call button. "Something's about to happen."

Bo watched out of the corner of his eye as Eddie hit redial.

The man dressing tables continued as he was, but Bo observed him glancing over his shoulder, keeping a visual on the activities behind him. The second man didn't seem to follow any pattern at all; he just stared into the scattered boxes spread out on the floor.

The next moment, however, he moved – reaching forward, he plunged his left hand into the box, and Bo could clearly see the handle of a gun as the man partly withdrew it.

The realization that they had concealed weapons hit him at the same moment he comprehended what Eddie was about to do.

How on earth they got those weapons past security – especially in a place as secure as the White House – he had no idea, but he did know one thing: the shit was about to hit the fan in a big way.

Bo was reaching for Eddie's hand to stop him

pressing the call button when his phone started ringing in the other man's pocket – who immediately froze from dressing the tables – the knowledge that they'd been rumbled printed across his face as he turned.

Bo waited with bated breath to see what would happen next – would they pull out a gun and fire on him and Eddie? Or were they waiting for the President to come back?

The man on his knees didn't seem to be involved, what was going on in his mind didn't relate to what was going on in the room, he now had a small hand gun cradled in the palm of his left hand, just staring at it

Without warning, Ron Champion and the President swung into the room through the open door, and as soon as he saw them, Bo's stomach dropped.

"Mr President, leave this room immediately!" shouted Bo, but before anyone had chance to react, the man on his knees looked up at the commotion. Then, with a distant, lost expression on his face, he lifted the revolver up, and – in a moment of madness – pulled the trigger, firing a shot at the men in the doorway.

Bo's reactions were quicker than a fighter pilot's. He had anticipated what was going to happen, and had launched himself at the assassin at the exact same moment the bullet left the chamber of the revolver. In what seemed like slow motion, Bo managed to get himself in the path of its trajectory, a human shield in front of the President.

The slug hit Bo full in the chest forcing him

backwards. He staggers and falls, hitting the ground at the Presidents feet.

It was strange. He knew he'd been shot, but it didn't hurt – not like he thought it would. In fact, it felt more like a punch to the ribs than a bullet wound, one that had caused a tremendous pressure to weigh heavily on his chest.

He clutched at his ribs, staring down as a deep red liquid leaked out over his hands. Around him, everyone was shouting, their voices so distant he thought they couldn't possibly be talking to him.

Looking up he could see Ron Champion, peering down on him, his expression was of deep distress but just then… there was something else. Some*one* else.

Bo's heart felt the warmth of his beloved Becky, she had just appeared at Ron's side, smiling with so much love in her eyes, he reached out his hand to grasp hers, but just could not reach her, he tried again, but she seemed further away this time.

As Becky's image started to fade, tears filled his eyes. He'd never get to say goodbye, never get to see her again.

The pain of knowing that was far worse than the pain in his chest.

The last thing Bo Nick Olsen thought about as he drifted away was Becky, *his* Becky, *his* life.

And then he was gone.

*

Bo's death was just a moment in time, and as he was slowly leaving this world, the White House was falling into chaos.

At the same time Bo was shot, the second FBI agent rushed through the doorway throwing himself in front of the President, Bo's body lifelessly beneath him, his gun already in his right hand. With impressive speed he fired a shot at the man squatting on the floor, the bullet passing straight through his temple. A second bullet entered his rib cage, just under his left armpit. He was killed instantly.

White Knight is now shouting out, "Don't shoot, don't shoot," as the FBI agent's pistol is now leveling up to his face. White Knight's hands are waving frantically above his head. "Don't shoot; please don't shoot."

The FBI agent's aim is now locked on White Knight's forehead.

The President intervenes, "Don't shoot him Agent Bering."

Bering nodded, though he didn't lower his gun. "Stay where you are," he ordered White Knight.

Secret Service Agents began to pour in through the door. The President gasped, struggling to comprehend the events. He and the Vice President – both of whom were in shock at what had just happened, as well as how fast it had all happened – were escorted out of the room, being taken away to a safe, secure location.

Back in the Vermeil room, the mayhem hadn't stopped, and Eddie in particular was panicking. He was kneeling down next to Bo, trying to tidy up his best friend's body so he'd look respectable when the paramedics arrived, but the truth was, he had no idea what to do.

Just what the hell was he supposed to do in a situation like this?

Ten minutes ago it had all seemed like a bit of an adventure story, but now the reality of what had happened was beginning to sink in.

He looked around the rest of the room, the scene in front of him surreal and dreamlike. Evans was most definitely dead, but his body was still kneeling, as if in a praying position. The far side of his skull had been completely blown away, the remnants spread out on the floor next to him.

White Knight was now being dragged out of the room, his arms having been tied behind his back, and the FBI agent who'd left his post for a share of the booty was being frog-marched away. He'd never work in the White House again.

Photographs were being taken for the investigation as the crews came in to remove the bodies.

Eddie watched all this happen as though a spectator at a play, and when a man walked over and offered to help him up, it took him several seconds to realize he was being spoken to.

Eventually, he let himself be escorted out, both his mind and his body now completely numb.

In the underground rooms beneath the White House, the President was trying to get his head around the recent events. It was not going well.

"Who the hell orchestrated this?" demanded the President, who was sitting at the head of a large, oval table. "This is madness – sheer madness! A gunfight in my house – in my 'EFFING HOUSE! *Where my wife and children live!"* He was trembling.

The people sitting around the table – some security staff and several senior politicians – had no idea how to respond.

Neither did Ron. He was absolutely devastated, and all he could think about was the moment he'd watched the life seep out of Bo, his good friend. He'd offered so much to mankind, and now he was gone.

"Excuse me Mr President, I need to attend to someone very dear to me." Ron stood up leaving the room, flanked by two FBI security agents.

He stopped in the doorway, the two agents almost walking into him. "What the hell are you doing?" he asked, turning around to face the two men.

"We're your security detail, Sir," one of them replied. "We've been deployed to protect you."

Ron glared at him. "To protect me? You're a bit late coming here, making that statement young man!" Ron growled. "We had a Dutchman protecting the President not ten minutes ago, and he sacrificed his life to do so."

He left before the agent could say anything else, walking into a nearby office and locking the door behind him.

He sat down at the desk, staring at the blank wall opposite as though expecting to see the answer to his problem. He knew what he had to do, but he didn't know *how* he was going to do it – not without completely breaking down, anyway.

After a minute or so he picked up the phone on the desk, to speak to the White House Reception. He waited for the call to go through to the time travel complex in San Diego.

After what seemed like an age, the phone began to ring, bringing Ron out of his trance. He wasn't ready to do this – not by a long shot – but he knew he couldn't wait any longer; it wouldn't be fair. Knowing the lady, Ron decides the best way to go with this is to tell Becky straight.

"Hello, Becky speaking. How can I help?"

Ron paused for a moment before replying, in a much quieter voice than usual, "Becky, its Ron."

"Oh, hi Ron!" said Becky, her professional tone immediately vanishing. She now had a warmth to her voice, and Ron could tell she was smiling.

This was going to be much, much harder than he thought.

"Becky," he said, his voice cracking. He paused, taking a deep breath. "Becky, I'm so, so sorry to tell you this, but I'm afraid there's been an… incident. We've… we've lost Bo. He's been shot by a mad man in the White House."

He paused, waiting for an answer, but none came.

"He died saving the President's life. I'm so sorry, Becky."

He paused again, and this time he heard her sharp intake of breath.

Ron holds on to the open line, "Becky are you there? I've got to get back into this meeting with the President."

Becky finally answers the request, "I'm here, Ron.

Just give me a minute. Let me take all this in."

"If you can, I think you should get on the next flight to Washington. He'd want you here, Becky, and I'd like to see you. I can explain everything then."

There was another brief pause, and then Becky whispered, "I'll be there."

Putting his head in his hands, Ron tried not to cry.

Chapter 20

Have you given it the last rites Mr Champion?

It seemed to take forever for Ron to get to the White House the following morning; his dear wife hadn't been too good of late, and at the moment she was completely bedridden. On top of that, although the normal 6.15 alarm got the family up, from 6.16 it all started to go very much downhill.

As soon as Ron got out of bed, he stubbed his big toe on the doorframe, which immediately received a torrent of abuse.

"It's no good blaming the doorframe, Ron; it's been there for twenty-three years," his wife said, trying to make light of her husband's dilemma.

Ron just scowled.

Down in the kitchen, someone had tried to boil the kettle without enough water in it, burning the element out, and the toaster – which was still smoldering – had been put in the back yard. A rather thick slice of bread that was really more suited as a doorstop had wedged itself in the frame of the toaster. The appliance, not knowing any better, had tried to cremate the bread until it caught fire.

This had set the fire alarm off, and Ron's answer to the whole thing had been to throw the damn thing out the back door.

Problem solved.

"Morning Mr Champion." Alice the maid had just arrived in the back yard, and was now studying Ron's handiwork. "Have you given it *the last rites* Mr Champion?"

"Very funny Alice," Ron loads a mug with coffee from the percolator, "at least this is still working."

"I think you'd better just leave things to me, Mr Champion," Alice said sympathetically. "Your car's parked at the front."

After downing his coffee, Ron said his farewells to his family and headed out to the car.

Some days you are just glad to get away from the stress of the family house, thinks Ron as he meanders down the path, still limping from his bruised big toe.

*

Ron was now at his desk, going over the events of the previous day's carnage. He had instructed a handpicked group of his trusted FBI investigators to sift through the evidence.

From reading the initial first day's report, one piece of the puzzle which had become clear was that the dead man, Evans – who had been a trusted orderly from the kitchens – was in fact a known MI6 operative.

Because British and American Governments always worked so closely together on various covert missions, it was felt acceptable that each Country would have undercover agents employed in both Governments. America supposedly having undercover CIA people in various roles in the British Government, and likewise the British have MI6 undercover agents in the American Government. Just a friendly way of keeping an eye on what each other were doing.

Evans was part of this practice, and was well known to senior personnel. However, he had been at the White House for so long, the surveillance that was kept on his movements had been relaxed, as different senior personnel had come and gone. A problem in both Governments.

The second man involved – the one who had pleaded for his life – also turned out to be an MI6 Agent. He had told the FBI that Evans seemed unbalanced right from the start, and that he should have declined continuing with the mission when he realized Evans was mentally disturbed. However, his handler had stressed to him that there was a time limit on the mission, so he had to continue hoping Evans might come around enough to be a full participant.

The agent said that he had no knowledge of the full extent of the mission; the only instructions he'd been given were to replace one fully loaded Presidential black box with the empty one.

Ron wasn't sure whether he believed that, not that it really mattered now.

During the morning Ron had received a message from Becky saying that she would be flying into Washington Airport around eleven-thirty. He had sent one of the Presidential cars to pick her up, and they'd made plans to have lunch together.

Ron had now finished reading the initial reports on the shootings at the White House, and it had become clear to him that it was the British Secret Service who were behind the ill-fated events of yesterday. But why for God sake?

Speaking on the intercom to Hannah his secretary, "Can you arrange a meeting with the President for this afternoon? I don't know what his diary is for today Hannah you may need to go through Joan to find me a slot."

"OK, Mr Champion, I'll arrange that," replied Hannah. "Oh, and there's a Miss Fining waiting to see you in the West Wing restaurant."

"Thank you," said Ron, looking at his watch. Time was running away from him, and he didn't want to keep Becky waiting.

Locking the FBI file away in his desk, "You don't know who's about these days," he says to himself. He then sets off to meet Becky.

FBI agents have been deployed to all senior staff within the White House, after the previous day's security breaches.

As he left his office Ron had been questioned about his travel intentions – where he was going, who he was meeting. He was not a happy man.

Accompanying Ron was the agent who had

crossed his path the day before. Ron hated this, and he had a strong dislike for the man following him just two paces behind.

Entering the restaurant, Ron spotted Becky immediately. She was sitting near to one of the windows, looking out over the White House gardens.

Pointing his index finger determinedly at the FBI agent, "You can leave me now," Ron tells him with a stern expression on his face.

The agent – remembering the incident the previous day – just stood down, and sat at the restaurant bar.

Becky had seen Ron enter the room and stood up to greet him, they embraced, and Ron invited Becky to sit back down at her table.

There were a few seconds of silence while Ron pondered what to say, before Becky asked, "Do you remember when we first met, Ron? When you took us for a walk in the gardens?"

Ron nodded, smiling. "I do, Becky. It was one of those nights when everything became clear to me."

Becky smiles. "Well Ron, it was that evening after we left you, that Bo and I made a pact with each other, we realized then, we had something special. It had been a whirlwind romance, yes. But the events of that night made us appreciate what true love really was, and the effect it had on both of us.

"We talked about marriage, children – grandchildren even! It was so, so romantic, almost like a Peter Pan fantasy. However, Bo and I, you could almost say, were not living in the real world.

You see Ron – and you must have thought about this yourself – as we are so close to the events of what has happened, and the fact that those events will be changed *forever*, by the launch of the missile… We…"

"…will never have met anyway," finishes Ron

"Exactly." She shrugged. "Not that it helps, of course… I'd rather he be alive and not know who I am than… well, you know…" She trailed off, a tear sliding down her cheek.

"You and Bo will of course know each other, but the topics we spoke about that night will never become a reality, because you and I will never meet Ron. I am so, so, sad and heartbroken at the loss of Bo, you may think that I'm not showing it, and that is right, but inside I can feel a heartbeat is missing. I sit here knowing that another lifetime is my destiny, and I'm to live in that lifetime without ever knowing the man I fell in love with."

Ron had listened to Becky's portrayal of events with tremendous care and respect. Given that she still kept the appearance of control and sincerity, filled him with pride to have known this person. He caught the eye of one of the waitresses and organized a pot of coffee for them both.

Waiting for the coffee to percolate, he took hold of Becky's hands. "I was going to start by trying to explain what we think happened here yesterday, but as I have listened to you I realize that it will not make any difference, and my best approach is to address those problems myself in a diplomatic way, so my other option is to explain my thoughts on what we should do. That's you and I Becky. Whichever time zone we end up working in, I am still going to be the party's nomination for the White House, and I feel that I would still need you to be with me, although I won't even know who you are."

Puzzled, Becky begins to pour the coffee, gazing at Ron, not sure where this is going.

"Well," said Ron, leaning forwards and lowering his voice, "what we need to do is put a message into the black box, private and confidential, just for Bo. Of course, he might think the whole thing is crazy, but if we don't try…" He trailed off, shrugging.

"Basically, we need to let the past Bo know about you, about your relationship. Hopefully he'll seek you out and if we can all meet again, who knows what we can achieve?"

He smiled at Becky, "It's strange, you and I talking like this. If anyone was to overhear this conversation, they'd think we were crazy." The two friends are now more hopeful. "I'll speak to the President, to okay it. What do you think?"

After a moment of thought, Becky smiled too. "We have got to try Ron, Bo is the only person I've ever loved. He will be the same gentle man in an alternative time zone as he was in this one. But would he feel the same towards me? Who knows? Could I love him again? Who knows? But if I do, I would take better care of him."

A few moments of silence follows. Ron cares very much for Becky, almost like a daughter, and feels he must do whatever he can for her happiness.

"Ok Becky, I will arrange access to the black box. Now, what I want you to do is come with me to our communications office where you can record a message onto a disk."

Without warning, Becky sprung up from her seat, running around the table and hugging Ron where he sat. "Thank you," she whispered as more tears filled her eyes. "Thank you."

"Ok Becky, you have less than thirty six hours. The black box is being moved to the launch site tomorrow evening." Ron, with his hands clasped in front of his chest, raises his eyebrows, creating the map of Africa on his forehead, "Any thoughts Becky?" he says.

"My only thoughts at the moment Ron," she replies with a deep sigh, "are that Bo was not a person who would dismiss any challenge, so I could set him the challenge of finding me."

Lifting her eyebrows, and shrugging her shoulders, Becky says, *"If only I had the man who wrote this novel to help me."*

Becky and Ron leave the restaurant. The FBI agent is still talking to the bargirl and doesn't see them leave.

Ron keeps quiet, so as not to attract his attention. As they leave the area Ron punches the air. "Yes got rid of him! I always work better without a shadow."

Suddenly, a voice from behind startles him. "Mr Vice President I would appreciate it if you would work with us! It's for your own protection," says the six foot two agent, Ron stops dead in his tracks, spins round, his fists in a sparring position, ready to defend himself verbally, but with a bit of bravado as backup. Becky takes two more steps, then she too pivots round.

The lone FBI agent is very cock-sure of his actions, but as Becky spins she catches him, staring at her derriere.

"Don't be so disrespectful," she says, catching his eye line as he looks up. "I'm not a piece of meat for you to fantasize about, little man! Mr Champion and I have very private and personal issues to address, and given a choice I don't want you anywhere near me, I won't say please leave us. All I will say is leave us. Now!"

The agents' mouth drops open, his eyes wide in shock. He didn't expect that! He felt about two foot two, not six foot two.

Ron had lowered his fists. No need for that now, he thinks. The agent makes eye contact with Ron, and all Ron has to do is nod his head in an F-off expression, and the FBI agent turns tail and skulks off. Ron and Becky carry on to the communications office.

"I'm glad I wasn't on the end of that one Becky," says Ron smiling, Becky also smiles.

"I've had to put up with that most of my life Ron, and that response is one that I've practiced in the mirror many times."

Ron starts laughing as they enter the communications office, Becky is introduced to the manager of that department who sets up a personal recording booth for her to transcribe the information onto disk.

"OK Becky," said Ron, "I'll leave you here while I go and meet the President. Stay here until I get back."

"Thanks Ron," said Becky, and once he was gone,

she got down to business.

It's a pretty straight forward operation for Becky as she uses her office skills to transfer the information onto disk. But it's the words she can't get right. What if she couldn't convince Bo to look for her? It was an awful thought.

After some time, she finally comes up with the solution that she feels will fit every aspect of what events may occur.

Becky produces two copies of the disk, one for her and one to place in the time travel capsule. Calling across to the manager, she informs him that she has completed her task.

"Ok young lady," says the manager as he walks over. "Now what we need to do is fit the disk into one of these data transfer cassette holders." Becky watches him closely, making sure that no mistakes are made. The manager continues, "Then we insert a second blank disk into the cassette which sits alongside the master copy." He carries out that task then closes the device shut and locks it, turning the package over he points out that a message can be embossed on the cartridge in the box provided 'if you so wish'.

Becky finds this amusing, "Right," she says, "in the box provided…"

The manager frowns, points his finger at the cassette. "Yes," he repeats, "in the box provided."

Becky smiles, thinking, *my sense of humor must have hit a generation gap there.*

The manager then inserts the cartridge into the

reader and printer device that will emboss a message into the *'box provided'*.

Becky punches the keys 'PRIVATE AND CONFIDENTIAL. BO NICK OLSEN', taking the cassette out of the printer, Becky looks over it. There is a plastic cap clipped over the forward end of the package covering a bank of electrical connections.

"Could you please explain what I'm looking at here?" asks Becky as she is examining the cassette. "I know this will sit in the black box, but why is there such an elaborate way of storing it?"

The manager shrugged, shuffling his feet a little in a nervous fidget.

"What?" asked Becky, frowning.

"Look, young lady," the manager says eventually, "I don't know if I should tell you this, but we've had full instructions from Dr Banner as to what he requires in the White House communications box. We've had to go through all our inventories to ensure that the items being used in this section of the project, have been manufactured before the estimated time period that the missile will arrive back to planet Earth – six months prior."

Becky, looks very intrigued at the lovely little man, she gestures with her hands to encourage him to continue.

"So, everything you're looking at existed before that moment in time. This, Dr Banner says, is a precaution to ensure that nothing will just dissolve into a soup of mixed-up atoms as time travels backwards." He edged closer to Becky, whispering his next words, "You know, it's not very often I meet someone who I can really talk to, someone who thinks the same as I do." He placed his hand on Becky's knee. "Do you think the same as I do?"

Becky tensed up, though she managed a small smile. She could feel the heat coming from his hand through her skirt, and his face was beginning to shine as perspiration leaked through his pores. Ignoring his question, she said, "Please go on. Then what happens?"

As a precaution to ensure his hand doesn't wander, Becky places hers over his. She smiles, holding his hand tight. She repeats, "Then what happens?"

He is now having a problem with his breathing. Reaching into his jacket pocket with his free hand, he takes out his inhaler, and after a few deep puffs on the device, his blood pressure comes back down from ultra-silly to just silly. He nervously smiles at Becky, praying he's not going to have his predicted heart attack, well not just yet, anyway.

He continues, "Well the only thing that has not been produced before that moment in time is…" he waves his free hand over the items on the table.

Becky realizes where this is going, gripping his hand tighter to stop it shaking, she speaks up, "The messages we have added to the disks."

Becky lifts his hand from her knee as her leg is becoming damp and uncomfortable.

"I knew you'd think the same as I do," he continues. "When the black box is first opened – and before any actions can be taken using its contents – a code has to be entered to activate the data transfer cassette holders; this ensures that the information you are all sending back, will, for a second time, be recorded, so whatever changes happen in the timeline continuum, it will never be lost as it's copied and preserved in the so-called *'real time'*."

Standing up, the manager opens a normal black box which is sat on the table. "This is a bad example to show you but inside the box you're using there is a bank of electrical plug-in connections. All you do is remove the plastic dust cover off the cartridge, line it up to the electrical receiver, push, and it will snap tight into the retaining brackets."

Becky peers into the empty black box, having to use her imagination to picture what the manager was describing.

He continues, "Now, I'd appreciate it if you didn't tell anyone I've been giving you top secret information," he said, a little sheepishly. "If Dr Banner found out, I'd be in for it."

Becky smiled. "So why did you tell me?"

The manager laughed nervously, staring down at the ground. "I've always been a sucker for a pretty face."

Feeling less disturbed and more flattered by the guy now, Becky leaned over and kissed him on the cheek. "Thank you for your help. And don't worry about Josh Banner – leave him to me." With that she picked up the cartridge, slipped it into a velvet sleeve, and placed it in her shoulder bag.

The manager – who was still blushing from the kiss – glanced up at her. "You know Dr Banner?"

Without saying a word, Becky winks at him, turning to leave the communications department.

Knowing that she is leaving one very happy little man to his dreams. Job done.

Very satisfied with her evening's work, Becky settles down in the reception area with a coffee and a bite to eat, where she knew Ron would see her. After waiting for half an hour, however, the early morning and the stress of the past twenty-four hours started to catch up with her. Soon, she was fast asleep.

Happy with her thoughts, she began to dream of Bo on the beach in San Diego, trying to jump the waves as they crash onto the shore. Becky's arms are full of clothing, just watching Bo living the dream on the water's edge, *what is it about this man that makes you warm to him?*

"Becky, Becky," came a sudden voice, making her jump. She looked behind her on the beach – there was no one there.

She can hear a voice and now feel her arm being touched and shaken, "Becky, Becky."

Ron had arrived back at the reception area. Due to circumstances he had been longer than he expected, and was trying to wake her.

"Are you OK Becky? We've got a problem. Becky are you with me?" As Ron wakes her from her sleep, she drops all the imaginary clothes she was holding, onto the imaginary beach.

"Bo," she shouts out, "here's a towel for you." Her eyes open and sat holding her out-stretched hand, is Ron.

He was standing next to her. "Sorry, I didn't mean to startle you. We've got a problem."

Becky was immediately alert. "What is it?"

Ron ran his hand over his face, feeling the stubble on his chin. "The President has turned down my request to reopen the black box."

"He's what?" says Becky, knowing full well what Ron had just said, but was hoping that she was mistaken.

"His concerns were that if it was only for my personal reasons, then he could not risk damaging or contaminating the contents, as we have no time to replace the disks. I'm sorry, Becky," said Ron, who did indeed look incredibly regretful. He reached out, taking her hands in his. "I can understand the President's view, but I know that doesn't help you. Anyway, the black box has already been moved – earlier than I was told – and it's en-route to Cape Canaveral as we speak."

Becky could feel her eyes filling with tears. She couldn't believe this! To come so close to getting Bo back – or trying to, at least – only to have her hopes dashed at the last minute… It was devastating.

Standing up, Ron places his hands onto Becky's shoulders and with a meaningful expression on his face he continues, "Right Becky. How well do you know Josh Banner? I know you've worked with him for many years, but how well do you really know him?"

"Josh Banner?" Becky is puzzled. "Well, he's a good friend and colleague. Sometimes he can be a bit difficult, but so can most people. Once upon a time he was a bit sweet on me, but I didn't encourage him. He fell out with me a bit at that time, but other than that we get on very well. Why? What is the significance with Josh?"

Becky is trying to evaluate the meaning behind this new direction of thinking. She observes Ron, he is deep in thought.

"Becky, please listen," Ron says determinedly, "I have one last plan. If you can get in touch with Banner, do you think he would help you?"

"Ron, I'm sorry, but what can Josh Banner help me with?"

Ron paused then, looking around them as though checking the coast was clear. Noticing the change in his demeanor, Becky leans forwards.

"Well Becky, I cannot interfere in this as it would raise too many suspicions, but Josh Banner is at Cape Canaveral waiting for the black box to be delivered, so he can fit it inside the time travel missile. I know this because Bo arranged it all before… Well before he was…"

Becky rests her hand on Ron's arm. "Don't worry Ron."

Cautiously, he slips his hand into his jacket pocket, his eyes fixed onto Becky's teary face.

Becky feels something is about to happen, and one last ray of hope begins to erupt from her heart as Ron takes from his pocket a re-sealable foil envelope and passes it quickly to Becky.

"This is a set of Presidential seals for the black box. I've had them officially date stamped, and this…" he said as he pulled a small parcel out of his other jacket pocket, "is the tool you'll need to remove the existing seals on the black box we fitted yesterday, and to refit the new set." He passed the small box to Becky.

She was staring at him intently, hope now rushing through her entire body.

Ron, feeling the emotions of a father figure continues, "Right Becky this is what you need to do, you must get into Cape Canaveral's rocket propulsion center."

With a look of desperation on his face, he continues, "You know the set up in these establishments, play the game Becky." Her facial expression now matches Ron's – *desperate*. "Banner is an intelligent man, he knows what's at stake here, try and get to him, try and appeal to his beliefs of right and wrong. Ask him for help."

Adrenaline is now rushing through Becky's body, pushing her on, *whatever it takes I must try to do this. But how? I'm on my own now. Think Becky. Think!*

Ron's arms drop to his sides. He continues, – "It's worth a shot Becky – we don't have any other options on the table."

Becky composes herself. "Right Ron if the black box is on its way then I should be." Becky grabs her raincoat, getting ready to leave.

His expression still serious, Ron takes out of his pocket a government pass that features all of Becky's details. "I've taken the information from your time travel complex files and had a friend of mine transfer them onto this pass. It will get you so far into Cape Canaveral, though how far, I'm afraid I don't know. I'm sorry, Becky, but it's the best I could put together in such a short space of time."

Becky reaches forward and gently places her fingers over Ron's lips, "Don't you ever say sorry to me, Ron," whispered Becky, her eyes sparkling under the bright lights. "Without you I would never have got this far. I know you care, I really do. When you become The President of the United States, your torch will shine so bright, the people will follow, and I wish I could be there with you."

A small smile appears on Ron's lips. "I wish I could do more, I really do."

Nodding, Becky slips the seals, the tool, and the pass into her shoulder bag.

"There is a White House limo parked outside for you Becky, and you're booked on the 20.35 flight out. I knew you'd have to go for this." Ron reaches out both arms to embrace Becky, holding her close he whispers, "We may never meet again Becky, but if this succeeds, who knows…"

The two friends part, for the last time.

Perhaps.

Chapter 21

Becky, is that you?

The taxi ride from the airport helped Becky regain her thoughts, though after trying and failing to get in touch with Josh, she was starting to get nervous. How was she going to play this? Was there even a chance she could pull this off? And how on Earth was she going to contact Josh, let alone find him when she got to Cape Canaveral?

The flight from Washington had helped Becky catch up with some rest. After freshening up and a change of clothes at the airport upon her arrival, she now felt ready to tackle the next set of hurdles – though how high they'd be was anybody's guess.

Her taxi arrived at the huge engineering complex – on the Cape's launch site. It was allowed into a secured entrance causeway, where a two man security team approached the vehicle.

Dressed in a very well fitting three-piece pinstripe suit, a white shirt, and a black tie with a classic Windsor knot, Becky looked distractingly attractive, and every inch the professional lady she was.

Stepping out of the taxi, she placed her favorite six-inch-heel stilettos on the ground – after all, she needed all the help she could get, and these shoes always, always got people's attention.

The security men are caught off guard, they didn't expect to see the vision before them. Marching very militarily towards the taxi, the one on the right stumbled from seeing Becky, catching one size ten on the other and down he went. His colleague could do nothing but laugh as his friend was sprawled out on the concrete. To hide her smile Becky held the fingers of her right hand to her lips. The taxi driver was practically crying with laughter.

Suddenly, Becky realized that the man on the ground was injured, she rushed across to help him, and both she and his colleague helped him up onto his feet. He had taken the skin off the palms of his hands as he scraped them over the concrete. Blood was flowing quite rapidly from his open wounds.

Springing into action, Becky ran over to the taxi, taking out the first aid kit she'd noticed on the ride over. She then began applying sterilizing lotion and bandages to the man's hands, who was trying very hard not to whimper. As the lotion stung his exposed flesh, however, he yelped out in anguish.

"Come on, Logan, be a man!" his friend said, making Becky smile.

"No pain, no gain," she said, the injured man laughing in response.

After returning the first aid kit and paying the taxi driver, Becky rushed back over to the injured man, helping him to the security office along with his colleague.

As they enter that area the two men go straight in, but Becky has to step through a metal detector which of course, sounds the alarm. As the ice has already been broken over the man falling, she is not refused entry, but is asked to step into the office. All the guys look up as she sweeps in, a comfortable chair is brought across for her to sit at the security manager's desk. *Had they never seen a woman before?* Becky thought to herself.

The manager thanks Becky for looking after the injured guard who had been taken to the medical center, then he says, "He's only a young kid, I don't really know what was up with him." Becky smiles. "Or maybe I do… Sorry, sorry I didn't mean any disrespect, sorry, what can I do to help you?" says the manager, spluttering his apologies.

Becky lifts her shoulder bag up on to her knee.

"I'm Becky Fining, and…"

One of the guards' interrupts, "I've poured you out a nice cup of coffee Miss," as he places it down on the desk in front of her.

"Thank you that's very kind. Oh, and it's Becky."

The Manager looks up at the guard. "What are you doing Fletcher?"

"Just getting the lady a drink Sir." Becky is smiling at both men with an expression of amusement on her face.

By this time Becky has got the pass out that Ron had given her, handing it across to – "Sorry I didn't catch your name," says Becky.

"It's Steve, oh, and I would just like to check the contents of your bag to see what set the alarm off, if you don't mind that is," replies the manager. He takes the pass off Becky as she is emptying the contents of her bag.

There's no point in trying to hide anything as everything is an official item, the only thing she does need to keep secret is the purpose of why she is there.

Steve spots the foil envelope, "It will be this that set the alarm off Becky. If I can call you Becky?" he says opening the parcel, which allows one of the copper disks to slip out on to the desk. It lands face up showing the White House Eagle symbol. "Oh you're from the White House!"

Becky is thinking fast, if he thinks I'm from the White House then who am I to argue? "Yes Steve, I need to see Doctor Josh Banner. It's very urgent."

Steve looks closely at the fake pass, seemingly scrutinizing every letter, looking up at her, then back down to the pass.

Becky waited, her heart thumping in her chest. What had he noticed? She hadn't had time to study it properly. Perhaps it says *Time Travel Complex, San Diego*, she hadn't checked. But she remembered Ron saying that was the file where he had got the details from, and copied them across to the fake pass. Now more nervous than ever, she held her breath as she waited for the manager to speak.

Steve looks up once more, "The thing is," he said, hesitating and making Becky's heart leap into her throat, "you won't get very far on this pass. Fletcher!"

he yelled, as he is checking his computer for Dr Banner's whereabouts. "Take Miss Fining to see Doctor Banner, would you? He's in loading bay five."

The nauseous feeling that had been working its way through Becky's body suddenly faded away, and she watched in relief as the manager placed the copper disk back into the envelope. *The good guys are on my side today,* she thinks. After issuing an official day security pass with her details on, he hands everything back to her.

"Thank you," she replies, hardly believing her luck.

"You're welcome. Now, Fletcher, take my car; we can't have Miss Fining traveling in that rattling old Jeep."

Smiling again at the manager, Becky left with Fletcher, and soon they were pulling up outside loading bay five.

"The entrance is just through those doors on the right," says Fletcher.

"Thank you so much, and thank you for the coffee." She pats the back of his hand as it rests on the gear-shift lever. Smiling at him, Becky then leaves the vehicle.

Fletcher watches her walk across to the entrance doors, there's so much elegance in the way she moves. Looking down at his hand he imagines Miss Fining's hand still resting on his, a stupid smile appearing on his lips.

Becky was smiling too – phase one: complete.

*

The start of Josh's day hadn't been quite as

eventful as Becky's, but nonetheless it was all happening in the place where dreams were made.

The entire team had been rocked by the dramatic events at the White House, which had robbed the project of their driving force. Shell-shocked and disturbed, his friends and colleagues had stepped up their efforts; none of them wanted Bo's unexpected and violent death to be in vain.

The time travel capsule was now being prepared for launch by NASA technicians, who were testing, checking, and double-checking all of the circuitry. Every system had to work perfectly – they couldn't afford any mistakes. They had one shot at this, one short window of weather before the time travel capsule absolutely *had* to be in orbit if they wanted it to get back in time to save the RAF transport plane.

Following the bungled attempt to substitute the black box at the White House, no one was taking any chances with security anymore.

Needless to say, the man who was meant to have been keeping watch over the black box had been fired on the spot, and the Vice President had given that job to a team of no less than six people. The capsule itself was being kept safe in a sealed container, away from prying eyes and away from anyone else who might have it in mind to stop this mission.

With a heavy heart, Doctor Josh Banner was overseeing things, moving from team to team and working with the dedicated NASA technicians.

He looked up as a group of NASA security officers and Secret Service agents approached, carrying the black box containing all of the information relevant to the mission. Josh eyed it, aware of what it had already cost them to protect the co-ordinates of the destroyed RAF transport plane, the information about the death of Princess Diana, and – now – a carefully worded addendum that was close to all of their hearts.

It was concealed inside a non-descript wooden packing case, for safety's sake.

There was a sort of reverent silence between the two groups of security men, born out of respect for one another. The NASA technicians, too, were quiet, each for their own reasons.

"We need to see that all the Presidential seals are intact," said Josh, somberly. "Has the packing case been opened at all?"

"No Sir, we've come straight from the White House," said the most senior Secret Service agent present. "I've been with it at all times, Sir. No one has tampered with it."

They handed the case over to Josh, who opened it carefully and examined the black box inside. Satisfied that all four Presidential seals were intact and that all the date stamps were accurate, he nodded. "A good man gave his life for this mission, so the least we can do is dot all the 'i's, and cross all the t's," he said. "I'll have to ask you gentlemen to leave now – security protocol. You understand?"

He watched as the Secret Service agents left, escorted by grim-faced NASA security officers. Then, turning his head back towards the capsule, a figure crossed his path – a very familiar figure indeed. "Becky, is that you?" he whispered, as she stepped forward out of the darkness.

"Hello Josh," she said, smiling, "I see you've almost got your creation ready for launch."

"Becky, I'm so sorry for you over the loss of Bo." Embracing her, he turns to the security guard who had accompanied Becky saying, "Please leave now, I will take full responsibility for this lady."

Becky now had unfamiliar feelings of emotion as her eyes began to fill with tears. She couldn't believe that she had got this far and now all she had to do was convince Josh to help her over this final hurdle.

"Josh," she said after a moment or so, "we need to talk." She pulled back from the hug. "I want you to listen to what I have to say, without interrupting me."

Holding Becky at arm's length, Josh studied her face. He'd never seen her like this in all the years they'd known each other, and he was pretty sure it wasn't just because of Bo's death. There was something else going on here.

Nodding, Josh let go of Becky and walked over towards the capsule. "Time out, you guys. Take twenty." Then, he covered the black box and the missile, instructing a guard to stay with the equipment.

Josh then takes Becky to a rest area that is pretty quiet, organizes two coffees and settles back to hear what Becky has to say.

Taking a grateful sip of the hot coffee, Becky proceeds to tell Josh everything that had happened to her over the past couple of days – all the help she'd been given by Ron Champion, recording the message to Bo, to tell him that she was waiting for him to find her, the President refusing to let them add anything to the capsule, everything.

Taking the velvet pouch out of her bag, Becky looked pleadingly at Josh. "So will you please help me get this data transfer cassette holder into the black box? I've got all the replacement copper seals, and the tool to refit them. I've only got this one chance! Please, Josh."

Sighing, Josh took a few seconds to think it over, eventually saying, "The thing is, Becky, I really believe that this will work – I really do – and if I help you, I may get in trouble…"

Becky could feel the tears coming back in her eyes. "Please, Josh," she said again. "You can see how much this means to me."

Josh stared at Becky, and after a couple of seconds, the corner of his mouth turned up in a cheeky grin. "What the hell, let's do it. But we have to be careful."

Becky could have kissed him, but instead she just gave him her winning smile. "Thank you, Josh, thank you!"

After finishing their coffees, Josh and Becky returned to the crate that held the black box.

"You can leave now," Josh instructed the guard, who left without even questioning the demand.

Once he'd walked away, Josh removed the lid of the crate, exposing the black box. Carefully, Becky took the tool and the replacement copper disks from her bag, before passing Josh the removal cutters. She felt like they were conducting a surgical operation in a hospital theater – they couldn't let even a single thing go wrong.

Josh used the cutters to snap the four copper seals, freeing the hinged lid of the box, which he then lifted up. Revealed below was the protective cushioned pad, which he removed.

Looking at the ultra-tough black glass panel, Josh reaches into his pocket and takes out a pair of fine silk gloves. Putting the gloves on, he begins to release the retaining clips to lift off the panel, being extremely careful not to damage the wiring looms. He placed it on the black box's open lid, the whole thing rocking and beginning to fall when he let it go. Josh's heart skipped a beat, but Becky, quick thinking as always, placed her hand on it, making sure it was safe.

"Thank you," Josh whispered, before focusing back on his task. But at the back of his mind he knew that a procedure should have started when Becky's fingers touched the glass panel. He decided not to say anything as Becky would have been heartbroken if she had known there was another problem to overcome.

There were ten electrical plug-in connection slots in the device, but only six were being used. "Give me the cassette holder," he said, and Becky obliged.

Before handing him the velvet pouch, however, she lifted it up to her lips and gave it a short, sweet kiss. "Good luck Bo," she whispered, before giving it to Josh.

Josh slid the cartridge out of the pouch, removed the dust cover, and lined it up with the electrical receiver. Pushing it forward, it snapped into place, the retaining bracket locking around it.

That was simple enough, thought Josh, as he looked over the device as a whole. So many thousands of connections. Which one is it…

"Yes, Yes! Found it" he said, noticing a small wire that had come adrift from the battery pack. It was the link connecting two of the battery pods, and it was extremely important. "It's a good job we're doing this, Becky," he said, trying to keep calm. "If we hadn't opened the black box again and discovered this bad connection, the whole thing would have been a waste of time."

"Oh, I don't know," said Becky, smiling, "I believe Bo is looking after things for us."

Smiling, Josh reconnected the cable before checking it was a tight fit. He redressed the wiring loom then lifted the glass panel back into place, securing it with the retaining clips. Job done.

"Thank you, Josh," Becky said sincerely. She could immediately feel a huge weight being lifted off her shoulders.

"You're welcome," he replied as he placed the protective pad back and closed the box.

Becky passed Josh the replacement copper seals and he began to refit each one individually. He was nearly done when they heard voices approaching – the engineers returning from their break. Throwing a meaningful look at Becky, Josh continued refitting the seals – he just needs a few more seconds… Becky pivots round, the three men are only yards or so away.

"Ah, gentlemen!" she started, "On behalf of the President of the United…" She trailed off, starting to cough violently. "Water!" she spluttered, "Can someone get me…"

One of the men rushed off to the rest area to get some water while the other two helped Becky over to a seat.

"Are you OK, lady?" asked one of the engineers, and she managed a quick nod before the other man came back with a small bottle of water.

"Ah! Thank you, thank you," Becky said, taking a small sip of water. "Oh, thank you. That saved the day." She glanced over at Josh, who was standing next to the crate, with that smile on his face that said, *mission accomplished*. "Yes," she continued as she stood up, "I just wanted to say, on behalf of the President, that he'd like to thank you for all your efforts in this project."

"OK lads, let's get this show on the road!" Josh said enthusiastically.

Going over to Josh, two of the engineers lifted the black box out of the crate. Feigning interest in the object – as if she'd never seen it before – Becky walked over too, and when she looked down into the crate and saw the split copper disks lying in the bottom, she caught Josh's eye, nodding down at them.

Just then, the third technician – who'd seen Becky's strange gesture – moved over to the crate, and thinking fast, Becky beamed at him, staring at him intently.

He immediately changed course, walking over to Becky and smiling back, as though about to try his luck.

"Adam," Josh said, interrupting their little moment, "give me a hand to open the missile, would you?"

A little reluctantly, Adam proceeded to help Josh, giving Becky the chance to collect the damaged seals from the bottom of the crate. She slipped them into her pocket, then winked at Josh when she was sure Adam wouldn't see her. He smiled back in relief.

Becky watched as they installed the precious black box in the time travel missile, her stomach churning in excitement as she imagined Bo receiving her message.

Once it was secure, Josh laid a hand over it, closing his eyes for a moment. "God bless America. This one's for Olsen," he murmured. "Alright," he said, "your turn."

The nearest NASA technician nodded and set about embossing an important message on the exterior of the craft. Josh stood back, watching him work.

This was a momentous day for America – and for science. It was, however, rather hard to be excited about it anymore, after it had cost the life of a man he had begun to think of as a friend.

At that moment, he felt a rush of gratitude for the dauntless, irascible man who had pushed them all into making this possible. It had hit them hard when they'd found out he'd been shot – particularly when they'd been told his assassin had been ineptly trying to replace the black box in the first place. What a waste.

His thoughts, of course, were also with Becky. In all the years he'd known her, she'd never managed to have a serious boyfriend, and then – by sheer chance – her knight in shining armor had come along. They seemed so happy together, but she'd only been able to hang on to him for a few precious months. It was just so unfair.

Josh glances round to see Becky, it was the happiest he'd seen her since she had arrived. "You've still got it, girl." Stepping closer, he took her hand. "We've done all we can," he said, "and I believe it will work."

Becky nodded back, smiling. She was currently unable to talk, so many emotions were whirling around inside her.

Getting back to work, Josh helped the technicians slot the missile into the magnetized force-field heat resistant shields that would protect it from the extreme heat and radiation produced by the sun. He also oversaw the progress of the installation of a friendly radar signal that would be recognized at the time it should arrive.

That was if everything went to plan, of course.

"Well," said Josh. "That's it. It's all up to God now."

The winches were engaged to transport the missile down to the decontamination area, then made ready for loading onto the Shuttle.

Josh and Becky watched it go.

"I can't believe I'm here doing this, it's a boyhood dream. Isn't it funny though, I feel we have all grown up in these past few months," says Josh.

Chapter 22

Oh shut up, you blithering idiot

Ron is leaning against a window frame in his bedroom at the American Embassy, looking out over the rooftops of London as the rain pours down. *Another shitty grey day*, he thinks, drinking his first cup of coffee.

The Vice President is dressed very smartly knowing it will give him an edge in the meeting that is to follow.

His mind begins to drift, *one thing I would like to do, is own a ranch in Texas. That would be something so rewarding, I would love that. Or maybe I could just retire and sit on a beautiful open deck porch, looking out over…*

"Mr Champion" … *my orchards…* "Mr Champion!" … *and the flower beds…*

He felt someone tapping him on his shoulder.

"Mr Champion, Sir are you Ok?" Ron looks round, startled, an Embassy aide had been trying to attract his attention, "You Ok Mr Champion?

Breakfast is being served in the dining room if you would care to follow me, Sir."

Picking up Ron's jacket he pulls a few imaginary threads off the shoulder then presents it to Ron who slides his arms into the sleeves.

"I don't get this sort of treatment at the White House," said Ron, amused, "or at home, for that matter."

"No Sir? Well, we like to look after our guests here. Please follow me."

Ron settles in for breakfast, he always enjoys his full English of bacon, eggs, sausages, fried bread, mushrooms, tomatoes, and even a small piece of black pudding. Delicious.

Eric – the American Diplomat to London – invites Ron to sit with him. He looks down enviously at Ron's plateful, as he is pushing *Cornflakes* around his bowl. He even has low fat milk, thinking I must be doing the right thing here. As long as I don't get run over by a Limo, *I must be winning.* "You always have that for breakfast when you're over here Ron. I don't know how you can eat it I honestly don't."

Looking down at his friends unexciting, uninviting bowl of wet cardboard. Ron's replies, "I love this, it's the highlight of my visit. They won't let me have it back in the States, what with my blood pressure and high cholesterol."

"I'm not surprised," replies Eric, "there must be half a pound of lard there."

With breakfast over, Ron briefs Eric over the forthcoming meeting. "I need you there Eric just for moral support. Something unpleasant is about to happen."

"When the going gets tough, Ron, the tough get going," said Eric, trying to lighten the mood.

Just then, an aide approached their table. "All your guests have arrived, Sir. We have shown them into the end state room, as you requested."

Ron acknowledges the statement, "Thank you."

Eric enquires, "Why have you put them in there Ron?"

Ron gives a crafty grin. "Well Eric, what have we got in there?"

Eric thinks for a moment. "Nice antique tables, chairs, beautiful decorations. Yes, no? It's a nice room to entertain Royalty."

"Yes Eric it has all that, but you're missing something." Ron smiles. "It has the biggest American Flag we have here draped down the wall at the head of the table, so when I am sat there everyone will be looking at the Stars and Stripes behind me, looking so dominant. Tactics Eric. Tactics. Remember Kennedy and Cuba?"

Eric shook his head, laughing.

The two friends marched into the meeting like men on a mission. Ron had been high up in politics for long enough to know that there was a permanent game of cloak and dagger going on – even between friendly countries – but he had lost a friend in Washington, and he had a reasonable idea of where to lay the blame.

There were several people in London who would

be smarting when he was done with them. He just wished he'd been able to get here sooner.

Waiting for him – and looking pretty annoyed and bewildered – were the British Deputy Prime Minister; Samuel Graves, the Director of MI6; and William Harcourt, the oafish British Foreign Secretary, along with several other high ranking politicians and their aides. Shuffling about in the splendor of the room where they had been escorted to, they looked up to see a man fired with righteous anger.

Given that the American Vice President was generally an easy-going sort of person, this level of anger took them aback, and they exchanged nervous glances, much like soldiers about to go into battle.

Not wasting time on pleasantries, Champion sat at the head of the table, with Eric to his right, and the Stars and Stripes hanging proudly behind them. The door was closed as the invited guests settled down to take their seats. Each and every one of them seemed utterly nonplussed.

Ron gives it a few seconds, then standing he takes the floor to complete silence.

"I want answers!" he snapped, banging his fist on the table. Several people jumped. "The President is going to make an official request to your Prime Minister for a top level meeting between just the two of them, and believe me when I tell you he'll be spraying the brown stuff all over the room!" He shook his head, incensed. "My job is to make sure it doesn't come to that, do you understand me?"

He wanted answers, but it was fairly obvious from their baffled expressions that hardly anyone on the

British side of the table knew what he was talking about. The Director of MI6, however, had gone very pale, rather giving the game away.

"I don't have to look too far to see who is the guilty party in this room, do I, Samuel?" Champion growled. "I knew you'd be behind this." He'd met Graves several times throughout his career, and every time he'd come away with the distinct impression that he was a deeply unlikable man. As it turned out, he'd been right all along.

As the two men made eye contact, there were a few seconds of silence. The Vice President rocked forward, pivoting on both fists as they rested on the tabletop, the vein in the side of his temple pulsing rapidly. He looked furious.

"For Christ's sake, Graves, what the actual fuck have you been doing?" he demanded. "Two men died! *Evans*, Graves, *Evans* – does that name mean anything to you? No?" He shook his head, frustrated. "We knew Evans was working for you – we've known for years – but it's just a bit of tit for tat. You have people in our organization, we have people in yours. That's how it works."

There was a long moment of silence, everyone's eyes glued to either the Vice President or the Director of MI6. Ron watched the other man carefully; he could almost see the moment when he decided that his career was over – the spark in his eyes went out, leaving behind a dull, ugly, muddy brown color.

"Clear the room of unnecessary people, Ron," said Graves, tightly.

Champion nodded and all the aides vanished,

deciding that on the whole, they didn't want to know – in some jobs, the less information you were privy to, the better. The Deputy Prime Minister and the British Foreign Secretary watched them go, puzzled and more than a little rattled at what was unfolding in front of them.

"We can no longer keep this conspiracy going," said Graves, heavily. "I need to make a clean slate of it, whatever the cost."

"What do you mean, make a clean slate of it?" asked the Deputy Prime Minister, sharply. "Samuel, what have you done?"

"Go ahead, Graves," said the Vice President. "It's a good question, and one that I'd very much like the answer to as well. The floor is yours. Tell us: what the hell have you lot been doing? I mean, we had a Wild West goddamn shootout inside the White House last week involving the President. I was there! I watched him standing toe to toe with an armed madman, a madman that hailed from these very shores. I swear to God, if he'd shot him you guys would be re-opening those old underground bunkers beneath Whitehall to hide from us! Right now, we'd be fighting World War Three!" He was almost spitting he was so furious.

"I know, Ron," moaned the Director of MI6. "I know, I know. I cannot apologize enough – Bo Nick Olsen sacrificed his life to save the President. I can't tell you how sorry we are. A very brave man – and he wasn't even an American!"

Ron shook his head, remembering his friend's face as he died. 'Sorry' really wasn't going to cut it. Not here, not now – maybe not ever. There was just no coming back from something like that. Usually.

"Look, Ron, we know all the details of what you lot are trying to do and there is no way we can allow you to change history. The implications are too far-reaching," said Graves, bluntly. "Things have happened in a certain way because we wanted them to – the time travel missile had to fail – it just had to."

"Time travel missile?" the British Foreign Secretary interrupted. "What are you talking about? There's no such bloody thing! You never told me about this the last time we spoke – for Christ's sake. Graves, does this thing actually exist?" he carried on without waiting for an answer, "When I told you what Ron had said about them having all the time in the world, you replied with a huff and a puff, saying it was typical of them. Bloody Yanks! They've no respect for protocol. Arrogant and slipshod, it was all a load of rubbish!"

"Oh shut up, you blithering idiot," Graves exclaimed, turning a furious glare on the British Foreign Secretary. "You politicians are all the fucking same! You lot think that you run this country, but it's people like me and the Civil Service who keep it running and keep it safe. You have no bloody idea what it takes, now shut your stupid, privileged, molly-coddled mouth!"

There was a slight pause, and Ron Champion almost laughed – would have, if the circumstances had been different. It was no secret that he and Harcourt didn't get on – especially after the rather public argument at the White House (luckily without anyone actually hearing what they were saying) – and it was good to see him get knocked down a peg or two. It almost made this trip worth it in itself.

Pulling his gaze away from Harcourt, Ron looked around the table. The Deputy Prime Minister's eyebrows had vanished into his hairline. Going by the man's expression, after today Samuel Graves would most likely be pensioned off to some obscure, countryside backwater where no one knew his name. He was out, and he knew it, which made him unpredictable and dangerous.

Ron had dealt with men like this before, and it hardly ever ended well.

The British Foreign Secretary, for his part, looked like he might actually explode. Wisely, however, he kept his mouth shut for the moment, possibly sensing the jeopardy he would likely be in if he said anything.

"Our attempt to disrupt your plans by exchanging the black box that was to go on the time travel missile was in an effort to prevent you from screwing up months of undercover work," said Graves, sounding angry. "We were ordered to ensure that the future King's mother would never marry her boyfriend, who was a Muslim. There were rumors of an engagement and we had to stop it before it could be announced."

He continued. "Needless to say, the operation didn't go quite as we had planned. The outcome was regrettable, but ultimately unavoidable. Afterwards…" he trailed off and shook his head, scrubbing his hands wearily across his face. "When I figured out that the time travel missile had been commissioned, in an attempt to save the transport plane, and the Princess I realized we had to stop you at all costs. We couldn't allow you to have so much power. To change history. *Are you mad?*"

Graves paused to catch his breath. "It may not work, of course," his tone here indicating that if it *did* work, he would eat his hat, "but we just couldn't take that chance."

The British Foreign Secretary – who was sitting next to his MI6 colleague – was becoming increasingly incensed by the whole situation.

It wasn't just being treated like a child by the Head of MI6; it was the implication of the man's confession. Ron Champion watched as he slowly began to turn puce.

After a few seconds or so of mulling it over, Harcourt shot to his feet. "This has got nothing to do with our government, Mr Vice President," he assured Champion, angrily. "*Nothing!*"

He then swung around to face Graves. "What the *hell* have you done?" he shouted, incandescent with rage. "You murdered our Princess! The most loved Royal we've probably ever had! A national treasure! Someone's going to pay for this, I can tell you that right now. *Just who the hell do you think you are?*"

"That the Princess was killed in the car crash was unfortunate," said the Head of MI6, licking his lips nervously. "But in other respects, the operation was a success."

"*Unfortunate?* A bloody *success?*" Harcourt demanded, astonished. "You just murdered three people – one of whom was the Princess of Wales, for Christ's sake – as well as putting another one in hospital with brain damage, and you just calmly sit there and say it was *unfortunate*? Do you realize what you've actually done? Do you have even one shred of sanity in your entire body? Do you feel no remorse? No regret? No shame?"

Ron Champion almost laughed again, for the first time feeling a slight bit of warmth towards old Harcourt. At least he had his head on straight when it came to the ridiculous plan that had ultimately killed the Princess. He and Champion shared the same views on that part of this whole mess, at least.

The head of MI6 also got to his feet, clearly feeling threatened, and Champion watched the scene unfold before him with an air of resignation.

The Deputy British Prime Minister put his head in his hands, giving up entirely; things had escalated quickly, and to be honest, he wasn't entirely sure what was going on here. He was used to dealing with more mundane issues than this.

Champion sighed as Graves began to poke the British Foreign Secretary in the chest. Honestly, it was like he was back in elementary school. Both men's briefcases, dislodged by their movement, slid to the floor with a clatter.

"Look, we are where we are with this," Graves hissed, finally pulling back his finger and placing it on his lap under the table, as though worried it might start poking someone again, with a mind of its own. "It can't be helped! The Princess is dead and we can't change that! We have to find a way to move forward, so why don't we do that instead of sitting here rehashing the past?"

William Harcourt threw his hands up in a

'whatever' kind of gesture, but as he did he gently caught the edge of the other man's chin. It was barely a graze, but Samuel Graves didn't seem to realize this – or at least, he pretended not to.

He stood up, grasping the older man's lapels. "What do you think you're doing?" he roared, spit flying from his mouth and landing on Harcourt's cheek.

Very quickly, the entire room was in uproar.

"What the bloody hell?" cried the Deputy Prime Minister, astonished at what he was witnessing. Graves was most definitely becoming unhinged – and fast too. "Let's just all calm down, shall we?"

"*I am calm!*" shouted Graves, proving that he clearly, was anything but.

The Deputy Prime Minister then sprang to his feet and backed away to the wall, wisely deciding that there was nothing he could really do about the fight breaking out in the center of the room.

Several CIA agents – who had been posted outside the doors – responded to Harcourt's bellowing and rushed into the room in case the Vice President was in trouble. They did a professional sort of double take upon seeing the actual combatants involved in the fracas, then rushed to haul the two men apart.

The British Foreign Secretary allowed himself to be removed from the fight with something like relief before wiping the spit off his face with his sleeve. He and his new escorts then backed up a few paces, away from the still furious-looking Graves. The Director of MI6 appeared to have lost his mind, and he started attacking the CIA agents, throwing a punch at one of them and bloodying his nose in the process.

"What the fuck is wrong with you, Graves?" the Deputy Prime Minister cried, having to shout to make himself heard. "Stop it this instant, do you hear me?" He then ran over to Harcourt, who was still looking a little dazed by the whole thing. "Here, Will, sit down."

Ron Champion watched everything unfold with despair. *If this was how they did things in England, he thought he was much better off back in America.*

Graves was eventually restrained and held by three CIA officers, but there was still a tremendous atmosphere of tension and ill will in the room.

"Just sit back, old man," said the Deputy Prime Minister, helping the CIA agents treat the elderly British Foreign Secretary. "Just let them look after you."

"In all my years of politics, I have never witnessed anything like that!" Ron Champion exclaimed. "How you guys think you can preach at us for messing anything up after that display of infancy, I have no idea – I've seen better behavior in school children. More sense, too."

"I have to agree, Ron," said the Deputy Prime Minister. "That was absolutely bloody unacceptable, Graves! And after what you've just admitted – well, I think it's safe to say that you can kiss your position goodbye! You've become reckless and, frankly, a liability to your country. You should be ashamed."

Graves just stared at him, saying nothing.

"Shall I contact the British Police, Mr Vice President?" one of the agents asked.

"No," Champion said firmly. "No. The less publicity this debacle gets, the better. Just get their cars round to the front – these gentlemen are leaving."

"Thank you, Ron," said the Deputy Prime Minister, soberly. "And I can assure you that any action Samuel Graves has instigated has absolutely no support from the British government. This is the first I've heard about any of this, and I can only extend my sincere condolences over the loss of a good man." He shook his head and Ron Champion decided that he was telling the truth. Like his late friend Bo Olsen, he was good at reading people, after all.

"I'll have to confirm it with the Prime Minister, but I think the least we can do after this whole tragic episode is to support you in your Time Travel Project," he continued, though his voice wavered a little over the words 'time travel'. He sent a glare in Graves's direction.

"Whatever the MI6 have deluded themselves with, the rest of the UK would be ecstatic if you can somehow prevent the deaths of all of those RAF personnel – and our beloved Princess and her companions." He smiled. "Time travel... I never thought I'd see the day."

"Thank you," said Champion as they shook hands. "I think it's fairly obvious that the only person with any knowledge about the murder of my friend – and whatever happened in Paris – is Graves."

"He will be dealt with accordingly, I can assure you of that."

Champion nodded. "I'll have them call your car,

Sir," he said gravely, confident that he had made a sane ally at last. Well, there had to be at least one within the British government, he supposed.

He eyed William Harcourt, who looked a little worse for wear after being grabbed and hauled up to his feet. Then spat on. "Might be worth having the British Foreign Secretary sent home," he added, feeling a little sorry for him. As much as he usually disliked the man, he hadn't started the fight himself, and he had been just as appalled at Graves's admission as any normal person would be. "Everyone who has witnessed this – we need total discretion. Do you understand? *Total discretion*," added Champion.

The others nodded their assent, glad that this nightmare of a meeting was finally over.

Champion waited until a few of the agents had left the room to make arrangements before turning and addressing Graves, "Now, I don't want you to come near this building ever again, do you hear me, Mr Graves?" he barked. "And as for the Princess being dead, we're going to do all we can to ensure that the Time Travel Experiment succeeds. I can assure you of that."

"Don't," the Director of MI6 pleaded. "Don't – I beg you! Leave things as they are – you've got to. Tell the President that no good will come of this. You should just leave things as they are!"

The disastrous meeting ended with the Head of MI6 being forced out of the room and then the building, much to the surprise of every staff member they passed.

The Deputy Prime Minister and the British

Foreign Secretary then stepped outside the front door of the American Embassy together, one supporting the other, a strange kind of couple.

Graves attempted to continue the row, but Harcourt was having none of it. He hadn't joined politics just so he could be spat on by the likes of him. Without saying a word, he walked over to his car and got inside.

Ron Champion watched them go, sadly. It seemed so ridiculous – and Bo had died for this. It really was ludicrous.

He glanced up at the clouds above the city. Somewhere above them, the time travel missile was waiting in orbit, locked into its enormous launch pad. He knew they would be filling it with fuel as the shockwaves of the meeting died down, and that in a few days it would be propelled off to complete its goal.

They couldn't let it fail. There was too much to lose.

Shaking his head again, Champion went back inside.

Chapter 23

A Skeleton Crew

The time travel missile was in almost total darkness as the refueling shuttle approached the orbital launch pad.

The Shuttle – named the Enterprise in honor of the late Bo Nick Olsen and his passion for science fiction – was going through its last minute checks. They made their approach slowly, creeping up on the time travel missile as if they wanted to catch it by surprise.

There was a skeleton crew on board, because NASA had felt that this would be the most dangerous aspect of the whole Time Travel Project, and they weren't taking any chances with their staff. Loss of life on a NASA mission was an ever-present danger, of course, but their first priority was always the safety of their astronauts.

For the sake of transparency, NASA had divulged the dangerous nature of this mission, and they'd had only three astronauts volunteer for the potentially treacherous trip into space. Now these three astronauts were watching the stars above them, strapped securely into their seats in the Space Shuttle Enterprise.

For Chuck Mason, Shuttle Pilot; Eugene Cochrane, Crew Engineer; and Poppy Willis, Flight Lieutenant, this mission was anything but routine. Still, they had to keep morale up, and Poppy ran her operational checks cheerfully, humming as she carried them out. She was one of the few female astronauts in the space program, and she had put herself forward for this particular mission hoping it would be the start of many years of service working in space.

It was her lifelong dream, and in this job, if you wanted to stand out from the men, you had to show them you had balls. It was rather ironic, but it was true.

That was why she'd volunteered for this, and that was why they were going to sit up and take notice of her, no matter what happened. She thought she could afford to be a little cheerful.

She had wanted to be an astronaut ever since she was a little girl, and she had made that dream a reality by working two part-time jobs in order to put herself through school. She had trained long and hard beside her fellow applicants, pushing herself to the max to be part of the next wave of new astronauts. It hadn't been easy; although NASA was one of the most progressive organizations in the world, being a woman in an engineering class could be trying at times, and not just because of the work – because of the men too.

Luckily, Poppy was a hands-on, do anything type of woman. She was ambitious, and she was going to achieve her goals at NASA, she just knew it.

Her part of the mission was to couple up the refueling hoses to the time travel missile. It sounded relatively easy, but as with anything in space, it was not. As was standard procedure, she had been practicing the operation for the last month in the deep training pools, feeling the strain of working underwater – the closest simulation to working in a no-atmosphere situation they could get.

She was prepared, but nothing could prepare her for actually being in space, and she was currently fighting a wave of irrepressible excitement. This was her first time, and she was – quite literally – over the moon.

The shuttle's microphone crackled into life. "All OK, Houston," Chuck Mason announced. "That was one hell of a launch, always gives me a tingly feeling down low, if you know what I mean. You guys have done a great job."

Poppy rolled her eyes. "I think you can put that tingly feeling down to your blood pressure, Chuck."

"It's Captain Marvel to you, Cadet Willis," Chuck Mason grumbled. While he didn't think of himself as having a problem with women, it was a little weird going up into space with one, and it was safe to say he was having a bit of a hard time adjusting. He felt like he couldn't be himself, like he couldn't joke around like he usually did with the guys. Up here, you needed to feel good in order to work well, and he was usually the joker of the pack.

He was brought out of his thoughts by the crackle of the mic. *"Affirmative, Chuck – we see you on radar, looking good for approach."*

"Copy that, Houston, we can see her," said Chuck, all business now. "Radar says she's at the eight mile point, so I'm switching to on-board autopilot. Co-ordinates locked and loaded – here we go!"

Chuck focused on the instrument panel in front of him, concentrating on setting up the on-board computer. He was one of the best shuttle pilots in the team, and he'd jumped at the chance to go on this mission – a mission that most of his colleagues wouldn't even consider signing up for. He also had an ego the size of the sun, so no one was surprised when he volunteered for the job.

"We're reading your input there, Chuck. All looking fine," Houston responded, before adding, *"message from the Controller – don't give Poppy any grief or he'll be on the phone to your wife. Copy that, Chuck?"*

"Ooh, Poppy," he said, careful to turn off the radio first. "Poppy, you're the girl of my dreams! You'd better start changing your gear for your space walk on the robotic arm – let me know if you need any help with that!"

"No help needed, thank you," said Poppy sharply. "Don't think I haven't heard those rumors about your octopus hands – you can keep them well away from me, Mason. Hey, Eugene, help me, will you? Keep Captain Dick away from me."

"Copy that, Poppy," said Eugene Cochrane. "Don't worry about Chuck; he's always like this when he's away from the wife. I'll protect you." He laughed, trying to lighten the mood. "Well, we better get suited up together. No rush, though: one hour to rendezvous point."

"You'll be safe there, Poppy," Mason joked. "With a name like *'Eugene'* he's got to be a transvestite anyway."

"Shut up, Captain Dick," said Eugene, almost lazily. "You wouldn't even know how to spell transvestite, never mind recognize one if you fell over him."

Chuck Mason laughed. At least Eugene got the banter, even if Poppy hadn't quite warmed up to it yet. He and Eugene were actually best friends – had been since the day they met – and he was sure that in the future, he and Poppy would be good friends too. Well, maybe not in the *immediate* future…

The journey went on, and after a while – once the banter had died down a bit – Poppy and Eugene got suited up with their spacesuits in the rear compartment of the shuttle, testing out all the accessories and components of their equipment and ensuring that they'd be fully functional in the ravages of space.

As beautiful as space was, it could become deadly very quickly and very easily. This they all knew, but it wasn't until you were actually *in* space that you really began to believe it.

They felt the shuttle begin to slow down as Chuck's voice came over the radio, his joking manner replaced by true professionalism. It was something of a relief all-round.

"Eugene, Poppy – approach to missile in 10, 9, 8, 7, 6, 5, 4, 3, 2, 1 – and all stop. View's looking good, can you see her?"

Poppy whistled appreciatively. "That thing sure is pretty, boys!" She grinned as she checked out the orbital installation, and any doubts she may have had about coming on this mission abruptly vanished. This would be one hell of a dinner party anecdote.

"Sure can, Chuck," said Eugene. "Doesn't she look magnificent? Poppy, how are you doing? Nervous, I bet."

"Not bad, Eugene. This is it," she said, excited and raring to go. "This is what I've been training for all these years. I've wanted to do this my whole life!" She took a deep breath, trying to get her excitement under control. She had to be professional now, and if Chuck Mason could do it, then so could she. "Chuck, can you check the levels in the decompression chambers?" she asked. "We're moving through now."

"Looking good, Poppy. Pressures are coming up, all telemetries from your suits are go, go."

Poppy and Eugene carefully made their way into the airlocks, their progress made more difficult by the bulky spacesuits. For EVA work they were perfect, but inside they could quickly become cumbersome and awkward.

"We're in the chamber now, Chuck," said Eugene after a moment. "The airtight hatches are closed and sealed."

"Copy that. All incoming telemetries are 100%. Are you both ready for this?"

"Eugene, you ready?" Poppy asked.

She and Eugene met one another's eyes and he nodded, making a thumbs-up sign. Poppy could sense the start of what felt like a million butterflies flying around her stomach and right up to her heart. This was really it.

"All ready, here we go," she said. "Pressure dropping and 5, 4, 3, 2, 1 – zero pressure. Stabilized. Copy that, Chuck?"

"Affirmative, Poppy, my readings are the same. Do you confirm, Houston?"

"We can confirm, Enterprise. All systems are go for space walk."

"Opening outer hatch now," said Eugene. "Repeat, opening hatch now."

The outer hatch slowly inched open, and although Poppy and Eugene had practiced this moment time and time again, it was never the same as the real deal.

For one thing, the only sounds Poppy could hear were the static from the radio transmitter and her labored breathing; they seemed to fill up her own personal universe. Space was beautiful to look at, but it was the silence that really got her. Nowhere on Earth could you experience this kind of absolute stillness. It was incredible.

Slowly, she stepped out into the working bay of the Shuttle, seeing the two high-pressured envelopes that contained the rocket fuel before her. The equipment had been tested several times in vacuum chambers on Earth many months before to ensure that the technology could cope with the zero pressure in space, and Poppy felt confident about what they had to do.

When you were dealing with extremely volatile

fuel, it paid to be safe rather than sorry.

Even so, the whole apparatus looked a bit menacing, hanging there in the Shuttle's docking bay like some kind of vast sea creature, and for the first time, Poppy felt a slight shiver creep up the length of her spine. Taking a deep breath, she told herself to calm down.

It wouldn't do to have a massive freak-out when there was work to be done, and she had to keep her cool. Yes she was in space, and yes it was extremely weird, but she had a job to do, and a hell of a lot of people were depending on her to do it right.

She looked again at the equipment in front of her. It was a complex system; it had to be. It was an experimental two stage fuel, and dangerously combustible – the two liquids were completely safe when kept apart from each other, but when they were mixed together in the engines of the time travel missile, they would become one of the most powerful and potent fuels known to man. Highly unstable – and highly explosive.

With practiced calm, Poppy and Eugene latched their safety harnesses to the sliding rails in the bay and slowly set off towards the robotic arm.

"Making our way to the arm, Chuck," said Poppy, as she walked. "Steady as we go."

"Copy that, Poppy – I can see you in the viewers. Let me know when you're ready to open the cargo bay doors and I'll get right on it."

"Affirmative, Chuck," Eugene replied calmly. "Let's just take this one step at a time, folks. Easy does it." Although he could tell that Poppy was more than capable for the mission – obviously she was, or she wouldn't have been allowed up here, low volunteer numbers or not – he also felt a little protective of her. Part of it was the fact that she was a woman, sure – he had two little sisters back home – but the first time a person went into space was always a bit of a weird one, and he wanted to make sure she was OK, and that she'd stay OK.

After a few seconds – which felt much longer out there – Eugene and Poppy reached the robotic arm, with Poppy allowing herself a little smile of triumph. First bit over.

The arm was currently folded into eight extendable sections with a seated workstation area on the very tip. The seating area was secured to the arm in several places, fitted with explosive bolts in case of emergency. There were also two flexible hoses from the fuel envelopes, designed to be carried with the astronaut as the arm extended outwards.

Carefully, Poppy maneuvered herself into position. She went slowly, suddenly terrified that she was going to screw up. Little flashes of self-doubt started to bloom in her mind, and she made herself take a deep breath.

"I'm watching on the view-screen, Poppy. You don't look very comfortable there. You OK?"

"You're not kidding, Chuck," she said. "It ain't comfy at all. You want to swap?"

Chuck's cackling came over the radio. *"Sorry, you're on your own."*

"Ready, Poppy?" Eugene asked, staring at her intently in case he noticed anything wrong. "Here come the seat clamps."

He operated the hydraulic levers that secured the seat clamps around Poppy, latching her firmly to the seat on the robotic arm. She could still move just enough to operate the refueling hoses, and for this task that was all they needed.

"OK, Poppy, we're doing great so far," said Eugene, grinning at her from inside his spacesuit. "You're totally secured in the seat. Chuck, can you give me a countdown start to open the Shuttle Bay doors from sixty, please? Releasing your tethers now, Poppy, hang tight – here we go."

"Copy that, Eugene," said Poppy, beaming. "I'm feeling quite giddy at the moment." And she was. Whatever she'd been feeling moments before – the fear, the doubt, the panic – had gone as soon as she'd been clamped to the seat. It was amazing what difference a few seconds could make.

Eugene gave her a slow-motion thumbs-up and released Poppy's straps; he could see her grinning from the platform and he smiled to himself, remembering his delight at his own first mission. This was good. He'd been worried she might have drawn a blank when it came to the work, or that she'd maybe have a full-on panic attack, but she seemed pretty good at the moment.

He made his way to the operating end of the robotic arm, locking his tether onto its base, and he reached the station just as Chuck's voice came over the radio: *"5, 4, 3, 2, 1 – and open sesame!"*

The Shuttle gave a small wobble as the bay doors began to open, the pneumatics releasing with a hiss of air that instantly vaporized in the vacuum of space. Eugene whistled. He'd done this process many times, but it was always exciting.

He counted himself lucky to have the kind of job where he could never, ever get bored. If he had to work a 9-5 job in some mundane office somewhere, he thought he'd probably have cracked up by now. No, he was the kind of guy who lived for adventure, and what better adventure was there, than space?

"Steady Eugene," said Chuck over the radio. *"I can see your heartbeat picking up on the monitors. Calm down. Same with you, Poppy. Try to keep calm, folks. We've got a job to do."*

Of course, there was always the worry that being too excited about your job could end in disaster, and it was always weird to think that someone was actually monitoring your vital signs.

Just as Chuck suggested, Eugene took a moment to ground himself – though, not literally, of course.

Almost in slow motion, the bay doors crept open and the unreal vastness of space loomed before them. Even after years of doing this job, it didn't seem real at all: it was like something out of a dream.

It seemed to take forever for the doors to open and lock into place, and while they waited, Eugene and Poppy quietly admired the Earth, hanging above them like a vast, glittering jewel. This was definitely a view that never failed to make Eugene smile, and he always got that strange feeling deep inside him – of how lucky he was to live on Earth, but also of how tiny and insignificant he was in the grand scheme of things.

Not today, though – today, his job was pretty damn important.

Poppy stared at the Earth as though she had never seen anything quite so beautiful. No amount of simulations or pictures in books could prepare her for looking at the actual thing, and it was quite simply mind-blowing to think of the billions of people down there, doing everyday things – working, eating, sleeping, dreaming. Perhaps dreaming of going into space, like she did when she was a little girl and she used to look up at the moon, mesmerized.

It was quite incredible to think how far the human race had come in so few years, and it made her excited for the future of space travel, for all the things she would witness and experience in the years to come.

The two of them continued to watch, patiently, as weather systems slowly migrated across the surface of the planet – their wonderful, amazing planet.

"Man," Poppy breathed, "have you ever seen anything so stunning?"

"Not on the Earth, or off it," Eugene remarked, looking down to check the telemetry on his workstation. "You know, sometimes I wonder if this is the life for me – I mean, I spend months away from my wife and kids, I miss birthdays, weddings, christenings… but the truth is, there is nowhere I would rather be. How many people get to see the Earth from above like this? We are in the privileged few, and don't you ever forget it."

"You got that right, Eugene," said Chuck, sounding like he, too, had one eye on their awe-inspiring home. *"There ain't nothing better!"*

"Wow, call the President," Poppy laughed. "I think this is the first time we've ever agreed on anything, boys!"

Eugene nodded inside his spacesuit, which wasn't the easiest thing to do in the world – or above it. "We should call a national holiday," he agreed, over Chuck's distant guffaws, before glancing up as the vibration from the opening door ceased travelling up through his legs.

"We have it!" Chuck announced. *"Doors are open and locked in place. Eugene, I'm checking telemetry from the robotic arm, so just hang tight for a few moments before we go for it."*

There were a couple of seconds of silence then, as all three astronauts waited for their equipment to finish moving, mentally preparing themselves for the tricky procedure ahead.

Now that the Earth-gazing moment was over, Poppy was starting to feel those small blooms of fear again.

Annoyed, she tried to mentally push them away, but physically, she was obviously giving off some worrying signals, as at that moment Chuck enquired, *"Are you OK, Poppy? Your vital signs are off the scale."* There was a brief pause before he added, *"Are you happy, Houston? Poppy doesn't seem too well."*

"Let's go for this, I'm just a bit anxious is all," Poppy assured them. "You guys have done this before – it's all still new and exciting to me, my readings are bound to be a little off, right? Let's do it – come on, let's do this!"

"Are you sure, Poppy?" Houston asked. *"Are you really sure?"*

"All OK at this end, Houston. I'm feeling calmer now," she said, though she wasn't sure if she really believed what she was saying. "I know that if I abort this, it will spell the end of the whole project. Y'all passed me for EVA duty and I've not changed my mind, so let me finish this. I don't want to let anyone down."

That was true, but she also didn't want to let *herself* down. She needed to prove to herself that she could do this – because if she could do this, then she could do anything. "There's a limited window of opportunity here, so let's move it, move it, move it!"

"OK, here we go," said Eugene. "Opening the robotic arm – deploying arm now. See you on the other side, Pop!"

Eugene operated the hydraulic systems that controlled the eight sections of the arm, and as each part of the jigsaw lifted and locked into place, Poppy verbally ticked it off, still sounding nervous, but more in control now. He watched her move off, slowly travelling out towards the time travel missile.

"One down, seven to go. Two down, six to go. Three down, five to go."

The flexible refueling hoses lifted alongside the robotic arm, gracefully uncoiling and following Poppy, like obedient pet snakes. It was quite the image.

"Four down, four to go. Five down, three to go. Six down, two to go."

It had all gone very smoothly so far, and Eugene was calm as he oversaw the equipment panel. Soon they'd be heading back to Earth, where Poppy could really celebrate the success of her first mission. There might even be cake, thought Eugene happily – even though he could look down and appreciate the world as a whole, he could still appreciate the little things in life. You had to, really.

"Seven down, one to go, Eight down – locked!" Poppy announced. "See, nothing to worry about – easy-peasy," she said, sounding a bit giddy again. "We can do this. Chuck, Eugene, how're things looking for fuel envelope release?"

"Slow down, Poppy," Eugene chuckled. "One thing at a time. I'm making my way across to them now – you know how long these things take in a suit. Chuck, how far is Poppy away from the missile fuel tanks?"

"Don't you worry about that, Eugene, she's bang on target," came Chuck's voice over the radio. *"Just concentrate on those fuel envelopes – I'll keep an eye on Poppy."*

It took some time, but eventually Eugene managed to position himself on the working platform that held the fuel envelopes inside the open shuttle bay. He could hear Poppy humming over her radio, her eyes still on the planet turning above them.

The propellant necessary to get the missile up to the required velocity – faster than planet Earth – was felt to be so volatile that the best thing to do was to get it as far away from the shuttle as possible before the transfer pumps were activated – particularly as the fuel had a tendency to explode upon mixing.

Locking the feet of his spacesuit to the fuel transfer platform, Eugene went through the system release procedures on the remote control panel.

"Copy that, Chuck," he said when he was ready.

"Do you read the same? All systems go for piston release."

"Looking good from here, Eugene. Just check on tether seven – I'm getting a low reading on the continuity of the circuit. Worth a second look."

"I see it, Chuck," Eugene nodded, moving to improve it. "I just need to reattach it, hang on… is that a better reading?"

"Copy that, Eugene. We are all go for piston release. Repeat, piston release: all go, all go."

Eugene returned his attention to the operating panel, satisfied. "Here we go, Poppy. You ready?" he asked, hoping that she was. She seemed OK, for now at least.

"Cocked, locked, and ready to rock, Eugene."

"Great," said Eugene. "Here we go – piston release in 5, 4, 3, 2, 1 – and release!"

He flicked a switch and the platform released with a small, controlled explosion from each of the four corners that held the fuel envelopes. As the pistons thrust the whole fuel tank framework into the void of space, it slowly rose to a position some three hundred meters above the shuttle and approximately three hundred and fifty meters from Poppy, who was awaiting her connection to the time travel missile fuel tanks.

"Enjoying the ride, Eugene? It's one hell of a dark night out there!"

"It's beautiful, Chuck," Eugene enthused. "I can see your house from here! Who's that in your swimming pool?" He laughed.

"*It's your Mom!*" came Chuck's voice over the radio, causing Eugene to laugh again. Chuck could be annoying sometimes, sure, but he also knew how to keep morale up in a difficult situation, and for that Eugene was very grateful.

"Come on, you two, let's get a wriggle on so I can come back inside," said Poppy tersely. "This doesn't seem to be quite as easy as it was in the rehearsals. I could just do without the banter from you jokers for a couple of minutes, if that's OK."

Eugene winced; so apparently the banter didn't comfort everyone, and he really didn't like the panicky tone of voice Poppy had started adopting – they couldn't afford to lose her now.

Chuck was clearly thinking the same thing. "*OK, keep it cool, Poppy. I can see your body telemetry is going up and up – cool it. Just take a minute and calm down.*"

"Yeah, Poppy, cool it, everything's fine," said Eugene encouragingly. "Chuck will be lifting the shuttle up to bring you closer to the refueling dock in just a second."

"I know he will," said Poppy, sounding more frustrated than anything else now. "You don't have to tell me what we're supposed to be doing, Eugene – I haven't lost my head."

Yet, thought Eugene rather darkly, before mentally berating himself. He was sure Poppy could handle this; she just had to keep her cool, that's all.

"*Poppy, please calm down,*" said Chuck firmly, all trace of his joking tone completely gone. "*We don't have to do this – release yourself from your tethers and I will bring you both back in. Copy that, you two?*"

"We can't, Chuck, you know we can't," said Eugene, really feeling for Poppy. "We've got to see this through. Besides, Poppy can handle it – just give her a minute." He tried to send her positive thoughts – well, anything was worth a try.

Poppy had beads of sweat rolling down her face, and by now she was terribly stressed and uncomfortable in her restrictive spacesuit. She hadn't realized just how claustrophobic it would be when she was wearing it for real, and the thought that she needed to breathe – *really* breathe, as in getting some fresh Earth air – was overwhelming. As hard as it was, she made an effort to calm herself down, and she closed her eyes for a moment, thinking of the ocean back home. It was her happy place.

"I'm sorry, Eugene, I didn't mean to have a go at you," said Poppy, after opening her eyes again and coming back to the present. "It's just that I'm not happy with this – something about it doesn't feel right." There was a pause. "Come on, Chuck, move me closer and let's get this done. Do you copy?"

"I copy, Poppy, and can I just say, you're one of the bravest ladies I've ever known," said Chuck, sounding like he actually meant it.

At any other time, Poppy would have rolled her eyes at the pulsing masculinity that seemed to come throbbing off that kind of statement, but she couldn't even think of that kind of thing right now.

"Here we go," he added.

Just then, the apparatus began to move, and Poppy shuddered slightly as the seating rig began to crawl lethargically towards the refueling dock on the time travel missile.

"Up, up and away," she muttered, as she began to rise.

"I've got you on my viewer, Poppy," said Chuck. *"Just two more clicks and it's all yours, baby. 5, 4, 3, 2, 1 – full stop. Looking good from here. Do you copy, Poppy?"* He laughed, trying to cheer his friend up. *"I've always been a bit of a poet!"*

Poppy reached across to the fuel docking port and operated the auto-open, auto-close fuel tank covers. The work was painfully slow in the vacuum of space, and all she could think was, that she wanted this to be over, right now.

Eugene could hear her verbally counting off each action, trying to keep her voice as level as possible.

Carefully, she inserted the male connection of the red hose into the docking port, her hand shaking as she did so. He could tell she was a little surprised at how much harder this was in zero gravity compared to working on the practice rig back home, and he felt for her. He'd thought exactly the same thing during his first time. His second, too.

She was calmer now, and less angry with herself for what she felt was letting the team down.

"Copy that, Chuck," she said. "I'm attaching the red refueling hose now." She turned it until it clicked. "Locked and loaded – do you have that, Eugene?"

"Affirmative, Poppy," replied Eugene. "Reading a good connection there; I told you there was no need to worry. We can do this."

Poppy didn't answer while she concentrated on

connecting the blue fuel line, but she was definitely feeling much more confident now. Just as she was lining up the hose with the docking port, however, she started to frown.

"Damn!" she swore. "God dammit! What happened there? We've drifted twenty millimeters. Chuck – what happened?" She paused for a moment. "Aw shit, I've damaged the brass locking rings! Chuck, what the hell happened?"

"Nothing doing down here – we ain't moving! The missile must be rotating," Chuck said, a frown in his voice. *"Hang on a tick, I'll compensate for the roll."*

"Too late, Chuck, I've smashed the locking rings up! We don't have any replacements for them, do we? Shit! Now what?" Her voice was becoming more and more panicked, her breath more and more stunted.

She watched helplessly as the damaged locking rings drifted off into the void of space. She reached out and tried to grab them, but all she succeeded in doing was flicking them further away. She was seriously panicking now.

"Shit, now what are we going to do?" she gasped. "Shit, shit, shit, I've let you down! I've ruined everything!" If she'd had the energy to cry, she thought she would have started sobbing right there and then, not caring what the guys thought of her anymore.

"Poppy, calm down!" Chuck cried. *"Calm down, for Christ's sake! Just increase the oxygen input to your suit for a minute, will you? Do that for me."*

"Poppy, it's OK," said Eugene calmly, though he felt nowhere near calm himself. "We can enter the hose into the tank and wedge it with the robotic arm – do you copy that, Poppy? It's unconventional, but it'll get the job done."

"Just give me a minute, Eugene," she said, fighting her panic. "Give the oxygen a chance to get to my brain." She inhaled and exhaled a few times, steadying herself as much as she could. She just hoped it would be enough.

After a few moments, she was ready to talk again. "Might as well give it a try. Right, here goes – entering the blue fuel line now," she said, her voice sounding more or less normal again. "It's holding in place… bringing up the robotic arm and cage now. Yes, it's working – the hose is wedged in." A little laugh escaped from the corner of her mouth. "You can go right to the top of the class, Eugene! I don't remember reading this in the do-it-yourself space shuttle guide."

Eugene reached down to open the valve on the fuel storage envelope that was connected to the red hose. "Fantastic, Poppy," said Eugene, more cheerfully now. "Fantastic! Right, I'm opening the valves at my end. Steady as she goes – red hose fully open now."

He shuffled towards the blue fuel valve. "I'm just giving that fuel line half pressure to maintain the proper mix," he said. "Keep an eye on it at your end, Poppy; let me know if it gets a bit excitable."

"Will do," replied Poppy, finally allowing herself to relax a little.

The others did too; things were going well – or at least as well as could be expected. No operation ever went off without a hitch, and so far the problem with the locking rings was only a minor one. If Poppy could stay calm, they were going to complete this thing, Eugene could feel it.

He kept a careful eye on the amount of fuel that was being transferred while Poppy kept an eye on the connection at the missile and Chuck monitored the rotation of the craft.

After a few minutes, the voice of Mission Control came over the radio: *"We're reading the fuel transfer loads, Eugene – red at eighty-eight percent, blue at thirty-five percent. You will need to increase the transfer pressure on the blue or you won't get the correct mixture when fermentation begins."*

There was a moment of silence.

"Do you copy, Eugene?"

"Yes I copy, Houston," said Eugene, frowning. "Poppy, you know what I'm going to have to do. It might come away – are you watching at your end?"

"Affirmative, Eugene," said Poppy. "Take it slowly. Can you drop the pressure on the red line to help balance it out?"

"Yeah, thought of that, Poppy," said Eugene, already on the move. "Reducing pressure on the red nozzle now, and increasing pressure on the blue. Keep a close watch on that connection – we might lose small amounts of the blue accelerant. That's an acceptable risk, but be careful."

As Eugene had feared, when the pressure increased, Poppy's bodged connection came under more stress. It was fairly obvious that the red connection was sound, but the higher the pressure, the more the blue connection began to chatter and vibrate in its locking mechanism. Small trickles of fuel began to spill out, forming tiny globules of floating blue liquid, which quickly burned off in the vacuum of space.

"We're losing fuel, Eugene," Poppy announced, sounding terse. "Not much yet, and the spillage is evaporating instantly so it doesn't seem too bad so far, but I'll let you know if the situation changes."

"Copy that – I'm just increasing the flow pressure slightly," said Eugene, trying to keep his voice under control. The last thing he wanted to do was alarm Poppy again. "Keep an eye on it, OK? Now Chuck – watch that rotation problem, buddy, it's critical. Let's get this thing in the bag and then we can go back home!"

There was silence for a few moments, and Eugene was just beginning to think that they might really be able to get out of this mess when Poppy shouted out, her voice full of panic.

"What? What's wrong?" asked Eugene, almost too scared to hear the answer.

"I can't see!" said Poppy, almost screeching the words at him as she watched her visor cloud over.

"*What? What's going on?*" asked Chuck, a slight panic coming through in his voice too.

"My visor, it's covered in a thick blue mist – I can't see a thing!"

"Stay with it, Poppy, it's just the fuel condensing on you. Not to worry – it won't ignite on its own," said Eugene, with what turned out to be an unusual level of prescience. "Let's do this. We're nearly there now – red is at ninety-two percent and blue is at eighty-three percent."

Poppy tried to focus again, but just as she thought she'd got her head back in the game, a strange assortment of sounds suddenly bombarded her ears. *Zing! Ping! Ping! Ping! Zing!*

As far away as he was, Eugene saw the moment that Poppy looked up, confused.

She shook her head. It seemed like someone was messing about on the coms – the sounds were emanating from within her helmet. "Pack it in, Chuck!" she complained, annoyed. "Don't you think I've got enough to think about without you messing around right now?"

"Hey Poppy," said Chuck, sounding perplexed, *"give me a break! I don't mess about up here – what are you talking about?"* He wondered if she'd started to go a little mad, hoping for all their sakes that she hadn't.

"Well, one of you is messing about, making stupid noises on the coms, and it's unlikely to be Eugene!"

"I can't hear anything, Poppy," said Eugene, a note of concern in his voice. "What's the problem?"

Poppy frowned and turned slightly in her frame, the blue mist on her visor beginning to clear. Out of the very edge of her helmet she saw tiny silver flashes heading her way, each no longer than a couple of millimeters, streaking towards the fuel docking rig.

Her heart dropped into her stomach.

No, no, this couldn't be happening.

She swore as the tiny slivers of aluminum began to

bounce and ricochet off her helmet, her spacesuit, and the fuel lines. They were beginning to get bigger, travelling in orbit faster than a speeding bullet.

"Eugene!" she squeaked. "I've got major problems over here! We've got satellite remnants travelling through space like micro missiles – they're hitting the fuel lines, and one of them could puncture the hoses. You'd better turn off the fuel flow!" Her voice came out high-pitched and hysterical, but she didn't care. The only things she could think of right now were the deadly aluminum slivers, floating around her like tiny little space daggers.

"I can't!" Eugene cried. "We're almost there now! Red is at ninety-eight percent and blue is at ninety-six!"

"No, Eugene, you have to stop it now – it's going to fracture the hoses!" she told him. "For God's sake, turn it off! Oh Christ, no!" She shrieked in terror as a particularly large chunk of debris tore through the red fuel line. "It's gone, it's gone – it's all over me! Oh shit, it's changing color – they're mixing and fermenting on my suit!"

"Hold on, Poppy!" yelled Eugene, as both Chuck and the team in Houston started shouting over the radio, demanding to know what was going on.

His heart in his mouth, Eugene moved towards the fuel switches, but it was far too late – the fuel was turning a deadly yellow color on the outside of Poppy's suit.

No matter what he did now they wouldn't be able to save her, but knowing that and giving up were two entirely different things. So, he plunged doggedly towards the fuel switches, desperate to save his friend. He couldn't let her first spacewalk end like this, he just couldn't.

Above him, the shower of satellite debris sparked against Poppy's suit and solar power pack, and Eugene watched in horror as her shrieks were swallowed into silence.

Her whole suit went up in a matter of seconds, blowing her up and away from the time travel missile like she was nothing more than a ragdoll.

Almost in slow motion, he watched as the fuel lines disengaged, the internal valves of the missile protecting it from any damage. The fuel spill slid down the robotic arm like lava, rapidly fermenting and eating up the apparatus as it went. The fuel hoses themselves ignited, the fierce fire travelling back towards the fuel envelope platform with a speed that alarmed even Eugene.

Without conscious thought, he released the clips holding him to the platform, glancing at the sections of fire hose that were burning towards him – since there was no oxygen out here, he knew that the fire couldn't travel too fast out in the void of space, giving him the vital seconds he would need in order to survive. It was just enough time to push himself clear of the fuel envelope platform, which he did, kicking hard against the deck plates and trusting his continued existence to the tether line connecting him to the Space Shuttle.

He leapt off the platform with as much force as he could muster, trying desperately to put as much distance between himself and the burning rig. Just as he reached the full extension of the tether he twisted his body, watching the explosion feed back along the hoses and into the fuel envelopes.

The explosion was intense and vast, though it traveled out into space almost ponderously. At least it was fairly contained, as these things always were in the vacuum of space; a small silver lining in a vast stormy sky of shit.

Eugene turned his back on the sight – in order to protect his visor – and then braced himself, preparing for the pressure wave that then knocked and spun him on the end of the tether.

He used his suit jets to slow and stop the spinning – which was something of a relief – and then turned back to gaze at the remains of the fuel rig, thinking mournfully of Poppy.

He took a moment to collect himself, but as distressed as he was for his friend, he knew he couldn't let it swallow him; there would be time to grieve for her later. Right now, his priority was to get safely back to the Space Shuttle, otherwise there'd be people grieving for him too.

Frantically trying to concentrate, Eugene reviewed his options. He was aware that a lot of people were shouting over the radio, but at that moment they were all just a blur. Slowly, he forced himself to focus, and the noise resolved itself into individual voices once more.

"Eugene, are you there?" came Chuck's now desperate voice.

"Chuck, Chuck, we've lost Poppy," he said, once he'd recovered his own voice. It cracked and wavered alarmingly, his calmness gone completely. "All hell has broken loose out here!"

"Eugene! I can't see!" came Chuck's voice, sounding a little panicked. *"What's happening? Where are you, man? No visual, no visual!"*

"It's breaking up – the robotic arm's breaking up!" Eugene cried. "It's exploding!" he added, breathing hard. "You'll need to jettison it. I'm winching myself back to you right now."

Eugene began guiding himself back in, using the in-suit winch, and as he inched his way back to the Shuttle, Houston came over the radio: *"What the hell happened out there, Enterprise? You're beginning to roll, Chuck – better correct that before you throw Poppy off the end of the arm!"*

"Poppy's gone, Houston," said Chuck, sounding really pained and sober for the first time since the mission had started. *"She's been lost – we have major problems up here. The robotic arm's screwed. It's on fire – must be the hydraulic oils igniting. Eugene's out on his tether – I have no visual, but I can hear him on the radio. He's winching himself back in."*

There was a pause while Mission Control digested this information. *"Where's Eugene?"* Houston asked. *"He was on the fuel envelope platform! What's he tethered to?"*

"The platform's lost, Houston – Eugene's been blown almost three hundred and forty meters away from the Shuttle. He's trying to winch himself back in."

"I'm tethered to the deck plating of the robotic arm," said Eugene, distantly, his voice small and – quite frankly – scared.

"He's tethered himself to the robotic arm," Chuck relayed to Houston.

Eugene let the conversation wash over him, concentrating instead on winching himself in while at the same time keeping one eye on the robotic arm. Another section of it exploded as he watched, rolling the Shuttle even more.

"What was that, Chuck?" Houston gasped. *"Hell! Your roll is getting heavier – better correct it or you'll lose it altogether!"*

As the controller spoke, another section of the arm collapsed and Eugene began pulling himself along the line using the manual winder – it was hard work in the spacesuit, but the electrical winch was taking far too long. Time was something that was most definitely not on his side here. His battery packs were running critically low.

"That's the robotic arm," Chuck's stunned voice filtered over the radio. *"We're losing it, we're losing it!"*

"Jettison it! Jettison it!" Houston instructed.

Eugene gasped. He wanted to scream, but he was too afraid – instead, he concentrated on pulling himself closer to the Shuttle.

"Let it go or it will take you with it. Do you hear me, Chuck? Let it go!"

"I can't," replied Chuck. *"Eugene's lines are fastened to its base!"*

There was a harrowing pause.

Nobody needed to calculate Eugene's chances outside the Shuttle: they were negligible. He would spin away – even if the explosions failed to take him out – and then Chuck would never be able to pick him up again. He would be a goner. He'd be alone, in space, until he died. This sure as hell wasn't how he saw this mission ending up.

"You've got to make a decision, Chuck," said Mission Control, sounding like they felt utterly wretched.

"I just need a few minutes, Chuck!" shouted Eugene frantically. "Just give me a few minutes, I'm on my way in now. I'm going as fast as I can!"

In desperation, he turned off the life support inside his suit so that all the remaining power in his battery packs could be channeled to the electrical winch, hoping if he did that, it would operate faster than the manual one. His last chance. He'd only have a few more minutes of air, but if he didn't make it back to the Shuttle before the rig was jettisoned, it wouldn't matter anyway.

It seemed to take forever, but soon the winch sped up and all of a sudden Eugene began to race back towards the Shuttle's open bay doors.

"Two hundred meters!" he yelled, the adrenaline coursing through him as he shouted at Chuck. "One hundred and fifty!"

Another explosion ripped through the local area of space, tearing through the robotic arm.

"One hundred and twenty meters! One hundred!"

The winch in the suit began to heat up now, generating a trail of smoke that streamed behind Eugene into space.

"Seventy-five meters!"

Another section of the robotic arm went up.

Eugene tried to fight his rising panic, but he could hear the dread in Chuck's voice when he said: *"I can't hold it off any longer, Eugene! I can't! I can't! I'm sorry! Jettisoning the arm in 5, 4, 3 —"*

Unable to even speak, Eugene listened with horror as his friend counted down the seconds to what would essentially be his death sentence. This couldn't be the way it ended — it just couldn't. Was losing Poppy not enough? They had to lose him, too? And possibly Chuck as well? No, this wasn't right. This couldn't be happening!

"2, 1 — robotic arm away!"

Around the base of the robotic arm, small exploding bolts released the mounting brackets, and the doomed base lifted away from the cargo bay. The six small launch pistons fired simultaneously, pushing the remnants of the robotic arm away from the Shuttle.

Eugene watched, helpless, as fifty meters of tether began to drift in the wrong direction.

"Release your lines, Eugene!" Chuck shouted, his tone more desperate than ever. *"Release your tether — let your trajectory bring you home!"*

"I'm going to miss the open bay!" Eugene cried, after a quick assessment of his trajectory. "I'm heading straight for the engines!"

"No, you won't!" Chuck ordered, trying to comfort his friend. *"Just trust me, Eugene! Do it!"* His words were encouraging, but he didn't sound entirely convinced, it had to be said.

Eugene looked back at the explosions that were, even now, consuming the platform, and decided that he'd rather suffocate than blow up, if he had to choose. Man, what a choice.

After only a split second of further hesitation, Eugene released the lines, which snapped away from his suit just in time as the robotic arm flew away from the Shuttle. He fell towards the spacecraft, spinning now, around and around.

He began to panic in earnest – there was no way this would work, surely! The extra velocity he'd gained from speeding up the winch was working against him now, hurtling him towards the side of the Shuttle and threatening to wipe him out entirely.

"Here we go, Eugene!" came Chuck's voice over the radio, sounding way too ebullient, given the circumstances. Eugene realized that he had a plan – and that, whatever it was, he wasn't going to enjoy it. *"Just reach out and grab something! Anything!"*

At that moment, Chuck fired the mini thrusters with practiced precision, tipping the nose of the Shuttle over just enough so that Eugene was directly above the open bay. He bounced against the walls, crying out from the impact, then reached out to grab whatever he could: metal stanchions, framework – it was all slightly beyond his grasp. Dazed and battered he was finished, *this is it,* he thought, *I can't slow myself down.* He was hurtling towards the bulkhead of the craft with enough force and energy to bounce him back into space, when the airlock door swished open ahead of him.

Chuck stepped out, locking the winch line of his suit onto the rail, and squatted down, bracing himself for what was about to happen. Then he reached his arms out to Eugene, who didn't even have time to be astonished at the unexpected sight before him.

"Come to Daddy!" bellowed Chuck, an almost manic glint in his eye.

They collided with immense force, knocking them both off the platform, the visors of their helmets pressed together. Eugene's face was a mask of terror, while Chuck was grinning from ear to ear. They hurtled across the open bay until Chuck's safety line caught, bringing them to a gut-wrenching halt.

"You're low on air, buddy," said Chuck, as he manually restarted the life support in Eugene's suit, increasing the volume of breathable air. Eugene took a great, welcome gulp of it. "Come on, let's get you inside."

He activated the winch in his suit and held onto Eugene until they reached the airlock, where he pushed his friend through it, half stumbling, then followed and sealed the doors behind them.

Eugene leaned heavily against the wall as his friend re-pressurized the chamber. He couldn't believe what had just happened.

Chuck took off his helmet and then came over and helped Eugene remove his. He was still grinning, but Eugene couldn't stop crying. He was shaking all over – a huge, hysterical mess.

"You saved my life," he choked between sobs.

With no words to say in response, Chuck embraced him, awkwardly patting him on the back of his spacesuit. They stayed like that for a few seconds, then began to remove their suits.

They had work to do. There would be time to freak out later.

"Oh God, Poppy," said Chuck after a moment, stopping what he was doing. With all the drama of getting Eugene back inside, he'd pushed that particularly horrifying fact to the back of his mind.

Eugene nodded, struggling out of the outer layer of his suit. "She didn't stand a chance, poor woman." He shook his head. "She was a good kid, a good astronaut." He paused, staring at Chuck's face, his own completely still. "It could have been any one of us."

Chuck sighed heavily.

"Let's just go home, buddy; it's been a long day."

Eugene nodded, now both physically and mentally exhausted. "The longest."

Chapter 24

A true adopted all-American hero

Following the chaotic meeting at the American Embassy in London, the Vice President had returned to America, immediately arranging a high level meeting with the President and all key personnel. He still couldn't believe what Graves had told him – or how the imbecile had responded when faced with what Ron Champion could only describe as reasonable objections. He was amazed that the buffoon hadn't been fired earlier.

Champion had just finished telling the group of senior politicians about the scenes of lunacy he had witnessed at the Embassy, and as he sat back in his seat, he sighed heavily. Just going over it all again was exhausting, and he hadn't felt this tired in a long time.

He wished Bo were there. Bo always knew what to do, and he always picked Ron up whenever he was running low on energy. He'd had that effect on most people.

After hearing Champion's speech, the President

couldn't believe his ears. "You know," he said, "since you've been over there, I've had several communications from the British government – one begging me to abort the Time Travel Project, and another to ignore the MI6 and do whatever we have to in order to clear up this mess."

"Sounds about right," said Champion, sighing again. "You really should have seen it, the two of them arguing in the Embassy, getting physical – we had to pull them apart. If it wasn't so serious, it would have been comical. Then Graves whacked one of our men – what a farce! We almost had to throw them out on the street!"

The President whistled. "I wish I'd been there to see that," he chuckled. "It must have been a real eye-opener into European government diplomacy."

"It was," said Champion, rubbing his forehead tiredly. He could feel a big headache coming on – a migraine, maybe – and he didn't have the time or the energy to deal with one. What he really needed was sleep, but even if he could afford to lie down for a few hours, he knew that sleep wouldn't come. It never did when he was dealing with things of this magnitude – and this was the biggest he'd ever had to deal with.

"I felt kind of bad for Harcourt, though," he continued. "I mean, the guy's a ridiculous old blow-hard, but he didn't start that fight, and it was pretty obvious that he thought Graves had gone insane sending those agents into the White House. Let alone organizing that little 'accident' in Paris. And the Deputy Prime Minister seemed pretty adamant about committing to the success of our project, so they weren't all completely mad."

"Hell, that's something," the President exclaimed. "It's good to know we have at least some decent men over there. Now, more importantly, what do we do next?"

"Well," said Champion, "Graves pleaded with us to abort the Time Travel Project, but the rest of them I met with are still pretty steamed about the RAF transport plane and would love to see that resolved, no matter how we do it." He shrugged. "How MI6 will see it, I don't know."

"Ron, when have I ever been bothered by what MI6 think?" the President asked. "As far as I'm concerned, they can take their so-called 'special relationship' and shove it. We lost an astronaut yesterday, and from what Houston have told me, it was a close call for the other two as well. Very close. *Too* close.

"I'm just glad they managed to complete their task before everything went to hell, or we'd be having a very different conversation right now. We lost a good friend when Bo was shot for no sane reason, and *now* they want us to abort the mission?"

Champion raised his eyebrows, shrugging slightly. It was the only physical movement he could be bothered with at that moment.

The President shook his head dismissively. "To hell with that!" he scoffed. "Let's do it – launch the thing. Launch it! We have a chance to save more lives than we've lost setting this up; we've got to launch the time travel missile!"

"I think that's the right decision, Mr President,"

said Champion, smiling for the first time in hours.

*

Mission Control was never a place that could be described as quiet, but today, with the influx of Time Travel Project personnel and *Microsoft* technicians, it was particularly busy.

The activity was centered around a hive of technicians who were working with NASA scientists and boffins from Redmond, pre-programming the on-board computers on the time travel missile. It was taking a while, but it was a tiny drop in the ocean considering how much time it had taken to get the project to this stage.

There was a window of only one hour and thirty-five minutes of launching from Earth's orbit before the time travel missile was beyond radio contact, and they needed to make the most of that or it would all be for nothing.

Several technicians – including three of the senior scientists from the Time Travel Project – were clustered around several computers where simulated models of the time travel missile's flight plan were being run.

A few steps behind them, Eddie Einstein was watching. His current concern was ensuring that the proper codes were imprinted into the software to ensure that the missile would not be shot down by any of Earth's defense systems as it approached the planet, and particularly by America's air defenses, which – like the country – were always quick to respond. He had the codes from twenty-five weeks earlier memorized now.

The whole project had been a bit of a learning curve, even for someone as experienced as Eddie. For one thing, he wasn't used to managing people – his skills were more in managing information – but Bo's untimely absence had pushed him to branch out, as it were.

The only thing they had stopped working for in the past couple of weeks was Bo's funeral, which had been packed to the rafters with friends and colleagues. If a man could be measured by the number of people at his funeral, then Olsen was clearly one of the greats.

Although the team had only known him for six months, Bo Nick Olsen had had a tremendous impact on them all, and he seemed to have had that effect on most people, from the stories that had been passed around at his wake. Eddie smiled at the memory.

He owed it to his friend to see this project through to the end, and if he had to be a bit uncomfortable managing his scientific peers in order to do so, then so be it. He just had to suck it up and get on with it.

Even though Champion could handle the politicians, and John Dillon was adept at controlling the funding and logistics of the project (he, too, had thrown himself into his work following Bo's death, which had hit him particularly hard), both men lacked a key skill that Eddie most definitely had: he could speak 'scientist'.

Around here, that skill was worth its weight in gold.

As Zack, Louis, and Jerry watched the simulated missile approaching the sun on their workstation computer screen, they started talking amongst themselves. There was definitely an air of great anticipation and excitement in the room. Ten years' worth of work – not to mention two deaths – had been leading up to this, making it a bittersweet moment, but one that was incredibly thrilling nonetheless.

Eddie left them to it, knowing that they'd call him over if they needed him, and joined Bill Gates at his temporary desk.

"Come on, Eddie, let's go through the numbers again," said Gates. "We've got to be sure – one mess up here and we're up shit creek without–"

"Yeah Bill," Eddie interrupted, tensely. "I know, I know – that's where it's got to arrive. That's it, that's it – don't let it get too close, Bill, it's going to scare the pants off them anyway; we don't want them to try and shoot it out of the sky."

Gates nodded before turning to face his old friend. "Working on this project with you, Eddie, has given me an extra buzz," he said happily. "If we can succeed with this, I'll be throwing a fantastic party for the whole lot of you! It's been too long since we got to puzzle something out together."

"Great!" Eddie said, though in truth he wasn't paying much attention – all of his focus was on the task at hand. "Now, download all that onto the mainframe, Bill – that's the end point where we need to be. If those newly-designed chips can look after all of this information then we've got it, Bill! Job done!"

"We've doubled up the chips and software," Gates told him, professional once more, though his smile still remained. "Program A will be covering program

B, which then cross-checks with program A. You're not dealing with an amateur here, Eddie!" he added, once again back in geek-happy mode.

Eddie laughed sadly, his expression growing wistful and distant. "That's something my old friend Bo would have said," he whispered softly, remembering his buddy.

Gates patted his friend's shoulder, gently. "I was sorry to hear about Bo. The way he stepped in front of the President like that – he was a true hero."

Eddie sighed. "To me, Bill, he was a true adopted all-American hero. Not only did he save the President, but he saved the black box too, and you could even say that he's the man who's saved the transport plane and all those on board." He smiled. "It's amazing really, how one man has made such an impact on so many."

Bill nodded in agreement, not needing to say anything in response. Eddie was spot on.

"Back to it, I guess," said Eddie, and in order to attract everyone's attention, he stood up from his seated position, waving his arms around as he cleared his throat. He moved towards the center of the room as everyone turned to look at him.

"Right, you lot," Eddie called. "It's now or never! We've got to upload all of this information to the time travel capsule. Everyone ready? Bill – has your team sent the data to the mainframe?"

"All coming across, Eddie," said Gates. "We just need to give it a few seconds."

Eddie, Bill Gates, and the scientists from the Time

Travel Project watched with bated breath as the mainframe computer downloaded all of the programs developed for the missile, including the launch sequence, the projected encounter with Mercury, the changes in velocity required to counteract the sun's gravity, the jettisoning of the spaceship's rocket engines and fuel tanks, and its expected final approach into Earth's orbit, twenty-five weeks earlier.

Everyone breathed a little easier when the computer announced, in a pleasant female voice reminiscent of Star Trek: *"Processing! Processing complete!"*

Then: *"There is an eighty-four percent possibility of success on this mission."*

There was a moment of fraught silence then, before an anonymous scientist in the back of the room broke the spell.

"What the hell?" he cried. "Eighty-four percent? That's not good enough! We can't let it go under those parameters. We've worked too damn hard not to be more certain of this!"

Gates frowned at Eddie. "He's right, we need it higher than eighty-four. In the nineties at least."

Eddie nodded reluctantly. He wanted it to be higher too; he was just wondering how high they'd actually be able to get it. So near, yet so far.

Everyone dashed back to their stations in order to re-calculate everything they could to try and improve their odds of success, while Eddie and Bill walked back to their station at a more leisurely pace.

They settled down in their chairs and watched the frantic industry around them with a more philosophical air. These were some of the biggest brains on the planet: they could do anything if they put their minds to it.

Right now, they didn't need any interference from Eddie or Bill; sometimes, you had to know when to just step back and watch.

"I don't know what more we can do, Bill," Eddie complained. "Looking at all this again isn't going to change our influence on the journey…"

"Hang on, Eddie, hang on, buddy," said Gates, a small smile playing on his lips. "Instead of us running the Shuttle and the time travel capsule head on together, why don't we program the capsule to enter the time zone from the rear of the Shuttle? Then we could just have them run parallel in orbit. That should iron out any discrepancies in trajectory. What do you think?"

Eddie shrugged. "Give it a go, Bill, we've got nothing to lose." He didn't mean to sound so defeatist – usually, Eddie was the most positive guy around – but you could only go so many hours without sleep, and Eddie was beginning to flag.

Still, he couldn't rest yet, so he made himself sit up straight in his chair and tilt his head back and forth, working out the cricks in his neck.

Other units in the room had, by now, improved their parts of the programming enough to give an overall probability into the ninety percent range. Bill entered his new parameters, which gave everyone a bit more of a confidence boost, and finally, they were ready to check it again.

All of the team leaders downloaded their section

of the journey back onto the mainframe computer, and then everyone gathered around the unit once again in order to hear its verdict.

Eddie just hoped the percentage hadn't gone down – how absolutely perfect would that be? He laughed to himself, thinking of the look on Bill's face if that were to happen.

"Processing! Processing complete!" chirruped the computer. *"There is a ninety-three point five percent possibility of success on this mission!"*

The room rippled with relief; everywhere people were high-fiving and congratulating one another, big smiles on their faces.

Bill and Eddie ignored them, even when they took out the bottles of champagne someone had bought. No one opened them just yet, however – their job wasn't complete, and they all watched the connection from the mainframe computer to the *Microsoft* programs on board the time travel missile carefully, making sure than no data went astray.

"Downloading! Downloading! Program transfer complete!"

As one, Eddie and Bill grinned and shook each other's hand.

"Good news, Eddie; you can relax a bit now!"

Eddie rolled his eyes. "I'm always relaxed, Bill – you know me. Now, if you'll excuse me, I've got to go and make a rather important phone call."

He left the room, stopping in the corridor and bringing out his cell phone. After he'd pressed number five on his speed dial, he waited for it to ring out.

"Yes?" came the rather abrupt greeting on the other end of the line, almost causing him to jump. Champion sounded more exhausted than Eddie, and that was saying something. He knew that Ron Champion had been waiting in the White House for news, and he also knew that he'd be with the President right now.

"Mr Vice President, Eddie Daniels here."

"I know who you are," said Champion, a little irritably now. Eddie didn't really think he could blame him. "Is it good news?"

Eddie smiled into the phone. "It's good news. Very good news. We're all good to go down here."

He could almost feel the relief coming through the line. "Thank you, Eddie." And with that, the Vice President hung up.

"Man of few words," Eddie said to himself as he put his phone back in his pocket and walked back into the main control room.

He returned just in time to hear the Mission Controller launch several Blackbird Spy planes to send home television footage of the time travel missile launch on a secure channel, and he looked over at Bill, who was now standing and chatting with one of the scientists.

They'd done all they could do. Now they just had to wait.

"Well Bo," murmured Eddie to himself, "this is it, man. This is it."

Chapter 25

If this works

The atmosphere in the White House's Oval Office was tense, and that would be putting it mildly.

Doctor Josh Banner, Ron Champion, and the President of the United States of America were watching a television someone had just wheeled in. Putting cameras in orbit – close enough to watch the launch – had been a clever move. It was the only way they would know that this experiment had worked; with any luck, they wouldn't remember any of this.

"I can't believe what we're doing," said the President eventually after staring at the screen for several minutes. "We're watching this on TV! I mean, it's actually happening – we *are* doing the right thing, aren't we?"

He turned and made eye contact with Josh, who gave him an anxious smile.

"What do you say, Josh?" he asked Doctor Banner. "Am I doing the right thing?"

Josh couldn't speak for a moment – a few months ago he was planning golf trips and worrying about losing his job, and now he was sitting in the Oval Office with the actual President. He had grown from a Boy Maverick to a Maverick Man in those few crazy months, though he didn't know how on earth it had happened. "You must be, Mr President," he told him. "Just look at all the lives you're going to save: Bo Nick Olsen, Poppy Willis, Princess Diana, Dodi Fayed, the driver and the bodyguard from the crash, not to mention all those people on the RAF transport plane. Anyway, this project doesn't directly hurt anyone, and I think those lives are worth the risk."

"Yes, I know," said the President. "But if this works…" He trailed off, clenching his fists. "I'm scared to death that it will change how we think about the future."

Frowning, he carried on. "Just think about it: we'll have no need to be careful in what we do, because at the back of our minds we'll always be thinking that if we get it wrong, we can go back and change it if we want to. The future will be fluid, and it could make us reckless. As individuals, and as a country. Where does this stop? Where – and *when* – does it all end?"

The Vice President raised his arm to interrupt then, which Josh Banner was very pleased about – he hadn't a clue how he would have responded to what the President was saying. It was all getting a little deep for him, and Josh usually tried to stay away from those kinds of thoughts.

"Mr President," said Ron Champion, "we are the most responsible nation on this planet. When we mess up, the rest of the world shivers – if, in the future, we can make this planet a safer place, then the rest of the world won't be having kittens over it. This Time Travel Project shouldn't change how we view the world – it just means that we need to take more care and responsibility for it. As with anything this powerful."

"Of course, Mr President," said Josh. "If this works, this conversation will never have happened. This timeline will have been erased, you understand. The rest of the world never has to know we succeeded – hell, they probably wouldn't believe us even if we tried to tell them. That's the beauty of the whole operation. Plausible deniability."

The President ignored him – in truth, thinking about time travel and the paradoxes it created gave him a headache – and picking up the direct line to Mission Control, he fixed his gaze on the TV's live feed.

"Let's do it," he said, into the receiver. "Let's do this! Is everything ready?"

"Yes, Mr President," said the Mission Controller.

"Then launch!"

Everyone gathered around the television, a few seconds passing before a blast of incredible magnitude pulsed through the orbital launch pad. Saturn Five's vast inverted engines ignited and the time travel missile commenced its journey, quickly picking up speed before zooming away further into space.

Ron Champion nodded, satisfied. "Are we ready to release the prepared statement about a spy satellite exploding in orbit?" he asked.

The President nodded in affirmation, and one of the aides scurried away to make the appointed phone call. Of course, if it worked, there would be no need to release a statement, but they had to cover all bases.

Doctor Banner watched the remnants of the explosion, a curious sense of anti-climax filling his heart. He'd spent ten years of his life on this project – though the last few had been more about golf than physics – so now what?

Now it was all done, what was he supposed to do?

He smiled, thinking he'd leave that decision up to his past self.

Chapter 26

You're goddamn right I'm taking pictures

Mission Control was having a very strange sort of day. There had been a shower of orbital satellite debris to watch out for, and now the Space Shuttle was in trouble; it had been a fairly standard mission up until the point a large, unidentified object had appeared on the radar, almost level with the Space Shuttle itself.

"Christ! Where did that come from?" the Mission Controller exclaimed. "There's a foreign body, an object catching you up from behind! It's going to hit you in the rear, look out!" he shouted, and when there wasn't any immediate response, he added, *"Mason! Take evasive action!"*

"Where in hell did that come from?" the pilot – Chuck – replied over the radio, sounding just as stunned and mystified as the Mission Controller. *"Hang on, guys! Hang on! Grab something to hold onto! Here we go! Here we go!"*

Everyone in Mission Control held his or her breath as the Shuttle banked and the unidentified object drifted past, narrowly missing crashing into them.

There was an explosion of swearing from the cockpit of the Space Shuttle, and then a tense, baffled silence.

Finally, just when the Mission Controller was about to start panicking, the pilot broke it. *"What the hell is that? What's going on, Houston? I don't believe my eyes! There's a freaking UFO on our six!"*

"No, Shuttle, it registers with a friendly radar blip," said the Mission Controller, frowning at a printout an intern had just handed him. "What *is* that? You must have a visual by now – what does it look like? It must be right alongside you!"

He waited impatiently as the astronauts several miles above him had a hurried and bewildered conversation.

"Well?" he asked, more intrigued than ever.

One of the other astronauts on board, Eugene, responded, *"Yes, Houston, we have it in view now."*

There was another pause, causing the Mission Controller to groan in frustration. "Well? What is it?"

"You are never going to believe this, Joe…"

"What's that, Shuttle?"

"It looks kind of like a missile, but there's a message on the side of it – and an image of the stars and stripes!"

Joe gaped. Visions of first contact missions swam in his mind – but then, how would they know about the flag? He quickly tried to pull himself together, to stop his wandering mind from wandering any further. "A message? A message? That's ridiculous! What does it say?"

"This has gotta be some kind of weird joke – it must be," said Chuck Mason, who sounded truly and completely baffled, especially considering he was normally the joker of the pack. *"It's gotta be Russia or China pulling our leg, it's just gotta be! It says 'Please return to the President of the United States of America: for his eyes only'."*

"It says *what?*" He waited for the Shuttle pilot to repeat the message and decided that if the world had in fact gone insane, he might as well go along with it. "Abort re-entry program, Columbus – abort re-entry program!"

"Please confirm, Houston, was that abort re-entry?"

"Affirmative, Shuttle," he confirmed. "Abort re-entry and await further instructions!"

"Copy that!"

"And take pictures!"

"You're goddamn right I'm taking pictures!" came the reply. *"As many as I can!"*

The Mission Controller – Joe – sat back in his chair and exchanging a glance with his colleague who was sitting next to him, said, "What do you think about that?"

His friend Mike shrugged, laughing. "I think we'd better get on the phone to the President."

It took quite some time for Joe to get in touch with the President, and when he finally did, it took even longer to explain the situation. The President just couldn't grasp the gist of what Joe was saying.

"You're telling me there's a… a what, a missile? In space… with my name on it?"

"That's about the long and short of it, Mr President," said Joe, still wondering if this was actually happening or if it was some really weird, vivid dream.

"But how? And why? And *who*?"

Joe tried to stop from laughing – talking to the President was no laughing matter, despite what the conversation was about. "That's what we'd like to know, Sir, but as I told you, it's apparently for your eyes only."

There was silence at the other end of the line, though Joe could just about hear the President mumbling to someone – the Vice President, probably – before he came back on the phone.

"Okay, as long as it's safe to do so, I want that object captured and brought in. As soon as you can."

"Copy that, Mr President!" said Joe, forgetting the whole professionalism thing for a moment as he almost shouted at him in excited joy.

"Keep me updated," was the only response, and then the line went dead.

Hurrying back into Mission Control, Joe flicked the switch that allowed him to communicate with the astronauts on the Space Shuttle.

"Columbus, we are looking at having you bring the object back down to Earth with you," the Mission Controller announced. "Direct order from the President." He paused for a moment, thinking. "Chuck, how does it look for size? Will it fit in your

Shuttle bay?"

There was a brief pause, and when the voice came over the radio, there was more than a hint of humor in it. *"This is no joke, Mission Control, but it looks like it was built to fit in the bay,"* the Shuttle pilot replied. He and his crew had clearly been having as close a look as was feasible without going EVA. *"It even has grab brackets for the robotic arm!"*

Joe gaped, and all four men in the meeting at Mission Control nodded their assent at the Mission Controller.

"It's like we built it!" continued the astronaut.

"Space Shuttle Columbus," said the Mission Controller, now even more excited. "Await computer upload for new mission parameters. We've got the technicians working on it at the moment."

"Copy that!"

*

The object had been brought down to Earth, but it was still a mystery.

Houston was baffled by the device, so – having decided that it didn't present any danger (despite its war-like shape) and having cleared it with the President – they put out feelers to certain members of the scientific community.

On closer inspection, the embossed message on the side of the craft also told NASA which personnel should be present at the opening of the device.

These people were from an unknown project in San Diego – a project that seemed to have been given a great deal of funding even though no one knew what they were working on.

The four nominated scientists had been flown urgently to Houston.

It was all highly mysterious.

The very eccentric Professors were clustered around the mysterious missile in a nearby hangar, muttering excitedly to one another and glancing at the object with identical looks of awe on their faces.

The President had gathered his key advisors, who had gathered *their* key advisors, and subsequently, the President, Vice President Ron Champion, Bo Nick Olsen, John Dillon, and Eddie 'Einstein' Daniels were all stood there, watching the scientists thoughtfully.

Whatever this was, it was a nice break from the normal routine.

Bo thought that the people surrounding the object had the look of men whose scientific universes had just been turned upside down. He had a good grasp of physics – for a layman – and after an in-depth two hour conversation with John and Eddie on the flight over from Maryland, he had the sneaking suspicion that this object had something to do with time travel.

The only other alternative – extra-terrestrial life – was just so unlikely as to dismiss it outright. After all, how likely was it that ET would write all over the thing in English? Time travel, though – that was an idea he could sink his teeth into. That was exactly his kind of thing, in fact.

He caught John's eye and grinned, aware that the man would dearly love to be teasing him right now for having his head stuck in an episode of *Star Trek*, but there were too many other people in the room. Plus, he was unwilling to even mention it in front of the President.

Instead, Bo turned his attention back to the huddle of boffins. They were all highly intelligent people in their field of work, so he was pretty sure they knew what prize was on the table.

Eventually, they seemed to elect one of them to step forward and speak.

Bo, who made a habit of looking people up before he met them, recognized the man as Doctor Josh Banner, who specialized in engineering and theoretical physics. He had spent an evening listening to him rambling on about black holes and Quasars some years ago at one of those government funded seminars.

Bo looked across at Eddie, pointing his finger towards Banner and mouthing, 'We know that guy.'

Eddie nodded in response. He had been the compere at the event.

"Mr President," Banner said, scratching the back of his neck in a rather nervous manner – Bo supposed he'd be nervous too if he was directly addressing the President of the United States for the first time, and under such strange circumstances too. "What you are looking at here is the future. Or to be more accurate, an object *from* the future."

The assembled advisors shared looks of disbelief at this dramatic proclamation – all except Eddie, who was wearing an expression of deep fascination. He just couldn't take his eyes off the capsule.

"This is our time travel missile – the result of almost ten years of painstaking research and development in the field of time travel. It has clearly been refined and put into operation at some point in the near future in order to get some kind of message back to you, Mr President." He paused, frowning. "It must have been pretty important to put this project in motion and risk sending it back in time."

The expression on the Presidents face is one of: *have I just entered an asylum?*

"What are you talking about?" the President demanded, unimpressed. "It's just one of our prototype missiles – look at it! This message on the side is… well, I don't know what that is, but I can tell you it's not from the future! It's clearly some kind of ridiculous practical joke," he declared, suddenly angry that these men – these men who were going on about time travel as if it were the most normal thing in the world – were taking up his valuable time.

"Mr President," Eddie gallantly interrupted, before he could get any more irritated. "I've studied some of the research into the time travel theory that these gentlemen have been working on – that the government has been funding, by the way – and the doctor's right; this is part of their time travel rig."

"That's right, Mr President," Bo interjected quickly, "I've just been appointed to oversee the Government Funding Agency to sort out where all our money is going, and I assume that this is one of the projects we've been sponsoring. I'll be able to tell you more about it once we overhaul the accounting offices. They're – uh – a little behind in terms of organization."

There were a few seconds of silence, with no one daring to speak. Everyone was watching the President, whose gaze swept around the room, landing briefly on every person there before finally coming to rest again on the missile. He seemed to be waiting for one of them to admit that this was all some kind of elaborate prank. Of course, no one did.

Finally, his chin in his hand, he nodded decisively. "Right, has this missile been scanned, x-rayed, given an internal examination? What I'm asking is, is the damn thing safe?" Looking across at his FBI team, exasperated. "Yes, No?! Tell me for Christ sake! That's what we pay you for!"

An FBI man responds, not knowing the correct terminology. "It's got a friendly bleep Mr President." He looks at the President hoping he had given the right reply.

"A friendly bleep?" the President repeated. "A friendly bleep! My wife says I've got a friendly bleep, but we still sleep in separate beds! Open the capsule, young man – let's see what secrets it holds. I've had enough of this."

A sophisticated-looking set of tools were produced then, obviously having been brought over from the nearby workshops. The missile itself was hanging from the roof girders, sustained by an array of pulleys and chains.

Given the choice, Josh would have preferred to be in a proper lab, but as he well knew, you couldn't always have it your own way.

A sonic wrench was used to remove the twelve bolts that held the inspection covers on, and once these had been taken away, a second compartment was exposed. This was then opened in a similar manner.

Given the bulk of the inspection panels, these pieces of the missile had to be lifted away by mechanical means, and as they were removed, an ever so familiar piece of kit was revealed.

Everyone held their breath as Doctor Zack Bookerman lifted out the White House secret communications black box, complete with Presidential seals and date stamps.

The four scientists looked up at the President, whose grasp on the laws of physics appeared to be becoming a little shakier. "What the hell is *that* doing there?" he demanded, dumbfounded. "*What the hell?* I didn't order this!"

"It's a White House secret communications black box, Mr President," said Banner, taken aback, "and you may well have ordered it."

"I know what it is, young man," the President spluttered, "but what the hell is it doing in *there*? And what *exactly* does this all mean?"

"I'm certain that the contents of this black box will explain everything," said Banner decisively, though the President still didn't look convinced about opening it all up, despite what his experts had told him about it being safe.

Bo studied him thoughtfully. Clearly, Banner was sufficiently convinced of its authenticity; this piece of kit came from the White House, and it seemed that Banner would stake his career on that. Bo knew more than most that no one stood up to the President about something unless they truly believed in what they were saying. Unless they were an idiot, of course, and Doctor Banner looked nothing like an idiot.

With no more objections, the black box was passed to the FBI agents who were accompanying the President. Putting it gingerly down on a table they invited him to examine the device.

The President appeared utterly dumbstruck: it was clear that he just couldn't believe this was really an object from the future. It strained credulity.

He peered closely at the four seals on each of the edges. "Yes… it's from the White House," he said, eventually. "These are my personal seals, dated – good God!" He exclaimed weakly, floundering a little. "How can that be? They're dated… six months into the future!"

His gaze wandered over to Josh Banner. "You were right?" He asked it as a question, though going by the look on his face, he was starting to believe it anyway.

Ron Champion approached the black box in order to get a closer look, while everyone else mutely watched the battle between consternation and amazement currently taking place on their President's features.

It was quite a sight to behold.

"Can someone bring a set of tools to remove these copper seals?" asked Ron, to which one of the FBI agents responded with a nod before leaving the room.

"Well," said the President, after a minute or two, "it's our turn to sort things out from here. Doctor

Banner, you and your team had better salvage what you can of the missile and take it back to the facility with you; I have a feeling you'll want to take a very close look at that capsule."

"Yes, Mr President," said Banner, stuttering a little. "The thing is, we already have one at our time travel complex, so with this one, we now have two." He looked both excited at what had happened and bitterly disappointed that he wasn't going to be there to see the contents of the box. Still, he might be able to see them at a later date, and that had to be enough for now. He smiled at the President and the other men, nodding dutifully.

"Bo, you're with me and Ron," says the President.

*

The President, Bo Nick Olsen, and Ron Champion, left the scientists crowing over their obvious achievement in the hangar – now arguing about how to transport the thing all the way back to their facility in California – and headed for a nearby building. A pair of Secret Service agents followed behind, one of them pushing a buggy loaded with the black box and the toolkit.

Upon entering a secure office, the President instructed the agents to lift the box onto a workstation, before instantly dismissing them.

While the President and Ron looked on, Bo searched through the tools for a set of cutters. When he was ready, he began to snap the four seals.

"Be careful, Bo, don't damage it!" said the President, suddenly nervous.

377

Bo nodded, then continued at a slower pace. Finally, the seals were removed, and Bo stepped back.

"Right," said the President, meeting the eyes of his associates, "let's see what we've got here."

Leaning over, he opened the box and removed the padded protection to reveal… nothing. All he was looking at was a highly polished black glass screen. "What's this?" he asked, looking around at Bo and Ron for help.

Glancing at the glass screen, Bo realized that it was one of *Microsoft's* latest – and as yet, not on the market – touch screens. He'd heard about these from Eddie, who was a good friend of Bill Gates.

Reaching forwards, Bo touched the glass, making the President gasp. Usually, there would be a lot more discussion before a course of action was decided. But Bo was Bo – he just got on with things.

The three men watched as the polished black screen began to scroll through all the colors of the rainbow. It was faintly mesmerizing, but finally, a window opened on the device, stating the words:

INCOMPATABLE ACTION CARRIED OUT – PLEASE TRY AGAIN

The screen returned to black, and Bo looked across at the President. "You touch it, Mr President. I know these things have state of the art intelligence."

Moving forward, the President placed his hand on the blank device, which responded instantly. Turning a deep red color, another window opened on the screen.

HAND PRINT IDENTIFICATION CONFIRMED

In the blink of an eye, the message fades, instantly being replaced by a new window:

WELCOME MR PRESIDENT

BEFORE YOU CAN PROCEED YOU MUST CONFIRM

THE SECURITY CODES THAT WILL ALLOW YOU TO CONTINUE

PLEASE INSTALL THE SIX DIGIT NUCLEAR LAUNCH CODES

FOR THE USA NUCLEAR SUBMARINE 'DREADLOCK'

With that, a small window with a keyboard opened on the screen, and the President looked across at Ron.

"Dreadlock?" asked Ron. "We haven't got a submarine called Dreadlock!"

"Oh, yes we have," the President replied, smiling. "Dreadlock was the name of one of our submarines in a comic I used to read as a lad. For some reason I can always remember the nuclear launch codes we used to frighten the Ruskies; it scared the pants off them."

Ron frowned. "Never heard of it."

"You know what this means!" said the President, suddenly excited. "Within this group of people, I am the only one who knows those codes!"

Bo nodded, smiling. "So this question must have come from you. From the future you! It *must* have, Mr President."

He nodded in response; if he'd had any doubts as to where this device had come from, they had all but vanished now.

With a trembling hand, he began to tap the nuclear launch code sequence for the Dreadlock – 2 2 7 2 2 7 – onto the glass keyboard.

A few seconds passed, the numbered window slowly faded, then the screen suddenly zapped to a bright red image, with the following words written in black:

IMMEDIATE LAUNCH – ALL MISSILES LOCKED ON TARGETS

The President smiled. "That's how it used to be written in the comic, every time we nuked them!"

The words faded, quickly being replaced by a more practical message as an electronic buzzing noise came from the device:

DATA TRANSFER PROCEDURE STARTED

PLEASE ALLOW EIGHT MINUTES FOR COMPLETION

"What's this all about '*Data Transfer*'?" The President gasps. "Bo," he added, "What do you think?"

Bo shrugged. "I think… duck if it goes bang!"

Shaking his head, Ron sat down at the workstation. "I met the previous commissioner of the agency a few years ago, and he was telling me about this Time Travel Project we were funding. I was fascinated at the time, but it soon turned into a huge waste of money. I never got around to scrapping it…" He shrugged. "And now look where we are."

"Maybe we should leave the science projects to the scientists to decide what should be done with them," remarked the President.

"Another job for Eddie, I think," Bo said, smiling.

Ron nodded. "You might have a point there, Bo – Eddie Einstein '*Head of Headaches*' I'll make a note of that."

Just then the black box started bleeping, and when they looked back at the screen, a new message was being displayed:

DATA TRANSFER COMPLETE

INFORMATION NOW PRE-RECORDED IN PRESENT TIMELINE.

PLEASE CONTINUE

This message faded, and then – after a few heart-stopping seconds – a new display showed the image of a handwritten letter.

Bo and Ron craned over the President's shoulder to get a look, but he waved them off in a distracted kind of manner. Bo backed up a couple of paces; though he was desperate to see what information the letter held, he knew when not to push his luck, especially where the President was concerned.

"It's in the image of *my* handwriting," the President says, his voice hollow. "It says: *'You will now have opened the black box. I know you won't be able to understand all of its contents straight away, but you must trust my words and take immediate action. There is going to be a devastating air crash resulting from friendly fire…'* Hell," he added, "it even gives the date! *The American Air Force will shoot down a British RAF transport plane carrying high-ranking British personnel to peace talks in Astana, the capital city of Kazakhstan.*"

He stopped reading and looked up at his advisors, confused. "What's all this about?" he asked. "Does anybody know anything about this friendly fire incident?"

"Mr President, I believe you're reading a statement from the future," Bo pointed out, gently. "My guess is that it simply hasn't happened yet."

"There *are* peace talks in Astana," said Champion, rubbing his head. "They're beginning tomorrow – but I don't know anything about the transport plane."

The President's frown deepened as he continued reading the letter.

"*This friendly fire incident happened on March 4*[th] *at 19:25 hours, local time. You must get the attached co-ordinates to the field of operations ASAP.*" The President paused. "*'You must not delay – by our calculations, you will only have a matter of hours to achieve this.'* I can't believe I'm reading this. What date is it?"

"Its March the 4th today Mr President," said Champion, slowly. "So that incident doesn't happen until this evening."

Bo frowned. Being Dutch he was always conscious of the time zones between Europe and America, "That would be true, except… wait a minute," he said, a tone of urgency in his voice. "It's already evening in Kazakhstan – that's on the other side of the world!" Bo looks at his wrist watch, making a quick calculation, "Mr President, yes, it's already evening time over there" Bo again looks at his watch, and carries out another quick calculation. "Mr President, Sir! We only have minutes, it's 19:12 hours in Kazakhstan now!"

The President pauses, just for a moment, gathering his thoughts, "Ron quickly, cell phone," reaching out his hand.

Ron had already anticipated this, and is pressing speed dial to the White House hot line, which overrules all other calls, he passes the phone to the President, "Joan patch me through to Bob Williamson in Flight Command immediately."

The President looks up, making eye contact with Ron and Bo, pointing at the planes co-ordinates on the touch screen, "Read these figures out to me Ron, how's the time doing Bo?"

"Seven minutes Mr President."

The call continues with the President giving all the details from the screen, "Call me with an update Bob, as soon as you have one." The President ends the call. "It's in God's hands now."

Chapter 27

Two missiles, oh shit!

Things aboard the RAF transport plane – which was high above Kazakhstan – were not looking good.

"Break radio silence, Singhy, and transmit today's Security codes. Tell them who the fuck we are," Newson roared.

Ali replies in an almost mocking manner, "Yes sir, at once Sir."

As Ali is fumbling in his flight case to retrieve the Codes, Luke is trying to attract the Captain's attention to tell him of his suspicions. He knew Ali wouldn't have the codes as he'd missed the pre-flight briefing. But would it make any difference, is the Transport Plane doomed anyway?

The Captain is now urgently shouting **"COME ON!** Singhy **COME ON!"**

Ali breaks radio silence, opens the microphone and begins transmitting the plane's details and the security codes for the day; however, he changes his well-spoken English accent to an accent of his Motherland.

Disturbed by the change in Ali's voice, the captain thinks for a few seconds, then realises what has just happened. He shouts at the co-pilot, "Hang on a minute, I recognise those codes: they're yesterday's! You bastard, you've stitched us all up! It's you that's been fucking about with the transponder. You bastard and now that stupid accent!"

The tension in the cabin is like a standoff at the 'OK Corral'. Who is going to make the next move?

Suddenly, another high-pitched bleeping omits from Luke's instrument panel. He clocks the readings and in a strained desperate voice says, "They've launched missiles. **TWO MISSILES! OH SHIT!"**

The captain makes a lurch for the radio; it's not too late he can still save the plane. If only he can get to the mic.

Ali thrusts his hand into his flight suit, pulls out a small handgun and shoots the Captain dead, Luke stares at him in horror, unable to move, Ali wasted no time in turning the gun on him. "Sorry Luke, but you're just another heathen."

Luke launches himself at Ali knocking him off balance the gun fires again but the bullet harmlessly lodges itself in Luke's seat, where he'd been sitting just moments before.

The flight deck door bursts open and two burley SAS men rush in. They see Ali with the gun but they are moving so swiftly that he does not have time to react to them and the first SAS man piles into him with such force that Ali is smashed against the cockpit windscreen rendering him unconscious.

Slowly, Luke picks himself up. Then, glancing over at Ali's motionless body – and trying to avoid looking at the remains of Ben Newson – he reached across to the plane's instrument panel, turning on the autopilot.

In the distance he could see two missiles, harmlessly drifting off, away from the plane.

*

They waited with bated breath for the phone to ring, and when it finally did, all three of them jumped.

The President answered it: "Yes Bob? Yes. Yes?" He beamed, and Bo Nick Olsen let out the breath he'd been holding in.

"Yes, thank you. Fantastic!" He turned to the other men, smiling. "They're safe, thank God. Now what else is in here?"

Staving off the incident in Astana had been all the confirmation they'd needed to believe that the time travel missile the scientists were arguing over back in the hangar was the genuine article.

It was unbelievable, but it was – apparently – true.

Now that he'd begun to accept the reality of the missile, the President was behaving rather like a young child – extremely excited to have this gift from the fates.

Touching '*continue*' on the screen and revealing page two of the letter, the President continued to read it out loud.

"'*Hello Mr President, Eddie 'Einstein' Daniels here,*'" he read, and then paused, looking over at Bo.

"*I'm standing here in front of you, dictating this section of your letter – though, in fact, I'm standing in front of you roughly twenty-six weeks into the future. However, if you have been able to save the British RAF transport plane, then the future that I was standing in will never happen.*"

The President paused as he and his companions tried to wrap their heads around Eddie's sentence. He shook his head and plunged on.

"*The words you are reading only exist for you because they have been pre-recorded onto a disk in your time zone when you inserted the launch codes. I know this is difficult to believe, but your present actions are changing the future, sending it off in a different direction – a different, alternate timeline, if you will. When you launched the missile back in time, you were very concerned about the possible misuse or abuse of this technology, so you must conduct yourself with caution and discretion, as I'm sure you would anyway. Back to you, Mr President.*"

He stared at his Vice President. "I'm finding this very difficult to take in. My head is swimming. Just give me a few minutes."

"I'll read on, Mr President," Champion offered, and the President nodded.

Staring at the screen, the Vice President continued, "*You now have to move onto our next problem, though you do have a little more time to sort this out,*" Champion read aloud. "*Fifteen hours after the incident in Astana, a member of the British Royal family – Diana, the Princess of Wales – is going to be murdered. Due to the circumstances surrounding these events, our country unfortunately got dragged into the situation, and we must prevent this tragedy from happening at all costs.*"

At this, Bo, Ron, and the President exchanged almost identical looks of alarm. What on earth did the

Princess of Wales have to do with America? And anyway, the idea of her dying was something that was very hard to take in – the death of someone of her importance would send shock waves all around the world.

The President nodded at Champion to continue.

"*The remaining contents of this black box will give you all of the information you will require in order to accomplish this,*" he read on, with a frown.

"*The CIA in our time zone have manufactured a mission protocol for their counterparts in your time – all of the information is on the disks enclosed. At all costs, you must get back to the White House and review these disks with the Head of the CIA to ensure that he follows all of the instructions to the letter. After all, they've come from him – only twenty-six weeks into the future.*"

Ron glances at Bo. "It's taking some believing is this." Reading on: "*The time to act is now: remember, no one must ever know what we're doing. We are changing the future.*' That last sentence has been underlined several times," added the Vice President, before pausing, a strange expression crossing his face.

"What now?" the President asked, but Champion ignored him, staring straight at Bo Nick Olsen, who was beginning to get a rather funny feeling in his chest.

"It's a personal message to Bo," he said. "*Bo – I'm assuming you're alive and well in your time zone. I'm sorry to inform you that we lost you in ours – we hope that our efforts will ensure that you will be safe this time around! Best wishes, the President.*"

Bo gaped at his friend, not quite believing what he'd just heard.

"I feel like someone just walked over my grave," he said, his mouth dry. "And I've got the weirdest feeling it might have been you, Mr President."

Bo was now standing alongside Ron, viewing the black box and looking at the words on the screen. Reading that paragraph again in his mind's eye, '*Best wishes, the President,*' shaking his head, "Something crazy happened in that future that's for sure," he says.

After touching 'continue' for the next page, two loud bleeps emitted from the device while the following message appeared on the screen:

INCOMPATIBLE ACTION CARRIED OUT

CLOSING DOWN PROCEDURE ACTIVATED

YOU HAVE EIGHT SECONDS TO STOP THIS AND CONTINUE

"Shit Bo, what happened? We've lost the information!" said Ron, panicking as the device counted down from eight seconds.

"Stand aside, gentlemen," the President commanded, holding up his index finger. "When you are a Jedi, you have special powers!" With that, he touched the screen, bringing it back to life:

FINGER PRINT IDENTIFICATION CONFIRMED

PLEASE CONTINUE

The President smiled – looking very much like a child with a new toy – while Bo laughed. "So the leader of the free world is really a Jedi Knight!"

Looking back at the monitor, Bo saw that page three had now opened on the screen.

He read out loud: "*You may open this device now. There are four retaining clips, and these need to be unlatched. Then you can lift the screen up and away from you. Be careful not to damage the wiring looms, and be aware that you have twenty-four hours of battery supply, after which you will need to connect to mains power. Inside you will find the data transfer cassette holders, which hold all the information you require in order to help the Princess. We believe that the master disks that were pre-recorded in our time zone will have had their information erased by now, because if you managed to save the transport plane, our timeline will never happen.*"

Bo continued: "*However, if you have followed our instructions, they will have transferred this information across to the secondary disks upon your insertion of the launch codes. This was done in your time zone before you had chance to change the future, so the information will be safe.*"

Bo stopped talking, staring at the two words now on the screen:

PLEASE CONTINUE

"Well, shall we open it up, Mr President?" asked Bo. "Are you ready to see what treasures it may hold?"

"Do it, Bo. We've got to get off back to the White House." He turned to Ron. "Make some calls, get everyone in who needs to be there."

Bo removed the glass screen that was still operating, placing it down on the black box's open lid.

Peering inside at the array of electronic circuitry and battery packs, he suggested, "I think we should leave this to Eddie," before pointing at the components. "I'm assuming these are the data transfer cassette holders." Each one was embossed with a title and a number, and each one was complete with a small, glowing green indicator. He could see ten compartments for the data transfer cassettes, but only six had been used.

"You'd better put that all back together, Bo," said the President. "Let's pick up Eddie and get back to Washington."

Nodding, Bo was just beginning to replace the glass screen when he noticed one of the data transfer cassette holders sitting on its own, looking rather lost in the tenth compartment. He had to squint to read the embossed title on the side, and it was partly covered by the retaining bracket, but he could just about see the words: **'PRIVATE AND CONFIDENTIAL.'**

"Come on Bo let's get going," says Ron as the FBI agents enter the room.

"Hang on Ron, I just can't see what this says. No good I can't make it out."

"No, come on Bo, leave it. We've got to get packed up and moving!" The President exclaims.

Bo gives up trying to focus on the remaining words.

If only he had taken two more seconds to read the name on the cassette; if only he had, things would have turned out so different, or would they? Poor Becky, after all she had gone through.

With that, the black box was closed up, ready for its journey back to the White House.

As they left, Bo thought again of that cassette holder, but he pushed the thought from his mind.

It probably hadn't been anything important.

Ron was now on the phone frantically trying to arrange for CIA Personnel to meet with him, the President and others back in Washington to evaluate the contents of the Box, and to finally put into fruition the mission to save the Princess, if they could.

Chapter 28

A Few Breaths of Chloroform

Two CIA agents waited nonchalantly in the dimly lit corridor – one of the very few in the entire hotel that wasn't surveyed by CCTV cameras. They'd double checked.

The fashionable end of Paris had become a place where the wealthy wanted their welfare checked up on, but not all places were under surveillance; there had to be some locations left that weren't under 24 hour scrutiny. Well, this was one of them.

A man in a sharp suit and polished black cap emerged from one of the rooms at the end of the hall, and one of the agents nudged the other in the ribs. They detached themselves from the wall as he passed.

"Bonjour, Monsieur," the first agent said, in a perfect French accent. "Do you 'ave a light? All my matches got wet in the rain."

The chauffer stopped, affably, outside a door that appeared to belong to a linen cupboard, and he was just fumbling in his pockets for a lighter when the second agent whacked him in the kidneys from behind. This made his knees buckle, and down he went like a sack of potatoes, a quiet '*whoomph*' sound escaping from his lips as he fell.

The two agents surveyed their mark, now a crumpled heap on the floor.

"It looks like you've been practicing that, Beckman," said AJ, approvingly.

"It's all in the timing. I've been watching a lot of Bruce Lee films; it's all about that one inch punch!"

AJ produced a drug-soaked cloth from his pocket, covering the winded chauffeur's face for a few seconds – just long enough to knock him out. The CIA agent then went through his pockets, quickly extracting a set of car keys.

Beckman – his partner of almost five years now – unlocked the linen cupboard before sprinkling whiskey all over the floor from a bottle they'd stashed there earlier. He then smashed the bottle against a heating pipe, causing glass to shatter everywhere.

"Right, let's dump him in," said Beckman, satisfied with his handiwork.

They manhandled the chauffeur into the cupboard, piling towels on top of his body as if they'd simply fallen onto him. Beckman then took a second bottle of whiskey from its hiding place and doused the chauffeur's clothing before wedging the bottle into the chauffeur's right hand. He took a moment to carefully clear away any fingerprints.

"There's a lovely sleeping beauty," he remarked, once he was finished. "Sweet dreams, man." He turned to his partner, "Let's go – we've got work to do."

The two agents wandered cheerfully into the hotel foyer, pausing at the front desk where a pretty young woman was presiding over the staff and guests.

"Hey, mademoiselle," AJ called, beckoning her over. "We've just seen a drunk falling into a linen cupboard up on the fifth floor." He spoke the words quietly, so as not to disturb the other guests. "He looked half unconscious – there was glass all over the floor. I think someone better check on him."

They left the scandalized woman furiously telephoning security and walked out into the Parisian drizzle, turning up their collars to keep out the chilly night air.

AJ stood for a few seconds on the plush *fleur-de-lis* tiles – stamping his feet to keep out the cold. Beckman joined him a few seconds later. Looking up, AJ knew he'd been clocked by his colleagues, who were watching proceedings from a parked van, a safe distance away.

Taking a handkerchief out of his pocket to blow his nose, was the signal to say that everything had gone to plan – so far.

He raised the cloth to his face, and as he smothered his nose, it suddenly dawned on him that he had used the wrong cloth. "Oh no," breathing in a few breaths of chloroform made him stumble on the top flight.

Laughing, Beckman grabbed the contaminated cloth from his colleague, stuffing it safely into his pocket. "Come on, old man," he said to AJ, "I'll help you down these steps. Let's take them one at a time, that's it. We'll soon have you back at the old folk's home."

AJ took a few deep breaths of fresh air as he walked down the steps, trying to clear his head. "Next time, Beckman, you do the drugs and I'll be the heavy."

Upon receiving the signal, a CIA Agent slips out of the truck, dressed in black, looking similar to the chauffeur taken out by AJ and Beckman.

He set off across the parking lot, on an angle that will coincide with the two agents travelling in the opposite direction. As they inconspicuously pass each other. AJ, by sleight of hand passes the limo keys that they had taken from Arnett's pocket, across to the third agent without even making eye contact.

To all concerned, they could have been just three men passing on the street. No relation, no connection.

The job done, Beckman and AJ paused at the corner of the building, watching the entrance of the hotel.

After several minutes, the doors opened as Princess Diana and her partner, Dodi Fayed, walked out. They were holding hands, and they smiled at each other as they descended the steps of the hotel.

Moments later, the Princess's bodyguard joined them, escorting them to the limousine that was waiting at the side of the road. The CIA chauffeur stepped forward, opening the car doors for his charges.

"Ma'am," he said politely, smiling at the Princess as she got inside. He easily reached past her and unlatched the seat belt clasp from its housing. As the spring loading of the device began to retract the belt, the Princess took it from him, extending it she locked it into the retaining bracket. Smoothing the belt out across her torso she was now safe.

The CIA chauffeur was not staring at the Princess, he was just watching her in his peripheral vision. He had been briefed that the Princess' safety was paramount to this mission, and whatever it took to ensure this result would be acceptable. Ensuring that she had that seatbelt on was crucial to the operation. Every care had been taken to look after her, and you don't mess with orders straight from the President of the United States of America.

"Thank you," the Princess replied in her soft timbre.

As the rain became heavier, Beckman looked up at the sky. The clouds were covering the moon, its pale light only briefly breaking through long enough to illuminate the scene below.

AJ and Beckman watch as the car pulls away onto the slip-road towards the carriageway. Safe – for the moment...

Taking his cell phone from his pocket, AJ pressed a button and held it up to his ear. "It's done."

With that the two men turned, satisfied, and walked into the night.

The rain becomes heavier as the vehicle rolls smoothly off the carriageway; making a turn onto the slip-road joining the motorway, it picks up speed.

Whatever you say about the German Car industry they make some of the best and most balanced vehicles on the road, the *Mercedes* is hugging the tarmac beautifully as it powers its way through the tunnels and flyovers of the motorway.

The CIA chauffeur is watching the headlights of a car in his mirrors. It's catching the limo up very quickly – too quickly.

As it approaches, the car starts to cruise almost at the same speed, it pulls out to overtake, now running parallel with the limo. As the passenger window lowers, a very stern face appears, making eye contact with the chauffeur.

A second car? he thinks. *But that was never in the briefing, is that new for tonight? No it can't be. This is how it happened, there must have been another vehicle involved all along. Keep focus watch for events.*

The cars are travelling at eighty kilometres per hour quickly approaching the entrance to another tunnel.

On the footpath above the tunnel, leant on the railings are a group of tourist-like people; watching the events?

One man is talking on his mobile, "Yes Mr Graves, the cars are approaching now, everything looks good, there's no other traffic."

As the chauffeur headed towards the tunnel entrance, he saw the two men on the footpath above. One was talking on his cell phone, while the other pointed at the limo. He knows that this is the tunnel entrance where the accident is planned.

It's all happening at break neck speed – first the two men – then the adjacent car reducing the road's width as it inches closer to him, leaving no room to manoeuvre. *Shit! They must have stitched Arnett up to make sure he didn't betray them,* the agent thinks, as he looks down at his speedometer which now reads eighty five kilometres per hour.

It's all happening fast now, very fast, he glances at the two men now stood on railings to get a better view, then he is aware that the adjacent car is now only inches away, he manoeuvers as far to the right as he can, running on the rumble strips on the edge of the road. The stern faced man is now gritting his teeth and looking very angry towards the chauffeur; he is pointing towards the tunnel entrance holding his fist up.

The limo's tyres are now rubbing the kerbstones, no room left, only fractions of an inch, he is being pushed towards the concrete stanchions as they are approaching the tunnel entrance, he can now feel the adjacent cars' pressure so great on his steering, pushing him closer and closer towards the concrete, he is fighting it, but the heavier off road vehicle is going to win.

To continue would be suicidal. Finally, the CIA agents' training kicks in, and he hits the brakes, stopping the limo almost instantaneously. This action rips all the mirrors, handles, metal outer skins off the doors and wings of both vehicles, a huge array of sparks erupts from the friction as the cars rake along the side of each other.

The problem for the heaver adjacent car was that the fuel tank and filler cap were on that side, and as all the parts and panels are ripped off – it exposes the fuel lines to all the sparks.

A large jet of flames engulfed the car, eating away at the passengers within, and causing the main tank to ignite, blowing the car into a fire storm in the tunnel's entrance.

Crashing through a barrier to its right, the *Mercedes* manages to find a small service road. It is now hidden by the flames of the fire storm, and is lost out of sight.

The whole tunnel entrance is now burning with black plumes of smoke and stench from the exploding car; the driver and passenger instantly blown to fragments as the fires of hell ignite.

The sun roof leaves the exploding car as if fired from a rocket launcher soaring up at the two men above the tunnel. They instantly try to duck from its path. One succeeding, the other a bit too slow as the sun roof catches him in the throat lifting him off his feet and almost decapitating him.

The surviving MI6 Agent scrambles back to their awaiting car screaming over his phone, "Yes Mr Graves, all hell has broken out here! We've lost both cars. Our Agents are gone, but so is the car carrying the Princess!"

Suddenly, the smashed-up *Mercedes* roars up the slip road, pulling out onto the roundabout above the tunnel. "Oh my god!" said the Agent, as he scrambled into his car to give chase.

Trying to catch his breath, he instructs his driver, "Follow that limo!"

"What the hell is happening?" roared Graves over the phone. The agent gives him a rundown of events as they race through the streets.

It's easy to follow the *Mercedes* as bits keep falling off it, leaving a trail.

The CIA agent driving the limo has now taken a cell phone from his pocket and is pressing an emergency code which he knows will activate a pre-planned procedure to hopefully finalize his mission.

He turns the com on between himself and his passengers thinking, *what shall I say?*

"Please keep calm and remain in you seats until the vehicle stops."

Shrugging his shoulders at the Princess's bodyguard sat in the passenger seat, "It's the best I could think of at the moment."

He knows that the MI6 car is right behind him now. "Just keep going, one mile that's all, one more mile," he whispers to himself.

His hands were gripping the steering wheel so hard he wasn't sure he'd ever be able to take them off. When suddenly, part of the smashed up rear wing drops down onto the rear tire, twisting the steering wheel from his grasp.

Black smoke plumes from the burning rubber; then with a loud explosion the tyre disintegrates; he's now running on the rim of the wheel as red hot sparks are cascading down onto the car behind them, hindering their view.

He's struggling now to keep control of the *Mercedes* as it snakes back and forth across the road – *come on, come on* – turning the last corner his destination is before him – the rear entrance of the American Embassy!

Having received his emergency signal, the barriers are already raised, waiting for him. There are four heavily armed Marines guarding the entrance. *Nearly there, nearly there.*

As if he hadn't had enough problems already, the car suddenly lurches to its right as the rear wheel disintegrates from its axle causing the car to drop onto the rear metal sub frame. There is a huge array of sparks as the vehicle is now scraping the road.

Come on, come on. Thinks the agent. *Nearly there. Yes, I'm home!* As he passes under the raised barrier, the four Marines rush to block the path of the MI6 vehicle following, with a very aggressive – and impressive – display of weaponry.

As the wrecked *Mercedes* comes to a halt, the MI5 bodyguard exits the car – immediately being sick in the nearby bushes – and the CIA agent scrambles out too, darting to the rear door and flinging it open.

With his heart in his mouth expecting the worst, but no there she was, still seated with her safety belt on looking a bit ruffled but never the less still very composed.

"Have you had a spot of bother young man?" says the Princess as he reaches across to help her exit the car.

"Not really Ma'am just a normal day at the office."

Everyone is safe apart from feeling a bit travel sick.

*

It would have been so different if the
Time Travel Missile hadn't made its
'Journey in Time'.

Is this the end of the story?
What about Becky?
What about Bo?
Does he find her?
Or,
Has Romance lost another heartbeat?

Printed in Poland
by Amazon Fulfillment
Poland Sp. z o.o., Wrocław